The KING

KADER ABDOLAH

Translated from the Dutch by
Nancy Forest-Flier

CANONGATE

Edinburgh · London

Published in Great Britain in 2014 by Canongate Books Ltd,
14 High Street, Edinburgh EH1 1TE

www.canongate.tv

1

Copyright © Kader Abdolah, 2011
English translation copyright © Nancy Forest-Flier, 2014
Map copyright © Joanna Dingley

The moral rights of the author and translator have been asserted

First published as *De Koning* in the Netherlands in 2011 by De Geus BV,
Post office box 1878, 4801 BW Breda

British Library Cataloguing-in-Publication Data
A catalogue record for this book is available on
request from the British Library

ISBN 978 0 85786 295 2

Typeset in Sabon LT Std by Palimpsest Book Production Ltd,
Falkirk, Stirlingshire

Printed in Great Britain by
Clays Ltd, St Ives plc

This book is printed on FSC certified paper

The
KING

Also by Kader Abdolah

The House of the Mosque
My Father's Notebook

Dedicated to the two most distinguished Persian
prime ministers of the late nineteenth century:

Mirza Abolghasem Ghaemmagham Farahani
and
Mirza Tagi Khan Amir Kabir

Contents

The Main Characters

The shah
Mahdolia, mother of the shah
Taj Olsultan, daughter of the shah
Mirza Kabir, the grand vizier, the prime minister
Sheikh Aqasi, the shah's spiritual vizier
Jamal Khan, leader of the resistance group
Mirza Reza, Jamal Khan's right-hand man

Introduction

In the tea houses of Persia, tales of the ancient kings have been the constant fare of storytellers for the last thousand years. The storytellers played fast and loose with chronology and gave their fantasy free rein so the history they depicted would be strong and colourful. They relocated events, made the occasional omission and sometimes added a thing or two.

They were elaborating on the narrative art that had been perfected by the great medieval Persian storytellers. When the Persian Empire fell fourteen centuries ago, however, the stories also came to an end. Persian pride was dealt a fatal blow.

But then life brought forth the poet Ferdowsi. Ferdowsi wrote a great book called the *Shahnameh*, or *The Tales of the Kings*. In order to cover the vast number of events that had taken place in the former kingdom, Ferdowsi created the hero Rostam. He had Rostam live for about nine hundred years, thereby rescuing the nation's lost heritage from oblivion.

The teller of this story is following in that poet's footsteps.

1. The Kings

I n the beginning was the Cow, and the Cow was with God, who bore the name Ahura Mazda.

The Cow did not yet produce milk. Ahura Mazda blessed the Cow, saying, 'We have appointed no one to have dominion over you. We have created you for those who care for the four-footed beasts and for those who tend their pastures.'

A few thousand years later, life brought forth the man Kayumars. One evening, as Kayumars was standing near his cave, he looked up at the stars and the moon, casting their light on the cattle and people in the never-ending pastures. 'Someone should take command of this mystery,' he thought.

As he was standing once again near the mouth of his cave on a sunny afternoon, dark clouds appeared without warning and torrential rain began to fall. Churning rivers destroyed the pastures and swept away people and cattle alike.

'Someone should take command of the rivers,' Kayumars thought.

On another day he saw the men fighting and beating each other to death with sticks. He saw that the women were afraid and the children were crying, and he said to himself, 'Someone should take command of those men, and protect the women and children.'

One morning, just as the sun was coming up, the women

and their children came to him and gave him a crown of young branches and fragrant blossoms. He put the crown on his head, stretched out his arms to the sky and spoke the following words: 'Ahura Mazda! Grant me your strength, that I might take command of everything that is motionless and everything that moves upon the earth.'

Then he went down from the mountain.

Kayumars reigned for seven hundred years. Many kings came after him. One of them was Astyages, the king of the Medes and ruler over the Persians. Astyages had a dream that a grapevine grew out of the belly of his daughter Mandane, casting a shadow over the whole world. He asked his dream interpreters what this could mean. They said that his daughter, who was the wife of a prince of the subjected Persians, would bear a son who would topple the king from his throne.

Astyages ordered that as soon as his daughter gave birth to a son, the child be put to death. But the child, who had been named Cyrus, was secreted away to be raised by a shepherd. Later, when Cyrus was fully grown, he killed Astyages and became the new king.

Cyrus conquered the whole world during his reign. He left behind a clay tablet bearing the following words written in cuneiform script: 'I am Cyrus, king of the world, great king, mighty king, king of Babylon, king of Sumer and Akkad, king of the four quarters.

'All the kings who sit upon thrones, from the Upper Sea to the Lower Sea, and those who live in districts far off, and the kings of the West who dwell in tents, all of them brought their heavy tribute before me and in Babylon they kissed my feet.'

*   *   *

Cambyses, the son of Cyrus, succeeded his father. After Cambyses there were three more kings until Darius the Third came to power. He established a strong empire on which the sun never set, and he built a network of new roads that brought together all the corners of his kingdom. He then decided to conquer Greece. Commanding an army of Indians, Ethiopians, Moschians, Thracians, Kissians and Assyrians, he entered the harbour of Athens.

Greece was terrified by his divine presence. The Greeks knew they could never win the war, but the gods were on their side. Defying all expectations, they broke the invincible army of the Persians and the king fled.

The flight of Darius the Third was an embarrassment to the gods of the East. They would sooner have seen him fall in battle, be taken prisoner or be hacked to pieces – anything but fleeing. There is an old saying that perfectly sums up what Darius did: a dead lion is still a lion, a wounded lion is a lion too, and a captured lion in a cage is a lion nonetheless. But a lion that flees from his enemy is not a lion.

After this the gods turned their backs on the kings of Persia and the decline of the empire began.

Later Alexander the Great dealt a staggering blow to the Persian Empire. He set all the palaces on fire and plundered the vast royal coffers. Then he left for India to subjugate that land as well.

A few centuries after this the Muhammadans, with their freshly written Quran, descended on the weakened Persian Empire. They managed to seize power in three weeks. The deposed king, Yazdegerd, mounted his horse and galloped to the farthest eastern border, to Herat. There he planned to revive his disintegrated army and to drive the Arabs from his land. Deep in the night, the exhausted king sought rest at a mill. The miller strangled him in his sleep and stole his royal robes and jewels. Thus the great Persian Empire was brought to an end by a miller.

Later still Genghis Khan journeyed from east to west, laying such waste to the land of the Persians that nothing remained of its former glory. It wasn't until the Safavids came to power that Persia underwent a revival, but it was short-lived. The land fell into decline. The tribes fought each other for power.

At the beginning of the nineteenth century one of those tribes succeeded in gaining control.

This story is about one king of that tribe: Prince Naser.

2. *Prince Naser*

Once upon a time there was a Persian prince who later on, after he had become king, went to visit Paris.

While meeting with a group of French businessmen he was introduced to the engineer Gustave Eiffel. No one suggested they go and see the great iron tower, however, since neither the city council nor the people of Paris were particularly happy with that useless pile of scrap.

The prince's official name was Naser Muhammad Fatali Mozafar. These were the first names of his father, his grandfather, his great-grandfather and his great-great-grandfather.

His mother, Mahdolia, was a powerful woman.

The prince had 374 brothers, for his father had married over 1,200 wives over the course of his long life – 1,235 to be exact.

Tehran had become the capital of the country during the reign of the prince's grandfather. Before that it had been a large village at the foot of the Alborz Mountains. In no time at all it had grown into a city of magnificent palaces, with the bazaar at its vibrant heart.

In the northern part of the city there were princes living in exquisite country estates, while in the centre wealthy merchants had built spacious houses for their large families. The rest of the inhabitants worked for the merchants in the bazaar or they had little shops or workplaces where they busied themselves with handicrafts. There was also a mass of unemployed people who had left their villages and come to Tehran to seek their fortune.

At that time Persia was bounded by Russia to the north and India to the east. To the south was the Persian Gulf, where the British sailed their big ships to India and back.

The country was wedged between two great powers. Now that the old king was dead and a new king was about to ascend the throne, both Russia and England were trying to wrest some of the power for themselves.

Although the late king had 375 sons, only eight of them were of any consequence. These were the sons whose mothers were from the same tribe as the king. In keeping with tradition the king had appointed each of these eight sons *wāli*, governor, of the most important districts. The crown prince was always the *wāli* of Tabriz.

Prince Naser was the crown prince. His mother Mahdolia was the cousin of the late king and had been his favourite wife and closest kin. Accordingly she enjoyed special status in the royal household.

Following tradition the crown prince resided in Tabriz. This city, which lay close to the Russian border, was the second most important in the country.

On his deathbed the king had arranged for both Russia and England to recognise and support the crown prince as his heir. After the king's death the Russians – with hundreds of horses and coaches – would accompany the crown prince from Tabriz to Tehran, where his coronation was to take place. This caused great irritation among the British. They too wanted to play a prominent role in the transfer of power.

Prince Naser was an adult when he became shah and he had acquired sufficient life experience, but the real power lay in the hands of his capable vizier, Mirza Kabir. So the vizier arranged for a British army brigade to escort the prince from the city of Qazvin to Tehran. This seemed to satisfy the British embassy. Word got around that England would cover the ceremonial costs as a gesture. In an elaborate and elegant ritual held in Golestan Palace, the prince placed his father's crown on his own head, ascended the throne and was given the official title of Shah Naser. The Russian and British representatives in Tehran congratulated him and personally presented him with gifts from Moscow and London.

The festivities in Tehran continued for forty days. The bazaar was decorated and the army musicians played day and night in the bazaar square with great enthusiasm. Many tents were erected in the middle of the city where people could come and eat.

While the shah made merry, Mirza Kabir governed the country. On the forty-first day after the coronation the vizier went to the palace to discuss the most important affairs of state with the shah. At the end of a long talk he alerted the shah to one burning issue.

'The British and the Russians may have reached an agreement with your late father to support you, but they are also supporting your brothers in an effort to promote their interests in India.'

'Which brothers?' asked the shah anxiously.

'All seven. The brothers have risen up in revolt. They have declared their independence. The three brothers who are governing the border regions – Mozafar Khan on the Russian border, Muhammad Khan and Jafar Khan on the borders with Afghanistan and India – have established open contact with the British. The country is in danger of splitting apart.'

'What is the nature of this support?'

'The Russians and the British are providing them with money and weapons.'

'Traitors!' cried the shah.

..ier urged him, as commander-in-chief of the army,
. the order to crush all pockets of resistance, ruth-
y and without delay. After Shah Naser had signed the
.der the vizier bowed to his king, put the paper in his
leather bag and walked to the inner courtyard where
his horse was saddled and waiting for him.

Now that the long period of festivities had come to an
end the shah was finally able to rest. He withdrew to the
official sleeping quarters, where a special bed had been
prepared, one in which all the kings of his tribe had spent
their nights.

3. The Harem

The new king had inherited a ponderous legacy from his father. The country was in dire straits: the treasury was empty, the army was poorly equipped, and the population was largely illiterate and living in poverty and uncertainty. And always there was a threat of war on the border with India, where the British were in control.

These were the issues the shah would have to deal with during his reign, but he didn't know where to begin and he preferred to leave it all to his vizier. Mirza Kabir did have a plan. It was a grand plan for which he needed the shah's consent. But as long as the shah was busy with his own affairs, the vizier was free to make whatever preparations had to be made in order to implement his reforms and set the country on the road to growth.

The king's first concern was the housing of his wives. His father had kept more than twelve hundred wives in his harem, but Shah Naser had only 230. They had already been travelling for two weeks to get from the Russian border city of Tabriz to Tehran.

The shah received Khwajeh Bashi, his harem's overseer. This man's father had been a faithful servant of the deceased king, and when his son was still a child he'd had him castrated to enable him to work in the harem as a eunuch later on. Once the boy was grown the old king sent him to Tabriz to serve in the harem of the crown prince. His loyalty later earned him the title 'Khwajeh', a high royal distinction for a eunuch.

Khwajeh Bashi received his instructions directly from the shah. After the shah he was second in command in the harem, where his word was law. He took care of all the women's needs, and knew all there was to know about their bodies and their secrets. None of the women were allowed to take a single step outside the harem without his permission. It was Khwajeh Bashi himself who guarded the entrance. The shah was able to get to his bedroom from the harem by means of a special passageway.

Khwajeh Bashi had now been summoned by the shah to report on the new accommodations. The shah was standing in the middle of the hall of mirrors when his chamberlain, a taciturn man in a long, tight-fitting black coat, asked permission to admit the harem overseer. The shah nodded.

Khwajeh Bashi had an ugly, sallow, hairless face as a result of the castration. The fact that he plucked his eyebrows did not improve his looks. He wore a filthy, dark blue coat, from which he was inseparable, and a white, unwashed scarf. The shah accepted his stench and distasteful appearance because it was the only way to keep the women away from him. Under his arm he carried a stick for keeping impertinent women in line. The shah allowed him to keep hold of the stick while standing in the royal presence.

Dangling from Khwajeh Bashi's thick leather belt was a ring with dozens of keys. Anyone within earshot who heard the jingling keys knew that Khwajeh was approaching.

Once inside, Khwajeh Bashi took off his cap, bowed and remained standing at the door.

'Tell us, Khwajeh Bashi, where are the women?' cried Shah Naser.

'They are just outside Tehran. I expect them to reach the palace by midday.'

'It was a long journey,' said the shah. 'They must be very tired.'

'They have been travelling for seventeen days now. It was difficult having the children with them, but they were able to get plenty of rest in the tents along the way.'

'See that they are lavishly entertained now that we have ascended the throne,' said the shah.

'Everything has been arranged, Your Majesty. A great feast will be held as soon as they arrive. They are not tired. They spent the evening in a spacious caravanserai outside Tehran and the harem's large hamam has been made ready.'

The journey had been unforgettable for the women. Usually the only outings they were permitted were brief pilgrimages. The rest of their lives were spent within the harem's four walls. Now they had traversed a vast section of the country on horseback, wrapped in black chadors and blue niqabs. Their children were transported in coaches and the servants rode behind them on mules. A column of armed soldiers escorted the procession. As this extraordinary caravan approached the great gate of Tehran, the local police cleared the way. One of the horsemen blew his bugle and cried, 'Best behaviour, everyone! The shah's harem is riding into the city.'

A large group of musicians with drums was standing at the ready. Curious bystanders pressed forward on both sides of the road. Boys climbed the trees and men searched for higher elevation. Some of the women stood on the roofs to get a better view.

Riding at the head of the procession were the soldiers, followed by the veiled wives of the shah. They passed the spectators in an endless column, and no one knew how to react. A silence had fallen; all you could hear were the sounds of the horses' hooves and the wheels of the coaches and carts on the paving stones. Every now and then a laugh rang out from a boy sitting somewhere in a tree. It was quite a spectacle, the wives of the shah in their blue niqabs, silhouetted against the colourful fabrics that adorned the horses.

You could tell from these decorations just how important each woman was. The first horses had silken cloths draped over their heads that glittered with a profusion of beads. Special ornaments covered their legs and beads were woven into their tails. The women on these horses were from the same tribe as the shah.

Bringing up the rear was a group of young eunuchs who worked in the harem as servants. These men acted like women. When they passed the silence was broken and everyone began to laugh and point at them.

The women were received in the palace with great fanfare. Female musicians accompanied female harem singers, who sang joyous songs of welcome. Now that there were no longer any strange men about, the women were able to take off their niqabs and chadors. They talked with one another, laughed and shook the dust from their clothing. They were curious about their new home.

The shah appeared unannounced at the top of the stairs with the royal crown on his head. As soon as the women saw him they began to scream with delight. Relieved and happy that his wives had all arrived in good health the king came down the stairs to greet them.

The children ran up to their father, who opened his arms but did not embrace them, motioning instead to Khwajeh Bashi to take them away and indulge them with sweets.

The women gathered round the shah, congratulating him and admiring his golden crown. It was said to be the same crown that had been worn by Cyrus, the king of kings. The shah enjoyed the attention of the country's most beautiful women, who laughed and then complained to him about their long journey. He caressed them, stroked their cheeks and necks, and after a while he retired.

The disappointed women let out a cacophony of screams until the harem overseer shouted, 'Ladies!' They immediately fell silent, for when Khwajeh Bashi spoke, he spoke the words of the shah. 'Ladies! You have seen how happy His Majesty is that you all arrived in good health. Everything has been properly arranged for you to his satisfaction. For my part I expect you to comply with the rules. Here in Tehran, and especially in this harem, nothing is as it was in Tabriz. This palace is the most prestigious and most beautiful in the land. And your harem is the most imposing. His Majesty is no longer the crown prince. He is king now – *the* king. This means that my words are the words of the king. And the words of the king are the words of God. So I am asking you to behave yourselves and to listen closely to whatever I say. Not a single mosquito leaves the harem without my permission, and not a single mosquito enters the harem without my permission. I will talk about the rest later on. Your rooms are ready, the beds are made and the hamam is warm. Take your time and get some rest.'

He asked all the mothers to stand with their sons and daughters, and he let them enter the harem first. Then he sent the women without children in one by one, where they were met by servants who took them to their rooms.

The women gazed in amazement at their new accommodation. It was a gigantic oval-shaped building three storeys high, with more than a hundred rooms. There were countless passageways leading from one part of the building to another, with many covered courtyards onto which dozens of rooms opened out. There were tea rooms, resting rooms, reading rooms, medical treatment rooms, dining rooms, music rooms, massage rooms, hookah rooms, storytelling rooms, a hair-dresser's and a very large hamam where more than a hundred women could bathe at once. There were more rooms than women, so everyone had plenty of space. It was easy for newcomers to lose their way in this vast maze of a building during their first weeks until they learned to find their rooms almost by instinct.

Behind the building was a large garden with fruit trees, long avenues lined with fragrant flowers, and benches for sitting and lying in the leafy shade. In the middle of the garden was a large pond filled with colourful fish and surrounded by wooden divans. Majestic carpets were scattered everywhere, and everything was decorated in fine, colourful silk.

The women with children were given spacious apartments at the back of the building, and the young women who had recently joined the harem had rooms off the long corridor on the first floor. So if the shah wanted to sleep with any one of them he never had far to go.

Most of the women in the harem came from the country-side. The shah had noticed them among the spectators during his travels and had taken them along with him. At first the women were very happy that the shah had chosen them; they felt as if luck had come to perch on their shoulders like an eagle. Once they arrived in the harem, however, the shah would spend only a few nights playing with them. He fondled them, bit them, pinched them in the neck, in the breasts and in the thighs, and then brutally took them by force. After that he usually never returned. These young, illiterate women found themselves in an intricate labyrinth of religion, superstition, disease, gossip, power games, female deception, spying and shady political intrigue. They were kept prisoner day and night, and killed time by putting on make-up, smoking hookahs, eating and quarrelling with each other.

Once the women had fixed up their rooms Khwajeh Bashi took his place at the entrance to the harem. To his delight the move had occurred without incident. A young servant brought him a hookah. The overseer leaned back on a cushion and looked at the women, who were getting themselves ready for the evening meal.

Slowly darkness fell. The servants lit the candles in the lanterns. A hint of sadness hung over the harem. A cat, the shah's cat, crept inside and jumped up on a ledge. She too watched the women in the twilight.

4. The Grand Vizier

Having received the shah's approval, Grand Vizier Mirza Kabir sent a couple of army units to the eastern and southwestern provinces to arrest the shah's rebellious half-brothers.

When the shah's father had felt his end was near, he had expressly asked Mirza Kabir to help his son until he was able to assume total control. The father of Mirza Kabir had been the first vizier of the late king, and the young Mirza Kabir had served as his father's assistant. Later he succeeded his father as vizier to the old king. He was quite aware of what state the country was in. Mirza Kabir was beloved by the people, but he had many enemies in high places, including the corrupt princes and politicians. He followed developments in Russia, England and France, and he knew his own land was lagging far behind the countries of the West. The unemployment, illiteracy, disease and extreme poverty in Persia grieved him deeply, as did his inability to prevent a small elite from enriching themselves and gaining enormous power.

One of his most influential opponents was Mahdolia, the mother of the crown prince. She had formed a shadow cabinet made up of several old, experienced politicians. She also had ties with a number of clerics, who claimed they were in contact with the divine energies.

The vizier had done everything he could to limit Mahdolia's power. He tried to keep corrupt people away from the old king. His goal had been to centralise power in order to make the land governable, but in this he did not succeed. Now, as grand vizier to Shah Naser, Mirza Kabir saw a new opportunity to realise his plans to modernise the country. He wanted to create businesses, construct roads, build hospitals and introduce a western educational system, and he had educated the future shah to go along with his plans for renewal. But without the shah's approval his dreams would never come to fruition. He certainly didn't expect any support from the ruling elite. They backed Mahdolia, the mother of the shah, in an effort to fill their own pockets. They had done well for themselves under the rule of the shah's father, and now they owned houses, castles and even entire villages.

Mahdolia tried to frustrate the man at every turn. She was determined to limit his influence on her son, whom she constantly belittled with remarks like, 'You're not your own man; you're the slave of your master.' Or: 'You're the king, but you behave like that man's errand boy. Don't be so servile.' And: 'That vizier is using you to advance his own plans. Don't forget that he's supposed to obey *you*, and not the other way round.'

Mirza Kabir came from a distinguished and independent family whose men had always exercised considerable literary and political influence. For five generations the family had produced viziers to serve the country. Mirza Kabir himself tried to act with only the interests of the country at heart. According to tradition the shah held the reins of power and the vizier was subordinate to him. It was the vizier's task to inform the shah of the latest events and developments, which always had to be done with the greatest caution.

One day, after the shah had undergone a neat beard

trimming, the vizier requested an audience with him to bring him up to date.

'Your Majesty, we are living in turbulent times. Russia is ready to attack the kingdom from the north. The British army is in the east, waiting to seize upon any pretext to use our country in order to safeguard their presence in India.

'Being king is a weighty responsibility. I have taught you about the nation's past and I have openly discussed your predecessors' strong and weak points. I have spent a great deal of time in Russia and I am aware of the changes taking place in England. Now more than ever a statesman is responsible for the welfare of his subjects. The time when people could get by with a cow, a bit of land and some wool to spin is over. The world is plunging ahead, but we are standing still. We must build factories, just as England and Russia are doing. With factories we could provide jobs for thousands of people. We will have to send our clever young men to France, England and Russia to be educated. Our children must learn to read. That is why we want to set up seven schools in Tehran. The French can help us create a new school system.'

'Is that all?' asked the shah with irony.

'I would like the shah to endorse these plans. Pay no attention to those who don't understand such things.'

'And who might the vizier be referring to?' responded the shah, greatly irritated by this indirect indictment of his mother.

'The Persian Empire is like a terminally ill patient who has been handed over to you and to me. Rule like a Russian tsar and like a British king, not like your forefathers. I appeal to you to limit the size of your harem. The women you already have are enough for all eternity.'

'The vizier is not to meddle in our private affairs. The

vizier would be wise to understand where his limits are,' said the shah. Somewhere in the back of his mind he could hear his mother reproaching him.

'Your Majesty must excuse the vizier. He is only doing his duty. I was told by your father to be tough and honest with you. And to alert you to your responsibilities.'

'We are the king now and the vizier is no longer under any obligation to instruct us,' answered the shah.

'I am not instructing you. The contact between the vizier and the shah must always be straightforward, honest and professional. I only ask Your Majesty not to come to any decisions without first consulting his vizier.'

'No more insults. The vizier is speaking to the shah. Watch what you say. We will decide what must be decided.'

'The vizier would never presume to insult the king. On the contrary, I value your discernment. Your reading know-ledge of French is excellent, so we have ordered French books for Your Majesty. They concern the astonishing changes that are taking place in Europe. Your Majesty must keep himself informed.'

'There is nothing we *must* do,' said the shah.

'Of course, there is nothing the shah must do, but the shah might like to know that millions of his subjects in the countryside are working like slaves for the large land-owners. They have nothing, while their masters live in resplendent castles. There is nothing the shah must do, but the shah might like to know that beyond the walls of his palace thousands of poor people are fighting for their existence while the princes lead blissful lives in Tehran. There is nothing the shah must do, but the shah might like to know that he cannot rule the land as it was ruled in his father's and grandfather's day. Should you decide to do so, I am afraid it could mean the end of your dynasty. You know I am serious. The shah must distance himself from the forces that are working against us. I need your help to modernise the country. I believe that in the near future you will have to undertake a journey to England or France.'

The shah was silent. He loved to travel. He travelled through his own land a great deal and had already been to Russia twice. But as king he did not dare leave the country. He knew its history and he knew what could happen if the shah were absent.

'The shah may want to think this over,' the vizier added.

Shah Naser rang his little bell. The chamberlain came in and the shah motioned to him to lead the vizier out.

5. Mahdolia, the Mother

Mahdolia was very young when she fell pregnant. She protected her son, the crown prince, as a lioness protects her cub. She never left him alone, afraid the other women would harm him in some way out of jealousy. Because she and the king were from the same tribe Mahdolia was the chosen wife, queen of the nation. She was the king's confidante and she knew the country's state secrets. When her husband took ill she became the decision-maker. The only thing standing in her way was Mirza Kabir. Now that her husband had died she tried to rule the land through her son.

Mahdolia mirrored herself on Catherine, the tsarina of Russia. Deep in her heart what she really wanted was to be the Catherine of Persia. She knew how important it was to tread a cautious path between the Russians and the British. She did not trust the British. They were cunning politicians who cared about nothing but their own interests. And the Russians weren't much better. Over the course of two wars they had seized a couple of large cities in the province of Azerbaijan. But Mahdolia knew that if she wanted to exert any influence at all, she would have to side with one of the two great powers. She had chosen the Russians.

Mahdolia wanted to hold the shah's allegiance and keep him out of the hands of the vizier. She had told her son on several occasions that at a suitable moment she was going to confide a secret in him. That moment had now come.

Her coach was stopped at the palace gate by the new head of the guards. 'Who is in the coach?'

'The queen,' said the coachman.

The guard was about to check, but Mahdolia forestalled him. She opened the little hatch and shouted, 'What's going on here?'

The guard was startled by the force of her personality. He saluted and let the coach pass.

'Mother! Your Highness!' cried the shah as Mahdolia entered the hall of mirrors.

'What is this all about? Is the shah a prisoner in his own palace?' she shouted angrily.

'What do you mean, Mother?'

'It's as if no one was allowed to move without the vizier's permission. Not even the shah.'

'No, Mother. No. It's not as bad as all that.'

'I don't feel comfortable here. The walls have ears. Let's go and sit somewhere else.'

The shah led her to his conference room.

'You've ended up in a snake pit. Not only do you have enemies in England and Russia, but you have them here under your own roof as well. First of all, let me warn you again about the vizier. My informants have proof that the vizier wants to seize power. He is sending boys to England and France to study. He wants to introduce reforms that leave no room for the shah, and he wants to change the army so it owes its allegiance to him. What is the shah doing in the meantime? Signing all the papers the vizier thrusts under his nose?'

'Mother, what you say is not true. I am aware of everything that is going on, and the vizier does nothing without my knowledge. He is like a father to me.'

'The shah must never use such words,' responded Mahdolia sharply.

'Whatever he does, he does for the good of the country and for us. Mother, someone must think of the people. It shames me just to go outside. I feel as if I were king of the beggars.'

'You are not king of the beggars. You are king of a magnificent land, king of great and extraordinary cities, majestic bazaars and castles. You live in this palace that is described in the *Thousand and One Nights* as a garden of mystery.'

'Mother, the vizier wants to build factories. He wants to send children to school and to bring in machines from abroad for printing books. He's going to outfit our soldiers in new uniforms and make sure they're properly armed.'

'So that's what the vizier wants, is it? And what does the shah want?'

'He is doing this in consultation with us,' replied her son.

'Was it with your permission that he reduced our allowance – and that of the princes – by half? If this is the way the shah feels, then what have I to add? What am I doing here anyway?'

'Mother, you were going to tell me a secret.'

She sighed deeply and leaned back in her chair. The shah poured her a glass of water. She sipped slowly, tilted her head forward and said in a muted tone, 'Son, you know history. Nader the Great, the founder of the previous dynasty, invaded India more than once. The last time the shah of India held him off with a large army and with elephants, but he lost. The shah of India knelt before Nader and handed him his crown. Thus Nader became the shah of India.'

'Mother, this is well known. Why are you speaking so quietly?' asked the shah with impatience.

Mahdolia continued: 'After fifty-eight days the Indians rose up in revolt against the Persian soldiers. When the resistance became widespread and violent, Nader had more than a hundred thousand people killed. He did not give the shah of India his crown back until he had plundered India's treasury.'

The shah sat bolt upright.

'According to documents in our royal archive,' his mother went on, 'Nader the Great brought great riches with him back to Persia.'

'What documents are these? And exactly where are they being kept?' asked the shah, who had never shown any interest in the royal archive before. 'Mother, what kind of riches are you speaking of?'

Mahdolia pretended to ponder the question. 'I will mention just a few,' she finally said. 'Chests full of gold and Indian jewels, a royal bed inlaid with precious green stones, a chair in the form of a great peacock, adorned with gems of many different colours. Sacks filled with large Indian diamonds. And two separate boxes containing the largest diamonds in the world, nestled on soft fabric of dark purple. One diamond is called the Sea of Light and the other is called the Mountain of Light. There are also a number of small figurines: elephants, peacocks, snakes and cows, all pure gold and inlaid with little precious stones.'

'Whatever happened to these treasures?' asked the shah with excitement.

'They are in our possession,' said Mahdolia calmly.

'In our possession?' he gasped.

'Lower your voice. The documents I spoke of contain a binding agreement which stipulates that the shah can do nothing with these divine gifts. You may see them, but you may not sell them except in cases of emergency. If the British or the Russians knew this, they would scour our land and plunder it to lay their hands on these riches. It is the work of the greatest Indian artists and metalsmiths who ever lived. The spirit of India is preserved in these treasures. Your forefathers took this secret to their graves. It is a secret you will have to carry too, but your heart must be big enough.'

'What good is all this if we cannot make use of it?' asked the shah.

'I am only passing on the words of your late father. I am but a messenger. The late king said, "My son! The treasures of India are a wonder that must remain buried underground until our land is stable and powerful once again. Only then may you let them be seen. Otherwise they will crumble and disappear."'

Shah Naser was unable to stay in his seat. 'Mother, where are they? Who else knows about this?'

'There must always be three living people who know about the treasure.'

'And who is the third person?' asked the shah.

'Sheikh Aqasi, your father's counsellor.'

'Why that man?'

'He has magical powers, and he always helped your father and me when it came to making difficult decisions. He can read the future. Someday you will make use of his strength, his honesty and his insight.'

'Enough about the sheikh, Mother. Just tell me where the jewels are.'

His mother took a small Quran from her bag and said solemnly, 'My son, place your hand on this holy book and swear that you will protect the jewels as if they were your own eyes.'

The shah hastily did as she bade him. 'I swear.'

'The treasures are here in this palace,' Mahdolia then revealed.

'What? In this palace?'

'This palace was built by the first king of our dynasty,' she went on. 'He built a secret cellar beneath the existing cellar. An invisible underground tunnel runs from that cellar to the mountains.'

'Here, beneath the cellar of this palace? May I see the treasures?' asked the shah impatiently.

'Not now. It must be dark, and there can be no one else in the palace.'

'But Mother, please!' he cajoled. His patience had run out.

'It is a man's job. I will ask Sheikh Aqasi to take you to the cellar tomorrow evening,' said Mahdolia, and with that she took her leave of her son.

Once she was gone the shah's cat stuck her head out from behind a curtain and padded up to him silently.

6. Sheikh Aqasi

The father of the shah had been a superstitious king. When the situation demanded that a decision be made, he never had the nerve to act. Usually it was his wife Mahdolia who cast the die. She would then consult with Sheikh Aqasi, who had an unorthodox view of things.

Sheikh Aqasi had been the late king's confidant. He was neither a minister nor an advisor, but he was in contact with invisible forces. If the king was at his wits' end, Sheikh Aqasi could calm him with his insights, prayers and cryptic holy writings. The king saw him as an extension of a divine power.

Sheikh Aqasi had a long grey beard and he always wore a long coat of thin white cloth. It was known that he could see into the future and that he had the gift of prophecy. Rumour had it that by reading the stars he could make the impossible possible. On one occasion the king had demanded the head of one of his enemies, and Sheikh Aqasi made sure he got it.

The sheikh dwelt in a peaceful country house in the mountains, where he could withdraw from the world. He lived simply and had no other property or possessions. The late king believed in him unquestioningly, which is why he was chosen to hear the king's royal secrets. The new shah was afraid of the sheikh's otherworldliness, but at the same time he knew he might need him in the future.

On the evening that he was to take the newly appointed

shah to see the Indian treasures, Sheikh Aqasi went to the hall of mirrors. Opening his arms like a father he walked up to the shah and pressed a kiss on his shoulder. 'Your Majesty, your father has gone down like a full moon and you have risen like a young moon.'

'You are dear to us,' said the shah. 'Father has passed away, but he left us with you and your wisdom.' He then walked into the adjoining room where he held his confidential conversations, sat down on a green satin chair and bade the sheikh sit beside him.

'We are listening,' said the shah, who could barely contain his excitement.

'Your mother has ordered me to show you the cellar,' said the sheikh calmly. 'But first I would like to present Your Majesty with a confidential letter. It is the royal last will and testament that your father left for you.' And with that he took a sealed envelope from his inner pocket.

The shah broke the lacquer seal and read the letter, which was indeed written in his father's hand.

My son, the glory days of the Persian Empire are over. Circumstances have made me a weak king. I have been forced to relinquish two large parts of the country to the Russians, and it was as if they had chopped off both my legs with an axe. I will have to take this interminable pain with me to the grave. You know the British have taken possession of Herat, the jewel in our crown, to impede the Russians in their passage to India. They want to give Herat to the Afghanis in order to maintain full control of the area. My son, do all you can to regain our precious Herat. If you fail, Herat will cause you everlasting torment and our descendants will never forgive us. It will be very difficult, but I hope you have the courage of your grandfather. My tears have fallen on this letter. Long live Persia.

The shah sat motionless in his chair for a moment, the letter in his hand. His father's last will and testament was a serious directive that he could not simply ignore.

Sheikh Aqasi, who thought he saw traces of distress in the shah's face, turned to him and intoned, 'The stars promise a glorious time for the shah. Your mother and I know the contents of the letter. I have seen in the movement of the stars that the shah will recapture Herat and that he will humiliate the British and push them deep into India.'

The shah looked at the sheikh and smiled. He folded up the letter and tucked it away in his inner pocket.

'Your Majesty, allow me to perform my duties. For a long time the Indian booty was in the hands of one of the grandsons of Nader the Great. Your grandfather beheaded almost all of Nader's male descendants until he finally discovered where the booty was hidden. He built a cellar beneath the cellar and put the treasures there.' Then the sheikh picked up a lantern.

The shah thought he was going to bring him to the palace's regular cellar, but to his surprise the sheikh led him to the shah's own bedroom and locked the door from the inside. He closed the curtains and opened the shah's closet. Then he took the clothing out of the closet and put it on the bed. Reaching into his jacket he produced a long key. He then shone a lantern into the closet and found a hole in the back panel into which he inserted the key. A small door opened and a cold draught blew in that made the shadows on the walls quiver.

'The shah must be careful,' said the sheikh. He wriggled his way through the opening with difficulty and disappeared into the darkness. Curious, the shah followed him.

'There is a small stairway here,' said the sheikh.

Shah Naser followed Sheikh Aqasi along the narrow tunnel, groping the wall with his hand.

'At the end of this tunnel there is another stairway, followed by an even narrower tunnel, another stairway and a short tunnel. Then we will be in the treasury,' said his guide.

At the end of the short tunnel a small door became visible, which the sheikh opened with another key. Once again he went first and the shah followed.

The shah was astounded. He saw a large room filled with jewels and golden objects that glittered in the light of the lantern.

'Welcome to history,' announced the sheikh.

'This is truly astonishing. A remarkable secret. But why did they make the door so small?'

'To make it difficult to remove the large objects. There's another secret door, however, that serves as the exit. That's for emergencies – if the shah suddenly has to leave the palace. The tunnel ends in a small cave, through which you can flee in safety. Someday I will show you the cave,' said the sheikh, lighting a couple of candles in a niche.

Shah Naser was overwhelmed by the riches that were revealed in the dim light. He saw gold and silver chests and a magnificent chair shaped like a peacock, studded with precious stones. Everywhere there were golden sculptures, plates and candlesticks. Then the sheikh opened a box before the shah's very eyes and said humbly, 'Your Majesty.'

The shah was struck dumb at the sight of the largest blue diamond in the world, the Sea of Light. He did not know a precious stone could be so big and so enchanting.

The sheikh opened another box and said, 'Look, Your Majesty!'

There lay the second wonder, the second-largest diamond in the world, which bore the name Mountain of Light. Once again the shah was speechless. He looked all around him. It was just as his mother had described: rare antique gold crowns, bracelets, necklaces, earrings and robes that had belonged to the kings and queens of India. Shah Naser opened a bag full of rubies and emeralds and let them run through his fingers. 'Delightful,' he murmured. He walked up to a large bed made of special hardwood and inlaid with precious stones, and he inspected the firmness of the well-stuffed mattress. Dropping onto it he stretched out full length.

'Exceptional,' he said. 'It's as if I had landed in a fairy tale.'

Lying there he looked at the abundance of swords, boots, plates and glasses arranged on the shelves and hanging from the walls. This profusion of heavenly colour couldn't have come from the kings and queens; it must have come from the gods. These were bits of history, of life. Fate had brought them here and preserved them. Now he must protect them and keep them safe.

'This is the spirit of India,' said the shah to himself, 'the India that the British, the Russians and the French want for their own. No one is to know what lies hidden here. No one. It is ours, Persia's.'

Sheikh Aqasi nodded and handed him the two keys.

7. Herat

Because the late king had had so many wives, there were hundreds of families who could claim a royal connection. Together they formed society's noble class, and all of them sided with Mahdolia. They occupied important positions in politics, in the army and in the nation's commerce. Almost all of them maintained secret contacts with the British and Russian embassies. The series of measures that the vizier had taken to limit the power of these families had encountered much resistance, and they had made their dissatisfaction known to the shah.

The shah had sent for the vizier to explain the situation to him. Early in the evening Mirza Kabir rode into the palace grounds on horseback. The head of the guards took his horse's reins and helped him dismount. They then exchanged a few words, something that did not escape the shah, who was keeping an eye on the courtyard from behind the curtain.

The vizier went inside. The chamberlain greeted him, bowed his head, took his coat and brought him to the hall of mirrors.

Mirza Kabir was wearing his prime minister's robe and his tall cylindrical hat. The gems on his clothing glittered in the light of the great chandeliers. His hands clasped behind him, he impatiently walked the full length of the hall several times, back and forth. The shah's cat followed his pacing. Every now and then the vizier would pause before the great mirrors and look at himself. With his cylindrical hat, his robe and his long salt-and-pepper beard he bore a striking resemblance to the portrait the court painter had once made of his father. It irritated him that the shah was making him wait more often, and for longer periods of time.

The hall of mirrors was an exceptional example of power, light and eastern art. The walls were decorated with thousands of little mirrors cut in mysterious shapes. Out of sheer boredom the vizier began studying the multiple reflections of himself. Famous Persian artists had painted the walls and ceiling with war tableaux, important battle scenes from the nation's history. Covering the floor were carpets made especially for this hall in natural shades of purple and emerald. The vizier came from the Farahan region, where the most beautiful carpets in the country – if not in the whole world – were made. He knew exactly which villages the carpets had come from. Kneeling down on one carpet of gold, green and dark blue silk, he ran his hand along the surface, feeling how fine the threads were. The shah's cat rubbed herself against him. The vizier picked her up and stroked her head and back.

'What a pretty jewelled necklace you're wearing. Just like a princess.'

The chamberlain then let the vizier know that the shah was waiting for him. Mirza Kabir took one more look at his reflection and went into the shah's conference room.

Shah Naser received the vizier in his military uniform with his hand on his sword. The atmosphere was tense. Mirza Kabir removed his hat, bowed and said, 'Your Majesty!'

The shah turned his face and spoke with his back to the vizier. 'Tell me what this is all about: the vizier removes certain persons from our entourage and replaces them with his own relatives. We are under surveillance in our own household.'

'You are angry, Your Majesty. But your intelligence is incorrect. You are the heart and the brains of the country. Traitors and enemies are trying to get closer to you. It is my duty to keep them out of the palace. Whatever I do, I do for you. I am your vizier, so in your presence I may speak plainly. I always showed great respect for your father. Because you are the king I am obliged to tell the truth. The court of your late father was riddled with corrupt politicians who had only their own interests at heart. Your father was surrounded by thieves, fools, superstitious clerics and spies from England and Russia. I have dealt with them all. In doing so I made many enemies, but that does not frighten me as long as I have the shah on my side.'

'The vizier has reduced the income of my mother and my family members by half. Are they also thieves and confederates of evil-minded forces?'

'I hold your mother in great esteem, but with the expenses she incurs I can build factories that would provide work for your subjects. The shah is entitled to know the truth. Your mother's palace is a hotbed of old men who are hungry for power.'

'Watch what you say, vizier. You are talking about my mother!' cried the shah, greatly offended.

'I am talking about Your Majesty, about the country. It's not personal,' said the vizier.

'We hear quite different rumours,' replied the shah, this time more calmly.

'What rumours, Your Majesty?'

'That it is the vizier who is trying to seize power from us.'

'Your Majesty, those are the words of my enemies. They

are thirsty for my blood. I knew the shah would bring this up, so I brought a Quran with me.'

The vizier pulled the holy book from his bag. He placed his right hand on it and said, 'I swear by this book that whatever I do, I do it for the glory of the shah. If this is not enough I will step down and the shah may appoint another vizier.'

The shah motioned to the vizier to put the Quran away. Evidently the vizier's words had restored his trust. The shah walked to the window and pulled back the curtain slightly. He needed the vizier's advice.

'We have been given a letter written by my father, a very personal letter. He was distressed about Herat. He asked me to do everything I could to recapture the city.'

'Herat is our national heartache,' agreed the vizier, 'but we are not in a position to drive the British out. Not only that, but times have changed. Afghanistan is a sovereign state and England has equipped all the Afghan tribal leaders with weapons. And they have stationed an Indian army in Herat. We cannot recover the city by force of arms.'

'Is the vizier suggesting that we must abandon our beloved city to the British, the Afghans and the Indians?' asked the shah. 'This is not about the city. It is about our country's honour. It surprises me that the vizier does not realise this.'

'Certainly I realise it. There is only one solution: the path of diplomacy. We must be just as cunning and clever as the British.'

'Every king has a mission in life,' said the shah. 'My mission is to reclaim the city of Herat for the nation. This we will do, at any price. I do not want to go down in history as a cowardly king.'

'I share the shah's sense of purpose, but Your Majesty

also knows that our country has been constantly at war for the past fourteen hundred years. Our strength is exhausted. Another war would cause us to lose our honour, not to regain it. The British have all of India in their possession. It is not India that is our eastern neighbour now, but England. The Russians and the British have cannons and rifles and other war machines beyond anything we can imagine. Our army is an army of beggars. The Persians have played out their role on the battlefield. Fighting a war against our Afghan brothers is exactly what the English are hoping for. It would put an end to all our plans for renewal. I have a series of projects in the cities—'

'What projects? Why do we know nothing of these projects?" asked the shah with suspicion.

'You will be told everything, of course, when we're further along. Now we're preoccupied with the struggle against your rebellious brothers. We had not expected that their resistance would cost the army so much time and trouble. But once this is behind us our hands will be free to pursue other projects. It all boils down to this: we think we ought to promote the development of our own products and make them great, just as the powerful nations do.'

'What products?'

'Carpets, for example. There are none better anywhere in all the world. Our saffron, caviar, pistachios, tea leaves, tobacco, dates and much, much more are of exceptional quality. If we could produce them on a large scale we would help thousands of people earn a living. Now we are negotiating joint venture agreements with entrepreneurs from European countries. Our mines are rich in gold, silver, copper and precious stones.' The vizier paused a moment to catch his breath.

'I have good news for the shah. Even before your father's

death we were involved in talks with the French to bring our army up to modern standards. They have reviewed our proposal in Paris and their reaction is positive. The future looks bright. A war now would be disastrous. If the talks begin to bear fruit I will submit the draft of our agreements to the shah for your consideration.'

'The French have never been trustworthy,' replied the shah. 'They deceived my father so many times. They sign an agreement with us, and as soon as they patch up their friendship with the Russians they renege on their promises.'

'What the shah says is true. But France is our closest ally. That country is the enemy of both Russia and England. The French want access to India just like everyone else, and the shortest route is through our country. We have to steer our own political course if we are to remain on good terms with everyone. France is the best option. We will not purchase weapons from them. Instead they will build factories for us so we can make our own weapons and ammunition. They have a very versatile industrial sector. They produce furniture and porcelain, leather and silk. They make the best precision timepieces in the world. And the French have come up with a machine that sews clothing in a most amazing way, and at high speed. They also have a kind of spinning machine that can spin as much as a hundred women working together, and in a very short time.

'We can bring all those machines and expertise to our country. The French are prepared to cooperate with us. If there is a desire to get at the riches of the East by way of Persia, we really ought to profit from it to get our country back on its feet.'

The shah was silent. The cat, who had slipped behind the curtain, decided the discussion had come to an end. The shah motioned to her and she jumped up on his lap.

8. Sharmin the Cat

It was evening. The shah was sitting in his chair, reading a book about Napoleon. He was a great admirer of the general's strategic genius. His grandfather had met him once and had always spoken of the French emperor with adulation. When the shah's eyes became tired he clapped his hands and the chamberlain entered the room.

'Hookah,' said the shah.

The chamberlain went to fetch the hookah, and the shah sat down in the special place reserved for smoking. The finely decorated hookah was placed on the carpet before him, on a round silver tray next to a small table. On the table was a pair of little golden dishes filled with assorted delicacies. The chamberlain put the teapot in the warm ashes of a brass chafing dish and asked if there was anything else the shah desired.

'The storyteller!' answered the shah. He raised the pipe to his mouth. There were many things on his mind and he did not know who to trust, his mother or the vizier. According to her the vizier was opposed to invading Herat because he was in league with the British. The vizier, she insisted, was going to replace all the warlords with officers who followed him implicitly.

There was a knock at the door.

'Come in,' said the shah.

The storyteller was a man well over fifty. He wore a special robe embroidered with gold thread and a traditional headdress that storytellers in tea houses always wear when they tell their stories. The man recounted a tale from the *Shahnameh*, the great Persian book written by Ferdowsi about the legendary kings of Persia from the country's golden age.

The shah listened to the tale of King Zal, hoping he could find in it an answer to his questions. The storyteller began.

King Sam hoped for a son who would help him consolidate his kingdom. But fate decided otherwise. He was given a son whose skin was completely grey and whose name was Zal.

The king was thunderstruck by this 'demon child' and ordered a servant to kill him. But the servant did not kill him. He secretly took the baby to the mountains and left him there. Then the Simorgh, a mythical bird, appeared. She took Zal to her nest and fed him. Zal grew up and became an extraordinary young man. One night, the king dreamed that his son Zal was still alive and that he was living in the mountains with the birds. Filled with remorse and joy, the king set off for the mountains. He found his son and crowned him.

A few years later, Zal and his army were journeying to Kabulistan to fight against the enemy. There he met Rudabeh, the dazzlingly beautiful daughter of the king of Kabulistan. These two people were made for each other. But because their two countries were embroiled in a history of hostility, their love was forbidden. One night, Rudabeh stood at her window in the castle and let down the long plait of her black hair. Zal climbed up the plait and entered her room. There they spent one of the most beautiful eastern nights together that has ever taken place. Nine months later, the birth of their miracle child was imminent. But the child was too big and the birth was impossible. Rudabeh wrestled with death. Suddenly Zal remembered that the Simorgh bird had given him one of her feathers in case he was ever in need of it. Zal burnt the feather and the Simorgh appeared. The bird told Zal what he must do: 'Give Rudabeh a great deal of wine. Cut her side open with this knife, take out the child and sew up the wound.'

The miracle child was born and was called Rostam. Later he would be the saviour of Persia's glory and the guardian of the crown.

The shah had heard enough, but he did not know how this tale could help him make a decision. He tossed a few gold coins to the storyteller. The man picked up the coins, bowed and took his leave. Shah Naser put down the hookah pipe and wandered wearily through the corridors of the palace.

'Sharmin! Where are you?' he called.

Every now and then he would pause and open a random door, calling softly, 'Here, kitty, kitty. Sharmin!'

Finally he saw Sharmin come in through an open window.

'Where were you? Outside? You're not allowed to do that. None of your tricks, you hear?' He lifted her from the floor.

Sharmin always kept the shah company and slept in his bed. Sometimes she stayed away for long periods of time, but she always came back to her master.

He strolled through the corridors of the palace with the cat in his arms. 'Mother says we should watch out for the vizier. But the vizier only wants what's best for us, don't you think? You love him too, don't you? My mother says he has a secret agenda, that he wants to seize power. Do you believe her?

'And the vizier only says nasty things about my mother,' he continued. 'I can't trust anyone but you, Sharmin. You are no one's spy. You are mine alone and you keep my secrets.'

When they walked past the kitchen the cat jumped from his arms in search of the cook, who always gave her treats.

It was late in the evening and the shah decided he wanted some human company, so he went to the harem. Usually he would notify Khwajeh Bashi, the harem overseer, when he was planning to visit. Khwajeh Bashi would then warn the women so they could make themselves up to receive the shah. But tonight the shah was not himself.

Khwajeh Bashi, who was sitting on a sofa next to the entrance and smoking his hookah as usual, sat up abruptly. He hastily began searching for his slippers. 'What can I do for Your Majesty?'

Shah Naser did not reply. Clasping his hands behind him he walked further into the harem. The women, who had not expected this visit, flew giggling to their rooms so as not to surprise him in their night-time attire.

The women's rooms were decorated with symbols from their respective cultures. The rooms of the Azari women from Tabriz were quite different from the rooms of the Kurdish women, and those of the Kurds in turn looked nothing like those of the Baluchis. The women from Kabul had different taste than the women from Herat. Often they did not understand each another's language and customs. But those who spoke standard Persian treated all the other women with proud condescension.

Chaos reigned in the harem. All the women began rushing around, trying to make themselves beautiful in order to tempt the shah. But he was not in the mood for women.

Khwajeh Bashi followed the shah at a respectful distance and apologised for the fact that the harem was not ready for his arrival.

'Which woman does Your Majesty desire?' he ventured.

There was no answer, and the further they walked into the harem the more indifferently the shah looked at the closed bedroom doors.

'There are a number of women with whom Your Majesty has not yet slept,' said Khwajeh Bashi cautiously.

'Are there any women from Herat among them?'

'I, I . . . don't know,' stammered Khwajeh Bashi. 'I'll go and find out, if that is your wish.'

The shah said nothing and Khwajeh Bashi hastened to his room.

The doors of the rooms were now opening one by one, and the women who hoped to seduce the shah came to stand in their doorways.

'Your Majesty,' whispered a woman with expressive dark eyes as the shah walked past.

But the shah ignored her.

'My king, you are so handsome,' said another woman who was dressed in garments of bright, gleaming colours.

The shah did not respond.

'If I may be permitted to receive the king, I will recite his own poems for him,' said a lady with black hair, lips painted red and a revealing gown.

The shah stopped. The woman began to recite:

Jamshid koja raft? Cheh shod taj o kolah-ash?
Ku farr-e Fereyduni o ku heshmat o jah-ash?
Aya beh kojayand kaz-ishan khabri nist?
Ku dowlat garshasbi o gula sepah-ash?
Bezhan beh koja raft? Gereftari jah-ash.
Aya beh koja-and, kaz ishan khabri nist?

The shah loved poetry. He himself was a poet. On some of the evenings he spent with his wives he took great pleasure in reading his latest verses. Besides as writing poetry he also kept a diary in which he personally recorded events for posterity.

The woman had recited one of the shah's most moving poems, about the great legendary kings. In it he wondered where they were, where their thrones and crowns had gone, and what had become of their glorious and mighty armies.

The shah turned to the woman. She stepped aside to admit him, but he did not enter her room. He stood beside her and stroked her left arm with the back of his hand. The woman had the audacity to take the shah by the hand and gently draw him towards her. The shah conceded to this gesture, lowered his face to her bosom, smelled the odour of her chamber and walked on.

With his hands behind his back he came to a woman who was standing shyly at her door. Her silence appealed to him. At that moment Khwajeh Bashi appeared with his list. Noticing that the shah was showing interest in this shy woman, he whispered, 'Your Majesty has not yet shared his bed with this lady. She is from Azerbaijan, from the region that was occupied by the Russians. She doesn't speak a word of Persian.'

The woman had light blue eyes and was dressed in the manner of Russian country women. The shah ran his hand down her dark blonde plaits. He smelled her white neck and brought his nose up to her ear. He seized one of her plaits with his right hand, pulled her head towards him, pressed his mouth to her dark red painted lips and bit her. In broken Persian the woman whispered, 'Hurt. It hurts!'

The king thrust his hand under her dress, pressed her against the doorframe and pushed his head between her breasts, causing his tall cylindrical hat to fall to the floor. Then he let her go. His lust had evaporated. The sadness returned.

Khwajeh Bashi picked up the hat and handed it back to the shah, who continued walking.

Now his glance fell on a young woman with very dark Afghan eyes. She had a mysterious aura about her and looked as if she had stepped out of an old fairy tale. Why had the shah not seen her before? He gave Khwajeh Bashi a questioning look.

'She has been with us for a long time, but she was still a child,' answered Khwajeh Bashi. 'Now – well, how shall I put it? – she has become beautiful. I beg your pardon; I should have noticed her earlier, but there are so many women and some of them blossom quite suddenly.'

'Where is she from?' asked the shah.

'From Herat, Your Majesty,' answered Khwajeh Bashi uncertainly, and he looked as if he had said it to make the shah happy.

Light twinkled in the shah's eyes when he heard the word Herat. He asked her what her name was.

'Jayhun,' she said anxiously, staring at the floor.

Her name intrigued him. It was the name of a mysterious river in Afghanistan about which the poet Rudaki had written an unforgettable poem a thousand years before.

The shah grabbed the girl round the waist and drew her towards him.

'I am afraid, Your Majesty,' said the girl with a sweet Afghan accent.

Her fear and her accent aroused the shah even more. He kissed her on the mouth and reached under her shirt to stroke her breasts.

'God, help me,' she cried.

The shah pushed her into the room and tore her shirt open. Her breasts tumbled out.

'Your Majesty, be gentle with me. Wait. Wait a moment.'

Khwajeh Bashi pulled the door closed and stood outside.

Suddenly screaming could be heard that had a note of joy. The harem fell silent and the women closed their doors.

9. The Brothers

The vizier had been working on two fronts to eliminate the danger posed by the rebellious brothers. He sent in the army to break the resistance of the armed groups, and at the same time he looked for a political solution to the national unrest, mainly by working with the British embassy in Tehran. He was certain that the British were supporting the shah's brothers in the eastern part of the country, so he abandoned all restraint and carried on hard-nosed negotiations to force the British to suspend their support of the rebels.

It was one of the few times that Mahdolia fully supported the vizier in a fight and provided him with important information. Army invasions in the province and the vizier's intransigence in his dealings with the British and Russian representatives finally bore fruit, and the seven rebellious brothers laid down their weapons and surrendered. They were brought to Tehran in chains.

The shah received the vizier in his military uniform at army headquarters, located in a barracks outside Tehran. His left hand was on his sword. With his right hand he spun a large, dark brown globe as he listened to the vizier deliver his report on the arrest of the shah's brothers.

It was the room in which the most important decisions in the wars of the past decades had been made. The globe had been a gift of Napoleon. Shah Naser stood beside an oil painting depicting his father in uniform, riding a silver horse. He was wearing his tall cylindrical hat, a red sash and a cloak over his shoulders, which fluttered in the wind. The painting was a copy of the famous painting of Napoleon shown seated on a rearing horse, holding the reins with one hand and pointing to some distant spot with the other as the horse prepares to jump. Behind him is a group of threatening clouds. The shah's father loved that painting, so he asked the court painter to depict him in the same pose.

In the palace library there was a book containing a series of paintings of Napoleon. The shah often took the book from the bookcase and leafed through it. In his youth he had been taught by the vizier that he must always emulate history's greatest examples.

The vizier reported on the negotiations he had conducted with the British and on the guarantee that the rebels would not be punished.

'So they are calling the shots,' responded the shah sullenly.

'The British are doing everything they can to secure their position in India. We've got to learn to live with that reality. We are trying to give the country a modern face, so there's no room for turmoil. The seven rebellious brothers will be brought to Your Majesty. They will kneel before you and ask your forgiveness, and Your Majesty may pardon them in the name of brotherhood. Thus peace will be restored – for the time being.'

'Brotherhood? These are no brothers of ours. What our father did not beget with my mother is not a brother,' said the shah angrily.

'This is the best solution to the problem. It would be good if you were to talk to the brothers and put the interests of the country above family matters. Your mother will not be amenable to a pardon, but in granting it you know you will have made a wise decision.'

The words of the vizier tempered the shah's rage. The brothers would kneel before him and beg for mercy.

Mirza Kabir then went on to explain the reforms in the army, for which the shah had already studied the contracts. The French did good work, but the costs were high.

'Yes, that has always been my concern,' said the shah. 'How are we going to cover the costs? The vizier keeps telling us the treasury is empty.'

'Your Majesty,' said the vizier with a smile, 'God loves our country. The empire has been truly blessed. We have immense riches: rough gems, gold and silver lying about everywhere. The French know that. We are now involved in talks with them, and when the time is right I will provide Your Majesty with detailed information concerning the proposals.'

The shah was satisfied with the vizier's course of action.

Now that the shah was in a good mood the vizier seized the opportunity and continued speaking: 'We have a beautiful country, a rich country, but there has not been a stable government here in centuries. The fate of the country is in the shah's hands. The wealthy families think only of themselves. They frustrate all our plans. If we want to build a factory, they refuse to part with even a metre of their property. Why do they need so much land, so many houses, so many villages? They bring in teachers from abroad to instruct their children in French and the new sciences, while the peasants are kept in ignorance.'

The vizier paused. 'I have invested all my hope for change in Your Majesty,' he said. 'All I desire is your active contribution.'

The shah had listened in silence. 'The vizier has poured

the same words into our ears over and over again,' he replied crossly. 'We have heard you. You may go.'

Upon his return to the palace at the end of the afternoon the shah was told by the chamberlain that his mother, the queen, was waiting for him in the hall of mirrors.

'Mother, what brings you here so unexpectedly?'

He embraced his mother and kissed her on the head. Dispensing with civilities Mahdolia took aim.

'I have heard that your rebellious half-brothers will be appearing before the shah tomorrow to beg for mercy. So I rode here in great haste.'

'They are my brothers,' said the king, trying to defend himself.

'Apparently the shah does not know the history of his own family. They are not your full brothers. Your father was ruthless in pushing his brothers aside, and your grandfather had his brothers butchered because they made a claim for power. Everyone is aghast that the king wants to receive these vicious men. The tale of the brothers is well known in Persian history. Kings have always had their brothers eliminated without mercy. Now it's your turn, and if you so much as hesitate they will destroy you. How often must I tell you that you cannot trust the vizier? You are the king, the representative of God on earth. This is all about the throne, and the throne is not yours alone. It also belongs to those who succeed us. You must show your brothers no mercy. For mercy they must appeal to God.'

There was nothing the shah could say. His mother's argument was unassailable. But so was the vizier's.

'Listen,' his mother went on, 'your half-brothers have received money and weapons from the British, and the vizier is secretly representing British interests. That is why he's trying to solve the problem this way. Your brothers should be hung, each and every one of them. That is the advice of Sheikh Aqasi. You are the king. I have said all I need to say.' And with that she left.

The shah stood in the middle of the hall of mirrors. He picked up the cat, who was pressing herself against his legs. 'Did you hear what she said? She wants to see blood. Woman is the mother of all misery. What should I do, Sharmin?'

The cat turned her head towards the library.

'Shall we consult Hafez?' asked the shah, and he let Sharmin jump down from his arms. The collection of poetry by the great medieval poet was a source of counsel for all Persians, poor and rich, if they had no one else to turn to. As tradition dictated the shah kissed the cover of the book, shut his eyes and opened it to a random page.

Mi-barad baran-e raham-at khoda-ye man
Pour over me, O Lord,
From the clouds of thy bounteous mercy
The rain of forgiveness
That falls ever faster on my grave,
Before I, like dust on the wind, from corn to chaff,
Rise up and fly away, past the knowledge of men . . .

Incredulous the shah read the poem through once more. Hafez was speaking in no uncertain terms to the shah himself. He was talking frankly about forgiveness – a rain of forgiveness, in fact – and about the principle of mercy.

He paced the room to and fro with the book in his hand. Should he try once more, just to be sure? If Hafez were to speak of mercy again, then he would choose the rain of mercy. He repeated the ritual.

Never have I laid my eyes on
More sweet-voiced verses than yours, O Hafez!

> This I dare to swear on the Quran
> That you carry in your bosom . . .

Hafez had not changed his mind, but now he advised the shah to consult the Quran. He mentioned the Quran by name; that was clear. The shah kissed the book of poetry, put it back on the shelf and turned his gaze to the Quran that was lying on a separate table in a green cloth slipcase. He went to the dining room and washed his hands under the small gold tap, dried them, went back to the library and picked up the holy book. He removed it from its slipcase with great care, kissed it, closed his eyes, opened the book reverently and studied the surah word for word.

> *Tabbat yada Abi Lahaben wa tabba*
> Destroyed will be
> the hands of Abu Lahab,
> and he himself will perish.
> Of no avail shall be his wealth,
> nor what he has acquired.
> He will be roasted in the fire,
> And his wife,
> the carrier of firewood,
> Will have a strap of twisted rope round her neck.

This surah was about the uncle of the Prophet Muhammad, a man named Abu Lahab, who had done everything he could to prevent Muhammad from carrying out his mission and once had even devised a plan to kill him. Muhammad had had him severely punished.

The counsel of the Quran was indisputable, and the shah felt a burden drop from his shoulders. He kissed the book, put it back on the table and walked to the dining room. Then he sat down and waited for the chamberlain to bring him his meal.

But doubt once again rose within him. To whom should he listen, Hafez or the Quran? Did Muhammad actually punish his uncle? He spoke harshly to him and wished for his hands to be broken, but he had not actually broken his hands. So what should he do now with his seven half-brothers?

His appetite had left him. Shah Naser walked to his bedroom. It was not yet time to sleep, but the shah crept into bed fully dressed.

The Persian elite and their kings were not committed believers as a rule. They had great respect for the text of the Quran but would have nothing to do with the culture of the Arabs, who had destroyed the Persian Empire, and this included the practise of Arabic rituals. The vizier was not a man of prayer, nor had he raised the shah to pray, but he did teach him to turn to God whenever he felt anxious or uncertain, as all the kings before him had done. And so that night the shah rose from his sleepless bed, washed his hands and face, and turned towards Mecca.

The next morning, after bathing, he went to the hall of mirrors. He ate a hearty breakfast and spent some time drawing as a diversion. To calm his nerves he drew a teapot and an apple in a fruit bowl. The sun was already at its apex. He put on his military uniform, pulled his sword from its sheath and played with it in front of the mirror.

The chamberlain came in and told him his seven half-brothers were awaiting him in the golden hall. The golden hall was where the shah gave great public parties and where he received officers and merchants.

The shah glanced at himself in the mirror once more, drew a white-gloved hand across his moustache and walked to the hall, where a pair of officers was waiting for him.

'His Majesty!' shouted a high-ranking officer.

A soldier blew on his trumpet and the shah entered the hall, accompanied by officers carrying the flag of the Persian Empire.

At the doorway he cast a glance at his seven brothers, who were standing with their heads bowed. The high-ranking officer made a gesture and all of them knelt down in a single movement with their heads touching the floor as a sign of humility.

'Rise!' cried the shah. There was a friendly tone to his voice that dispelled the oppressive atmosphere. His brothers summoned up their courage and looked at the shah. Addressing them he said, 'It is a blessed moment. Our homeland is unified once again, and we are happy. Our brothers must understand that whatever we do, we do for our country, and that accordingly we are following in the footsteps of the kings who went before us. The decision that has been made is a decision made for the country by God himself.'

He thrust out his hand and had his brothers come forward one by one to kiss it. Then he walked over to a table. On the table were a quill pen, an ink pot and paper. The shah picked up the quill and wrote a few words. He signed the document, pressed his signet ring into the ink-pad and placed his seal beneath his signature. Then he folded up the paper and handed it personally to the high-ranking officer.

That same evening the shah's brothers were hung in the bazaar square. The next morning the people who came to the bazaar saw the gallows and the seven men hanging motionless from the ropes.

As soon as he heard the report of the execution the vizier hastened to the palace.

'How could this happen?' he said to the shah.

The shah did not respond.

'I asked you to pardon them. By committing this deed the shah will unleash chaos in the country. Everyone is afraid. No one trusts us any more. It is impossible to hold the country together with bullets and gallows. We must engage in politics. Why did the shah make this decision?'

'We are the shah! England can go to hell. We do not have to answer to anyone.'

'But the country must be governed!' said the vizier in a fury.

Without saying a word the shah withdrew behind the curtain, leaving the vizier to stand helpless in the hall of mirrors.

10. Taj, the Daughter of the Shah

The king had many daughters, but little Taj Olsultan was different. She was born of the marriage with Foruq, who was a woman of the Qajar tribe, the same tribe as that of the shah. Foruq was also the shah's cousin.

Foruq was expected to bear a son for the monarchy who would later succeed the shah. Dozens of sons had been produced by the other wives, but they didn't count. Only a son of Foruq could be the crown prince. As fate would have it, however, she did not immediately become pregnant. The entire royal medical staff examined her, and all the aged women of the tribe included her in their lengthy prayers. Female shamans from every corner of the land were admitted to her bedside until finally she was found to be with child. Great was the joy. But instead of a son she bore a daughter, who was given the name Taj Olsultan.

Now there was hope and the shah could often be found in Foruq's bed. But to everyone's great disappointment Foruq bore four more daughters. After the last daughter was born the shah stopped sleeping with her.

Foruq complained to the queen, who called the shah to account. 'How dare you? What does this mean, seeking the solace of other women? Foruq is the only one who can give you an heir.'

'I am neither willing nor able,' said the shah.

'To do what?'

'I am not able to sleep with her.'

'Why not?' shouted his mother.

'I am a man, and I cannot function any more with Foruq,' he confessed.

'Then think of something. Or the sons of your other wives will rise up in revolt later on and tear the country into a hundred pieces.'

'That changes nothing. If I can't, I can't. It is undoubtedly God's will. We must not be ungrateful. Perhaps life has something else in store for us: perhaps our daughter Taj Olsultan will bear a son for us.'

'The shah must stop this nonsense. She is only a child.'

'When she is grown, we will look for a suitable husband for her from our own tribe. You know our history. Such things happen. Our father was a good example. He was not the son of the ruling king. No, he was the son of the king's brother. We don't know what secrets life holds. Let us be patient and wait.'

From that moment on Taj Olsultan was treated like a precious jewel.

The shah always went to see his daughter whenever he felt sad. According to custom the wife who bore the crown prince did not live in the harem. Her children were regarded as princes. Because Taj Olsultan was the shah's favourite and would one day produce an heir for him, she did not live in the harem with the other women and children. She had a separate apartment of her own, where one of the shah's old retainers cared for her as if she were a queen.

The night the shah's half-brothers were hung, the shah could not sleep. He had nightmares and dreamt that he too was hanging from a gallows and that the wind was playing with his body. Even though he had been hung he was still alive. Looking down from the gallows he could see masses of people gazing up at him. He tried to cry for help, but the cord round his neck stifled his voice, and his hands had been tied behind his back. His felt his soul slipping away. Gathering all his strength he tried to move his legs to show that he was still alive, but this just caused the cord to tighten even more round his throat. He woke up drenched in sweat.

Dazed, he drank two glasses of water from a pitcher on a nearby table. Then he pulled the curtain aside. It was still dark. Slowly he realised that he should not have had his brothers hung, that this act would unleash waves of hostility in the land and that God would punish him severely. He should have listened to the vizier.

The shah picked up the lantern. Followed by his curious cat he left the palace through the back door and entered the garden of the living quarters where his favourite daughter slept, pushing the door open with great care. The old servant woke immediately.

'Is she asleep?' he whispered. 'That's fine then. Let her sleep. I'm going to rest here.'

Straightaway the woman placed a mattress on the floor beside the girl's bed. The shah lay down and his cat nestled at his feet. The old woman pulled a blanket over him and bolted the door.

Early in the morning she gently wakened the girl.

'The king is sleeping here,' she said.

The girl smiled, got out of bed and crept under the blanket with the shah. '*Bonjour, monsieur*,' she whispered in his ear.

The shah opened his eyes and threw his arm round her. '*Bonjour, madame. Comment ça va, ma fille?*'

'Very well, Father.'

'Have you been working hard on your French?'

'Yes, Father.'

'And your English?'

'Not very hard, Shah-my-Father.'

'Why not?'

'Your doctor speaks to me in French whenever he sees me and it's funny. But I don't like English.'

'Like it or not – learn their language; you're going to need it.'

'But it's so difficult,' she complained.

'Enough. Come and massage my back,' he said, rolling over on his stomach.

The girl stood on his back and massaged his shoulders with her feet.

'How delightful to have such a daughter,' sighed the shah.

'But you have so many daughters,' she said with a smile.

'That's not true. They are the daughters of our wives. I have just one daughter and that is you. The other girls are not mine.'

'Why not?' asked Taj Olsultan with surprise.

'Because you are the only one I love,' said the shah.

'Why?'

'You are my own flesh and blood, and my firstborn. Let me tell you a secret. I want to revise the law so that later you can become the shah.'

'The shah?'

'You will succeed me.'

'But that's impossible. I'm a girl.'

'Catherine, the queen of Russia, was also a girl, but she became one of the most powerful women ever. I want you to become just as powerful.'

'What do you have to know to be shah?'

'We will teach you everything.' The shah was already looking forward to the lessons.

'But I don't want to be a queen. Why don't you ask my mother?'

'Your mother? We have no need of her.'

'And my grandmother? She's already queen.'

'But she will be dead before I die.'

'You mustn't speak of my mother and your own mother that way,' protested the girl.

The shah fell silent. It pleased him that this young girl made no attempt to disguise her opinions or to curry favour with him.

'It's light outside,' the old woman told the shah.

The shah kissed his daughter and went out to the garden, much relieved. With a stick in his hand he walked past the tall trees and returned to his own room, where the chamberlain had his breakfast waiting for him.

11. The Cannon

The matter of the hanging of the half-brothers had jolted the vizier awake. Mahdolia's influence over the shah was still considerable. The vizier had been able to calm the popular unrest after the execution, but now he had to be on his guard against the shah's unpredictable behaviour. The desire to retake Herat was still smouldering beneath the surface.

The vizier had instructed the shah in the ways of the world, but he had enough experience to know that some of a child's traits cannot be corrected by lessons. The shah was his father's son: weak. But he was also his mother's son: vindictive, hungry for power, obstinate and headstrong. And he was his grandfather's grandson: a valiant fighter, a hard man whose will was law. The shah was a mixture of his father, his mother, his grandfather and his tutor.

The vizier had to be able to cope with all these contradictions, not for the sake of the shah, nor for his own sake, but for the sake of the country, even though he knew he would probably have to sacrifice his life for his ideals.

In the meantime the shah had put his troubles behind him for the time being. He took pleasure in life and he was going hunting. He had his own cannon, a cannon that Napoleon had given as a gift for the crown prince just after his birth, and he liked to shoot it.

The French emperor had once written to the father of the shah.

Bonaparte, the Emperor of the people of France, writes to the King of Persia:

Greetings. *Je vous salue.*

You are the king of a noble land that God has blessed with his devotion and his mercy.

The inhabitants of Persia are magnanimous, clever and courageous, and they are worthy of good kings, but we know that the kings before you forsook their people and ignored the needs of the country.

I am sending you one of my best advisors, who will personally convey to you my views and feelings with regard to your country. You may also tell him anything you wish. He is the most trustworthy man on our staff.

May God help Persia.

Napoleon Bonaparte

What the British and the Russians wanted was nothing new. Napoleon Bonaparte already wanted to get to India by way of Persia, and he tried to form an alliance with the father of the shah behind the backs of the Russians and the British. The late king had hoped that with Napoleon on his side he would be able to attack Russia and to free Azerbaijan from Russian hands. But Napoleon was forced to give up his dream. He did not keep his promises, and in failing to do so he abandoned the Persians. Russia punished the shah and took possession of part of the country.

Napoleon was now a page in the annals of history, but he had left a tangible part of himself behind in Persia. During his Russian campaign he had sent Persia a cannon, a special gift for the young crown prince. The design of the cannon was new – it had two wheels – and Napoleon had arranged for the name of the crown prince and the royal coat of arms to be engraved on it in gold. It was clear from the elaborate ornamentation that this was a princely cannon.

When he went to Tabriz as crown prince, Naser brought the cannon with him. After his father died, the cannon came along in the move to Tehran. It was kept in well-oiled readiness at Golestan Palace. The king never left the palace without it.

'Sharmin?' called the shah.

The cat sprang from the chair.

'We're going for a little ride over the hills.' When he reached the top of the outer stairs he took a deep breath and said, 'Magnificent! You can smell the trees. What a fragrance!'

Three servants took care of the cat. They placed her in a basket covered with a sheer white cloth and carefully put the basket in a coach that was furnished just for her.

The shah climbed into his saddle and looked to make sure his cannon was ready. With great poise he rode to the gate, followed by a number of guards. His cannon was mounted on a decorated cart, which was pulled by two horses. The shah looked excited and happy.

No sooner had he left the palace than the drummers and the trumpeter announced to the city that the shah was approaching. It was the first time in a long time that the shah had let himself be seen by his people. He had been afraid there would be disturbances after the execution of his brothers, but except for a few minor scuffles it had remained peaceful. This led the shah to believe that his subjects agreed with his decision. Now he was going hunting in the hills outside the city, but he had mapped out a route through a number of busy streets.

The drummers beat their drums even harder and the

town criers shouted, 'Blind be the enemy, the king is approaching!'

The people tried to catch a glimpse of the shah's cat in her royal coach. It became more and more crowded, and the officers leading the procession had to lash the people with their whips to keep them away from the shah. Hundreds of blind, disabled and deformed people, who begged for coins or bits of bread in the street or in the bazaar, tried to get as closed as they could, crying out, '*Javid shah, javid shah*, long live the shah, long live the shah!'

The guards raised their guns and beat the beggars, but they threw themselves on the ground in front of the horses and stretched out their hands to the shah, weeping and imploring.

Deep in his heart the shah felt troubled. Recently he had complained once again to his mother, 'We keep having the feeling that we have become king of an endless procession of indigents.'

'You may complain, but what you say is not true,' his mother had said to comfort him. 'You are the king of a very special land. The king of the princes who live in mysterious palaces, the king of the enigmatic Persian women, the king of the rich carpet dealers who populate our beautiful cities, and the king of thousands of large landowners in the villages. And you are also king of your mother.'

He reached into his coat pocket and pulled out a handful of coins, tossing them into the crowd. The people fought for them.

'*Javid shah, javid shah*,' cried the multitude.

And once again Shah Naser threw out a handful of coins. The drummers beat their drums even harder and the trumpeters blew louder on their trumpets. Just like

Napoleon on his horse in the painting, the shah pointed to a spot in the distance. The horsemen surrounded the shah and galloped through the city gate.

Once they reached the hills the king took the lead, hunting for wild stags. Shooting from a galloping horse was a uniquely Persian feat. No one in the world could hit their mark on horseback the way a Persian soldier could. It was a skill acquired by all the future kings during their childhood years. The little princes practised it while hunting, and Shah Naser was a master. It made him happy when he shot and the animal fell.

The shah also loved fighting. He who was sometimes so frightened in the palace proved quite courageous on the front. He had fought in two wars with his father. The first time they lost to the Russians. The second time was the battle of Herat, which ended in disaster when the British took possession of the city and handed it over to the Afghan tribal leaders. Everyone knew that the grief over the loss of Herat was what had caused the old king's death.

Hunting was in the shah's blood. He used to hunt in the forests of Tabriz, searching for lions and tigers. Now he had to content himself with the stags of Tehran. While he pursued the animals his guards dragged the cannon to the top of the highest hill. When they reached the summit a sergeant blew on his trumpet to announce that everything was ready. The shah rode up the slope and, covered in sweat, sprang from his horse and thrust his arm in the air. 'This is an exceptional day! How good we feel!'

He stroked the cannon's barrel. One of the guards handed him a cannonball. The shah kissed the ball, placed it securely in the barrel and aimed it at a target on another hill. He was handed a burning torch with which he lit the fuse. Then he bent down, his hands over his ears. The cannon went off.

After he had shot the cannon seven times an officer threw a coat around the shah to keep him from catching cold. He was handed some sweet rose water. He walked up to a table on which a large dish of delicacies had been placed and ate his fill of dates stuffed with walnuts, crisp almond biscuits and ginger cooked in butter and honey.

When the servants had loaded all the bagged game onto the cart, the shah jumped back on his horse. He would have stayed longer, but he could tell from the eyes of his cat that she preferred to lie on her own sleeping spot at home.

12. The Reforms

The vizier had ordered local officials to build large carpet factories where hundreds of weavers could be employed. In the north of the country, near the Caspian Sea, small companies packed caviar in handy transportable boxes and pots.

The vizier dreamt that his unemployed countrymen would find jobs in factories, just like British labourers. He dreamt that Persian girls would go to school, just like the girls in Moscow. He could hardly sleep for all the work that had to be done. In the meantime his enemies did everything they could to bring him down. He presented his plans to his advisors.

'I have many dreams for this country, but we mustn't try to do too many things at once,' the vizier had said to the young men in his council of ministers. 'All of you have studied abroad. But our country is not Russia, let alone England. In those countries the power is centralised. Here the majority of the population live in villages. In the countryside we have no power at all; there everything is in the hands of the large landowners.'

'We are not losing sight of reality,' said one of the ministers, a man named Takhi Khan. 'That's why we're concentrating on the big cities, especially Tehran.'

'Actually Tehran is more difficult than anywhere else. Everywhere we go we're held back by the elite, who own all the property,' argued the vizier.

'We must work to establish a separation of powers, just like in the countries of the West,' said Amir, the vizier's young advisor. 'That is essential to carrying out our plans.'

'But we must not frighten the elite,' said the vizier in measured tones. 'We must move forward with caution. I will speak to the shah.'

Persia's wealth lay in the abundance of its gold mines, rubies, diamonds, spices and something that the Portuguese called *ouro negro* – 'black gold'.

The Portuguese had already tried their luck at extracting the *ouro negro*, or crude oil. They had drilled holes here and there in the Persian soil in search of the mysterious black liquid, but had found nothing.

Later came N.R. Darsi, an adventurer from New Zealand. His expedition was financed by a chemical company. He searched for sources of crude oil, but what he found was not worth mentioning. Darsi returned empty-handed.

It was then that people in the western countries began to understand what oil was actually worth. In a valley in Pennsylvania in America they had drilled down seventeen metres, and by the next day the well was filled with oil.

In Persia's southern province the nasty black liquid leaked up from the ground spontaneously. The local inhabitants called it *qir*, or pitch – they ladled it into crates and smeared it on the wheels of their carts.

The French were asked by the vizier to set up businesses, to reform the army and to teach science. A number of them, however, had been given a secret assignment by the French government: to search for oil. The French asked permission to conduct drilling operations in addition to the mining activities they had agreed to. No one could have known that underneath the surface lay one of the largest crude-oil reserves in the world.

The drilling produced nothing and the French brought this particular sideline to a halt. Then one day they happened to see a black substance glittering in one of their wells, so they resumed drilling – with no appreciable results. They ladled the oil out of the well, put it in vats and sent it to France. It was something, but nothing in comparison with what lay ahead.

The vizier made too many demands, but the temptation of the mineral resources and the chance to gain power over the Persian army was irresistible to the French. They agreed to all the conditions, and the vizier drew up a list of projects he wanted be carried out, namely the setting up of:

- Three technical schools in Tehran, Tabriz and Isfahan.
- A large library in Tehran containing modern scientific books on urban development and road construction.
- A mining school in the city of Sultanabad.
- Five printing offices in five major cities.
- A hospital in Tehran and a women's clinic in Tabriz.
- Several primary schools for the children of Tehran.
- Leather and shoe factories.
- A military training institute for young people.
- Schools for drawing and painting.
- Two boarding schools for orphans in Tehran.
- Textile, glass, iron, copper, paper, sugar and tobacco factories in various cities.
- A small spring factory in Shiraz for the suspension of carts and coaches.
- And last, a factory for the casting of medium-sized bells for the cities.

On top of all this he firmly demanded that a number of cannon and cannonball factories be built in Tehran,

Isfahan and Shiraz so the army would no longer be dependent on Russian or British cannons.

The vizier realised he would not be able to bring all his plans to fruition during his lifetime. He knew how great the opposition would be. But of all his dreams there were at least three that he wanted to see fulfilled.

First he wanted all the children in the country to be vaccinated against smallpox. This would bring a halt to the nation's increasing rate of blindness. His second dream was a technical school for gifted children, which he would later incorporate into his development plans. His third dream was highly personal. When he was still a boy, his father worked as a minister in the cabinet in which he would later be prime minister. After having travelled to Russia his father told him about the bells that hung high up in the churches there, the bells that rang so the entire city could hear them. Later, when Mirza Kabir was a young man, he was part of a delegation to Moscow. In the Kremlin he heard for the first time the bells his father had described. The whole notion of time made him tremble with happiness: time that advances, time that slips away.

That boyhood dream had never left him. He had met with the engineer of a French bell foundry to discuss the possibility of hanging a number of bells in big cities like Tehran, Isfahan, Shiraz and Tabriz. The bells could not be placed in the minarets, of course. That would be too reminiscent of churches, which would create ill feeling. The vizier thought of putting the bells on the great squares of the country's bazaars. Sometimes while riding to the bazaar he could almost hear the bells ringing in his mind. Time was standing still in his homeland. He wanted to use the bells to get time moving again.

He had made his wish known. The engineer would erect a foundry and start making bells as soon as the country entered calmer waters.

There was one big problem standing in the way of these developments: the country had no decent roads, only narrow tracks that had been beaten down naturally by horses and coaches. Long ago Persia had boasted the greatest roads in the world, but time and war had destroyed them and they lay buried beneath many layers of earth.

To stay on good terms with the populace and to quell their unease about the presence of the French, the vizier asked the Russians if they would be willing to build a new network of roads to connect the cities of Persia. They accepted the offer immediately and went straight to work. They passed over the southern cities and began with the roads that brought them closer to the borders with India. The vizier was aware of this, but he also knew that what the Russians were doing was good for the country.

The presence of the Russians in the northern and eastern parts of Persia was another thorn in the side of the British. They had no leverage with the vizier, who was eager to keep everybody happy. Another problem was that the vizier came from a family that was not easily bribed. So the British decided to wait. They provided the Afghan tribes with weapons and military advisors to block any Russian invasion of India that might take place.

At the same time the British tried to use their front men to set Mahdolia further against the vizier. They sent her false reports that the vizier was planning to weaken the position of the shah over time.

'He signs whatever papers the vizier puts in front of

him, without asking any questions,' complained Mahdolia to her confidant, Sheikh Aqasi.

'It is indeed disquieting,' agreed Sheikh Aqasi. 'It won't be long before the shah loses all his power. It is your duty to admonish the shah.'

'I will talk to him,' said Mahdolia. 'I must talk to him.'

13. The Russians

The shah often went on cross-country journeys, and he always took a group of his wives with him. During these journeys he gave his subjects the opportunity to admire him, and he also received local officials. He invariably paid visits to the army barracks.

He looked forward to receiving delegates from the various trades, which happened every now and then. He also had regular visits from clergymen, with whom such contacts were useful. He invited the imams with royal connections to come round on holy feast days, such as the birthdays of the Prophet Muhammad and the holy imam Ali, and the anniversaries of their deaths.

When the clergymen came the chamberlain had to make them wait for the shah in the golden hall for a long time. While they waited they were treated to tea and refreshments. When the shah came in the clergymen all bowed, and one by one they kissed his hand. The shah then gave a brief speech, chatted with some of them, asked them to pray for him and for the kingdom, pressed special gold coins bearing his image into their hands and withdrew once again. Then he would whisper in Sharmin's ear, 'A pack of fools. They all smell of goat droppings.'

Sometimes the shah didn't want to be shah any more. He envied those who were free to walk in the street and go to the bazaar, or to work on their land as farmers. He found life in the palace boring most of the time because one day was no different from the next. He read, he wrote, he studied the documents the vizier showed him, he ate, and sometimes he spent the evening in the harem. He went for long walks and visited his mother. Occasionally he looked in on his daughter to see if she was studying hard.

Today he strolled into the courtyard and went to the elegant structure that was set off by itself behind the tall trees and was known as 'Tableau Noir'. It was a single pleasant room decorated with French furniture and very fine paintings by the famous Persian artist Kamal-ol-Molk. Mounted on the wall was a blackboard, *tableau noir* in French. There were also a few chairs for the pupils, all of them children the shah had begotten by women of his own tribe.

The schoolroom had been built by order of the shah's father. When the crown prince was a boy he had learned French and mathematics there from an old French lady. The teachers had always been French: the wife of one of the staff members at the French embassy or a lady brought in from France for this special purpose.

Now Taj Olsultan was being taught by such a French lady. She was new. The vizier had arranged for her employment through the embassy. She lived in the French residence and spent a few hours every day giving lessons to Taj.

Looking through the window the shah could see the French woman standing at the blackboard. She was new and shy. The shah was not sure whether he should go in or not, but his cat sprang from his arms and boldly sidled up to Taj.

The teacher walked to the door. She greeted the shah and made a little curtsy. Then she stepped aside to let the shah enter. But he stayed where he was.

'Is everything to your liking?' he asked in French.

'Yes, indeed,' she replied politely.

'Excellent,' said the shah. 'Is Taj a good pupil?'

'Of course. She is clever and sharp-witted. A real princess.'

'You make us happy. If you need anything, please let us know.'

The shah called Sharmin and walked back through the garden.

Sometimes he painted to dispel the boredom. Kamal-ol-Molk had been his instructor. For one whole year the painter had come to the palace to paint a portrait of the shah in the hall of mirrors. Working on a large canvas Kamal-ol-Molk had brought to life the room's ceiling and walls, with their thousands of little mirrors. The heavy, dark green curtain behind which the shah always vanished and reappeared, the dark blue and red carpets with their hundreds of figures – all were realistically depicted. Finally the painter added the shah, seated in his royal chair.

By studying the paintings the shah learned several techniques that he himself applied as best he could. Sharmin was his first model and the painting that resulted was quite good. He was happy with it and hung it immediately in his study.

Another time he tried to immortalise Taj Olsultan, but was unsuccessful.

'It is a hopeless task. The shah has two challenges that cannot be conquered,' Kamal-ol-Molk told him. 'Firstly your daughter is breathtakingly beautiful. Secondly she has no wrinkles. I propose that the shah paint his mother. She is a dream model. Her beauty is emphasised by her royal wrinkles, she radiates power and her choice of clothing is perfect.'

'That is impossible,' the shah shot back. 'Our mother cannot sit still. She cannot be silent for even one minute.

She is always looking for an opportunity to reproach us about something. She in a chair and we with a brush in our hand: we can see it all now. It would be war.'

The shah limited himself to painting his cat and still lifes. He secretly tried to make a copy of Napoleon's horse, but it didn't look like anything.

'It's not a horse but a donkey,' he said to himself. 'Even so, the attempt has given us pleasure.'

He would never be an impressive painter, but the shah was indeed a true poet. He committed his thoughts to paper, but he had trouble making the words rhyme. When he was satisfied with the result and each letter was in place, he would set aside an evening and summon his chronicler and his lantern-bearer to make an official copy. One of the poems was the following:

> I dreamt that the body of my grandfather had
>   dissolved and turned into dust
> Except the eyes.
> Which were revolving in their orbits
> And looking about.
> The sages interpreted my dream:
> 'He is still looking amazed
> how his kingdom belongs to others.'
> He is thinking of Herat.

After the last word the chronicler sat with bowed head. He was always the first to hear the shah's poems. Anxiously the shah awaited his reaction.

The chronicler broke the silence and said, 'A regal poem. I am moved, Your Majesty.'

A smile appeared on the shah's face and he tossed the chronicler a couple of gold coins.

The vizier, who also loved poetry, had given the shah a beautiful, gold-tooled volume of poems by the medieval

Persian poet Abu Abdollah Rudaki. The shah read the classics and knew many poems by heart. Poetry was his salvation during the long boring nights in the palace. He read the magnificent collection attentively, and on one occasion he happened to stumble on one of the most beautiful of all Persian poems:

> *Buye juye muliyan ayad hami*
> *Yad-e yar mehreban ayad hami*

The shah was deeply impressed and made a detailed entry about it in his diary: 'Herat will not let us rest. No matter what we do, the city keeps occupying our thoughts. Today Herat skilfully revealed itself in a poem by Rudaki. The poem was about his favourite river, the Amu. Reading it brought tears to our eyes, and today we hummed it all day long:

"The wind carries the fragrance
of my homeland's river
and memories of the beloved.
Though the River Amu has a rocky bed, I still long
    for home.
Then the river will feel like down beneath my feet.
The shah is the moon.
Home is heaven
where the moon is bound to go."'

Winter came, and after a while the shah no longer knew how he was going to get through the long winter nights. He was pleasantly surprised by an invitation from the Russians.

The vizier had commissioned the Russians to construct roads between the cities, and they had been working day and night on the project for two years. The roads could have been made by the local population too, but the Russians had what the Persians lacked: discipline and perseverance. Russia's violent past and countless wars had created a people who no longer dared to believe in the future.

Before the severe cold set in the Russians wanted to please the shah with a special present. There was a shrine outside Tehran where Abdoldawood lay buried, a descendant of the Prophet Muhammad. For much of the year this shrine received thousands of visitors from Tehran, and it was the shah's favourite spot. He went there when he felt most desolate, kneeling at the grave of the saint to complain about life.

The Russians knew from the vizier how important the grave was for the shah's spiritual well-being. But in the winter the road to the shrine was impassable, rocky and dangerous, and no one dared attempt it by coach or on horseback. So the Russians had built a road for the shah that would always be passable: a track that snaked past the big rocks.

The riverbed had been bridged at twelve different places. Thousands of strong-armed peasants had levelled all the pits and dangerous slopes with earth and stones. Tea houses, eating establishments and houses of prayer had been built along the way.

The colder it got the harder the Russians worked. They built big fires and worked along with the peasants without interruption. When the road was finished it was covered by a thick layer of snow.

The vizier had arranged for the shah to receive the Russian road-builders on the first hill outside the city. He accompanied Shah Naser on horseback, and as they rode he reported on the work the Russians were doing throughout the country.

'We have already heard that they are hard-working people,' the shah remarked.

'We leave everything to God,' said the vizier. 'We ourselves do nothing.'

The shah thought the vizier was referring to his king's way of life and changed the subject.

'What are we doing here in the snow?'

'The engineers would like to give the shah a tour of the road they have built,' the vizier explained.

'And must that happen today?' complained the shah.

As soon as the Russian engineers saw the shah coming they formed a semicircle. The shah remained at a suitable distance, his stick in his hand, and the vizier introduced the Russian engineers to him. The chief engineer bowed his head slightly, rode up to the shah and asked if he might show him round. The road to the shrine lay under the snow and the shah did not understand what the engineer was suggesting. He cast an indifferent glance at the snow-covered hill and turned to the vizier for an explanation.

'If Your Majesty agrees, we will take him to the grave,' said the engineer.

'Where?' asked the shah with suspicion.

'To the shrine,' repeated the Russian coolly.

'Which shrine?'

'To the grave of the holy Abdoldawood.'

'In this snow? To Abdoldawood?' asked the shah incredulously.

'I assume Your Majesty's horse is able to gallop in the snow?'

'Our horse is strong, but it's late and soon darkness will fall.'

'Your Majesty will be back in the palace before dark.'

The shah looked distrustful.

'Is the vizier aware of this arrangement?' asked the shah, turning to the vizier.

Mirza Kabir nodded.

Shah Naser stared silently into the distance. Suddenly he turned to the Russian and said, 'Take the lead! Surprise us!'

The chief engineer spurred his horse to a gallop and raced down the snow-covered road. The shah followed the Russian past the great rocks, taking the turns with ease. He rode down the slopes without hesitation and passed a few tea houses. It seemed unthinkable that they could ride with such confidence down that unseen, snow-covered road.

After a short time the shah's eye fell on the golden cupola of the temple in the distance. It was no less than a miracle. In the past it would have taken a whole day to reach the shrine, even in the summer. Now it took them less than half an hour.

Just outside the shrine of Abdoldawood the Russian slackened his pace and brought his horse to a halt. The shah galloped past him and rode into the shrine.

14. The Spring Festival

It was spring, and the shah wanted to celebrate the Persian New Year as the Persian kings of old had done.

The festival had not been a lavish occasion in past years, but this time he was going to do it in style. His plan was to sit on the jewel-encrusted throne that dated from the time of the Medes and the Persians. Only the great Persian kings – Cyrus, Cambyses and Darius – had done that during their festivals. It was a simple but magical throne that was so old it was depicted on one of the stone walls in the ruins of the Persepolis Palace. This famous tableau shows Darius, the king of kings, receiving the other kings during the spring festival as they present him with gifts for the new spring season. Alexander the Great once set fire to the palace, but the throne was rescued and taken to a safe place.

According to the Persian calendar spring was arriving at ten o'clock in the morning that year. The guests who had been invited to the palace had made an early start. They were led to their places according to their rank by festively dressed servants. The guests stood in two rows facing each other so the shah could walk between them in order to greet them. The old, wise family members from the shah's own tribe stood in front, followed by the foreign delegations. Opposite them stood the warlords and a deputation of imams, led by the ayatollah of Tehran. Next to the imams were the military.

Then came representatives of the bazaar and of all the other professions and trades.

Everyone glistened in their New Year's finery, and all the beards were well combed and neatly trimmed. People smelled of roses, candles were burning and fragrant spices had been thrown on the fire. Happy voices and music could be heard on every side – all in anticipation of the shah's imminent appearance, which was to take place from behind the new long green curtains. Yet everyone was waiting for the foreign delegations. Something was wrong. They had arrived, but they were still standing near the pond.

The shah, who had been informed of the delay, looked past the curtain into the courtyard. He noticed that his vizier was involved in a serious discussion with the British ambassador.

'What's going on?' the shah asked the chamberlain.

'There is a disagreement between the vizier and the British delegation.'

'What about?'

'The British want to keep their boots on when they enter.'

'But this is not a stable. They have always taken off their shoes. Why not now?'

Everyone who entered the palace took off their shoes. The king was the only one who kept his shoes and boots on.

The British had chosen this way to express their displeasure about the activities of the Russians and the French. At first glance it seemed like such a little thing, but a very sensitive nerve had been touched. The vizier understood that it wasn't about the boots. He tried to control himself, but inside he was boiling with rage. The insolent British had provoked the vizier's ire once before when they recognised Afghanistan as a sovereign state.

'You will take off your boots!' the vizier said imperturbably to the ambassador.

'We have our traditions, just as the Persians have theirs,' responded the man. 'Britons never take their boots off, let alone at a festival given by the Persian king.'

His answer irritated the vizier even more. 'On other occasions you have greeted the king without your shoes,' he pointed out.

'Different rules apply for different occasions,' said the ambassador.

Mirza Kabir was faced with an impossible problem. Time was pressing, spring was about to start, the new calendar year had begun, hundreds of guests were waiting inside and the shah would lose his patience.

In the meantime the matter had reached the ears of all the guests and there was uproar in the hall.

'With their shoes on?'

'What an insult!'

'Those arrogant British again.'

'The shah will never allow it.'

The imams made it clear that this was unacceptable.

'It is forbidden,' the ayatollah of Tehran announced. 'The shah is the shadow of God on earth. His palace is as holy as a temple. If the British do not want to come in, then they won't come in.'

The vizier let the British stay where they were and went to talk with the other foreign representatives.

The Ottomans were used to taking off their shoes. The French ambassador let the vizier know that the French in Africa always took off their shoes out of respect. The Russians, who knew what the British were really annoyed about, walked in their stocking feet across the mysterious carpet to take their place behind the Turks and the French.

'Time is pressing,' said the vizier to the British ambassador.

'We realise that, but we have strict orders from London. The British do not take off their shoes,' said the Briton.

'I can offer you a pair of royal socks,' said the vizier in a conciliatory tone. 'You can pull them up over your boots.'

'Out of the question,' said the Briton.

The vizier noticed that the shah had disappeared behind the curtain.

'The hospitality of the Persians is world famous, but the shah has decided. This far and no further,' said the vizier.

The British ambassador motioned to his delegation and they walked to their coaches without taking formal leave.

The vizier waited until they were gone, hastened up the stairs, took off his boots and went into the hall. The cannons fired salutes, the orchestra began to play, spring had begun. Shah Naser appeared and walked to the royal throne.

He was wearing the oldest crown in the kingdom. He had a long, bejewelled cloak draped over his shoulders and a long, golden staff clasped under his arm. It was the staff that Nader the Great had taken from India after his victory at Delhi. This was the first time the staff had been taken from the Indian treasure chest and shown in public. Everyone gazed at the shah in awe.

As king of kings he took his seat and let everyone come up to wish him the happiness of the spring season, handing out gold coins as New Year's gifts that he took from the golden dish beside him.

15. The New Army

The French had taken great pains to transport all the separate factory components through the Persian Gulf and into the rundown harbour at Bandar Abbas. From there they had brought the materials by mule and on carts through the mountains and forests, which were almost impassable, to Tehran, Isfahan, Shiraz and Tabriz. With the same perseverance they had transformed the Persian army into a modern fighting force.

Some of the factories were now in operation. Now the vizier could proudly gaze on the manufactured products with his own eyes and hold them in his hands. He wanted to share the results with the shah, so he invited him to inspect the army.

It was a beautiful day. The shah was being led round by a group of officers. When they reached the top of the highest hill they stopped. From there they had a view of the entire plain, and the king was startled by what he saw: a large army in perfect formation. It looked every bit like the kind of French army he had seen in the French history books. He took his binoculars in hand to study some of the soldiers up close, and his open mouth betrayed his astonishment. He studied their berets, coats, gleaming boots and rifles. You could see the word 'unbelievable' forming on his lips. His eyes then fell on a row of brand-new cannons glittering in the autumn sun.

The vizier rode down the hill alone. A gentle breeze

played with the shah's coat. As soon as the vizier reached the army, one of the French officers shouted, 'Ready!'

The soldiers raised their new rifles and steadied them against their shoulders. The shah searched for the vizier's face through his binoculars and saw his smile.

'Fire!' shouted the vizier, sitting astride his horse and pointing into the distance. Shots were fired. The shah's horse whinnied and reared up. The shah struck him lightly on the flank and urged him to calm down.

At the vizier's signal a group of sergeants sped to the cannons and turned the barrels to the horizon.

'Fire!' shouted the vizier once more.

Seven successive shots were fired. The shah had to pull firmly on the reins to keep his horse under control. Then he went down the hill to join the troops.

The French officers saluted and were ordered to begin the parade. The columns of soldiers marched past the shah, who kept touching his hand to his hat. He was clearly impressed. The vizier had done good work, but the shah refused to compliment him.

'Has the entire army been reformed this way?' he asked.

'No, not the whole army, Your Majesty! We're not quite ready yet. It will be a while before we've reached that point.'

The impressive parade made the shah think of the discipline of the Russian troops during the last war, when he had fought side by side with his father. Clearly the vizier had enormous influence over the army. He seemed more like the commander-in-chief than the shah himself. A plan began to ripen in his mind. With these armed forces he would be able to free Herat from the hands of the British and the Afghans.

The vizier had the officers step forward and he gave a short speech in French, describing the activities they had completed. Then he introduced them to the shah one by one. The shah put his hand in his coat pocket and handed each officer a large gold coin on which his own image was depicted.

16. *The Russians Seek Contact*

T he British spies were busier than ever gathering information on the Persian cooperation with the French and the Russians. There wasn't a single influential aristocrat who hadn't been bribed by the British. And anyone with a bit of political ambition knew he wouldn't be able to achieve anything without British support. Over the past fifty years England had also forged ties with the imams in the mosques and with tribal leaders in every corner of the country. Very little escaped the British.

The vizier also had his own information network. He knew, for example, that Mahdolia was planning a secret chat with the shah within the confines of the harem. He suspected that the meeting had to do with a sensitive issue. The informant who had passed that message on to the vizier was an old woman whose job it was to remove unwanted hair from the faces of the women of the harem by using a fine thread. She had seen the shah's mother, fully veiled like one of the women of the harem, go into a room in the back of the building. The woman had hidden behind a cupboard to see what would happen next. Quite unexpectedly the shah came into the room. The old woman was so shocked she couldn't remember what had been said. The vizier had to find out for himself, and he didn't do that until it was too late – for him and for the country. Otherwise he would have learned that the conversation had unfolded like this:

'What did you want to tell me?' the shah asked his mother.

'The Russian embassy has a message for you.'

'From whom?' asked the shah.

'No names were named, but it's probably from the tsar.'

'What do they want to talk about?'

'The content of the message is still unknown.'

'Who is going to bring the message?' he asked.

'If the shah agrees, a highly placed Russian politician disguised as a merchant will come to Tehran with a group of tradesmen. He will want to speak to the shah on behalf of the tsar. Under no circumstances must the British get wind of this.'

'What's it all about?' the shah asked again.

'I have my suspicions, but it's better to be patient and to hear the message from them first-hand,' said Mahdolia.

'Where can we receive them?' asked the shah.

'The best place for the meeting is the country house of Sheikh Aqasi. He is the most trustworthy person we know. I think we can gather in his albaloo garden. If the shah takes his harem along it will be seen as an ordinary outing.'

The shah was silent. The idea appealed to him.

'May I arrange the meeting?' asked Mahdolia.

'Fine,' said the shah.

Mahdolia took the shah's hand and pressed it to her breast.

When Mahdolia was gone the shah walked back to the hall of mirrors and called for a hookah. He sat down amongst his cushions, and as he smoked he thought about what had happened.

His mother never let herself be used as a messenger unless it was a matter of the utmost importance. The shah decided to wait and not to inform the vizier.

17. The Albaloo Garden

An albaloo is a cherry, but it is somewhat redder, more delicate and more flavourful than other cherry varieties. The tastiest albaloos in the world can be found in the outdoor gardens of Tehran near the Alborz Mountains. In other cities the albaloos ripen in late June, but the cherries of Tehran are not fully developed until late summer and early autumn. There nature takes her time to make something outstanding.

Albaloos were very popular among the young lovers of Persia. The girls and young women would hang albaloos over their ears and the young men would long to pluck them. The albaloo was the shah's favourite fruit. Everyone near him knew this, and the rich merchants in the bazaar, who had large albaloo gardens at their country houses, were aware of it as well. They sometimes invited the shah and his harem to spend a day among the cherries. Like the aristocratic families they had built castles in the surrounding villages where they would spend the summer. These were outposts of paradise, constructed according to the conventions of Persian landscape architecture.

Sheikh Aqasi had one of the finest gardens in Tehran. He had made all the necessary preparations for the secret meeting to be held there between the shah and the Russians.

The evening before the meeting the shah lay in bed. He missed Sharmin. Only much later did the cat finally come into the bedroom, rush onto the bed and lie down. The shah felt her restlessness.

'Where were you, Sharmin?'

The cat crept up to her master. As he stroked her head he felt a piece of paper hanging from a cord round her neck.

'What's this?'

In the candlelight he saw that it was indeed a slip of paper. Two words were written on it that were barely legible: 'Beware! Tomorrow!'

What could this mean? Who would write such a thing? What should he beware of? Was it a warning, a threat or a joke? Who dared to use his cat as a messenger? He put the slip of paper in his coat on the coat rack and went back to bed.

'Sharmin, who did this? A friend? An enemy?' he asked. 'Was it one of the women in the harem? Someone who is jealous of you because you sleep with me every night? Could it be that Foruq wants to take revenge on me because I no longer want to share my bed with her? Perhaps I will never find out. But whoever it was, I will see that she is thrown from the roof.

'We are surrounded by enemies,' he went on. 'We are not safe. The piece of paper round your neck is proof. There is nothing to be done. A king is always in danger. He will never sleep peacefully.'

The shah woke early. His breakfast was waiting for him. A servant brought the cat's breakfast in on a large silver tray. It was fresh milk in a little porcelain bowl, roast mutton on a gilt-edged plate, a few small pieces of fresh bread spread with butter and a dish of water.

The shah looked to see whether his cat was eating her breakfast, and at the same time he kept his eye on the servant. Someone in the palace must have hung that piece of paper round the cat's neck.

After breakfast the chamberlain brought in comfortable clothing that he had selected with great care. The chamberlain did not know about the secret appointment with the Russians. 'No, it has to be more formal,' said the shah.

'But if the shah intends to partake of albaloos later on, perhaps it's better . . .' suggested the man cautiously.

'Formal clothing,' said the shah firmly without looking at him.

A short while later the chamberlain returned with a suit. He showed it to the shah with some hesitation.

'That's good,' said the shah.

He held the suit in front of him, looked in the mirror and said, 'This is excellent. We're going to get dressed.'

Meanwhile Sheikh Aqasi's country house had been made ready for the arrival of the shah and the women of his harem. It was quite warm in Tehran, but at the foot of the Alborz Mountains the temperature was pleasant. In Sheikh Aqasi's garden the branches of the albaloo trees were drooping under the weight of the ripe, red, full fruit, which gave off a delightful fragrance. As a child the shah had taken great pleasure in plucking albaloos. He never used his hands, but would stand under the hanging branches and pluck them with his lips.

Sheikh Aqasi knew how to please the shah. He had asked the old baker from the bazaar to make the albaloos even more delicious by adding sugar and fragrant ingredients. Sheikh Aqasi had ordered large carpets to be rolled out in the garden and the couches to be covered with colourful cushions so the shah and his harem would feel completely at home.

* * *

The shah was on his way. Behind him rode seventy-five women from the harem who had been selected especially for this outing. The women were veiled and covered in niqabs, and each of them wore a pair of binoculars round her neck, a gift of the English consul in Tabriz to the wives of the crown prince (as the shah was at the time).

The binoculars had been packed in a wooden box and inscribed with the English text, 'From the princesses of the British royal house to the princesses of Persia. Warm greetings.' It was the text more than the binoculars that had so delighted the shah. When he went out with his wives he had them bring their binoculars so they would have something to keep them occupied along the way.

The women who were selected to travel with the shah always had the time of their lives. These were their happiest moments, away from the seclusion of the harem. The father of the shah had never bothered to take his wives anywhere, for it required a great deal of organisation.

The shah rode in front. Remarkably he had left Sharmin at home. The women noticed he was peevish and kept their distance to avoid any angry outbursts.

'Something is bothering him,' whispered the women.

'Perhaps he misses his favourite cat.'

'Why did he leave her at home?'

'She probably doesn't feel very well,' said one of the women with a laugh.

'She gets a lot of fatty meat.'

'If she were sick, His Majesty would never go anywhere. She's not sick. I saw her on the roof this morning. She enjoys being with the wild cats when he's gone.'

'So it's something else,' whispered another woman.

'Didn't you notice? The shah has brought along a lot of extra balls for his cannon.'

The women held up their binoculars to look at the cannon.

'He's taking us to the front,' one of them giggled.

Once outside Tehran, when there was little chance that they would be meeting any strange men, the women took off their niqabs and enjoyed the warm wind blowing around their heads. This was how they rode to Sheikh Aqasi's country house. They all knew him. And because they didn't like the queen mother, they didn't like the sheikh either.

'She's got something going with him.'

'He's always with her.'

'She seems to need a great deal of his advice,' someone said with a wink.

'Come, advise me,' said another, imitating the queen mother. 'Come, read me my future, show me the stars.'

Sheikh Aqasi stood at the gate to welcome the shah. He was wearing a long, light summer coat, and his beard, which went all the way down to his chest, was neatly combed. He rushed up to the shah, who was still seated on his horse, and pressed a kiss against his right boot of light brown leather. The shah got down from his horse and the sheikh took the reins.

The women of the harem had put their niqabs back on and were waiting for a sign from the shah.

'The Russians will arrive in the afternoon,' said Sheikh Aqasi. 'Your Majesty has plenty of time to rest with his harem in the garden. The weather is splendid and everything is ready for you and your company. If Your Majesty agrees I will escort you to the garden.'

The shah nodded and motioned to his wives to dismount.

Sheikh Aqasi opened the great gate of his country house and said, 'Please come in and bless your subject's garden.'

The shah was impressed. The trees groaned under the

weight of the glorious red albaloos, and the branches were bent over so far that if the shah raised himself up on his toes he could, with a little effort, pluck the albaloos with his mouth. The ground was covered with elegant carpets, and beneath the trees lay large colourful cushions and small rugs. Big parasols cast shadows across long tables that were covered with a vast array of dishes, fruit juices, fresh vegetables and other delicacies. An unusually delightful fragrance filled the air.

'It is good,' said the shah to Sheikh Aqasi.

'Your subject grants Your Majesty his rest,' responded Sheikh Aqasi. 'The harem may make themselves completely at home. There are no strangers here, and later I will go inside. Should you require anything I will see to your needs without delay.' He bowed and retreated into the building.

As soon as he left the women began walking round the garden, full of amazement. They did not touch the fruits or foods until the shah gave them permission to have something to eat or drink. But the shah's thoughts were with the Russians and he forgot the women. One of them ventured to draw the shah's attention to the magnificent albaloos.

The shah looked at the waiting women and the albaloos. He put his hands behind his back and stood beneath the branches, searching for the largest one. It hung defiantly high. Standing on tiptoe he tried to reach it with his mouth but was unsuccessful. On the second try his lips touched the fruit. The women encouraged him light-heartedly. He tried once more and stretched himself out to his full length. You could see his legs tremble with the strain. The fat red albaloo was almost in his mouth when his tall hat fell to the ground.

The women clapped their hands over their mouths to suppress their cries of alarm. This was a highly unusual occurrence. No one was ever to see the shah without his hat. The women immediately averted their eyes, but in that flash they had seen that the shah had become a little bald and a little grey. He put his hat back on and cast an angry glance at the women. The festive mood had been spoilt. Still hanging high in the tree was the fat treacherous albaloo. The shah plucked it roughly with his hand and played with it for a moment between his fingers. Would he crush it and throw it to the ground, or pop it in his mouth? He popped it in his mouth and bit down. The taste alleviated everything.

'Wicked! Extraordinary!' exclaimed the shah.

The baker had done his work with consummate skill. There was no stopping the shah now. Forgetting the purpose of his visit he ate so much in so short a time that his stomach began to ache and he had to lie down on the couches.

'Bring me hot tea with rock candy,' he groaned.

Indeed that was the only effective remedy for stomach ache caused by eating too many albaloos. Once he had drunk the sweet tea and his stomach began to feel better, he looked up from his couch at the women plucking albaloos.

'No, not by hand. Pluck them with your mouth,' he kept shouting.

The women put their hands behind their backs and stood under the branches. The shah laughed at the sight of their lips, which the oozing juice of the albaloos had stained a deep red. It aroused him. He called one of the women over and sucked on her lips. He plucked a couple of cherries, squeezed them and let the red juice flow over the women's faces, necks and breasts. They enjoyed all the attention. It was one of the rare moments when they actually loved the shah. Now he belonged to all of them, and he kissed all the lips that came near.

Back in the palace they would talk about what they had experienced and how much they had enjoyed it. It would provoke jealousy among those who had not been kissed or touched by the shah in years. Discord lay in wait, ready to pounce.

The shah drank a few more glasses of tea and stretched out on one of the couches. He closed his eyes to take a nap.

Silence descended on the garden. The women sat on the big garden benches smoking hookahs. The shah slept restlessly, tossing and turning. Then all at once he stood up, left the women and withdrew into the building where he was to receive the Russian delegation.

'Does the shah wish to rest any more?' asked Sheikh Aqasi, and he accompanied him to a special room.

The shah picked up a book that was lying on a table, sat down in a chair, put his feet up on another chair and began leafing through the book.

'Does Your Majesty require anything else, perhaps?'

The shah said no, after which the sheikh gently closed the door.

Within the hour the sheikh returned, tapped gently on the door and brought in a cup of tea, with the shah's approval. The sheikh then led him to another part of the building where he was to receive the Russian guests unobserved. They could arrive any minute now, but apparently they had been delayed.

The shah waited in this guest room and Sheikh Aqasi waited at the back door, but there was no sign of the Russians. The shah looked out through a slit in the curtains at the fields along which the delegation would have to pass. For a meeting at this level an unreported delay was unusual. The shah paced up and down the room and took another peek outside. Sheikh Aqasi stood rigid at the door, as if he had turned to stone. He dared not approach the shah.

Finally the shah turned to him. 'Is there a problem?' he asked.

'No, not that I know of. Everything was meticulously arranged with your mother.'

'Perhaps they've lost their way?' said the shah.

'The Russian ambassador himself stopped in yesterday to go over the route,' he answered.

With his hands behind his back the shah returned to the guest room. Soon Sheikh Aqasi came to bring him another glass of tea.

'How much more tea do we have to drink?' said the shah, and waved him away with his hand.

The sheikh withdrew, afraid the shah was about to fly into a rage. His nerves were stretched to the limit.

The shah could take it no longer. He bounded down the hall and cast his eyes on the women resting in the shadow of the trees. Then he thrust his hand into his coat pocket and felt a scrap of paper. He had forgotten it, the paper hanging round his cat's neck. 'Beware! Tomorrow!'

He was stunned. Could this warning have to do with the failure of the Russians to appear? He turned back to the guest room, pulled the curtain aside and grabbed his binoculars. There was no one to be seen. A serene silence reigned.

Suddenly he heard a shot in the distance. Could he be mistaken? Had Sheikh Aqasi heard it too? He opened the window and strained his ears. Then he heard another shot, far in the distance.

'Sheikh Aqasi!' he cried.

The sheikh was at his side immediately.

'Did you hear that?'

'What?'

'The shots. We heard two shots.'

Sheikh Aqasi, clearly shaken, went over to the window. Another shot was heard.

The shah didn't hesitate. 'Get ready!' he ordered his wives. 'Back to the palace!' Chaos ensued. The women put on their niqabs and hastened to their horses. Surrounded by his regular guards the shah raced back to Tehran. The other guards escorted his wives to the palace by way of a shortcut. After a ride of unprecedented speed the shah and his guards reached the city. He noticed the agitation immediately. Everyone was indoors, looking out at the empty streets from behind closed windows.

The shah was told that there had been shooting and that a few people had been killed, but no one knew exactly what was going on. He wanted to ride to the centre of the city, but the guards held him back and brought him to the palace despite his protestations. There he summoned the head of the guards and had him call for the vizier. The messenger returned and reported that the vizier had gone to the bazaar square, where a serious incident had taken place that required the vizier's personal attention. He was not able to come to the palace.

'What kind of serious incident?' cried the shah.

'I don't have the exact details,' answered the messenger, 'but I heard that many have been killed.'

'How many?'

'More than twenty, maybe thirty.'

'Thirty killed? Who fired the shots? Who died?'

'What I am telling you is based on rumour,' said the man cautiously.

'Tell us the rumours then!' cried the shah in a rage.

'According to the rumours more than twenty Russians were killed.'

'What? Russians? What makes you think they were Russians?'

'I'm only passing on the rumours,' repeated the messenger.

'Go then, and come back quickly with the facts,' ordered the shah.

No one in the palace knew what had happened on the bazaar square. And if anyone did know he didn't dare open his mouth for fear of the shah's explosive fury.

If the rumour was true and the incident had something to do with the Russians, then the special Russian envoy himself could be dead. Russia would hold the shah responsible for this attack. He didn't know what to do next. He was prepared to crawl to the temple of the holy Abdoldawood on his knees to rectify the situation.

The messenger was probably too terrified to return. Doubtless the matter was a complicated one or the vizier would have come to him immediately to fill him in. There was no question of his mother having anything to do with this plot. His appointment with the Russians had been violently sabotaged. The shah, his mother and the Russians had walked into a trap. What if the Russian envoy indeed had been killed? What was he to do?

His mother's palace was a hotbed of spies, a pit of old, black, poisonous snakes, crawling with the imams' accomplices and British informers. Stupid. How stupid he had been. He was angry with himself and furious with his mother.

'Witch, vixen!' he cried aloud.

Hearing a horse in the courtyard, he looked outside and saw the messenger. The shah pulled himself together. He walked to the middle of the hall and waited until the chamberlain had admitted the messenger and no one else.

'Report!' he said impatiently.

'I have seen the following with my own eyes and heard it with my own ears: thirty-four Russians have perished, thirty-one of them staff members from the Russian residence and three Russian businessmen.'

The shah heard no more. The messenger saw him go pale and begin to totter. The man was about to call the chamberlain.

'Continue reporting!' cried the shah.

'It is said that last night three Persian women spent the night in the Russian residence. Haj Mirza Masih, the ayatollah of Tehran, got wind of this report. He announced it during Friday prayers and has called for a jihad. An angry mob led by a young imam went today to the Russian residence. The Russians bolted the gate of the embassy and drew the curtains closed. Stones were thrown, and the windows and doors of the Russian buildings were destroyed. The young imam climbed over the embassy fences and the people followed him. Just then shots were fired from an unknown location. Although the imam was hit in the back, the people cried that the shot had been fired from the Russian residence. They pulled down the fences and stormed the embassy garden. One Russian merchant threw gold coins into the raging throng to play for time so the people inside could flee through the back door. But the people forced their way into the residence and the Russians began shooting into the air in response. This inflamed the crowd even more and everything got out of hand. Five men were killed on our side and thirty-four on the Russian side. The tarts managed to escape.'

'Barbarians, they're all barbarians,' cried the shah. He was seething.

The terrified messenger remained standing until the chamberlain came to fetch him.

'Women are witches! All of them! From queen to tart!' cried the shah as he thundered through the palace corridors.

18. Fear

Late that evening the vizier came to see the shah. He found him sitting in his chair with the cat in his lap. As soon as the vizier entered the room the cat jumped down, went up to him and brushed against his leg. The vizier was tired and shaken. He reached down and stroked the cat. 'How are you, Sharmin?' he said.

The vizier came from a family whose men had often been through trying times like these. The incident at the Russian embassy would have serious consequences.

'With His Majesty's permission I would like to speak with him privately in his conference room.'

The shah stood up and the vizier followed him. They locked the door and sat down at the conference room table.

'We've walked into a British trap,' said the vizier, coming straight to the point.

The shah suspected that the vizier was aware of his secret appointment with the Russians.

'We won't solve anything by blaming each other. It only makes matters worse,' continued the vizier. 'A lackey from the British embassy went straight to the ayatollah and told him about the presence of the Persian women at the Russian residence. This ayatollah maintains good contacts with the British, who have him on their payroll. He took immediate action. Tomorrow the report of the thirty-four Russian corpses will reach Moscow. The British wanted to show the Russians in a bad light, but they never could have imagined that their scheme would end in this disaster. They're celebrating at the British residence right now, you can be sure of it. They took a chance and won.'

'What do you mean?' asked the shah.

'Now the shah has nowhere to turn,' said the vizier. 'But there's one question that puzzles me: what was the appointment with the envoy all about?'

The shah stared in bewilderment and said, 'We don't know. And the man is dead.'

The vizier could see that the shah was hiding something. He had a feeling it had to do with Herat. He wanted to keep asking questions, but the shah was clearly in a muddle. It was not the right moment to continue the conversation.

'It is better that Your Majesty go to bed. We do not know what tomorrow will bring,' he said.

The vizier left. Once he was alone the shah was overcome with a sense of the vizier's growing power and of his own powerlessness. Fear had the upper hand. He knew that many ayatollahs and princes were being paid by England, but he had never expected that the British would manipulate an ayatollah in order to carry out their plans. The vizier hadn't said it in so many words, but he had let the shah see how he was being used. What did the vizier mean when he said he had nowhere to turn?

'Sharmin!' called the shah.

The cat did not come.

The shah was tired, but he couldn't sleep. His head wouldn't stop churning. In the hall's gloom he looked into the mirror and raised a threatening index finger: 'Tomorrow we will teach that ayatollah a lesson. He will hang. But what about the thirty-four corpses?'

Suddenly the light of a torch was reflected in the mirror. The shah spun round and walked to the window. It was peaceful in the courtyard, but at the gate there were more guards than usual. He watched as two of them rolled a cannon to the gate. He also saw a few guards on top of the wall, their weapons poised. His glance fell on the stable, where a number of horses had been readied. Then he walked to his study, which afforded a better view of the gate. His heart began beating faster when he saw the shadow of the vizier's tall hat out on the wall. Something touched his foot and he jumped, but it was only Sharmin.

'You startled us. Where were you? Come, we've got to go away. We cannot stay here tonight,' he said, picking her up from the floor. 'I believe the vizier has imprisoned us. But maybe not. Maybe he is doing all this to protect us.'

He went to the bedroom, put Sharmin on the bed and turned all the locks. He opened his closet door, unlocked the secret hatch of the hidden tunnel leading to the treasury, and set out his boots and gun in readiness.

Ever since Sheikh Aqasi had led him to the treasury by way of this hatch, the shah could often be found there. And when the vizier had reduced the allowance for the shah, his mother and the royal relatives by half, and had imposed restrictions on the expenses for the harem, the shah had come to the cellar regularly to load up on gold coins. He had them melted down and made into new coins to cover his considerable expenses. The shah had already emptied several sacks of Indian gold.

He had also had the jewel-encrusted bed of the old Indian kings made up for himself, should he ever have to stay in the cellar for prolonged periods. Every time he came to the treasury he brought non-perishable food with him.

He checked the door and the windows of his bedroom once more and went to bed.

'As soon as you hear footsteps in the hall of mirrors

you must wake us up, Sharmin. Then we will flee together.'

And with that the shah laid his tired head on the pillow and immediately fell into a deep sleep.

19. The Ayatollah Who Committed Treason

That night the shah dreamt that he and his cat had fled to the mountains by way of the secret tunnel and found refuge in a small cave, from which he had a view of the palace. He followed every move by means of his binoculars. The vizier entered the palace with a procession of officers. He was wearing his tall hat, but when he came back out he was wearing the shah's golden crown.

In reality nothing happened that night. The shah and the cat slept better than they had during all the other nights put together. That was because of the draught of air that came pouring in from the cellar through the hatch, which made the shah and the cat creep down under the covers. The next morning the shah was awakened by Sharmin. He got out of bed, looked out the window and saw that the flags were flying at half mast.

'We overslept,' said the shah to the cat, who sat beside the door waiting to go out.

A knock was heard.

'Who's there?' said the shah sleepily.

'Your Majesty? . . .' It was the voice of the chamberlain. He sounded worried.

'We're coming,' said the shah.

He knew what he had to do.

*   *   *

Soon the shah appeared in the hall of mirrors in his military uniform. Although the traces of deep sleep were still visible on his face, he walked with his back straight and showed that he was ready to deal with the important matters of the day.

The shah had made up his mind. He must not appear weak right now, certainly not in the presence of the vizier. He was the shah and he did not have to wait for anyone. The vizier had often led him to believe that times were changing, that a king could no longer act on his own volition and that a ministerial council was needed. What this actually meant, however, was that the vizier wanted to rob him of his power. He had become a king who rubber-stamped the decisions of his vizier, a king whose only purpose was to sign and seal documents. But not any more.

This is why he had put on his military uniform. And although he always took enormous pleasure in eating breakfast, today none of the dishes interested him. With an empty stomach he shouted, 'Bring me the chief of police.'

The chamberlain obeyed without delay.

It wasn't long before the shah heard the rapid footsteps of the police chief on the stairs. As soon as the man entered the hall he saluted the shah, his left hand on his sword, and stood at rigid attention.

'You are the chief of the city's police force?' asked the shah threateningly.

'Yes, Your Majesty,' replied the man with a quavering voice.

'And thirty-four Russians were killed on your watch?'

The trembling man was silent and let his head drop to his chest.

'Loosen your sword and place it on the floor,' commanded the shah.

With shaking hands the soldier laid his sword on the floor at his feet.

'Take off your uniform,' continued the shah.

The man thought he may have misunderstood the order.

'Take everything off. You're not a soldier, you're a failure!' cried the shah.

With a pale face the man took off his uniform and remained standing in his underclothes.

'Now get out of my sight before I have you killed!' screamed the shah.

The man rushed out. The chamberlain took away the man's clothing and sword.

'Bring me the messenger!' cried the shah.

When the messenger arrived the shah gave him this order: 'Go to Shaban and whisper the following in his ear. "Take a group of your men to the home of Ayatollah Mirza Masih. Wrap his turban round his neck, drag him to the square in front of the Russian embassy and punish him in public. His humiliation must be so painful that Moscow hears about it tomorrow."'

Shaban was a criminal who sometimes carried out dangerous orders for the shah. He was known as Shaban Bimokh, a man without brains. He was the head of a group of violent men who did anything for money. After receiving the messenger's order Shaban acted immediately.

His men went to the ayatollah's house and smashed down the gate with a heavy beam. Shaban stood at the gate while his men took the aged ayatollah by surprise. They found him in his long white nightshirt, standing next to the outdoor pool. The ayatollah tried to escape through the roof, but one of the men ran after him and grabbed him by the leg before he could get there. The ayatollah's turban fell from his head and rolled down the stairs. Someone picked it up, twisted it round the ayatollah's neck and pulled him outside.

The powerless ayatollah stumbled and cried aloud, '*Allah al-aman, al-aman*: Allah protect me, protect me!'

Shaban's men ignored his supplications and dragged him to the square in front of the Russian embassy. The people in the street couldn't believe what they were seeing.

To keep an eye on all of this the shah had sent Sheikh Aqasi to the square in front of the embassy with this message: See to it that the ayatollah is punished so severely that his howling is heard in Moscow.

The sheikh positioned himself inconspicuously but made sure he had a good view from where he was standing.

News of the ayatollah reached the bazaar and the merchants were overcome by what they heard. It was an unforgivable insult to Islam to treat an ayatollah this way. They left their shops and made their way to the Russian embassy. Shaban's men had pushed the ayatollah onto his back with his feet fastened between two beams, and they were beating the bare soles of his feet with switches.

'*La ellaha ella allah!*' the aged ayatollah wailed.

A few of the merchants recognised Sheikh Aqasi in the crowd, and they asked him to help. But he told them this was a direct order from the shah, that he was only supervising the proceedings and that he was not to become involved any further.

A group of people tried to free the ayatollah, but Shaban's men responded by shooting. They made it quite clear that anyone who took a step forward would be punished on the spot.

The merchants from the bazaar rode to the palace by coach to speak with the vizier, but he was not there. He had a secret meeting with the warlords in the war room of the barracks outside the city.

The merchants returned to the embassy having achieved nothing. They begged Sheikh Aqasi for help once again.

'I'll see what I can do for you,' said Sheikh Aqasi.

He walked up to Shaban and spoke with him.

'That's enough!' shouted Shaban. 'He's learned his lesson.'

They loosened the ropes round the ayatollah's feet and left him lying on the ground. Ayatollah Haj Mirza Masih was lifted onto an open cart and taken to his home.

The shopkeepers closed their shops in protest.

20. Mourning

Three days had passed. The bazaar in Tehran was still closed. In the Jameh mosque, where the ayatollah led daily prayers, it was busier than ever. The old man's legs could no longer support him, so he was carried on a box to the mosque where he prayed sitting down while hundreds of believers stood behind him.

The army was put on a state of alert to meet any possible Russian attack. Fearing that the protest in the Tehran bazaar would spread to other cities, the vizier held talks with the bazaar's representatives. He managed to convince them to remain calm to keep the country from plunging into crisis. Then the vizier visited the aged ayatollah. He kissed his hand and extended his apologies.

The shopkeepers accepted this gesture of reconciliation. They returned to the bazaar and reopened their shops.

In the meantime the shah had turned to Sheikh Aqasi for solace. The man had a gift for soothing troubled souls. He spent the whole day and part of the night in the palace, and his presence had a sedative effect.

As a gesture to Moscow, Sheikh Aqasi advised the shah to commemorate the dead Russians according to Persian custom. He had large tents set up near the embassy, and on the shah's behalf he asked everyone to be in attendance. Large pans were placed on cooking fires and a common meal was served.

The ayatollah forbade his followers to attend.

Commemorating people who had invited Persian women into their home was simply unthinkable. It was said that the women had drunk alcohol that night and that they had sat on the laps of the Russian businessmen. The Russians had defiled the honour of the women of Persia. The ayatollah's words fell on eager ears. Even the beggars refused to be seen in the tents, despite the temptation of the royal meal.

To avoid humiliation Sheikh Aqasi sent soldiers to the tents dressed in civilian clothes, and he also invited the shah and his entire harem.

At about noon the shah rode to the Russian embassy dressed in black. His wives, in black chadors and black niqabs, followed in silence. A group of soldiers led the procession with flags at half mast, and a Persian dirge was played. When the shah came to a halt at the embassy gate the vizier rode up.

The vizier inclined his head towards the shah and said quietly, 'The Russians have invaded the country.'

Without a moment's hesitation the shah left his wives behind and rode to the barracks in silence with the vizier. Once in the war room the shah asked, 'Have the Russians officially declared war?'

'No, certainly not,' answered the vizier. 'They have seized part of Azerbaijan. We've been waging war over that region for centuries. Usually we win, sometimes we lose. But this time it's different.'

'What's different about it?'

'Russia isn't Russia any more. They have one of the mightiest armies in the world. Our army would be obliterated by so much power.'

'But the French have reformed our army, haven't they?' responded the shah.

'We're inexperienced, and we can't win a war with a

few hundred French cannons. Battles are not decided by guns and bullets but by the health of the country and the mentality of its army. Our land has financial problems, the politicians are corrupt, the imams are open to bribery and the population is enfeebled. We're standing on the brink of the abyss.'

'Has the vizier brought us here to share this bit of information?' asked the shah.

'Such truths can only be uttered in the war room,' answered the vizier, 'because war is not the answer. We will have to find a political solution to this problem. The most prudent option is to send a high-level delegation to Moscow to explain the situation and to prove our innocence in the affair. If Your Majesty approves I will begin selecting a delegation without delay. Later I have a meeting with the ministers and the warlords, and I will inform you of their advice as soon as possible.'

'The vizier has already made the decision,' answered the shah without looking at him.

'No, absolutely not, Your Majesty. You decide.'

'We're going to think this over,' said the shah. So he rode back to the palace surrounded by his guards.

In the palace the queen mother was waiting for him. She had made every effort behind the scenes to reach out to the Russians, but the Russians had slammed all the doors shut. They felt she had betrayed them. There was no question in their minds that she had walked into the trap with her eyes wide open, which is why they did not respond to the report Mahdolia sent. Even the shah did not want to speak with her. She had repeatedly asked for permission to come and see him, but to no avail.

Mahdolia had heard about the Russian invasion in Azerbaijan, and she knew that the vizier had discussed it with the shah in the war room. Now she was here to speak to him. The shah ignored her, but she followed him into the hall of mirrors.

'I can see the shah is upset,' said Mahdolia with concern. 'Speak with me. Ease your distress.'

'According to the vizier we've lost the war before we start. He thinks we ought to send a delegation to Moscow. Emergency talks are being held right now between the ministers and the warlords.'

'The vizier is right,' said Mahdolia. 'We cannot win a war with Russia. Sending a delegation is a wise decision, but the shah must take charge.'

'What do you propose? Travelling personally to Moscow to offer our apologies?'

'That will not be necessary. I will go in the shah's place.'

Her proposal surprised him.

'You are partly to blame for all this trouble,' answered the shah irritably.

'It does not become the shah to speak to us in this manner,' said his mother sternly. 'I am your mother, you are my flesh and blood. What I do, I do instinctively for the happiness of my child. No one can blame me for causing this disaster. Whatever I have done was in the shah's interest.'

'What interest? What happiness?' cried the shah. 'Your palace is a breeding ground of informers. Everyone around you has let himself be bought by the British.'

'The British are everywhere. That is a fact. Even here in the palace of the shah. We must learn to live with this reality. Send me to Moscow. We'll keep it between you and me, and the British will never get word of it.'

The shah sat down and tried to put his thoughts in order. Mahdolia knelt beside his chair, took his hand and said gently, 'Listen to me. I know the Russian royal house.

My mother met Catherine once. I went there as a child. If anyone can exercise influence it is I. If the vizier were to go to Moscow and persuade the Russians to withdraw from the borders, you would be turning him into a hero. I will bring royal gifts for the tsar, his wife, his mother and his daughters, and I will solve this problem.'

'Royal gifts?' asked the shah suspiciously.

'Indian rings and necklaces from the cellar, and a be-jewelled sword.'

'Out of the question! The Indian jewels belong here. It is our inheritance, and it is our duty to preserve them.'

'I know that. But this is a matter of life and death. You are trading gold for our land. And there's something else, something important that you and the vizier have lost sight of,' Mahdolia continued.

She stood up. 'The Russians wanted to speak with the shah, which is why they sent a messenger to Tehran. The messenger is dead, but the message is still alive. The Russian tsar wanted to tell the shah something important. Send me as your messenger to Moscow. I will listen to the tsar.'

The shah rose from his chair. The queen mother smiled, kissed him on the shoulder and whispered, 'I am always here beside you.'

21. The Báb

The shah was hoping to keep his mother's journey to Moscow a secret from the vizier. But since nothing escaped Mirza Kabir's notice the shah was finally forced to inform him of Mahdolia's mission.

The vizier did everything he could to convince the shah that it was not Mahdolia's job to negotiate with the Russians over such complex political matters. In the consultations he had conducted with the ministers and the warlords *he* was the one they had appointed to sit down with the Russians at the bargaining table.

'The decision has been made. Besides, our mother is not going alone. We have sent Sheikh Aqasi to accompany her. Only the vizier is aware of this. Should Mahdolia come back empty-handed the vizier will then be sent, but not before.'

With these words the shah put an end to the discussion.

Outside the palace the vizier met a messenger who had just arrived in the city. His head and shoulders were covered with dust. He led his horse up to the vizier and whispered, 'The Báb has risen up in revolt,' and he gave him a sealed envelope.

The Báb was a young mystical leader in Shiraz, a city in the southern part of the country about a thousand kilometres from Tehran. At one time Shiraz had been the capital of the Zandieh dynasty, until the Afghan ruler Mahmud swept in and destroyed everything. Shiraz had produced two great poets: Hafez and Saadi. Both were buried there.

It was a city filled with the most beautiful houses, built by wealthy merchants and the elite. These houses looked more like dreams of heaven than places to live in. They had turned the centre of Shiraz into a holy site where Islamic architecture was shown in all its glory and power.

A revolt led by the Báb could be even more dangerous for the country than an attack by foreign forces because religious resistance would wreck the country from within.

The Báb wanted to follow a route that was entirely different from that of the traditional Shiites. For centuries the Shiites had been waiting for a messiah, the holy Mahdi, who was seen as a redeemer. They believed that a series of twelve saints would follow the Prophet Muhammad, and that the Mahdi would be the twelfth.

Fourteen centuries earlier the Prophet Muhammad had gathered all his followers together. Standing on a stack of camel saddles he cried out, 'O people! Those who love me must also love Ali. Ali is my soul, my spirit and my heir.'

Ali was Muhammad's son-in-law. Later he became the fourth caliph of the Islamic world. One evening, while praying at the mosque, he was stabbed in the back with a sword.

The Persians, who opposed the Arabs, chose Ali's son Hasan as Muhammad's heir, a choice the Arabs rejected. Hasan was put under house arrest for the remainder of his life. Hussein, Ali's other son, raised a rebellion in an effort to follow his father as the Prophet's third successor, but Hussein was beheaded. Baqir, the son of Hussein, claimed power as the fourth successor, but he died of a mysterious illness. Musa, the son of Baqir, succeeded his father, but he was not allowed to show his face during daylight hours, nor to walk past a mosque to address his people. Jafar, son of Musa, was banned from ever speaking again in public, as his father had been. Kazem, son of Jafar, spent much of his life in prison, and Reza, his son, died from eating poisoned purple grapes. Little is known about Tagi, son of Reza, nor about Nagi, son of Tagi, nor about Asgar, son of Nagi. Mahdi, son of Asgar, was the twelfth successor. He managed to escape an attempt on his life and sought refuge in Persia.

After the flight of Mahdi, eleven hundred years before, a new faith took shape in Persia that later became known as Shiism. A strong myth was created based on the life of Mahdi. It was believed that the saint had hidden in a well, and that he was waiting there for God to call him.

Mahdi was the messiah. One day he would come to save the world from its suffering. Great feasts and religious gatherings were constantly being organised, at which believers came together and begged the messiah to come quickly and save the world from destruction.

Now the Báb had turned against the regime. He seemed to suggest that he was the long-awaited messiah, the man who would heal the sick and supply everyone with bread, meat and vegetables.

The vizier saw the Báb as just another cleric with an overinflated view of himself, a passing curiosity and not a serious threat. But the Báb emerged as a mystical leader who preached Sufism and could count on a growing number of disciples.

As soon as the vizier heard that the Báb's followers were walking around the city of Shiraz with shiny new rifles, he knew immediately that the weapons were English.

'We cannot pin this unrest on the British,' said Amir, the vizier's young advisor. 'The problem is poverty. In western countries change is causing hope to rise like the sun in the East. We are losing hope. Our people have no future. This is why a cleric like the Báb is so popular. If we can improve the lives of ordinary people they won't go running after a man like the Báb.'

'This is the purpose behind everything I do,' answered the vizier, 'but it's not easy. I'm standing here with nothing but the tail of the ox, while the real power lies elsewhere. What can we do to get the Báb's followers to change their minds? They're ignorant people.'

'We've got to get the Báb first! Then people will see for themselves that he's no messiah.'

Because the shah was more worried about the Russians than the Báb, the vizier decided to follow his own course. He sent the army to Shiraz to crush the movement. The order was to arrest the Báb and bring him to Tehran, but that didn't happen without a struggle.

The Báb was a charismatic speaker. He possessed all the qualities that the Persians attributed to the messiah. He was a handsome leader with dazzling dark eyes, long black hair and a salt-and-pepper beard. He wore a green scarf, rode a brown Arabian horse and carried a sabre that he waved at his followers. This old sword proved that he was a descendant of the holy Ali, since Ali also fought with a special sword like this one, with a point that looked like the forked tongue of a dragon.

'It's the sword of the holy Ali,' the people said, trembling with happiness.

'All the saints before the Báb carried this sword.'

'And to think that we should live to see this after a thousand years,' they said with tears in their eyes.

Every Friday morning thousands of peasants from the countryside would come to the city on their mules to admire the Báb in the great Jameh mosque.

'He is the messiah,' the peasants whispered during his fiery speeches.

'He's not ready to reveal that he is the holy Mahdi, but you can just see it in his face.'

'He's waiting until he has more disciples. Then he'll proclaim the good tidings to one and all.'

The city was pulsating. Hope shone in every eye. Everything seemed to indicate that the end of all the misery was in sight. People had become friendlier. They were quicker to reach out to each other, to embrace each other and wish each other luck. They claimed that every time the Báb gave a speech the air was filled with the fragrance of flowers.

Just as Mahdolia was arriving in Moscow the Báb seized control of the city of Shiraz. When the chief of police saw the Báb and his hundreds of armed men he knelt down and laid his rifle on the ground. The Báb occupied the city barracks and prepared his followers for the journey to Isfahan. If he could gain that city's support as well it would be a major breakthrough, and the army would no longer be able to control him.

The Báb was discussing the journey to Isfahan with his bodyguards, twelve young armed imams, when he heard that a large army unit had been dispatched from Tehran and was heading for Shiraz. The first troops would reach the city gates by the next morning.

The army arrived much sooner than expected, however. They destroyed a section of the city wall by firing their cannons at it, and then they stormed the city. But to the shock of the commanding officer the soldiers refused to fight the Báb. As soon as they saw him surrounded by rural country soldiers and by his own disciples, who broke into a hymn in Arabic, they knew right away that this was the messiah himself. They knelt down before him and laid down their arms.

*　　*　　*

After receiving the report that his men had surrendered to the Báb, the vizier left immediately for Shiraz with his cavalry. When he arrived he managed to convince the soldiers to listen to him. He delivered a fiery speech in which he demonstrated that the Báb was not a messiah but a traitor to his country.

'Just look at their brand-new rifles!' he shouted. 'These are weapons from England and they're meant to tear our country apart. Fight this imposter! Disarm him! And may God and the king reward you!'

The vizier's fervour was infectious. The soldiers decided to resume their struggle against the Báb. As a result fierce fighting broke out between them and the cleric's armed followers, who had thrown up sandbag barricades at all the city's strategic points. The vizier himself fought on the front line. Many were killed on both sides, and it took three days before the armed core of the insurrection was routed.

It was during the last skirmishes that the vizier saw the Báb for the first time. He recognised him from his scarf and the sword with which he fought, like a true messiah. The vizier put away his rifle, took out his sword and rode up to the Báb. His intention was to arrest him and take him to Tehran. But the Báb made a run for it. If he were to escape his disciples would turn him into a legend, so the vizier set off in pursuit. Yet the Báb got away. He was familiar with the area, and when evening fell he went into hiding.

'We've got to find him, even if he slithers into a hole like a snake,' the vizier told his officers.

The vizier ordered a search of all the houses and farms in the vicinity. After a few days they discovered the Báb hiding in a well at a goat farm. They pulled him out and took him back to the city in chains. There they propped him up backwards on an old donkey and rode him through the streets of Shiraz to show the inhabitants that he was not a saint but a false prophet. After that the vizier took the Báb to Tehran and threw him into prison. He put a heavy lock on the door with his own hands, handed the key to the head of the prison and said, 'Feed him and treat him well. He must be kept alive.'

When Shah Naser was informed that the Báb was now sitting in a jail cell in Tehran, he wanted to see him. The coming of the messiah had been the source of inspiration for all the great Persian tales. After all the things that had been said about the Báb, the shah wanted to marvel at the 'false prophet' up close.

One day in the late afternoon he rode to the prison with an armed escort. Carrying a torch the prison supervisor led him to the cell. They went down several dark, damp corridors until they came to a room that was so dark you couldn't see your hand in front of your face without a torch.

The supervisor went down a few more steps, pointed to a spot at the end of the corridor and handed the torch to the shah. The shah produced a couple of deliberate coughs and walked on hesitantly. He saw the iron bars, but he could not make out the Báb in the darkness. Then he held the torch aloft and saw a silhouette. A man in torn clothing was manacled to the wall with a heavy iron chain. His green scarf glittered in the torchlight like a riddle. The shah took another step forward. There was a momentary flash of lightning in the Báb's eyes. He had recognised the king.

'The messiah,' whispered the shah.

With childish fascination the shah touched the iron bars and whispered again, 'The messiah.'

Suddenly the Báb drew closer and spat in the shah's

face. The shah recoiled, wiped the spittle away with his sleeve and shouted, 'String him up!'

The next day the Báb, the false messiah, was hung from a gallows before the great gate of Tehran. His green scarf fluttered over his shoulder.

22. The Cats

The tsar received Mahdolia in his palace, and during one of their talks he revealed to her the message that the Russian delegation had planned to tell the shah at Sheikh Aqasi's country home.

The talks with the tsar were encouraging. Mahdolia had regained his trust. She spent two weeks on an estate outside Moscow, and whenever she left the estate to take a stroll in the city she was accompanied by a group of older ladies from the Russian royal family.

Her plans to return to her homeland were hindered by a heavy snowfall that struck the northern part of Russia. The roads were covered with a thick white blanket. The temperature plummeted, and no one dared venture out on the roads. Mahdolia was forced to remain indoors until the snow began to melt.

In Tehran winter was still far off. The shah walked through his palace in a panic. Sharmin had not shown her face that night, which had never happened before. She would walk through the palace and the gardens, but she always came back to the hall of mirrors to sit at the window.

When Sharmin failed to show up the shah was unable to sleep. He spent the night wandering the corridors, peeking into all the rooms and calling her name. He was afraid he might find her dead somewhere. He searched through dark storerooms and under old cupboards and couches, but she was nowhere to be found.

The next day he sent out the guards, but there was no trace of Sharmin anywhere. Tired and disappointed the shah lay in bed and listened to the outdoor noises. The wild cats were making a racket on the roofs of the palace. Had they seduced Sharmin? Would she have chosen the warmth of a feral cat over the warmth of her master's arms?

The caterwauling of the cats drove the shah to distraction. He got out of bed and went out to the courtyard. When he reached the pool he called out, 'Sharmin, are you there?'

The guards saw him. The head of the guards asked if he could be of any help.

'Bring us a torch!' ordered the shah.

The guard did what was he was told.

Torch in hand the shah climbed the stairs leading up to the roof. The cats, who saw the shah coming towards them, jumped to the other roofs of the palace. There must have been at least a hundred of them. The shah had never seen them in a group like this before. During the daytime each cat went his own way, but in the evening they all gathered together. Astonished, the shah held the torch aloft. The fat wild cats regarded the palace as their own territory, and each day they feasted on leftovers from the harem and the palace kitchen. These were the descendants of the cats that had been living on the roofs of the palace for generations. The animals knew where the borders were drawn. They never entered the palace; the roofs, the back garden of the harem and the rubbish shed at its far end were their domain. Now, face to face with the shah, they knew they were not to get any closer and that they had to behave themselves.

'Sharmin!' the shah shouted. The cats flew in every direction. Sharmin did not appear.

Back in his bedroom the shah could not bear the empty spot at his feet. He rang his little bell and cried, 'Taj!'

Rapid footsteps told him that the chamberlain was on his way to fetch the shah's daughter.

Taj Olsultan was still living with her servant in a separate apartment at the end of the harem, which had its own entrance to the gardens. The shah continued to pay regular visits to her classroom, where she was tutored by the French woman. An experienced statesman came to teach Taj the history of the country, but it was the shah himself who told her about events that had taken place during the rule of his father and grandfather.

'Remember everything. As princess you must know these things.'

The secrets that the shah shared with her strengthened the tie between father and daughter, but they also caused her to worry about his health and well-being.

Taj Olsultan had quickly slipped into a dressing gown when the chamberlain told her the shah was having another sleepless night.

'What is it, Shah-my-Father?' she asked as soon as she saw him.

He embraced her and kissed her long dark hair. 'Sharmin is gone.'

'What do you mean, gone?' asked the girl with surprise.

'I've looked everywhere.'

'She's bound to come back. You're tired. You really must sleep,' said Taj.

'I can't sleep,' replied the shah.

'I'll read to you then,' she said, and she put the shah to bed.

Taj picked up a French book from the stack on the

bedside table. She sat on the edge of the bed and began reading from the page where the shah had made a dog-ear.

'"*La vicomtesse était liée depuis trois ans avec un des plus célèbres et des plus riches seigneurs portugais, le marquis d'Ajuda-Pinto . . .*"'

But the shah's mind was elsewhere. He sat up and said, 'The women of the harem have a hand in Sharmin's disappearance.'

Taj pushed him back gently and continued reading.

'"*C'était une de ces liaisons innocentes qui ont tant d'attraits pour les personnes ainsi liées . . .*"'

'They take away everything that is dear to me,' said the shah, and he got out of bed.

'Where are you going, Father?' asked Taj, putting the book back on the bedside table.

'I still don't have an heir. No son of those women could ever succeed me.'

The girl poured out a glass of water and handed it to him.

'I don't need water,' said the shah. 'Taj, listen, you are my only hope. You must give me an heir. I must find you a suitable husband.'

'What are you talking about?' said Taj, clearly startled. 'I'm only a girl.'

'Your mother was also a girl. She was about fourteen when she gave birth to you. How old are you now? Almost fourteen, surely?'

'No, far from it,' said Taj.

'You'll soon be thirteen, and thirteen is the same as fourteen. You must watch what you eat. The older and prettier you become the more likely they are to poison you. They've taken Sharmin from me and with you they'll do exactly the same,' he said, and he left the bedroom.

'Where are you going, Father?'

'To the harem. Whoever harms Sharmin will die. You! Go to your own room. Watch what you eat. And keep the door firmly bolted when you sleep. I'll have them hung if they so much as point a finger at you,' he said.

It was deep in the night. Khwajeh Bashi, the harem overseer, was asleep. The shah kicked the door so hard that the man awoke with a start. Only the shah would ever do such a thing. Khwajeh Bashi unbolted the door. The shah probably had need of a woman.

'Your Majesty!'

The shah ignored him and walked on. The air of the harem was heavy with the smell of tobacco.

'Sharmin!' the shah bellowed.

Khwajeh Bashi's heart was in his mouth. He had heard that the shah's cat was missing. He knew the shah was capable of murder if he didn't calm down, but Khwajeh Bashi dared not open his mouth for fear that he would be the first victim. He followed him at a safe distance.

'Sharmin! Sharmin!' called the shah.

He stumbled over a chair and a bucket in the dark. Then he knocked over a hookah. Blind with rage, he kicked the pipe against the wall and it shattered noisily. Grumbling sounds could be heard from the rooms. The women had woken up and locked their doors from the inside, afraid the angry shah would come in.

Khwajeh Bashi, who thought there was a good chance that the women were behind the cat's disappearance, went to get help. The women fell silent.

'Where are you, Sharmin?' called the shah.

Suddenly the terrified whine of a cat could be heard and the creature tore past the shah's leg. The shah thought he had seen from which room the cat had been tossed, and he threw his full weight against the door.

'Stop, Shah-my-Father! Stop!'

Khwajeh Bashi had rushed to get Taj and warn her. The girl took the shah by the arm and led him out of the harem.

23. A Secret Message

Mahdolia was back. After a day of rest she received the shah in her palace. She wanted to keep their conversation beyond the knowledge of the vizier. The Russians had expressed negative opinions about him.

'Mother, how was your journey? How did they receive you?'

'Far beyond my expectations. I was accepted with open arms – just like a blood relation – by the tsar's wife, his mother, his sisters and his daughters. The atmosphere was one of trust. The tsar said he knew we had nothing to do with the attack on the embassy.'

'You make us happy, Mother,' said the shah.

'The visit to Moscow was another unforgettable experience. The majestic churches and the impressive historic buildings all underscore human mortality. Everything, from the streets and bridges to the theatres, is so completely different from what we have in Tehran. There were a few times that I found myself silently weeping in the streets of Moscow.'

'Why, Mother?'

'For you, my son. It wasn't until I reached the palace of the tsar that I realised the kind of misery in which my son, the shah of Persia, is living. That was when I became fully aware of what history has done to us, and especially to you. Once we had magnificent cities and palaces that made Moscow look like a simple village. Now my son has become the king of a land of ruins.'

The shah offered her a handkerchief.

'But in the presence of the tsar I behaved as if I were the mother of the mightiest shah in the world.'

'We are grateful to you for that,' said the shah. 'What did you discuss with the Russians?'

'Sheikh Aqasi has all the documents. Tomorrow he is coming to hand everything over to you. It all comes down to the following: the Russians are prepared to withdraw from the occupied regions of Azerbaijan, but under certain conditions.'

'I'm listening,' said the shah guardedly.

'They want access to the Persian part of the Caspian Sea, so they can freely sail there.'

'That's impossible,' answered the shah. 'We ourselves have no ships. Must we fully surrender our northern waters to the Russians? Must we stand aside and admire the Russian warships? No, never.'

'Son, if we have no ships, what do we need that sea for?'

'Mother!'

'Listen. The Russians are prepared to withdraw, but in exchange they want us to give up our authority over the islands in the Caspian Sea and the steppe above Afghanistan for a period of fifty years. We wouldn't be giving anything away; only lending.'

'I beg your pardon, Mother, but this is utter madness!'

'Madness? Of what use to us is that wild, uninhabited steppe above Afghanistan? Even the Mongolian donkeys detest it. And then that handful of islands. Has one single Persian even set foot on them since the creation of the world?'

'What do the Russians want with them, then? They'll be colonising our land. Aren't you ashamed of yourself?'

'Why? I'm doing everything I can to keep our land intact,' said Mahdolia defensively. 'I know what our tribe has sacrificed to serve this people. I have seen the bodies of so many of our brave men who were killed in the wars or murdered by the spies of foreign powers. You act as if I were betraying our nation. I want to protect you. I'm tired. I think you should go. Tomorrow I'll share the tsar's most important message with you,' said the queen mother, and she stood up.

'No. Sit down, Mother.'

'Only if you sit down too, and stop speaking to me from such a great height, like your father.'

The shah sat down beside her.

'You know the Russians want access to the Indian Ocean?' she continued.

'Let them dream. We're not giving them our land.'

'The tsar has made the following proposal: if the shah wants to free Herat from the hands of the British he can count on us.'

A light flickered in the shah's eyes. 'How do they think they're going to do that?'

'If we agree to their plans, they will withdraw from the occupied regions. The tsar will then provide us with cannons and rifles. If the shah requests it the Russian officers will assist our warlords and fight alongside them in our army uniforms.'

'Did the tsar really propose this?' asked the shah.

'He promised me this personally and no one else knows about it, not even Sheikh Aqasi. Listen, my son, if you can give our beloved Herat back to the nation you will go down in history as a hero.'

'But the Russians cannot be trusted,' said the shah.

'Son, what have we got to lose?'

'The vizier will never agree to it.'

'You are the shah. And by the way the tsar hasn't got a single good thing to say about the vizier.'

'What did he say?'

'The tsar told me in confidence that according to the report of the Russian embassy, a possible takeover by the vizier should be taken into account.'

The shah sank in his chair.

'But don't worry,' said Mahdolia. 'The Russians have agreed that if your throne is in danger they will step in and take action.'

The shah stood up, took his mother's hand, kissed it and left her alone.

On his way to his palace he wondered when he ought to inform the vizier of the tsar's proposal. While the shah saw the possibility of recapturing Herat just within reach, the vizier was concentrating on domestic concerns.

The shah decided to wait for a suitable moment.

24. The Print Shop

The shah was still living in Tabriz as crown prince when the vizier sent a group of bright students to Europe to study. Now that they had graduated the vizier needed them to build up the country.

The engineers, who knew all there was to know about modern technology, provided Tehran with a new road network. The doctors were put to work in new hospitals, where people stood in long queues day and night waiting to be helped. Those who had learned new languages and had been introduced to modern academic disciplines became the teachers of teachers and would later be sent to work in schools that were yet to be built.

One of the young men was of particular importance to the vizier. He was the son of their family cook. Long ago, when the vizier was helping his own children with their French lessons, he noticed the cook's son hiding behind the door and following everything he said. The vizier called him in, put the French textbook down in front of him, and said, 'Read this aloud.'

To his astonishment the boy began to read. Recognising an exceptional talent the vizier had made him part of the family and had him join his own children in their private lessons. Later he sent the boy to Paris, and now that he was back he worked as the vizier's right-hand man. His name was Tagi, but the vizier, who was convinced that this young fellow would later become a national leader, gave him an honorary name: Amir, a synonym for prince.

Another of the vizier's dreams for the country was to open a print shop. He wanted a newspaper for Tehran. He had seen newspapers for the first time in Moscow when he went there with his father.

The vizier wrote poetry, and he also kept a diary for recording the day's events. He hoped to publish his poems in book form one day. Poetry gave him peace of mind, and he always carried poems around with him to correct. It was a way of cutting himself off from the outside world. He also liked to write letters: letters as political documents, as historical markers.

The vizier wrote a new kind of prose. The Persian language was ponderous and complex, but the vizier's style had a unique clarity. It all came from serving as chronicler for his father and from translating so many letters from Russia, France, England and India into Persian for the father of the shah, work that brought him into close contact with the direct European style of writing. The father of the shah had once given him a royal quill as a reward for his beautiful handwriting.

His most moving writings were the letters he wrote to his wife.

My love,
When I arrived home yesterday you were not there.
Our house seemed like the empty nest
of a rare bird that had flown away forever.
Always be home, my love, when I return,
or I am forced to go from room to room,
calling your name until you come.

This brief, simple letter provided a whole new glimpse into the relationship between men and women. Persian poetry was full of men's declarations of love to women, but not a single man had ever written a letter to his own wife.

The vizier had asked Amir to start a newspaper that would deal with developments in the country and throughout the rest of the world. So it was with great pride that the vizier conducted the shah to the brand-new print shop. Inevitably the shah's cannon was dragged along behind him.

The vizier told the shah about the young Persian engineers who had remodelled the streets of Tehran along French lines. Before going on to the print shop the shah would be presiding over the official opening of one of the city's new squares.

The closer they drew to the centre of the city the more crowded it became. Everyone wanted to admire the king. His royal garb, and the way he rode his ornamented horse through the throngs of the poor, so tall in the saddle, made him seem like something from a different world. Having arrived at the square the shah was surprised to see all the important men of the city standing along the road in festive clothing. It was a relief to encounter these esteemed individuals after so many deaf and blind people, so many beggars. The shah got down from his horse to cut a ribbon. He had never been part of such a ceremony before. The square was paved with flat stones and decorated with large flower boxes, and in the middle was a fountain with leaping jets of water.

A pair of scissors were handed to the shah on a tray. He picked them up and walked somewhat awkwardly towards the ribbon. Making a royal gesture he grabbed the ribbon and slowly cut it through. Music was heard, followed by an outburst of cheers. The shah received the engineers, spoke with them briefly, pressed a few coins into their hands and proceeded to the print shop with the vizier. A group of young men walked with them.

The print shop was located behind the mosque in a new building. It was filled with an unfamiliar odour that stung the shah's nostrils and eyes. The vizier had been supplying him with documents about the progress of its construction, but seeing a print shop up close was something quite different.

He looked at the new machines and equipment, but his eyes lingered on the young engineer who was leading the tour. He had heard about this Amir, the vizier's right-hand man. The shah had no idea how the equipment worked, but he acted as if he knew everything. He looked at the lead letters in their cabinets and paused at one of the printing cylinders, running his index finger over it cautiously. The grease on the cylinder made his finger black. Not knowing what to do, he held the finger up in the air. Amir fetched a clean cloth. The shah wiped his finger and continued walking. He paused again at the type case, and the vizier motioned to Amir to provide the shah with an explanation.

Amir picked up a few lead letters from the type case, arranged them in a line on the composing stick and placed the stick in the printing machine. Then he handily sliced off a sheet of paper and laid it on the machine's paper holder. The shah watched the engineer with amazement and waited for the results. Amir turned the handle of the machine. It made a sound that was totally unfamiliar to him, after which the sheet of paper fell into a tray down at the other end. Amir picked up the paper and handed it to the shah. Speaking to himself the shah read the sentence that was printed on the paper: 'The shah is welcome to the first Royal Print Shop.'

He gazed at Amir in admiration. Then the vizier led the shah to another printing machine that already contained a fully composed text. He asked the shah if he would like to turn the handle of the machine to declare the print shop officially open. With one hand on his sword and the other on the handle, the shah turned the wheel three times. A large sheet of printed paper fell out of the machine. The vizier picked the paper up with both hands, gave it to the shah and said, 'The newspaper.'

The shah found it confusing to see his own portrait superimposed over the lion from the royal coat of arms with a sword in its paw and a dazzling sun on its back. A momentary smile appeared on his face. His eyes fell on a brief text printed below his portrait. It gave him goose pimples.

'Look! One of our poems is printed here!' He beamed with happiness and gave the newspaper to Amir, who was standing beside him. 'Read it aloud to us!'

Amir began.

'We can't hear you. Speak up,' said the shah.

With more feeling this time, Amir began to declaim:

'Said one among them – "Surely not in vain
"My substance of the common Earth was ta'en
"And to this Figure moulded, to be broke,
"Or trampled back to shapeless Earth again."'

'Excellent,' said the shah, 'but our eyes must grow accustomed to these letters. It's not like reading a book.' He pointed to an article that was printed beneath his poem and said, 'Read this!'

It was an article about telegraphy that Amir himself had written. He began reading with deep conviction: '"At one time the world's fastest communication system was a work of our own devising. The great King Darius had built an enormous network of roads, with couriers who rode ceaselessly day and night to bring reports to the palace with the utmost speed from every corner of the world. They even used echoes, gestures and mirrors to convey the messages across rivers and over mountains. Back then we were proud of our inventions, but now we have become dependent on the Russians to build donkey trails for us . . .'"

The vizier saw the look of unease on the shah's face. Amir hesitated a moment but continued, '"Telegraphy is the sending of a message by cable. It works as follows. The sender hands his message to the postal clerk, who sends it to its destination at exactly the same moment . . ."'

'Go on, go on,' said the shah impatiently.

'"England used to be dependent on ships. It took months for a message from London to reach the Far East, and it took even more months for an answer to be sent back. But now England sends . . ."'

'Yes, yes?' urged the shah.

'"The vizier has informed this newspaper that we won't have to wait for decades for telegraphy to come to us, if that is our desire. And if the vizier says this, we must believe that we too will soon be able to send our messages from one city to another in the blink of an eye, but— "'

The shah snatched the newspaper from Amir's hands, rolled it up and kept walking through the print shop. He inspected the cables, the ink pots and the lead letters, tossed the workers a few coins and walked out.

Once outside the vizier shed some light on the newspaper article. 'The information in the newspaper is not new to Your Majesty, of course, but we think our fellow countrymen also ought to be informed of these big changes.

The articles in the newspaper will cover developments in our own land. The British have told us informally that they are thinking about running a telegraph line to India via our country. Not so very long ago they laid cables along the bottom of the sea, a difficult and expensive method that takes a very long time. Now they have approached us, since the cheapest and shortest way for them to run their cable to India is through our country. It has also been drawn to our attention that they are considering a railway line that would run straight through our country and on to India. We have not had any official discussions with them, but we expect that very soon they will come knocking on our door.'

The shah listened in silence and thought about the tsar's message with regard to the invasion of Herat. He wanted to talk this over with the vizier, but decided not to. 'Keep us informed,' said the shah.

That night the shah awoke with a start, his heart pounding in his chest. Sharmin rubbed up against him. Sitting up in bed he thought about his visit to the square and the print shop. Only now did he realise that wherever the vizier went he was followed by a group of young men. These were the ones who had studied abroad. They looked different, they had a different way of sitting on their horses, and the way they walked was different from that of the merchants and princes. Together they represented the face of a land that the shah had never seen before.

'Perhaps our mother is right,' said the shah to the cat. 'You weren't there in the print shop, or you too would have seen how those young men are brimming with ambition. This won't be the last we hear from them.'

25. An Historical Decision

The shah, his mother and Sheikh Aqasi were the only ones who knew what had been discussed with the Kremlin. To prevent informers from discovering their secret they had formed a triumvirate. They never employed a messenger and never took notes. The shah had decided to become more actively involved in affairs of state. He attended important military meetings more often and kept the vizier outside the decision-making process whenever he could. To the vizier's great irritation the shah had relieved him of some of his military responsibilities, arguing that the vizier would need to have his hands free in order to carry out his reforms. In the meantime the shah had appointed Sheikh Aqasi as his official advisor.

The sheikh was now serving as a messenger between the shah and the Russians in the negotiations on the invasion of Herat. Ultimately the shah intended to transfer some of the power from the vizier to the sheikh. The sheikh advised the shah to make sure his subjects could see that he was ruling the land and not the vizier. He also tried to keep the shah from getting bored. He was constantly making plans for him and sending him to various cities on working visits. This change did the shah good; it cheered him up.

Sheikh Aqasi knew that if he could enter into a stable agreement with the Russians, and if the shah could take

Herat, he would undoubtedly become the country's next vizier.

It did not escape Grand Vizier Mirza Kabir's notice that Sheikh Aqasi was meeting with the Russians more and more frequently. He had warned the shah countless times about the sheikh: he was sly, superstitious and easily influenced. A man like that could pose a danger to the country.

'I would suggest that everyone mind their own business,' responded the shah sharply.

The vizier was forced to sit by and watch as his faithful warlords disappeared from the highest ranks of the army. The shah was the army's commander-in-chief, but the decisions he made revealed the influence of the vizier's adversaries. The vizier could do nothing to oppose them. The shah would not hesitate to use force to brush him aside.

Whenever the shah made an appearance Sheikh Aqasi was at his side. He also made it his business to be with the king whenever the vizier came to the palace for meetings.

It was late in the afternoon. The last page of the document that would seal the alliance with the tsar lay before him on his desk. Once he pressed his signet ring into the ink-pad and made his mark at the bottom of the page, the path to Herat would be thrown open. He walked around the room with the signet ring in his hand, looking at himself in the mirror. He would do what his father had not been able to accomplish.

'Sharmin!' he called, but Sharmin did not come. The shah looked out of the window towards the gate, where two guards were marching. He took off his hat, scratched his head and stood there with his hat in his hands. Resolutely he put his hat back on his head, walked to his desk, pressed his signet ring first into the ink-pad and then, with force, beneath his name. He rang his bell and asked the chamberlain to fetch Sheikh Aqasi.

The shah handed the agreement to the sheikh and sent him away without a word. Now that he had made this decision he felt the need to speak with the vizier.

'Sharmin!' he called again.

The cat remained hidden.

The shah was about to go into the courtyard, but halfway down the stairs he turned back and entered the harem unannounced. Khwajeh Bashi quickly put on his slippers and followed the shah, who walked further into the harem and then changed his mind. He turned to Khwajeh Bashi and said, 'Fetch the vizier!'

Khwajeh Bashi did not understand why the shah wanted to bring the vizier to the harem.

'Why are you standing there? Fetch the vizier!' shouted the shah.

Evening had just fallen when the vizier rode into the palace. He handed the reins to the guard and had the chamberlain inform the shah of his arrival. Once the vizier was inside the shah took him to his conference room.

'Have a seat,' he said, contrary to custom, but the vizier preferred to stand.

'Please, sit down,' repeated the shah in a friendly tone.

The vizier sat down. The shah walked over to the window. Standing with his back to the vizier he told him in general terms about the decisions he had made, about Herat and about the Russian ships in the Caspian Sea. After having said all this he felt as if a burden had been lifted from his shoulders.

The vizier sat silently, his head bent low, lost in reflection.

'What does the vizier think?' asked the shah.

'What the shah has done is irreparable,' said the vizier, and he stood up.

'Irreparable?'

'Opening the Caspian Sea to Russian ships is surrender, pure and simple. And as for Herat, the shah knows we will never be able to win a war with the British. The shah and his advisors are steering us into troubled waters.'

'We've made airtight agreements with the Russians,' said the shah in his own defence.

'No one is capable of making airtight agreements with the Russians. The generations before us have had plenty of experience in that regard.'

'Times have changed,' answered the shah unsteadily.

'For the Russians times will never change,' insisted the vizier.

'But what have we got to lose if we don't win the battle for Herat?' asked the shah, feeling his way.

'We'll lose a great deal, but exactly what is impossible to predict.'

'I wish the vizier would not speak with us in guarded terms. Let's have some examples. Give us an example,' said the shah emphatically.

'The tsar is taking a chance. The tsar has nothing to lose. But the shah must be very careful where he puts his feet. We may end up so deep in the morass that we won't be able to climb out.'

'I asked for a concrete example, but the vizier is speaking in riddles.'

'The gravity of the situation exceeds all examples,' answered the vizier. 'The war will bring unrest and uncertainty. We must reach a compromise with the British and not walk into the tsar's trap. The reforms—'

'Reforms, reforms. What good are all these changes if

we are no longer in control of our own country later on? Compromise? What compromise? The vizier knows better than anyone that the British don't understand the word "compromise". Only a cannonball can put them in their place. The decision has been taken. Soon we will invade Herat. You have been sufficiently informed,' said the shah, whose lower lip was trembling with agitation.

The vizier hazarded one last attempt: 'Excuse me, Your Majesty, but it is my duty to tell you that this is the most impetuous decision you ever could have made. I am against it. You are allowing yourself to be led by a group of greedy, deranged advisors. I am opposed to this war in every possible way. Tear up the documents. Don't jeopardise your crown. Don't endanger the nation!'

In his youth, when the vizier was his tutor, the shah had often been forced to endure his harsh scoldings, but those days were over now. The shah opened one of his desk drawers, took out a stack of papers and thrust it under the vizier's nose. There was no need for the shah to utter a word. It was a chapter of a translation of the French constitution that the vizier had been working on for quite some time. What it contained undermined the shah's power.

'Out of my sight!' he shouted, slamming the door behind the vizier with all his might.

26. Isa Khan

Deeply offended, the vizier left the palace. He rode through the dark streets to the hill outside the city, talking to himself: 'A pack of wolves is pursuing me in the dark. Why so many wolves? There's hardly enough meat on me to feed three wild beasts.'

He needed to talk to someone. He rode, he galloped and he talked out loud. Finally tears began running down his cheeks. Would he have to retire as vizier and spend the rest of his life at his family estate in Farahan, writing? Of course stepping down would be out of the question: that would play right into the hands of the corrupt elite, the politicians and the foreign powers.

He saw his plans crumble into bits. His dream of a railway line that would run from the deep south to the far east. Telegraph cables criss-crossing the entire country. He wanted to build bridges and hospitals, to send children to school and deliver women from their misery. So studying the French Revolution and reading the documents on the Assemblée nationale, the flight of Louis XVI and the French constitution had all been for naught. It seemed like an impossible wish, but he was already visualising a Persian Assemblée as the country's legislative power. It was his conviction that the legislative, executive and judicial powers would have to be separated. He understood that history could be shaped and moulded, and that man was the author of his own happiness.

The vizier had never been permitted to talk about these things in the presence of the shah. He spent his scant free time translating the French constitution into Persian. He thought no one knew, but his enemies had proven to be formidable opponents. Sheikh Aqasi had somehow managed to get hold of a chapter of the translation, the very chapter that dealt with limiting the shah's power. The sheikh had waited for just the right moment to pass it on to the shah.

The vizier rode to the home of his aged father, who had retired from public life and was living in a castle in a village outside Tehran. His name was Isa Khan. Having worked for the father of the shah as first vizier, Isa Khan was an experienced manager who had lived through many wars and political assassinations.

The small village lay at the foot of Mount Tochal. The villagers had no large pieces of land, but they farmed on small plots that lay on the slopes of the mountain. Because there wasn't enough room the villagers had built their homes in step fashion, so that the roofs of the lower houses formed the courtyards of the houses above them. For strangers it was always peculiar to see cows and sheep standing among the roofs.

The vizier's family had built the castle centuries ago. Now the vizier's father lived there, and some day the vizier himself might spend his last days there as well.

Advancing with caution his horse climbed to the village in the dark. At a certain point the vizier dismounted and made his way to the castle on foot. The gate was wide open as usual. An old woman who had worked in the house for years as a servant saw the vizier and wanted to warn Isa Khan immediately, but the vizier let her know this would not be necessary, that he wanted to surprise his father.

Isa Khan was in his room, sitting on a carpet at a small table and reading a book with a magnifying glass. The vizier stood there for a few minutes watching him, aware that this might well be his last visit with his father. He saw the decline in the way he sat, and that his hair and beard were completely grey. He couldn't believe this was the same man who had once fought the Russians at the front, who had held lengthy talks with the tsar in order to establish the country's borders with Russia – the same man who had also been forced to undergo the humiliation of signing a treaty in which the Persians were made to cede the state of Yerevan and the northern part of Azerbaijan to the Russians.

Isa Khan sat bent over a book as the yellow light from a lantern illuminated half his face.

'What is Isa Khan reading?'

The old man straightened his back, looked in the direction of the voice and said, 'I hear the vizier.' He tried to stand up. The vizier rushed up to him, held his two hands, kissed them and knelt down beside him.

'The vizier is sad. What is it?' asked Isa Khan.

'The country, the country, the country,' sighed the vizier, and he rested his face in the weathered hands of his father.

'I see you are troubled, my son.'

'I'm afraid they will kill me.'

'The men of our house have never been afraid of death,' answered Isa Khan.

'I am not afraid of death, but I am afraid they will kill me before I am able to finish my work.'

'You cannot set the course of history alone, and man is not capable of completing his work in its entirety, yet you must try.'

'I am doing that. I have always done that. But I fear that history will forget what I was trying to do,' said the vizier.

'Your words sound familiar,' answered his father with a smile. 'Don't worry. History has seen you.'

'But what if they kill me halfway through my mission?'

'Then that too is the course of history,' said Isa Khan.

The vizier smiled. He was relieved.

'I have never feared death,' said Isa Khan. 'Nor did my father, nor my father's father. These were men who served their country, just as you are doing. They did their work exceedingly well. Now it's your turn.'

The vizier went back to shut the door, then sat down even closer to his father.

'Father,' he whispered, 'the shah is running the country into the ground, and his mother is even worse, if that's possible. His counsellors are deceivers and the shah wants to be deceived. He's letting himself be led around by a pack of charlatans.'

'That's nothing new,' answered Isa Khan placidly. 'Didn't I go through the same thing with the father of this shah?'

The vizier walked back to the door to see if anyone was listening. 'Father, you served the weak father of this shah. Your father served the weak father of the father of the shah. Now I serve this shah. They cannot manage without us,' said the vizier.

'Unburden your heart, my son,' said Isa Khan.

'Father, we live in a time of electricity and trains. There is a need for new leaders. I think the shah should step aside, and I'm not the only one,' said the vizier.

The old man looked into the eyes of his son. 'Dismiss these ideas from your mind,' he said calmly. 'If you depose the shah the whole country will become entangled in tribal wars, something the foreign powers are just waiting to happen. This land is an ancient labyrinth of hidden power struggles, ancient resentments, convoluted religious currents, poisonous politicians, vindictive princes, stupid clerics and powerful women who pull the strings behind closed doors. Son, no matter what it is you want to do, you'll have to do it with this shah.'

'But the shah is a fool. Everyone is urging him to kill me, and he will do it without batting an eyelid.'

Isa Khan paused to reflect.

'I envy your ambition, my son,' he said calmly. 'I will not stand in your way. Perhaps you are right, perhaps someone should save the country by rising up like this. But because I am your father I am not the right advisor in this matter. You are clever and you don't need my advice. One thing should be clear, however: don't turn back. Use whatever strength you have and do your duty.'

The vizier was encouraged by his father's answer. The desire to live flashed in his eyes. He stood up and swung the door wide open.

27. Supernatural Forces

When King Darius the Great first announced that he wanted to send his vast army to the West by way of Athens, his counsellors studied the stars well ahead of time and provided Darius with wise advice.

But the country no longer had any wise astronomers, and all the high towers from which they had once gazed at the heavens had been destroyed by the enemy during the wars. Now it was mainly magicians who predicted the future.

Sheikh Aqasi was the last man of that tradition. He claimed that he could make contact with supernatural forces. The shah had instructed him to put his talents to work so that he, the shah, could feel certain about Herat.

Sheikh Aqasi climbed Mount Tochal to shut himself up in his cave. This had been his practice whenever the last king had asked him for advice. It was a place where magicians and fortune-tellers once came to pore over ancient texts and busy themselves with strange herbs, perfumes, dried animal paws, human skulls, snakes and other reptiles.

The opening to the cave was a narrow crack between two great rocks. Sheikh Aqasi had brought along a few pieces of dry bread, a sack of dried dates and a jug of water. He squeezed himself into the cave and crept down a narrow passage until he came to a space where he could not stand completely upright. He lit a candle and walked further. It was an oppressive, fearful place, but not for Sheikh Aqasi. He hummed a verse from a holy text to chase the poisonous creatures away: '*Ya rabb, ar-rabbok, en ma' rabbok, en inna rabbok, en allaha rabbok, en Muhammad-on rabbok, wa 'Ali-on rabbok en mahdi-on rabbok.*'

The walls of the cave were black with candle smoke, and hanging from them were dried herbs, plants, wolf paws, skulls, snake teeth and talismans. The sheikh sat down, and after he had taken a nap and was completely rested he began to concentrate on Herat. He always sat in the same place when making contact with the supernatural forces, as he had when preparing the mother of the king for her journey to Russia. On the opposite wall he had seen Mahdolia ride into the palace of the Russian tsar in a coach. He had seen scenes from the future long before the queen had left for Moscow.

After three days and two nights the sheikh had not received a single sign from above concerning Herat. It wasn't until the end of the third evening that he began to hear the voices and see the faces of the inhabitants of a Herat of the future. Soon scenes from the war began to appear on the wall. He saw the Indian soldiers marching near the gate of Herat under the leadership of British officers, and British flags fluttering above the gate. A strapping British commander, who was in control of the city, came up so close that his face imprinted itself on Sheikh Aqasi's memory. He heard the Persian cannons shooting over the city walls and saw the British flags fall. He saw the Indian soldiers take to their heels and the Persian warriors pursue them on horseback.

In another scene he saw the shah, alive and well, riding through the gate of Herat and into the city. It was so vivid that he could hear the horses breathing. The shah was still mounted on his horse when a severed human head was tossed to the ground in front of him.

Sheikh Aqasi recognised the big head immediately as that of the British commander. The message from above was clear. The sheikh went down from the mountain to pass the favourable prophecy on to the shah.

28. The Invasion

Herat was once called Aria. It was the first city of the Aryans, the founders of the Persian Empire. The ancient Greeks called the city Artacoana.

Alexander the Great once invaded the city on his way to India. He built a fortress there as a base of operations so he could rob India of its gold. He called the city Alexandria Ariana. A few centuries later the Arabs forced the population to accept the Quran, after which Genghis Khan arrived and razed the city to the ground. Many came and went in the years that followed. Now the shah of Persia was next in line to lay claim to this jewel of a city.

One month after receiving the good news from Sheikh Aqasi the shah travelled to the border town of Mashad, in the east of the country, where he was to meet with the Russian officers. These officers had painstakingly gone over the battle plans with the Persian warlords, and their strategy earned the shah's immediate admiration and approval. It was well thought out, which pleased the shah since he personally wanted to be present at the front. He saw himself riding through the gate of Herat and into the city with a great display of power, exactly as Sheikh Aqasi had envisioned in the cave.

The chosen moment was exceedingly favourable. The British had their hands full with protests in the cities of India and in the countryside. They saw their conflict with the Persians as a matter for the negotiating table. The

Persian army, they thought, would never be capable of occupying Herat by force of arms.

The Russians made sure that all suspicious movements in the eastern border region escaped British observation. At the same time the Russians sent an army unit by ship via the Caspian Sea to the steppe beyond the Afghan border to come to the aid of the Persians as soon as Herat had fallen into their hands.

The shah brought his storyteller with him to the border region. On the evening of the invasion he had him recount an old war story.

The shah slept in the barracks at the border, in his own tent. He was sitting on a sofa, leaning on great, soft cushions, and smoking his hookah, a vast assortment of delicacies within reach. He sent the servant away and summoned the storyteller.

The storyteller had dressed like a man of Herat with a milk-coloured turban wrapped round his head, the loose end of which rested on his shoulder. He bowed and waited for the shah to give him permission to begin.

'What does the storyteller have for us today?' asked the shah as the smoke from his hookah escaped from his mouth.

'With Your Majesty's permission I will talk about the journey of Xerxes to Athens, a true story based on the writings of Herodotus.'

'Begin!' said the shah.

The storyteller blew out a few candles and began his tale.

Xerxes, the king of kings, lived in a palace in Apadana, where he was watched over by seven thousand bodyguards. This was the glorious order of guards known as 'the Fadaian'. They carried long spears that had been specially designed for them, spears that were worked with gold and silver. Besides the guards there were seventy thousand cavalrymen who were called 'the Immortals'. And then there were elite troops from the various states of Persia and other subject nations such as Media, Bactria, India and the steppes of the Saks.

An army of a million and a half soldiers was on its way to Athens.

The king of kings rode in an open coach that was pulled by a royal horse, while a servant with a parasol stood behind him.

Xerxes had his coach rolled onto a majestic ship, where warlords in special uniforms awaited him. A deafening thunder of drums and trumpet blasts was sounded. A camel was slaughtered as a sacrifice so the coach could ride over the blood. The royal anthem was sung with great enthusiasm. The priest of Zarathustra gently tapped the coach a few times with his golden staff to bless the king's journey, and with his free hand he directed the smoke from the holy herbs towards Xerxes to protect him from the evil eye.

It was a display of power unlike any that had ever been seen before on earth. The Greeks understood that soon they would be striking the image of this great king onto their gold coins.

Xerxes, son of Darius, had remembered but one lesson from his father: 'Conquer the world.' Only when he had Athens at his feet could he proudly claim the throne of the Achaemenids. It was four hundred and eighty years before the birth of Isa, son of Mary.

After seven days the ships reached the harbour of Greece. As they approached the mainland Xerxes stood on the deck of the ship to admire his army. Wherever he looked ships appeared on the horizon. He was hardly a man any longer; he was a god who was revealing himself to the world. When he turned round he saw the coastline of Europe for the first time.

The king's ship dropped anchor. Xerxes remained standing on the deck and watched his soldiers go ashore. The local populace looked on, powerless.

'The King of Kings,' they whispered, as they held the hands of their children and shook with fear.

The shah knew the rest of the story: the humiliating defeat of Xerxes at the hands of the Greeks. It was not clear why the storyteller had chosen this particular tale, an event over which the Persians had remained silent for centuries out of shame. The storyteller was not yet finished when the shah threw a coin against the door. The storyteller stopped immediately, picked up the coin and disappeared.

'Idiot,' muttered the shah and put his hookah aside. He turned round, pulled the blankets over his head and tried to sleep. He would have to be up early the next morning to impart some words of encouragement to the first troops going to the front.

A dream wrenched him from his sleep. He had seen his father. He had embraced him in his sleep with tears of joy. It was extraordinary that the old king should appear in his dream now, but it was also to be expected.

All through the centuries the Persians had cherished Herat like an old gem. It was a very special city, where the Indian and Persian cultures met. The people spoke proper Persian, the customs were Persian, even the Indian rulers spoke Persian, but the British occupiers had done everything they could to make it an Indian city. It was no accident, then, that the dead king should have visited the shah in his sleep on that night of all nights. It was necessary, and it was a good sign. Later that morning, when the cavalrymen marched before the eyes of the shah on their way to the front, he felt in his heart that victory was inevitable.

As soon as the shah heard that the attack on Herat had begun, he pressed his forehead to the earth and begged God with tears for a successful outcome. He was not yet finished with his prayers when the Russian colonel ordered the Persian army to fire the cannons.

Thousands of Persian sharpshooters moved towards the city on horseback. This was the Russians' idea, since the Persians were unsurpassed in their ability to shoot from galloping horses. It seemed like a very disorderly way of fighting, but it was intended to throw the disciplined Anglo-Indian army into confusion.

The British, who had counted on every possible kind of attack, had not expected this strategic variant. The officers didn't know how to defend themselves against such a swarm of armed Persians. The Afghan and Indian soldiers who were standing on the city wall could not hold out for long. The cavalrymen dispersed to avoid the British cannon shots and reached the gate of Herat. This obstacle was soon demolished, and hand-to-hand combat began within the city walls. The British had never stood face-to-face with Persian soldiers before.

The fighting was painful for the Afghan soldiers. Deep in their hearts they did not want to fight their Persian brothers. The Indian soldiers too were short on motivation, for Persia was a nearby country and they were reluctant to take sides with the English against their own neighbours. The Persians believed that victory was within reach, and that gave them courage. They instinctively avoided the Afghan and Indian soldiers and pursued the British officers and sergeants, chasing them beyond the city walls.

A sharpshooter took aim at a British officer standing on the balcony of the army post and brought him down. One of the Persian warlords ordered that his body be placed in a cart, to be thrown at the shah's feet later on. As soon as the Indian soldiers saw this, they fled through the other city gate towards the Indian border.

The Afghan soldiers no longer knew whether they should be fighting against the Persians or with them. Herat was a city in which tribes of both Afghan and Persian origin had always dwelt, and many mixed marriages had taken place over the centuries. So the population awaited the outcome of the invasion with considerable tension.

Once the Anglo-Indian troops were driven out of the city, the Afghan soldiers were ordered by their own leaders to withdraw into the hills until further notice. And thus the Persian sharpshooters captured the city. Beyond the walls, however, the battle raged. There the British inflicted great damage on the Persian army, destroying their French and Russian cannons. The Persian army was shattered, with countless dead and wounded.

The British got ready to drive the sharpshooters from Herat. They had asked the Afghan tribal leaders to attack the city from all sides. But suddenly, to everyone's astonishment, the British colonel was told to pull his army out of Herat and retreat to Indian territory without delay. The British officers were furious. They could make neither head nor tail of the order, but apparently London had something else in mind.

One of the British officers had noticed that there were Russians fighting with the Persians. He sent his soldiers to look for Russians among the dead. The soldiers returned with three Russian bodies. These were placed on a cart, and with this booty the British army withdrew from Herat.

The report of the victory soon reached the shah. Surrounded by Persian officers he entered the city like Xerxes. The Persian inhabitants of Herat came out of their houses to admire their king. The shah, perched high on his horse, waved at his subjects, and he thought of Xerxes and how happy he must have felt to first set foot on European soil.

29. A Deathly Silence

Reports of the victory had reached Tehran. The joy was enormous. Town criers spread the happy news. The city was festively decorated by order of Mahdolia, the mother of the shah, and army musicians played merrily in the streets. Merchants had huge torches lit in the bazaar, and great pans were placed on fires in the bazaar square so food could be shared with the poor.

Mahdolia's retinue wished the queen happiness with this turn of events. The triumph was seen as a firm slap in the face of the vizier. Sheikh Aqasi's prestige rose, and he was treated like the new vizier by all and sundry. No one doubted that upon his return the shah would be transferring all responsibility from the current vizier to the sheikh.

In a speech at the victory celebration that the sheikh had organised on behalf of the shah, he went to great lengths to praise the shah's courage in the presence of all the princes, politicians and great merchants of Tehran. He explained how the Persian cavalry had forced the gate of Herat and taken the city. He announced that the shah would remain in Herat until the city's governing structure was restored and to enjoy his beloved city.

Sheikh Aqasi visited Tehran's Jameh mosque the next day, where the ayatollah of the city prayed for the health of the shah in the presence of thousands of believers.

Celebrations were held throughout the country for ten

days and ten nights. Trees were decorated and flags fluttered above the government buildings.

The shah took up lodgings in a castle in the centre of Herat where, until quite recently, the British commander had lived. He assumed personal responsibility for the running of the city. Now that he had so much to do he felt vital and energetic. In his own palace he had been bored, but in Herat he felt like a king of consequence. Every day he rode through the city, inspected the barracks and stood on the high tower, gazing through his binoculars at the Indian border where the British army was stationed.

Everything was going according to plan, except that it was suspiciously quiet on the Russian side. The shah knew the Russians could not stomach the fact that the British had taken the bodies of some of their officers back to India. It was also surprising that, one week after the victory, the Russians had returned to their own country and hadn't been heard from since. The shah tried to reassure himself with the thought that the Russians were preparing to march into Afghanistan to prevent a possible attack by the British. Or perhaps they wanted to see how London was going to react to the defeat.

Yet his sense of unease remained. For although the Persian army had done extremely well in Herat, the shah also realised that if the British had wanted to they could have stopped the Persian troops and beaten them. Had he walked into a trap whose scale was greater than he could imagine?

Then came the report that an attempt had been made on the tsar's life in Moscow. The tsar was unhurt, but the incident made the shah wary. His flush of victory vanished and was replaced by anxious nights. The shah sensed that something was about to happen.

Finally the Russians made contact. The Russian embassy

in Tehran sent a third-class civil servant to the shah's mother to tell her that the tsar was in good health, that the Russians were pleased with the victory in Herat, that the tsar sent his greetings to the shah and that Moscow was ready to meet any military response from London. The ambassador also wanted Mahdolia to know that if the British were to attack Herat again, the Russians would immediately deploy their troops across the northern Afghan border.

It was a curious way of sending a message. Although it could be interpreted as an insult, the shah was reassured and found he could sleep again.

A few days later the shah received news from one of his spies that filled him with happiness. The Indian soldiers along the border had risen up in revolt and were refusing to fight the Persians. The report was of such significance to the shah that he wanted to meet the messenger personally. The messenger was promptly brought to the castle. The man, who looked more Indian than Persian, stood trembling at the door, terrified at the sight of the shah standing in the middle of the room with a stick in his hand.

'*Farsi baladi*?' asked the shah.

'Yes, I speak Persian,' answered the man shyly.

'But you are Indian?'

'No. Yes. I am an Indian, but I am Parsi,' answered the man.

'Funny. You speak Persian with an Indian accent.'

The man was a descendant of Persians who had fled to India thirteen hundred years earlier as followers of Zarathustra when the Arabs invaded the Persian Empire. These Indian Persians were called Parsi.

'We have heard the report of the protests of the Indian soldiers, but we would like to hear it once again from your own lips. Listen carefully to what we say. If you are lying, if you utter one false word, we will have you hung. Do you understand?' asked the shah coolly.

'Your Majesty, I don't dare say anything. I'm afraid I'll say something wrong,' said the terrified man.

'Don't be such a baby. Tell us from whom you heard this report!'

'From an Indian soldier who himself is stationed in the barracks,' said the man.

'Did the Indian soldier tell you this personally?'

'Yes, Your Majesty.'

'That's good. That's clear. Tell us then, word for word,' said the shah.

'The Indian soldier said, "We were in the barracks cleaning and oiling our rifles when more and more of the men began to feel uncomfortable about fighting the Persians. The rumour spread that the oil we were using to oil our rifles was made of cow fat. Everyone was shocked. Later came the rumour that the oil we spread between our buttocks and toes to prevent blisters was made of British pig fat."'

'Fantastic,' said the shah, laughing. 'Keep going, tell us more.'

'The Indian soldier continued, "I saw everyone put down his rifle and stand up."'

'Splendid,' cried the shah.

'"We began to rub the oil from our hands and feet with dirt from the ground. The British sergeants tried to force us to pick up the rifles, but we refused. Finally they moved us to the rearguard."'

'And then?' asked the shah.

'That was all, Your Majesty.'

The shah walked up to him and ordered him to open his mouth. The man, who thought he had not understood the order, stared at the shah in confusion.

'Open your mouth wide!' repeated the shah.

Trembling, the man obeyed. The shah popped a couple of gold coins into his mouth and said, 'You may go now, but always remain a Persian.'

With the gold coins still in his mouth the man bowed and walked backwards out of the room.

Now the shah could go back to enjoying his stay. He gave himself permission to spend his nights with the women of Herat, who made him forget his loneliness. This peace and quiet soon evaporated when the shah heard that the Russian troops had left the steppes north of Afghanistan and had gone back to Russia via the Caspian Sea. No sooner had he recovered from the shock than he learned that England, with the permission of the Afghan tribal leaders, had billeted thousands of Anglo-Indian soldiers in Afghanistan.

What took place next was a nightmare. The shah was forced to stand by helplessly as decisions concerning his own country were made behind his back. The Russians had deserted him; they had sold him to the British. But in exchange for what? The shah was almost sick from all the uncertainty. He couldn't eat, his hookah lost its flavour and the beautiful women of Herat no longer excited him. He realised that for the time being he could not leave Herat.

In the meantime the people of Tehran were busy with other things. They had also heard the alarming news, and everyone was trying to secure his own future. Some of the princes sought closer ties with the British embassy, others with the Russians.

Sheikh Aqasi, who had heard about a treaty between England and Russia, tried to strengthen his position in this new balance of power. He managed to get hold of a document from the British embassy, which stated that the vizier was in close contact with the Russian People's

Movement. The go-between was one of the students the vizier had sent to Moscow.

The name of the student was mentioned in the report, and it was alleged that he had attended meetings of the Russian People's Movement. The report confirmed earlier reports that the mother of the shah had received through her informants.

Sheikh Aqasi wanted the shah to read the reports and documents as soon as he returned. Everyone in Mahdolia's circle was waiting for the vizier's death blow, now that the shah was stuck in Herat. Sheikh Aqasi fed the rumours by telling Mahdolia, 'The vizier has placed a number of cannons in front of his palace. He has sent his wife and children to his father-in-law in Farahan. Something is probably about to happen of which we have not yet been informed.'

30. England's Surprise Move

London had been eyeing the southern province of Persia for a long time. In much of the brutally hot, uninhabitable south, the soil was so dark brown that everything seemed to have been rinsed in crude oil. The fact that the shah was still stuck in Herat worked out very well for the British.

The report of the attack on the south had reached the British officers in India. It took a whole week before the shah heard about it from a messenger. The exhausted courier fell to the ground at the shah's feet and said, 'The British have invaded the port of Bushehr.'

'What did you say?' cried the shah.

The man was too frightened to tell him the rest. From his inside pocket he took out a letter from the vizier sealed with red wax and handed it to the shah. With trembling hands the shah removed the sealing wax and read the letter. The British had left Herat for what it was and had invaded the country six thousand kilometres away.

'Why there?' cried the shah, utterly perplexed.

British warships had sailed into the Persian Gulf and occupied the Persian island of Kharg. The British seamen had bombed the port of Bushehr from their ships and had driven off the local population. Hundreds of soldiers from the Anglo-Indian army had occupied the abandoned city centre, where British flags were now flying.

Although the vizier felt his opponents breathing down his neck, he could not desert his country. He set out for the south without delay, and in his letter he wrote, 'England has touched a nerve. The future of our homeland is in danger. It is essential that the shah return to Tehran.'

The shah promptly summoned his warlords and gave them the necessary instructions. He appointed a colonel as his deputy and let him know he was leaving. Early in the morning, when the streets were still dark, the shah left the city. Upon reaching the gate he got off his horse, picked up a handful of earth and put it in his pocket as a precious memory of Herat. He kissed the gate's wooden door and, with tears in his eyes, began his journey back to Tehran, which would take almost a week.

While this was going on the British managed to defend themselves against local resistance in the port of Bushehr and to strengthen their position. England's plan was to use the port as a military base in the Middle East and as their gateway to the Far East. They also had their eye on two important cities, Khorramshahr and Borazjan, suspecting there were large oil fields there.

Until five years before England had only been interested in India and had scarcely paid any attention at all to Persia. But now, although they couldn't be certain, everything they were learning about the soil along the Persia–Iraq border pointed to the presence of enormous oil reserves there. It was a British state secret that had not yet been made public. To realise their plans the British would have to come to an agreement with the Russians, and the invasion of Herat was a perfect moment to begin those negotiations.

For decades Russia had been at war with the Ottomans around the Black Sea, and the British had always sided with the Ottomans. England proposed to terminate this support if Russia would withdraw its troops north of Afghanistan and leave the shah of Persia high and dry. The tsar, who had his hands full with domestic uprisings, agreed to the offer. Russia withdrew its troops from the steppes north of Afghanistan and gave England a free hand.

Nor had the vizier been sitting idle. He managed to raise an army in the city of Khorramshahr to guarantee the safety of the population. In Tehran it was thought that England had invaded the country by way of the Persian Gulf as a retaliatory action. The vizier was preparing to fight like a lion.

The British showed no mercy. The vizier was defenceless in the face of the British cannons, so he changed tactics. He pretended to be defending Khorramshahr, but at the same time he ordered his men to hide in the cellars and passageways below the city and to prepare for hand-to-hand combat. He wanted to let the British capture the city so they would blithely make their way through the streets as victors. Then he would strike.

Working in great haste he sent messages to the tribal leaders and nomads in the area around the city, telling them that their country urgently needed them. 'Put down your glass and ride with your men to Khorramshahr.'

The tribal leaders joined forces. Following the tracks that had been left by the British horses, soldiers and war carts, they finally arrived at Khorramshahr.

The enemy was under the misapprehension that the Persian soldiers had abandoned the city via the side gate, so they raised their flags and began to ready their cannons for a possible counterattack. Suddenly the Persian soldiers popped out of their hiding places and opened fire on the intruders. The British soldiers sought shelter, but they were waylaid by sharpshooters. There was no other way to escape from the city.

The vizier tried to buck up his troops. He hoped that the tribal leaders would come to their rescue in time, and his hope was confirmed. Now the British found themselves between two fires. A real battle broke out, with the vizier spurring his men on. Suddenly a British officer recognised him, aimed his pistol and fired three shots. Two of the bullets hit the vizier. Someone managed to get him on a horse and move him behind the front lines.

The local tribal leader took command and pursued the enemy deep into the night past the fields of date palms. When the new day broke there wasn't a single British or Indian soldier to be seen.

England then sent its ships to the important southern port of Bandar Abbas and stormed the harbour. No Persian soldiers had been stationed there. Two reports were sent to the shah, neither of them good: 'The vizier has been fatally wounded, and England is in control of the Persian Gulf.'

31. The Woman

Before the crowing of the cock Mahdolia rode in her coach to the palace of the shah. She had been having trouble with her knees of late and could no longer walk long distances. She sought the support of the handrail and tried to pull herself upwards. The shah came to meet her and to offer his assistance. Still on the stairs Mahdolia threw her arms round him and wept, 'O, my son. O, my poor king.'

'Mother, where is your dignity?' whispered the shah. 'The guards are looking at us.'

'Let them look, son. Our country is in need. I weep for the country, I weep for the shah,' she said even louder.

Once in the conference room Mahdolia dropped into a chair with a sigh.

'O, my son, if only I were dead I would not have to see you in this difficult situation,' she whimpered.

The shah stood at the window, visibly moved.

'Your silence is crushing me, son. Talk to me. Pour out your heart.'

'What is there to say, Mother? My army is stuck in Herat. Our ports on the Persian Gulf are occupied and I haven't got a bullet left to fire. What am I to do? I don't trust anyone any more. You see, Mother, how the Russians have abandoned us? How they toyed with us? The tsar received you into his family. He spoke with you privately and then turned round and stuck a knife in my back.'

'I don't believe the tsar did this. He fought alongside us in Herat. You must look elsewhere for the cause. This plot was hatched within our own circles,' said Mahdolia vindictively.

'By whom?'

'Don't be naive, my son. By the vizier!'

'Mother, stop this morbid spitefulness. I often think we have treated the vizier badly, and that he does not deserve it. I have sent him a letter and thanked him for his courage. The man is seriously wounded. He may die.'

'He may be wounded, but dying is something else. Even that is intended to pull the wool over your eyes! Go out into the street. Put your ear to the ground. Then you'll understand what your mother is talking about. Your army is stuck in Herat, the Persian Gulf has been taken, our nation is being threatened, but people are talking about the vizier. He's become a hero, everyone is calling *him* the real king. Did anyone tell the shah? No, no one. No one dares tell you the truth. I am here, son, to remove the scales from your eyes. I am your mother, the only one who will not deceive you. The only reason I came was to comfort my child.'

The words of Mahdolia touched the shah. Tears ran down his cheeks. He turned to the window to hide his sorrow. The queen mother struggled out of her chair, hobbled to the king, took his hand, kissed it and said, 'This country didn't just drop into our lap. Great men from our tribe, men who came before you, held the country together with the edge of their swords. We will not give it up. The story of this ancient land is a long one. It did not begin with you, and it will not end with you. Stand tall and endure.'

The shah nodded without looking at her.

Mahdolia pulled her son closer and whispered, 'Think

carefully. Now it is your turn. It is your duty to save the throne. You must be as brutal as your grandfather was. Leave everything to the vizier for the time being. Give him the freedom to do as he likes. Let him be cheered as a hero by these thick-witted people. Then the shah must act. Later I shall return to tell you what to do. It will not be easy, but if everyone else abandons the shah someone must stand by him, and I am that person!'

The shah straightened his back and placed a gentle kiss on Mahdolia's cheek. He led her outdoors. The fresh air did him good. He took a deep breath, breathed out again and said, 'I thank you for coming, Mother.'

Mahdolia's visit had lifted the shah out of the doldrums. He felt good again, and after so many sleepless nights he was able to get a proper night's rest. When morning came he was ready for a hearty breakfast. As he ate he felt a poem taking shape in his head. Straightaway he called for a pen and paper.

He took his notebook, placed it on his knee and jotted down the poem in rough form before he forgot it. These were fragments that had come to him earlier when he was still in Herat, but because of the turbulent events they had slipped his mind. The poem was about the game of life, but he could not find the right words to make it rhyme. He wrote:

Kash mi-shod keh man azad budam
Chubi bar dast, pa bar rah budam
If only I were free like other men
I would walk away without a care, my stick in my
    hand.
Weary, I would take a nap in the shade of a tree
With my shoes beneath my head.

I would go away, away, far, far away
And one day I would come across a lovely peasant
     lass,
She would take me to her home
And there I would stay.
I would plough her fields,
I would hunt for her
And return with a gazelle on my back.

He was so engrossed in his poem that he didn't hear the noise and the uproar in the courtyard. When he finally became aware of it he put his poem down and walked to the window. Almost all the women of the harem were standing in the courtyard. They were looking up at the roof and shouting, 'Don't do it! Don't do it! Come down!'

The shah opened the window. 'What's going on?'

Not a single woman dared reply. Khwajeh Bashi, the harem overseer, pushed his way through the crowd of women and shouted, 'A woman from the harem is up on the roof.'

'What's she doing there?'

'She wants to jump because her mother is standing on the steps outside the palace.'

At that moment a woman's scream was heard behind the palace walls.

'Who was that?' asked the shah.

'The mother of the woman on the roof.'

'What's her mother doing here?'

'She wants to take her daughter home.'

'Why is she screaming then?'

'She's afraid her daughter will jump off the roof.'

'Who is the daughter? Do we know her?' shouted the shah.

'She is one of your wives.'

The women of the harem were now shouting all at once, 'Don't do it! Don't jump!'

But it was too late. The woman jumped from the roof and fell like a sack of flour beside her weeping mother. The woman wailed and ran out through the gate.

'It's a miracle. She's still alive! She's still alive!'

'Bring the woman here!' shouted the shah.

A few minutes later the woman, wrapped in a blanket, was brought to the hall of mirrors by two burly guards. The women outside strained to hear what the shah was saying to her.

'Take off your niqab and stop crying.'

The woman took her niqab off, but she pulled her chador over her face and continued to sob quietly.

'Stop that blubbering, I said!'

The woman put her hand over her mouth and was silent.

'Take your chador off. We want to get a better look at your face,' said the shah. The young woman was not especially beautiful.

The shah look at her with surprise and asked, 'Are you one of our wives?'

'Yes,' she said. Her eyes were red from crying.

'That's impossible. You're not our type of woman.'

She began to cry louder.

'When did we see you for the first time?' asked the shah.

'About three years ago,' the woman answered.

'Where?

'When you came to us in the village. I was standing in the crowd and you pointed to me. I was brought here and now I've been waiting for a very long time.'

'Waiting? For what?'

'For you,' said the woman.

'For us? Where were we then? We are often in the harem.'

'You were with me twice, that was all. My mother has tried several times to take me back home, but Khwajeh Bashi wouldn't let her in. Today I heard her call my name. I fled to the roof and then I jumped.'

There was a knock at the door.

'Come in,' said the shah.

It was Khwajeh Bashi. He had a golden hookah bowl in his hand.

'What's that?' asked the shah.

'The woman stole this golden bowl from your hookah. It was hidden under her clothing. I found it outside on the step,' he said, handing the bowl to the shah.

The shah sent Khwajeh Bashi away and held the golden bowl out in front of the woman.

'Why did you steal the bowl from our hookah?'

She was silent.

'We asked you why you stole our golden bowl.'

'I . . . I . . . I didn't steal it. I only wanted to take something of the shah's back home with me. When I ran to the roof I saw your hookah and I grabbed the bowl. I wanted to take it as proof – proof that I had lived in the palace, that I belonged to the shah and that I was his wife.'

The shah was touched by her words. He took the golden bowl in his hand, and with the other hand behind his back he walked round the room. At a certain point he turned to the woman and said gently, 'You are not the sort of woman we are attracted to. Why did we point to you and bring you back to our palace?'

'I was pretty then,' said the woman frankly. 'I was just the kind of woman you desired. But these past years in the harem have made me gaunt and ugly.'

The shah walked up to her, leaned over a bit, stroked her head and ran the back of his hand over her left cheek, and played with the neckline of her blouse. The woman shivered with excitement. He took three large gold coins from his jacket pocket and tossed them onto her lap, whispering, 'We have seen you. Go back home with your mother, if you like.'

A smile appeared on the woman's face. Now he could see something of her former beauty.

The shah opened the door, and the women who were eavesdropping scattered in every direction. He pretended he hadn't seen them and walked into the gardens as if nothing at all had happened. He thought for a moment that the woman's jumping was a sign, that the people were dissatisfied because the shah would have nothing to do with them, and that he should give them their freedom. But he promptly dismissed such thoughts. The people did not need more freedom. What the people needed was a leader. And that leader was the shah.

32. The Country Prays for the Persian Gulf

The British dared not show their faces outside the walls of the port cities. As soon as they did they came under fire.

The vizier, who was seriously wounded, was being cared for in the castle of the tribal leader. The local physician succeeded in removing the bullets from his body. After a month of treatment the vizier was still weak and unable to stand. When he was finally given permission to leave his sickbed he tried to walk by leaning against the castle's long walls. He was well looked after by the devoted old women of the Bakhtiari tribe, and gradually he regained his strength. Early one morning, much to everyone's delight, he even managed to heave himself onto his horse and cautiously pick his way across the pastureland.

For the vizier this period was a low point. He had to think of a way to get the British out of the country. With the help of a few powerful men he managed to raise a small army of martyrs. He told the warriors they would have to fight the mightiest country in the world with their daggers and outdated weapons, but that this had been decreed by history. He emphasised that while a victory was impossible, the whole aim of the mission was to torment the occupying forces. The martyrs were ready for anything.

When the vizier was sufficiently recovered he and his martyrs advanced on Bandar Abbas. Any confrontation with the enemy was prevented by the enormous barricades that the British had erected in the harbour area and by the artillery in the hills.

'Be patient and impede the enemy wherever you can,' the vizier instructed his warriors. 'Your only weapon is waiting, waiting and waiting some more.'

Indeed it was time that was Britain's Achilles heel. The factories in England were gasping for fuel, while millions of litres of crude oil lay unused in the Persian soil. England was in a hurry.

But the dangerous situation in the Persian desert was keeping the British from getting any closer to the sites they had considered for further soil research. The martyrs lay in wait day and night among the tall date palms, their guns in hand, or they sat motionless with their daggers in the mud.

The British thought their ships were safe in the Persian Gulf, but more and more of the vizier's men were willing to take to the water and jeopardise their lives by climbing onto the ships in the dark of night.

Stories of the warriors' heroic deeds spread throughout the region and heartened the inhabitants of the occupied port cities. The resistance gained wider and wider support. The British could no longer go out at night without risk.

The British realised they would have to make use of their experiences in India. They would have to negotiate with the Persians. Long-term security and stability were essential if they were to keep on searching for oil and digging wells, guaranteeing the supply of black gold to England. To everyone's astonishment the British unexpectedly withdrew from both port cities. They sat in their big cargo ships in the Persian Gulf and waited for instructions from London. The prayers of millions of people in the mosques had been granted. The vizier had scored a success.

Late one afternoon diplomats from the British Foreign Office paid a visit to the residence of the Persian representative in London. They had been meeting more frequently lately. The Persian representative received them with tea and refreshments, and they sat down at the table to see how England and Persia might do business.

Shortly thereafter the vizier received a telegram that had been sent from a British ship. It took a while for his eyes to adjust to the unfamiliar typescript. He picked up his glasses and read the report. Then, without delay, he sent a message to the shah.

Glory be to God, He who possesses exalted power and might. He is all-knowing, and nothing is hidden from His eyes – not anything that is whispered, nor anything that is concealed through silence. He sees all, and nothing exceeds his power, neither on earth nor in heaven. He is the ruler of all. The shah is the first to whom the vizier may send these glad tidings. We have reached an accord with England concerning a ceasefire. The British are prepared to discuss both Herat and the raw materials in the south. Next week we will speak with a British delegation in Bandar Abbas. The shah will be immediately informed as soon as anything concrete has been achieved.
Respectfully yours, the vizier.

33. The Chronicler

Since returning from Herat the shah spent a great deal of time in the barracks outside Tehran. He did not concern himself with the military activities there, but his presence gave everyone the impression that he was taking command of the armed forces. He sat in the war room and wrote poetry, and he had begun to record his memories of his stay in Herat. Usually he wrote in his diary in his own hand, but now he had engaged the services of a chronicler. Unconsciously he felt the need for a witness.

Writing always made the shah feel that he was working on something of significance, that he was writing history. He sensed that in the future he would be praised for his diaries, and that his pen would linger in the public memory longer than his other deeds. When he wrote he forgot everything. He enjoyed himself. And although he had a good style he envied the vizier his writing talent. He knew the man could do magic with words. When the shah received letters from him he sometimes paid more attention to the sentence structure than to the content of the text.

It was now the middle of the night. The shah, who had been sleeping poorly of late, decided to stay in bed and write in his diary. It was at about this time that the vizier's messenger reached the shah's palace. The head of the guards told the chamberlain that the shah was to be wakened straightaway. Gently the chamberlain knocked on the bedroom door. The shah dropped his pen and called out, 'Who's there?'

'Your Majesty, a messenger from the south with something important,' the man said.

The shah groped for his dressing gown in the dark. 'Let him in. We'll be right there.'

The chamberlain lit the candles of the lanterns in the hall of mirrors.

'Thanks be to God. It is my good fortune to bring the shah this good news,' said the messenger. He pulled an envelope out from under his clothing and handed it to the shah.

The shah walked over to a lantern on the mantelpiece, opened the letter and read it. A broad smile spread across his face, emphasised by the room's light and shadows. He wanted to reward the messenger out of sheer happiness, but he had no coins in his dressing gown. It was not fitting that a man who had ridden hundreds of kilometres non-stop should be sent away empty-handed. He searched his pockets once again, but could find no coin. Then he took off his royal slippers and handed them to the messenger, who was so tired he could barely stand: 'For you. Take them with you!'

The messenger, who had counted on a bit of money, didn't know how to respond.

'Take them. They are for you!'

The messenger took the slippers, kissed them, tucked them under his arm and stood there hesitantly, waiting for the coins.

The shah rang his little bell. 'Chamberlain, take this poor man with you. He is tired. Give him something to eat and a chance to get fully rested. Tomorrow he is to receive three coins from us,' said the shah.

The messenger wanted to kiss the king's hand, but he

gave him no opportunity. The chamberlain assisted the man on his way out.

Exhilarated by the report the shah could no longer sleep. He read the vizier's letter once again. He had been saved. He no longer needed to feel ashamed about a lost war. He picked up his diary and continued writing.

> God is with us. God has never abandoned us. God has saved us. It is the middle of the night and we cannot sleep for joy. We do not know exactly what the cunning British are looking for in the southern part of our country. Raw materials, the vizier says. Raw materials in a place where the sun incinerates everything, as if it were hell. God will always be on our side. He is guiding us.
>
> We have not lost the war. In fact we will be earning an extraordinary amount of money in customs duties.
>
> We, the shah of Persia, announce with these words that we have embarked on a new page in our history.
>
> We feel good again, and although it is the middle of the night, we are in the mood for a hearty breakfast.

The shah hid his diary. He needed to share his happiness with someone, but with whom? At first he thought of going to the palace of his mother, but he was the king and he had to restrain himself and wait until morning. He also thought of his advisor, Sheikh Aqasi, but he rejected that idea out of hand. There was only one person who understood him, who would be as happy as he was with this unexpected development, and that was his beloved daughter, Taj Olsultan.

The lights were out in the small courtyard of Taj's residence, but one candle was burning in her window. He tapped gently on the door. The old servant, who knew that only the shah would come knocking at such an hour, picked up the candle, took a quick look through the little hatch just to make sure, and opened the door.

The shah walked quietly into his daughter's bedroom. 'Taj, are you asleep? It is we, the shah, your father.'

The girl, who looked like a young woman under the covers, turned in her sleep. She pulled the blankets up over her shoulders and kept on sleeping.

'Taj, wake up. We have good news. The shah is happy, very happy.'

The girl opened her eyes. 'Did something happen?'

'Good news,' he whispered. 'England has abandoned the harbour. They want to do business with us.'

She hugged the shah and kissed him on the head. 'Father, I'm so happy for you,' she said, and she began getting out of bed.

'Stay where you are. I want to talk with you,' said the shah, and he knelt down on the floor beside her. 'Listen. I was often very sad in Herat because I have no heir. If anyone there had killed me I would have had no son of my own flesh and blood to follow in my footsteps. We must quickly find a husband for you.'

'But . . . but . . . Father, I don't want this. It is still too soon for me,' said Taj.

'Nonsense,' responded the shah. 'We've told you a hundred times that your mother was just your age when she was pregnant with you.'

'I have asked her. My mother was nowhere near as young as I am now when she married.'

The shah picked up a pillow and stretched out on the carpet. 'I'm going to lie down here for a little while. Suddenly I feel so tired. I haven't been sleeping well lately.'

'Father, I'm reading Russian, French and English books.

In those countries the girls don't marry at such a young age.'

'The stories you read are all made up. The fathers of the girls in those books are not kings. I am the king. When I die the sons I have begotten by other women will fight each other for our crown like wild dogs. They will tear the country to bits as dogs devour a deer. Think about what you are saying.'

'I understand you, Father, but can't you wait until I'm a little bigger?' pleaded Taj.

The shah looked her straight in the eyes and whispered, 'We have enemies. I trust no one – not your mother, not your grandmother, not my counsellors, not the vizier. You are the only one I trust. Do you hear me? Everyone wants to bring me down. We don't have much time.'

He glanced towards the door to see whether the old servant was standing there. When he was sure they were alone he said, 'Listen, the vizier wants to depose us. I have proof – documents. We've given him a free hand, and he is well liked by the people. But he is hatching a devious plot against us behind our back. He doesn't know that we know everything. First we'll let him finish the negotiations with England and Russia, and then at an unguarded moment we'll sting him like a poisonous scorpion.'

'Father, I don't believe any of the things that you have told me. The vizier is an outstanding man. I like him very much. What makes you think—'

'I have proof. You are still young. You have so much to learn. But soon you'll be the mother of our heir. You have to strike while the iron is hot, or it will be your turn next. What we need now is a crown prince.'

'To whom are you planning to give me, Father?' asked Taj anxiously.

'To a man from our tribe.'

'How will you find such a man?'

'We will work that out. We have dreamt that you bore a son for us,' he said, and he lay back down.

'Father, my womb is still too small. I fear I will not be able to give you a son.'

The shah refused to hear another word. He shut his eyes and fell asleep. Noiselessly the old servant entered the room. She pulled a blanket over the shah and took Taj to her own room to sleep for the night.

34. The Documents

The vizier had taken three of his young advisors with him. One of them was Amir. The British had asked whether the negotiations could take place on one of their warships because they had better facilities. The look of their glorious ship would increase the pressure on the Persian delegation. The vizier had rejected this request and in turn invited the British to meet in the old fortress where the great world conquerors Cyrus, Darius, Alexander the Great and Genghis Khan had spent time during their journeys.

The fortress was one of the oldest barracks in the country. It was built on a hill beside the sea. There were no conveniences in the old fortress, but you could feel the glory of history there and the spirit of ancient powers. From the tower of the fortress you had a grand view of the Persian Gulf.

Chiselled into the rock walls of the fortress were images of the wars waged by the world conquerors. There was a rare scene of Alexander the Great marching into India with his army. Behind his back was a cloud of smoke rising from the Persian palaces he had set ablaze. There was also an impressive scene of Genghis Khan looking west, with the conquered East in the background. It was common for a new oppressor to destroy all traces of the previous rulers, but miraculously the fortress had been respected by all of them. The wall images had been left alone.

The vizier knew that the impressive wheels of the Industrial Revolution had rolled into the country by way of the Persian Gulf. He wanted to have this event recorded in stone.

Mounted on horseback the vizier and his three advisors arrived on the beach. They refused to surrender their horses to a British sergeant and instead climbed the hill on foot with the horses' reins in their hands. Once they reached the fortress they ignored the British officer who was there to welcome them. They brought their horses to the stable and gave them food and water. Only then did they go to the tent to sit down at the negotiating table. The vizier could feel the pressure. Groping for something solid to hold onto he began to recite a holy text.

I repeat Your name.
You who created everything and who governs all.
You who determines fate and shows the way.
You who pours down rain in abundance.
You who cracks the earth open.
You who makes the corn to grow.
And vegetables and olive trees, dates, orchards thick
    with trees, and fruits and fodder.
Alif lam meem.
Alif lam meem.
Alif lam meem.
I pray to you and turn to you for help.
Guide me to the path that is straight.
The path of those on whom you have poured your
    mercy,
Not the path of those who have earned your anger.

For the vizier the first days of the negotiations were humiliating. The British delegation acted with supercilious arrogance, which was hard for the vizier to swallow. Every day at the end of each session the British negotiators would go back to their ship to eat, rest and sleep in preparation for day to come. The vizier and his advisors stayed in a tent in the fortress. After three weeks of difficult negotiations the following proposals were on the table:

- England is to withdraw its warships from the Persian Gulf.
- England is permitted to use the harbour of the Persian Gulf for trade with India.
- The French are to leave the Persian army, and in their place the British officers will assume the job of reforming the army.
- Mining contracts with the French are to be terminated and England will pay the insurance claim to the French.
- The British are given use of the southern harbour with accompanying customs duties for the next fifty years, but supervision will remain in the hands of the Persian customs office. After deducting the costs incurred for the construction of harbour installations, England will pay a monthly allowance to the Persian state.
- The British are given permission to search for raw materials throughout the southern province and to place the necessary installations there.
- Seventy-five per cent of the extracted product will accrue to England and the remaining twenty-five per cent to Persia.
- On paper Herat remains part of Persia, but leadership of the city will stay in the hands of the British.
- England will construct a telegraph line to India exclusively for its own use and will retain the monopoly for fifty years.

- England will construct a railway line from the Persian Gulf to the Indian border and will retain the monopoly for fifty years.

The treaty was not a victory. The vizier had made passionate attempts to have two decisive demands included, which the British had ignored.

He rose to his feet. 'Then we won't do it. If we go home with this agreement our wives will despise us.'

He demanded that the following sections be added to the peace accord:

- England will provide Persia with a telegraph network that will connect Tehran with all the major cities of the country.
- England will not employ Indian clerks to work in the hundreds of telegraph offices, but will hire local ones instead.

The head British negotiator was angry. He could not resist making the comment, 'In this country no one has even heard the word "telegraph". How, then, can they be expected to work in a telegraph office?'

'They'll learn soon enough,' responded the vizier.

The negotiations were temporarily put on hold and the vizier's demands were sent to London.

One week later London responded with a modified proposal:

- England will provide Persia with a telegraph network on the condition that the total customs duties in all the harbours of the Persian Gulf be transferred to England for the next fifty years.

This was a harsh and nationally sensitive demand, but after a long discussion with his young advisors the vizier agreed. The country was in no position to improve its outdated harbours. If the English ships wanted to use the harbours they would have to do the work of modernising them. It was also impossible to say what the future would bring. If the British ever left they wouldn't be able to take the harbours with them back to England. The buildings and installations would remain for the country's own use.

The British thought the final accord was now within reach when the vizier tossed one more demand on the table:

– England will construct a railway line from the Persian Gulf to India only on the condition that a national railway for Persia be built at the same time.

The vizier took everyone by surprise, even his own advisors, because this was an unrealistic and unreachable dream that no one even dared to consider. The British realised that if they did not go along with it the Russians would take over the construction of the international telegraph network and the railway line. After a day of fierce discussions they all relented and agreed to the following section:

– Should England ever begin constructing a railway line from the Persian Gulf to India, it will consider the possibility of a national railway system for Persia.

The accord was finally signed, and it took a week for the documents to reach Tehran by messenger. Begrudgingly the shah placed his signature and set his seal upon them.

After the vizier and the head of the British delegation had handed each other the documents and shaken each other's hands, all the British ships' horns were sounded. The vizier was deeply moved, but he held back his tears. The ships' horns were waking the people from a thousand-year sleep.

Reports of telegraph cables and trains rumbling through the land were already racing through his head. Now he gave his tears free rein. Seated on his horse before the old fortress he watched as the British warships left the Persian Gulf.

'A new page in our history has been written,' said the vizier.

35. Fagri

Ever since Alexander the Great had set fire to the ships of the Persian Empire, the country had lacked the wherewithal to build a great seagoing vessel. This is why the people did not grasp the importance of their own Persian Gulf, and why they grieved daily for Herat and for Afghanistan.

When they spoke of Afghanistan their eyes filled with tears, because Afghanistan had been the home of a handful of great Persian poets and because a few heroic love stories from the *Shahnameh* had taken place there. No one was ever able to accept the fact that Afghanistan was no longer part of the homeland. Nothing remained of its ancient grandeur. But among the people it was still very much alive.

At the same time many sons of rich families and wealthy merchants went to Istanbul, where they gazed in astonishment on a whole different world. The city served as a bridge between West and East. It was in Istanbul that new western inventions such as the telegraph, the train and artificial light were first used by Easterners.

The younger generation saw for themselves that Baku and Bombay had undergone enormous changes, while Tehran still looked like a big village. No other king had a harem, while the shah's harem grew and grew, constantly being supplied with new women.

Ideas from Russian resistance groups gradually reached

big cities like Tabriz, Rasht, Tehran and Isfahan. Young intellectuals in these cities got together more and more frequently to discuss the future of the country. The protest there was comparable to the sounds being heard in Moscow.

The resistance in Russia was growing in proportion to the industrialisation of the country, and Russian resistance leaders were succeeding in stirring up the workers to oppose the tsar. But in Tehran or Isfahan, the resistance groups couldn't count on anyone. The people were ignorant; they saw the king as the representative of God on earth. Opposing him was the last thing on their minds.

Like the vizier, the shah was following the changes that were taking place in neighbouring countries. He sensed the danger of an awakening people. And he knew that all eyes were on the vizier.

The vizier's enemies accused him of high treason. His advisors tried to convince the people that because of the peace accord the country would in fact be playing a greater role in the world. The shah didn't know whom to believe. He was becoming increasingly aware of the declining potency of his power. He still made trips to surrounding villages to show himself off to the people, but these visits had less and less influence.

In the meantime, after the signing of the accord with England, the vizier was being received like a celebrity as he travelled from one city to the next on his way to Tehran. Thousands welcomed him at the city gates with drums, flags and horns. Cows and camels were slaughtered as sacrifices for the vizier. There was a spontaneous sharing of dates and sugarbread in the streets, and the important merchants set up their tents in the squares and invited everyone in for a meal. In Isfahan, where the vizier stopped to rest for a few days, the residents carried him on their shoulders to the centre of town.

When he finally reached Tehran it seemed as if the whole city had come out to admire him. Children climbed trees and women stood on the roofs. Hundreds of carpets were laid down along the route from the gate to the bazaar square. Horsemen accompanied him and his entourage to a large tent on the square as the people sang him songs of welcome.

With a mixed sense of joy and pain the vizier surrendered to the happiness of the crowd. Important businessmen embraced him and congratulated him for his fighting and for the victory, but the vizier noticed that no one from the palace was present.

The merchants helped the vizier into a chair they had placed on a sumptuous carpet beneath a tree – just for him – and they all gathered round. He was offered fresh tea and cakes, and he fell into conversation with the curious merchants.

'The things we have accomplished will be to your benefit, businessmen,' he said with a smile. 'Make sure you're ready. Get yourselves a couple of new suits and some new shoes. Before long you'll have to start making trips to the telegraph office, and you'll be able to travel by train.'

Everyone took pleasure in the hope that emanated from the vizier's words.

'You have been warned. Don't stock any more candles in your warehouses. You're going to have to throw all those candles away, I'm afraid, because I've started purchasing electrical poles. Soon our houses won't be lit by candles any more but by lamps.'

He laughed, and everyone around laughed with him.

As evening fell the vizier finally arrived at his own house to spend the night with his family. It was a large house just outside Tehran in a small village called Velenjak. The house was an official residence where the viziers of the country had lived since the olden days. His wife was the daughter of a prominent family from his own tribe in Farahan, and the couple had two sons and three daughters.

The vizier had seen telegraph poles and cables for the first time in Paris, and in London he had seen his first train and railway line. Whenever he travelled abroad it was the women that always attracted his attention. He saw them in cafés, in playhouses and in political circles, where they kept company with their husbands. The inequality of the women in his own country was always brought home to him, because in fact they had no rights at all.

In Moscow he had spent many nights with Russian women in drinking houses, women who had pampered him like a Persian prince. He had known many women in his life, but he found peace with his own wife, Fagri. He loved her and missed her when he was travelling, so he always wrote to her when he was away for long periods of time. His letters were very personal.

> Sometimes I feel like an old tree
> In which birds alight, flight after flight.
> But I want only you
> To sit among my leaves
> And sing for me.

Now the vizier was home after a long absence. Despite the public euphoria that his deeds evoked he felt sad. There was something he couldn't put his finger on. History was devouring him – he knew that as he stood at the gate of his house. He got off his horse, opened the gate and brought his horse to the stable. He washed his hands and face in the pool as Fagri, his wife, looked out at him from a window. Then he walked slowly to the veranda. You could see from his shadow that he was lame.

Fagri saw it immediately. She came outdoors with a lantern in her hand. Silently he took her in his arms and held her for a long time.

'I missed your lantern, Fagri. Keep me home. Don't let me go away again.'

Fagri wept.

'Come inside, my husband,' she whispered between sobs.

She had heard that everyone in the shah's circle had branded her husband a traitor, someone who had sold the country to the evil spirits. Now she feared for her husband's life as never before. It felt as if every embrace could be the last.

'Come inside, my love,' she whispered, as she looked anxiously back at the gate.

36. In the Palace

The vizier waited in Velenjak for the shah to summon him, but to his chagrin there was nothing but silence. When it seemed to him that too much time had passed he decided to go to the palace on his own initiative.

The shah was not there. Even the chamberlain, who always came to meet him, was nowhere to be seen. With great suspicion he pushed open the door. To his surprise there were no candles burning in the wall lamps. He knocked on the door of the hall of mirrors and said quietly, 'Your Majesty, it is I, the vizier.'

There was no response.

'Are you there, Your Majesty?' he called, this time a bit louder. He considered going into the hall but decided against it. Instead he went outside and called the head of the guards.

'Where is everyone?'

'What do you mean?' said the man.

'There's no one here. Where is the shah?'

'His Majesty must be in the palace.'

The vizier went back in, walked through the empty corridors and called the chamberlain: 'Aga Moshir!'

He tried to get into the kitchen, but it was locked. Then he opened the door to the hall of mirrors. 'Your Majesty, are you there? Is everything all right?'

The only possible explanation was that the shah was spending the night in the harem. He could return at any moment. The vizier sat down in a chair and began massaging his complaining right leg.

Suddenly he heard a great clamour behind the building, and he went to see what was causing it. It was the shah's wives out in the harem courtyard. Whatever was troubling them must have been serious because windows were being smashed and the women and children were screaming.

He went to the end of the corridor and stood behind the door. Should he open the door a crack and look out? Should he call to ask if he could be of any help? It was too risky. If the shah were to regard his interference as an invasion of his privacy it could have far-reaching consequences for him. So he stayed behind the door and listened. All he could hear were the women, the children and Khwajeh Bashi, the harem overseer.

The vizier understood from all the tumult that the women of the harem wanted to go out, but Khwajeh Bashi and his servants were trying to keep them in. Things were getting out of hand. The women were pounding on the door of the harem and were about to break it down. The vizier couldn't just stand by and watch. He opened the door halfway and shouted, 'Ladies! What's going on?'

His voice was drowned by all the chaos.

'Ladies! It is I, the vizier. Allow me to come and help you.'

No one heard him. Were the women so upset because something had happened to the shah? Had he dropped dead? Had he been murdered by one of his wives? Was Khwajeh Bashi trying to keep the women inside in order to prevent the dreadful report from leaking out?

The vizier could no longer control himself. With his hands held over his eyes he went in.

'Ladies? Where is the shah? What is going on here?'

A deadly silence fell. The women were surprised by the

presence of the vizier. All of them were unveiled, without their niqabs, and they were in a state of total confusion.

'Cover your heads!' shouted Khwajeh Bashi.

The servants of the harem went to fetch the chadors and passed them out. When the women had covered themselves the vizier pulled his hands away from his eyes and asked once more what had upset them so.

The women burst out crying as if they were seeing their older brother or father, to whom they could pour out their hearts. The shah, the queen mother and the princes all despised the vizier, but he was beloved of the shah's wives. They knew he loved his own wife and that he wrote her letters when he was travelling. All of them knew the beginning of that one letter by heart:

My love,
Always be home when I return,
or I am forced to go from room to room,
calling your name until you come.

'Everyone is ill, everyone in the harem is going to die,' cried one of the women through her sobs.

'It's a plague,' cried another. 'The harem has been struck by the plague.'

'What did you say?' asked the vizier, who thought he hadn't heard properly.

'Plague has broken out in the harem.'

'How do you know that?' he said, refusing to believe it.

'A woman died tonight,' one of the women bawled. 'She's still lying in her bed.'

'A plague has broken out in the city,' cried another woman. 'Everyone knows about it but us.'

'It's not true. I've just come from the city, and there is no plague. Don't be afraid. They're just trying to scare you. The woman in the harem probably died of something else.'

'There are many women sick in bed and the shah has run away. He's taken his mother, his cat and his daughter with him and has left us all here to die.'

The vizier was shocked. He spoke privately with Khwajeh Bashi and came to understand what may have taken place in the palace. The shah's court physician had probably diagnosed plague among the sick women of the harem. He had then informed the shah in confidence, after which the shah had decided to go to his country house, where it was safe.

'It's going to be all right, ladies. I'll take care of everything,' said the vizier, and he turned to Khwajeh Bashi. 'Remove the dead woman from the harem and gather all the sick women together in the big room on the other side of the palace. I'll notify the doctor immediately.' Then he said to the women, 'The doors of the harem will be kept open. You may go to the garden for fresh air. Clean everything in the bathrooms and in all the other chambers. Wash your children and yourselves.'

The vizier's fatherly advice did the women good. Peace and quiet were restored. The body of the dead woman was taken away immediately and the sick women were examined by the doctor. The women launched a major clean-up operation in the harem, and the children began running freely through the palace gardens again.

The vizier was disappointed by the shah's irresponsible behaviour. He didn't believe that plague had broken out in Tehran, and he suspected that the resulting panic had caused the women of the harem to imagine things to be worse than they really were. He mounted his horse and rode towards the city of Qazvin, to a small village in the mountains where the shah had gone to stay.

The country air was good for him. His anger cooled and

he even began to sympathise with the shah for going away. Something quite serious must be going on.

He left the last hills behind him and rode through the open fields. At one point he noticed people lying on a path along the riverbank. At first he thought they were farmers resting in the grass, but when he got closer he couldn't believe his eyes. They were sick people who had been left there to die, thrown out of the village by others who were afraid of the plague.

The vizier was dumbfounded. Everywhere, men and women were lying on the ground like dead beasts. He saw mothers wrap their dead children in shrouds. He saw parents fleeing with their children to the mountains. Powerless to do anything he walked past three dead women whose bodies lay half in the river, their legs bare. The gravediggers tossed quicklime over the corpses to keep the wild dogs away.

Darkness had just fallen when he rode into the village and reached the castle. He rode straight to the gate but was stopped by the guards.

'His Majesty is not receiving anyone,' said the head of the guards.

'Will you please tell the shah that the vizier is standing at the gate?'

'Even the guards aren't allowed in,' declared the man.

'You can shout through the hatch that I'm standing here at the gate,' said the vizier, trying to control his rage.

'His Majesty does not want to see anyone. Not anyone. He gave me this order in person,' said the man resolutely.

The vizier saw himself standing at the gate. What was he doing there, anyway? What could the shah do about a plague that apparently had stricken the entire district? If there was anyone who could do anything at all, it was the vizier. Why come here like a mendicant, begging the shah to speak to him?

He decided to turn back and try to preserve Tehran from calamity. Perhaps he ought to ask the Russians and the British for help. He would go straight to the British ambassador to warn him. The ambassador could ask London to send British army nurses to Tehran by way of Herat. That was their only hope.

The vizier wanted to go to Tehran, but the thought of a carefree shah in his safe castle made him angry. The king had a responsibility for his people.

He began to scream, 'Shah! The vizier has come! The vizier has come! The vizier has come!'

The guards tried to chase him away, but to no avail.

The vizier shouted even louder, 'Shah! The vizier has come! The vizier! The vizier!'

The head of the guards picked up his rifle, but he didn't dare aim it at the vizier. The vizier in turn picked up his own rifle and began shooting it into the air, repeating over and over again, 'The vizier has come!'

There was chaos at the gate. The horses neighed, the watchdogs barked and the guards tried to keep the vizier from coming any further.

Inside the castle the shah was listening indecisively. He heard the tapping of his mother's walking stick. Mahdolia stood behind him and said, 'What are you waiting for? Kill him now. He's become too powerful.'

At that very moment the gate of the castle opened. Taj Olsultan, the daughter of the shah, went outside with a torch in her hand. She walked calmly up to the vizier and said, '*Salam*, Vizier. Is there something I can do for you?'

'No, no, my daughter. I am glad the princess is in good health, that is enough for me,' said the vizier.

'I heard you had been wounded in the south. I was

worried, but now I'm glad to see you again. How are you, Vizier? I have thought of you very often.'

Taj's words surprised the vizier. His anger cooled. He looked at her standing there in the dark beside the gate, part of her face visible in the light of the torch. The vizier saw that Taj had grown and that, although she was still young, she acted like a real grown-up princess.

'I thank you for your heart-warming words, my daughter. I am doing better. You have become an extraordinary princess.'

'Thank you,' said Taj, and she smiled.

'Go back inside, and take good care of yourself,' said the vizier. He tipped his hat, bowed and spurred his horse to a gallop.

37. The Black Blanket

Tehran was stricken by the plague, but England extended a helping hand to the vizier just in time. They sent Indian nurses to the villages around Tehran to cope with the epidemic. Russian army doctors also came over, pitching tents on the bazaar squares in the northern cities.

Thousands of people died in Tehran and the surrounding countryside. In the harem three more women succumbed. Every Friday the populace went to the Jameh mosque to ask for God's help, under the imam's direction. And their prayers were heard, for winter came earlier than expected and it was so cold that the rocks crumbled in the mountains. It snowed for one whole week, and the snow froze. The weather was so severe that it was impossible to know whether people were dying from the cold or the plague.

As if that weren't enough famine caught them unawares. Experience teaches that when hunger strikes you no longer think about death. The hunger was so intense that everyone forgot about the plague.

There was no sign of the plague in the southern part of the country. The British were working on the harbour in the Persian Gulf, and in the city of Masjed Soleyman they were laying the foundation for the first major oil installation in the Middle East.

All this time the shah stayed in his castle and sent his orders to Tehran from there. Just before a thick layer of snow threatened to cut the shah off from the outside world, he returned to the palace. He avoided the harem and refused to allow anyone to talk about the tragic deaths.

On one of those cold winter nights, when the streets were deserted and everyone had their windows covered over with blankets, the shah summoned the vizier. The shah had had no personal contact with him since that one evening at the castle before the invasion of Herat. A messenger had been conveying messages back and forth between them. It was strange that the shah wanted to see him just now, in this cold and so late at night.

'I have a bad feeling about this. It would be better if you didn't go alone,' said his wife, Fagri.

'Don't worry. I won't be long.'

'Listen to me. Think of something. Say you'll drop in tomorrow.'

'I can't do that. The shah needs me now. Otherwise he wouldn't have summoned me at this late hour.'

'God help us,' wept Fagri silently.

'*Vizier-koshan*' was a well-known hallmark of Persian history. It meant 'kill the vizier!' The murder of a competent vizier was not an unusual occurence in royal circles. Each vizier was fully aware that at any unexpected moment he could be killed by the king. There were also many examples of princes who had murdered a king, and of kings who had taken the lives of their sons and brothers.

The story of Grand Vizier Hasanak was an example everyone knew about. Hasanak was popular and powerful. On one ill-fated day the sultan summoned him. Hasanak knew that he was hated among the royalty, but he never suspected that the sultan wanted to kill him. As soon as he rode into the palace grounds the gate was closed and bolted from inside. Bayhaqi, the medieval chronicler, recorded the following scene in his book:

The next day, Hasanak the grand vizier was put on a shabby nag and taken to the gallows. He had never ridden on such a small horse before.

The executioner wanted to blindfold him, but Hasanak refused.

'Stone him!' cried the sultan.

But no one threw a single stone.

'Hang him!' cried the sultan.

The executioner hung Hasanak. For seven years Hasanak hung on the gallows. The Persian sun burnt him and the east wind carried his ashes away.

Another familiar example was the death of Grand Vizier Mirza Tagi Khan. Early one morning he went to the hamam to bathe. After his bath he sat down in the barber's chair. The barber sharpened his razor, removed the superfluous hair from the vizier's neck, placed the razor on his artery and severed it. He did this by order of the king.

Fagri knew those stories, which is why she was afraid that her husband would meet the same fate.

'Don't cry,' the vizier told his wife. He kissed her and rode to the palace.

When he got to the gate he noticed the guards were different. He had never seen this head of the guards before. It was customary that when the vizier appeared on the square, a horn would be sounded and the head of the guards would come out and salute him. This time there was silence, and the head of the guards did not move from his post.

Still seated on his horse he heard the sound of the bolt in the gate, which he suspected was being locked behind him. The branches of the trees bowed low under the frozen snow, the palace chimney smoked and the torches near the pond were burning. The shadow of the shah fell on the curtains of his study, as if he were spying on the vizier from the window.

The vizier dismounted and gave the reins to a groom who was also unfamiliar to him. He was a muscular man who lacked a groom's customary deftness.

The vizier cautiously climbed the icy stairs to the palace entrance. Inside the corridors were dark, but a small lantern was burning in front of the door to the hall of mirrors. There was menace in the air. A voice within him urged him to turn back before it was too late, but he couldn't turn back. The shah had seen him and was waiting for him. Instinctively he turned round, pulled the door open and was about to go outside. The man who had taken his horse away was standing at the top of the stairs.

'His Majesty is waiting for you,' he said calmly, and closed the door.

The vizier walked back to the hall of mirrors, knocked gently on the door and called out, 'Aga Moshir!'

Out of the darkness came a voice: 'Go in. The chamberlain is not here.'

All the curtains in the hall of mirrors were closed, but the candles were burning in the chandelier. The vizier walked across the big green carpet, sat down on the pomegranate-coloured satin chair and began to massage his leg, which was acting up again.

Every time he came here to wait for the shah he marvelled at the patterns in the carpet beneath his feet. It was one of the most beautiful carpets he had ever seen. Many thin threads of gold were woven into it, and hundreds of finely polished, colourful little jewels were worked into its floral patterns.

No one knew exactly when the royal carpet had been crafted, but it was thought to have come from one of the Persian palaces that had been set on fire by the

Muhammadans when they conquered the Persian Empire thirteen centuries before. Muhammad's disciples had plundered all the palaces and burned them down, but one servant managed to save this carpet. This distraction helped put the vizier at ease.

'The vizier was frightened for a moment,' he said to himself. 'This is not like you. You're tired. Why not go back to Farahan for a week and get some rest?'

Suddenly he heard footsteps behind the small door the chamberlain always used.

'Aga Moshir!' he shouted.

No one responded. He went to the small door to see who it was, but the door, which was always open, was now locked. He heard someone walk away.

'Aga Moshir, is that you?'

The silence that followed filled him with fear. Something moved behind the long curtain from which the shah always made his appearance. The vizier expected the shah, but it was Sharmin, sticking her head out from underneath.

'Sharmin!' he called, greatly relieved. 'Come, come here!'

The cat didn't budge. She seemed to smell that something was amiss. She stared at the vizier for a moment, then pulled her head back and disappeared. Sharmin convinced the vizier that the situation in the hall of mirrors was not as it should be. Otherwise she would have come up to him and rubbed herself against his leg.

The vizier hesitated. Perhaps he ought to notify the shah himself: 'Your Majesty, I'm waiting for you.'

He walked to the curtain.

'Your Majesty! Are you there?" he called again.

Perhaps the shah wasn't in the building yet and the vizier had been mistaken when he thought he saw the shah's shadow. He paced back and forth through the room with his hands behind his back. Something told him he had walked into a trap. His body had warned him right from the start, but he had ignored all the signs.

What else could he have done? He couldn't have disregarded the summons. He couldn't have stayed at home or fled. He had to obey the shah, so he had come to the palace.

The fact that his enemies wanted to kill him was something he always had to take into account. But he hadn't thought they would set the trap in the hall of mirrors.

He tried to rally his courage. Perhaps the shah was just angry at him and was trying to offend the vizier by making him wait too long. Besides, what could the shah do? When the shah's father had asked him to be his son's prime minister, the vizier had agreed under one condition: 'If the crown prince swears by the Quran that he will never kill me.'

The crown prince had laughed and said, 'I swear by the Quran that I will never have your blood on my hands,' at which the shah's father had happily placed his son's hands in those of the vizier.

'Now I can die in peace,' he said.

The vizier was startled to recall the shah's words. The shah hadn't sworn that he wouldn't kill the vizier, only that he would never have his blood on his own hands. He could leave that to others.

The torches around the pond had been extinguished and the courtyard was pitch dark. The gate was closed and there wasn't a guard in sight. The vizier had not been wrong. He had to save himself. He flung open the door and ran smack into the broad back of the guard, who was blocking the entrance like a brick wall.

'I believe His Majesty is very busy and will probably be occupied for quite some time,' said the vizier. 'I'm going to prepare myself for prayer.'

'You're not going anywhere. His Majesty is waiting for you.'

'It won't take long.'

'You cannot leave,' said the guard.

'I believe I am being detained?' said the vizier with a tone of irony.

The guard roughly shoved him inside and shut the door.

'Don't be weak,' said the vizier to himself. 'Stay calm.'

He stood in the middle of the room for a moment, then walked to the shah's water jug, which had been placed on a table in the corner. Meticulously he washed his hands and face for prayer, then turned towards Mecca. It was the only calming thing he could do. He said his prayers, taking longer than usual, but the shah still did not appear.

What was the shah waiting for? If he had wanted to belittle the vizier he had succeeded. And if he had something else in mind, why was it taking so long?

Suddenly he realised it was Friday evening: on Friday it was forbidden to kill anyone. The moon was hanging directly over the palace. It was almost midnight. He began to sing quietly: '*Ashhado anna la ilaha illa Allah, wa ashhado anna Muhammadun rasul Allah*. I testify that there is but one God and He is Allah. I testify that Muhammad is His prophet.'

These are the words you recite when you are certain that death is near. It was quite conceivable that the shah was spying on him to see how the vizier, the hero, the man who wanted to topple him from the throne, was now wrestling to escape from a tight situation.

With great composure he walked through the room. Now that he was prepared to die he had become calm. He observed the carpet once again. It was indeed the most beautiful carpet ever made by Persian women. Many other viziers had probably walked across it just before their death.

The moon had almost passed over the palace.

'It is time,' murmured the vizier.

The door opened. Three burly men came in. They were carrying a large black blanket and a rope.

'*La ilaha illa Allah*,' cried the vizier.

Two of the men ran up to him, grasped him from behind and tied his hands tightly together.

'*La ilaha il—*' cried the vizier again, but before he could finish his sentence the third man shoved a handkerchief in his mouth.

The vizier fought to get loose, but the three men forced him to the ground. In a few quick movements they wrapped him in the black blanket. He snarled and kicked, but the men bound the blanket with the rope, lifted him from the floor and carried him outside.

When peace returned to the room the cat came out. She walked across the carpet and sniffed it here and there. Then the curtain opened and the shah appeared. It was still night, but the torches near the fountain were burning again and the guards were standing attentively at the gate as if nothing had happened.

38. The Silence

After the murder of the vizier, Amir, his right-hand man, helped his wife and children escape from Tehran. All the friends and relatives of the vizier fled. And Amir went into hiding.

There was feasting in the palace. The vizier's opponents congratulated each other without mentioning the dead man's name. Mahdolia, who could barely walk now, spent the whole day on her feet receiving guests.

The country's change of power was observed in silence in foreign capitals. The vizier's death was not officially announced anywhere. The very question of his death was neither confirmed nor denied. Ordinary people did not take the rumours seriously.

Only when the vizier had been absent from the scene for a very long time did people begin to wonder where he was. It was suggested that he had been dismissed by the shah and that he and his family had moved away to his country estate.

There was a story making the rounds that the vizier had committed treason in the negotiations with England and that the shah had punished him for it. Some claimed that he had arrogated all the power to himself and had not been willing to give others any room to manoeuvre, much to their indignation.

It was now openly said that the vizier had had a double agenda. Sheikh Aqasi announced that the shah had been given written proof clearly showing that the vizier had made a deal with England in which they would provide him with support if he were to depose the shah. The vizier's opponents wanted everyone to believe that he was the one who had turned Afghanistan over to the British. They made him out to be a traitor and praised the shah for his courageous decision.

When the tension had died down and the dust from the rumours had settled, the shah threw a party. He invited all the princes, the prominent men from the bazaar and a few ayatollahs.

Not a word was uttered about the vizier. The hall was full and everyone was dressed to the nines. When the guests came in they bowed their heads to demonstrate their loyalty.

Normally the shah was not very talkative, but today he felt the need to say a few words to his guests: 'It is God's will that we have been permitted to see you all again in this capacity,' he said to his own astonishment, for he himself didn't know exactly what he meant. Because his words had inadvertently brought tears to his eyes, the guests were moved as well. No one asked any questions.

He walked past the guests, who were lined up in two facing rows. Very occasionally he would stop and speak at length with merchants from the bazaar, telling them in guarded terms that changes were coming and that the bazaar would benefit. He paused when he came to the ayatollahs and gave them the opportunity to preserve him from evil with their singing. One of them boldly pulled out his pocket Quran, recited a short surah under his breath and blew gently over the shah's face for extra protection.

At the shah's almost imperceptible command three

servants appeared, each carrying a dish filled with gold coins. It was customary to distribute new coins to guests at the New Year's feast, a gesture to symbolise the beginning of a new spring.

The feast had cost the shah five gold bars, which he had taken from the gold supply in the cellar. Sheikh Aqasi had used them to have new coins minted.

The guests, most of whom were from the upper class, laughed and admired the shah, kissed his hands and wished him luck. The princes, all of them decked out in new military uniforms, surrounded the shah and let him know that they were prepared to sacrifice themselves for the nation.

The shah listened to all of this in silence. He smiled. He knew the princes were in collusion with England and Russia. In his diary he later wrote, 'They're just a bunch of traitors. They'd kill me if they had the chance. They'd even do away with my daughter and Sharmin. We've got to render them harmless before they begin hatching plans.'

The guests were served fresh tea in gilt-edged glasses. The shah took a little coffee. It was the first time he had ever drunk coffee in public, and it was seen as the beginning of a new era. He put the cup back on the gold tray with a flourish and withdrew behind the curtain.

Sheikh Aqasi now assumed the role of host. Servants came in with huge dishes full of tasty morsels. The guests let him know they were aware of how he, in his wisdom, had stood by the shah in difficult times. Never before had they seen the shah so happy.

Sheikh Aqasi said the shah had spent a long time grieving over Herat, but fortunately he had put that grim episode behind him, and now the leadership of the country was back in his own blessed hands. He also told them that the shah had asked him to take on the responsibilities of the vizier. 'There have been many irregularities, especially in the army. Fortunately the shah has the expertise to deal with them all. That is not exactly my forte.'

With tears in his eyes Sheikh Aqasi swore by God to apply all his talents and strength in his service to the shah.

At first the shah tried to keep the vizier's death hidden from England and Russia. But the British ambassador had received the report of the murder from his spies on the day it took place, and he had alerted London. The ambassador saw it as an unfortunate event that was not wholly unexpected. The vizier had been ambitious and had made many enemies. His young advisors had been arrested or had gone into hiding, and the reformers had taken a hard blow.

England was not sorry about the change of power. From now on London could do business with the shah directly.

Forty days after the death of the vizier the ayatollah of Tehran made a brief announcement on behalf of the royal house during Friday prayers: 'We, the king of Persia, appoint Sheikh Aqasi the new vizier of the land. May Allah be with him.'

In his announcement the shah had not said a word about the vizier. The ayatollah too was silent. Sheikh Aqasi was praised as a God-fearing man, and the ayatollah hinted that Allah was happy with the choice.

Stories about the vizier were still making the rounds in the street.

'The vizier has fled.'

'He's in the British embassy.'

'The vizier wanted to depose the shah and place the crown on his own head.'

'He's gone into hiding among his own tribe.'

'His house is empty and boarded up. His wife and children have fled as well.'

'The vizier has been arrested. The agents have searched his house and have taken his files.'

'The vizier is soon to be hung on the bazaar square.'

The stories had made their way into the harem. One of them was accepted as the truth: 'The vizier rode into the palace grounds. All the guards had been replaced that night. They strangled him in the hall of mirrors. Then they buried him in great haste in a simple grave in the Abdoldawood Cemetery.'

No one knew the source of that report. It was a compilation of three facts that had been related by three different witnesses. The witnesses were an undertaker's man, a cleaning woman and a liveryman. They recounted what they had seen because their consciences were troubling them.

One night, as the undertaker's man was lying beside his wife in bed, he said to her, 'There's something I want to tell you, but it can't go beyond these four walls. Remember that evening when I had to prepare a grave for a burial? A coach with two horsemen brought a body wrapped in a black blanket. I got the lantern and went into the grave to lay the body on its right side. I wanted to pull the blanket away from the face, but one of the men jerked the lantern out of my hand and pulled me out of the grave by the collar. They threw earth over the body and filled in the grave. By the time they were finished it was daylight. In the glow of dawn I saw that it was a coach from the palace. The dead person was from there.'

The wife of the undertaker's man promptly told an old servant in the hamam, and the story made its way from the hamam to the harem.

One week after the vizier had been killed a cleaning woman from the palace found a crushed cylindrical hat in the hall of mirrors. It lay on the floor behind a curtain in front of the window. The cleaning woman immediately recognised it as the vizier's hat from the ornament decorating it. Her hands began to tremble. She dared not tell anyone about her find. She concealed the object under her clothing and took it back home with her, scared to death. Once she was home she wrapped the hat in a black cloth and hid it under the beams in the dark cellar of her house.

For three weeks she was as silent as the grave, but she had the constant urge to tell someone about it. One night, when she couldn't sleep, she went to see her old mother. She hid her face in her apron and began to weep. 'I have a hat in my house,' she said through her tears. 'I found the crushed hat of the vizier in the hall of mirrors. It was lying on the floor behind the curtain, but his jewel glittered in the light.'

Although the only person she told was her mother, it finally came to the attention of the shah's wives.

There was only one more thing the women needed to know to get to the whole truth.

The palace liveryman could no longer keep his mouth shut, and one evening he unburdened himself to his daughter: 'The vizier's horse has been in the palace stable for quite some time. This means that the vizier came to the palace on his own horse that night, but he did not leave on his own horse. I don't dare show the animal to anyone, so I've hidden it in the stable. The horse is becoming very restless, but I can't let it out. You're not to tell anyone about this.'

This report also made its way to the harem.

The shah's wives lined up all three of these facts and came to one conclusion: 'The vizier was killed in the hall of mirrors!'

The next Friday morning the shah's wives put on black

clothing and sat together on the veranda of the harem. The smoked their hookahs and drank tea. On the floor in front of them was a large dish of black dates, a sign of mourning. They looked sorrowful, but no one cried and no one talked about the vizier. It was appallingly silent.

39. Malijak

The country seemed unruffled, but just the opposite was true. The vizier's opponents said his death and the arrest of his supporters had saved the country from misfortune. But they had no idea what the vizier's death had unleashed. A wave of resistance slowly spread across the land.

It was at this time that Sharmin went missing. The shah looked everywhere for her, but she seemed to have disappeared off the face of the earth. He suspected that the women had stolen his cat to avenge the death of the vizier, so he asked the overseer of the harem to search all the rooms. But not a trace of Sharmin was found. Could Sharmin have left the palace herself? Had she not felt safe? Had she been afraid of the women of the harem, or was she afraid of the shah? Perhaps Sharmin had joined the wild cats.

The shah had a feeling she would never come back. It caused him pain, but there was nothing he could do.

A few months had passed since the death of the vizier. The shah often thought of him, but he threw himself into his poetry as a distraction. It didn't work. His latest poems were all about the vizier.

Take up a pickaxe, break down the wall
and flee this prison.
Escape, and surrender to the light.
Just like those who are gone
And are never coming back.

No matter what he did, the remorse he felt at doing away with the vizier grew stronger and stronger. No one had been permitted to mourn his disappearance, but the shah mourned him in silence. He consoled himself with the thought that other kings in his position had done the same thing. Someone had to hold the country together. Now that the vizier was no longer there he would have to go out into the country and show his face.

He asked Sheikh Aqasi to arrange a journey for him to the city of Sultanabad. The road to Sultanabad ran through the holy city of Qom, where the holy Masuma, a second cousin of the Prophet Muhammad, lay buried. Her tomb was one of the most important religious sites in the country.

Sheikh Aqasi advised the shah to spend a few days in Qom and to pay a visit to the shrine as a way of strengthening his ties with the great clerics of the city. The journey would take almost two weeks, and the shah and his wives would stay in the homes of the city's richest merchants.

Qom was a passionately religious city on the edge of the desert. Its inhabitants were mainly clerics and their relatives. The country's most important ayatollahs lived in Qom. The status of ayatollah was the highest that an ordinary imam could achieve. Those who held that position were usually of advanced years. The ayatollahs were powerful. They had thousands of followers. They lived simple lives among the people and their words were widely heeded. The mosque was the centre of their power. There were hundreds of imams throughout the country who kept them informed about what was going on at the grass roots. The shah hated that city, but he had to maintain good relations with the ayatollahs.

The shah spent his days in Qom in a castle just outside the city in a very special place among the old date palms, where it was pleasantly warm during the day and pleasantly cool at night. The shah was not really interested in visiting the holy tomb, but he had to let the ayatollahs see that he was the one with a firm grip on the reins of power.

Accompanied by a group of leading clerics the shah paid a visit to the holy Masuma and kissed the golden bars of the grave, as required by tradition. From there he visited a madrassah where students were training to become imams, and then withdrew to the castle so he would no longer have to have anything to do with saints, turbans and beards.

The next morning he rose early and continued his journey to Sultanabad. After a day of riding he and his retinue spent the night at a caravanserai, where a tent was set up for the shah. The thirty women accompanying him were put up in the travellers' lodgings.

Sultanabad was a provincial town and of little consequence in and of itself. The Farahan district, however, which contained a few hundred small villages, was a different matter. It was the native region of the murdered vizier, and for centuries the descendants of the vizier's family had lived there. The inhabitants of the region were proud of the family and were especially proud of the murdered vizier.

When the shah rode into the city the next day as evening fell, all the men he saw looked like the vizier. He may have been mistaken, but they all seemed to be wearing the same beards and the same hats. Tears sprang to his eyes.

The shah wanted to go to the city's old bazaar. The vizier had loved shoes, especially tall leather boots, and every time he went travelling he came back with a new pair. Once the shah had remarked on this practice: 'I see you had enough time to purchase a pair of boots.'

And the vizier had answered, 'No matter what I buy it never gives me as much pleasure as when my father bought me my first pair of boots at the Sultanabad bazaar.'

Everyone was surprised by the shah's visit. The shopkeepers didn't know how to react, for they had heard of the role the shah had played in the disappearance of the vizier. The chief of police cried, '*Javid shah*!' and the officers responded, '*Javid shah*!'

At the spice stands the shah stopped and inhaled the spicy fragrances. At a carpet shop he pointed to one carpet and asked, 'Where was that carpet woven?' And without waiting for the answer he walked on. He passed a number of jewellers and went into a shoe shop. He picked up a light brown boot, smelled the leather and put it back. After inspecting the other boots he walked out and left the bazaar by way of a side street. His guards never lost sight of him.

The shah wanted to visit the large carpet workshop just behind the bazaar. One of the vizier's big plans had been to promote the export of Persian carpets, and a proposal had been made to build a large number of carpet factories in various cities. The factory in Sultanabad had been erected as a pilot.

Much to the shock and joy of the carpet weavers the shah entered the factory with a train of guards and attendants. The shah was moved. Here he was, in one of the vizier's own dreams. An operation like this was unprecedented in

Persia. There was a beautiful gate leading to a classical enclosed garden with several ponds, around which were rooms where the workers wove carpets.

The shah stopped at the entrance to one of the work-rooms. He couldn't believe his eyes. Inside were hundreds of girls and young women, sitting side by side, knotting carpets on looms. Up until then the carpets had been made by women in their own homes out in the villages, but it had never occurred to anyone to gather the women together. The shah had the urge to reach into his pocket and toss out a handful of coins, but he realised this custom would be out of place here.

At first the women didn't know he was the shah, but even so, having a strange man among them was quite unusual. And he must be a very important man to have such a retine. Suddenly someone whispered his name. A tense silence fell. The women didn't dare look up. They remained seated and stared at the carpets in front of them. The shah walked past the unfinished carpets and glanced at the women. A lump rose in this throat and his eyes began to burn. Then suddenly he turned and went outside.

The next day the shah decided to go deer hunting in the mountains with his guards. The mountains of Farahan were the habitat of mighty wild stags who were no easy prey. Their colouration was the same as the stones', and they hid behind the rocks as soon as they heard a strange sound.

The hunters had spent half the day climbing around Mount Marzejaran and hadn't encountered a single stag. They'd probably have to content themselves with a couple of pheasants and a few wild ducks. The shah was a good shot. He brought down two large pheasants, which increased his desire to climb further and to reach the top of the mountain. After seven pheasants and nine wild ducks the group returned, fully satisfied, to enjoy a delicious kebab of fresh meat.

On the way back they spied a solitary stag. The shah motioned to his guards not to stir. He kept a close eye on the animal with his binoculars. Moving cautiously he picked up his gun and took aim. The stag stood with his ears cocked in the direction of the hunting party as the shah pulled the trigger. The stag started and momentarily lost his balance, so it looked as if he had been hit. But he recovered immediately, turned and bounded away. The shah released two more shots at the stag and set out in pursuit. The stag changed direction and ran into the woods.

The shah galloped to the spot where he had seen the stag disappear, and his fellow hunters heard one last shot. The shah could go no further on horseback. He dismounted and ran among the trees, the horse's reins in his hand. There was the stag, a short distance away, looking to see if the shah was still coming after him. Impatiently the shah shot, but he missed again. Refusing to let himself be beaten by such a beast, he jumped on his horse and rode to the rocks in order to head him off. Sweating and out of breath he reached the foot of the mountain, but there was no trace of the stag.

The shah was superstitious, and he was convinced that he had not crossed paths with this stag by accident. He had shot and missed five times, which seldom happened. In the old Persian tales, deer, stags and gazelles led the kings on mysterious adventures, but this stag was serving a higher purpose.

Because he was covered in sweat he wanted to keep moving. He was thirsty, and in the distance he saw a village. As he rode past the trees he heard a child crying in the bushes. He brought his horse to a halt and peered in. There he saw a dirty little boy, about seven years of age, standing in the bushes with bare feet.

'What's wrong? Why are you crying?'

The scantily clad boy couldn't see very well, or so it seemed. His eyes were oddly placed, too close together. His ears were larger than normal, and he was clutching a little bird to his chest with both hands.

The shah smiled and got off his horse. The little boy stopped crying and looked over the shah's head with his strange eyes.

'What are you doing here? Do you live in that house?' asked the shah, nodding towards a simple mud hut further down the road.

The boy didn't answer.

'What's your name?'

He didn't respond to this question either. Did he not understand the shah's language, or was he deaf?

'That's a lovely little bird you have there. What's his name?'

'Malijek,' said the boy.

'What did you say?'

'Malijek,' he said again.

The shah laughed heartily, for the boy had taken the dialect word for wild sparrow – 'malij' – and turned it into a diminutive: 'Malijek'.

'Splendid! You've come up with a delightful new word. We'll have to include it in one of our poems. Malijek, lovely, very good.'

He took a sugar cube from his trouser pocket and put it in the boy's mouth. Sucking on the sweet the boy grabbed the shah by the hand. It moved the shah, evoking a familiar feeling within him, and he gently stroked the boy's hair. The boy pressed his head against his leg, as Sharmin had always done.

'You're a sweet little boy,' said the shah. 'It's going to be dark soon. You have to go home, and we have to leave as well.'

As he began walking back to his horse the boy followed him. 'No, Malijek, don't follow me. Go home.'

But the boy said, 'Malijek, Malijek, Malijek!'

The shah looked at him and smiled. 'We like you. Come, we'll take you home with us.' He picked the boy up and put him on his saddle.

At that moment a girl's voice cried out, 'Give me my brother back!'

The bushes moved and out stepped a young woman with large, wild, black eyes and tangled hair. The shah took a step towards her, but she turned and ran away.

'Girl! Come here, and take your brother with you!'

Her long green skirt covered with red flowers, her bare feet in the wild grass, the fear in her eyes and her undaunted voice: all this intrigued the shah. He put the boy down in front of the mud hut. 'Go inside and ask your sister to bring us a bowl of water.' But the boy wouldn't move.

The shah mounted his horse resolutely. The hunting party had found him by this time and were riding towards him. The little boy began to cry. An older man came out of the hut. Seeing the horsemen at the door, he suspected that this was an important person. He bowed subserviently and pulled the boy away.

The girl walked up to the shah with a bowl of water. He took the water and looked into the bowl with surprise. 'What is this? Why is the water so filthy?'

'It's not filthy. I put broken sugar cane in it.'

'Why didn't you take the cane out?'

'You're all sweaty and the water is cold. You're thirsty. If you drink the water all at once you'll get sick. You must drink slowly.'

The shah drank the sweetened water, looking at the girl as he did so. Then he slid a gold coin into the bowl.

'Let's go!' he said, and he set the horse in motion. The little boy came running after him, screaming. The shah stopped and the boy grabbed his boot and clung to it. Then it occurred to him: he was in Farahan, the region of the vizier. A stag had led him here, to this mud hut. All this had meaning. He called for one of his guards to come and stand beside him. 'We're taking this boy with us. The girl, too.'

The guard rode back to the house, dismounted, talked with the peasant, pressed a sack of gold coins into his hands and was given permission to take his daughter and son back to the palace. The peasant spoke quietly with his wife, who looked at the shah with astonishment and bowed. She walked up to her daughter, talked to her, and kissed her on the forehead and on the eyes. A mule was fetched from the stable for the girl and her brother to ride on as part of the shah's retinue.

Five days later, back in the palace, the shah sent the girl to the harem. He replaced the 'e' in Malijek with an 'a' so the name would sound better. Then the shah instructed the chamberlain to give the boy a bath.

'He's filling the empty place left by Sharmin, and his name is Malijak.'

40. The Telegraph Service

Malijak became the shah's pet. His sister cared for the boy and was given a separate room with the servants, which she shared with her brother. During meals Malijak was allowed to sit on the floor next to the shah, just where Sharmin used to sit. At first the women took pity on Malijak and treated him kindly. But before a year had passed the child became troublesome. He hit the other children and pestered the women of the harem. No one dared say anything, and the shah let Malijak do whatever he liked. He poured out his heart to the boy.

Malijak ate more than was good for him and soon became big and fat. The undernourished child had disappeared. The servants kept out of his way, and the women of the harem popped sugar cubes in his mouth whenever he unexpectedly made an appearance. The boy always wore exactly the same clothes as the shah: the same jacket, the same boots and the same hat. In the evening Malijak played in the shah's company until it was time for him to go to bed.

The stories about Malijak spread across the land. You never knew what was true and what was false. It was said that whenever Malijak began to cry because he missed his mother and father, the shah would get down on all fours like a donkey and give the boy a ride around the hall of mirrors.

No one ever saw the shah without his tall cylindrical

hat, but it was said that Malijak was allowed to grab the shah's hat and play with it. The child was always dirty and he stank. He was afraid of water and never let anyone wash him.

'The shah washes him himself in a big tub,' people said. 'And he cuts his hair with a pair of scissors, since Malijak doesn't even let his own sister touch his hair.'

It was said that the shah didn't want Malijak to learn to read and write. Education was unnecessary because he regarded the boy as a pet. The only thing the shah taught him was to play a good game of chess so he could keep the shah amused.

Malijak also liked to play tricks on Sheikh Aqasi. The shah enjoyed it whenever anyone teased the sheikh, and Malijak quickly caught on. As soon as the sheikh came into the room Malijak would run up to him, hang on his clothes and search his pockets for sweets. He loosened the scarf that Sheikh Aqasi used as a belt and ran through the room with it. The poor man would have to chase him to get his scarf back – but carefully, so his trousers wouldn't fall down. The shah enjoyed this immensely and laughed out loud, and his pleasure egged Malijak on.

The shah felt good when Sheikh Aqasi was around. By getting rid of the vizier he had the freedom to be himself again. He had always felt inferior to the vizier, and the words of his mother echoed in his head: 'You act like the vizier's errand boy.'

With Sheikh Aqasi the roles were reversed. Now Sheikh Aqasi was the errand boy, and that gave the shah a tremendous sense of satisfaction. He could make decisions on his own.

There was only one thing that kept the shah from being fully himself: his mother. With her he was powerless. After all, you can't send your mother home, you can't sack her and you can't kill her. With his mother the shah would just have to be patient.

Now that Sheikh Aqasi was vizier, England had more room to manoeuvre, although he was not an easy man to work with. He was not a trustworthy partner. To maintain firmer control over developments in the country, London decided to replace its ambassador in Tehran with the gifted politician Sir John Malcolm. He was fascinated by Persian history and he spoke reasonably good Persian. He knew that the country's coffers were empty and that the shah's personal expenses were inordinately high.

At his official introduction to the shah Sir John made a good impression from the minute he walked in. He presented the shah with a hunting rifle, and the shah in turn invited him to go hunting.

Both men had a feel for language, and both loved poetry. During one of Sir John's tea visits to the palace the shah entrusted the ambassador with one of his poems:

> O wretched heart, I hear thy piteous groan,
> Since thou must pay for what the eyes have done,
> For had mine eyes not gazed on love's sweet face
> How could love by an innocent heart be known?

'It is a most regal poem,' Sir John had remarked.

One of the first things Sir John arranged for the shah was to cancel the construction of the domestic telegraph system. London had resisted the plan from the beginning, and Sir John promised the shah a monthly bonus in exchange for dropping it.

To avoid any appearance of bribery he replaced the word 'bonus' with 'tax', thereby obliging England to pay a monthly telegraph tax to the shah. The shah beamed with happiness. He was being given a large sum of money, right out of the blue. It was as if God were rewarding him for his deeds.

Sir John Malcolm realised that without the cooperation of the elite, England would not be able to maintain its position. So he invited the influential princes to the embassy and asked them for their support. He gave them all positions in the national telegraph scheme, which existed only on paper, and arranged monthly salaries for them.

This enabled England to make more headway with the activities arising from the plans it had agreed on with the vizier concerning the telegraph line to India. Several thousand men from the countryside were put to work chopping down trees, and hundreds of young men from Tehran learned how to install telegraph poles and cables. Experienced masons from throughout the land were called on to build scores of telegraph offices along the India line.

The shah had hoped that by scrapping the national telegraph system his subjects would be cut off from news of the latest developments. But this was far too simplistic. The merchants who travelled abroad kept coming back with impressive tales of new products, companies, cities, squares, bridges and newspapers. Wherever the shah went he heard people talking about these things. Even the royal circles were all abuzz.

The princes tried to add prestige and panache to their conversations by peppering them with the latest English and French terminology. Everyone was trying to give others the impression that they had seen or heard something new.

While travelling to Isfahan for a working visit the shah happened upon a group of Persian men in blue work clothes who were installing cables and insulators on telegraph poles. He saw policemen at the Isfahan gate walking about in uniforms that were unfamiliar to him. He was not aware of the existence of these officers, which surprised him. Upon enquiring he was told they weren't policemen at all but guards for the telegraph offices then under construction.

Curious, he spent some time visiting a company where the cables were cut to measure and insulators were fixed to iron bars. The country was changing before his very eyes. It distressed him, and he remembered how often the murdered vizier had told him he ought to go to France or England to see the industrial developments there first-hand. He had always dismissed the idea. How could he have travelled with an easy mind when the fate of Herat was hanging in the balance, and when people were lying in wait, ready to seize power from him?

During his visit to the villages around Isfahan he noticed that the villagers were gathering round the telegraph poles and debating with each other. How could a handful of poles and a few cables cause such a commotion?

'It's a miracle. They put your words in the cable, and in a flash it gets sent to the other side of the world.'

'What words do they send?'

'English words, I think, or Russian ones.'

'What about Persian words, then?'

'I don't think it works with Persian.'

'It's orders from the king of England. He says something and then they send it out to the whole world through these cables.'

'Can our king use the cables, too?'

'I don't think so.'

'Why not?'

'They're not for us. The cables belong to the British. The shah has only leased out the land to them to put their poles in.'

The peasants admired the shah for his wisdom, and the shah made it seem as if he was riding along the telegraph route to inspect the operations in person.

When it came to the telegraph system Sheikh Aqasi was of the same mind as the shah's mother.

'The British have laid more than two thousand kilometres of cable across our country,' she said. 'They've chopped down thousands of trees to make telegraph poles. Are they doing this for our benefit? No, they're marching down our back in order to reach India faster. Why are we letting them do this? I asked this question once, and I'll keep on asking it until I get an answer.'

'Mother, you're forgetting that England was in possession of the south. We had to negotiate. You have to see this collaboration on the telegraph project as a symbol of the changing times,' said the shah, and he ended the discussion.

The cables were laid with incredible speed. The British had gas lanterns, which meant that the work could go on all night. When people got up in the morning they saw that the workers were already hundreds of poles further along.

When the telegraph headquarters in Tehran was finished, Sir John Malcolm asked the shah to officiate at the opening. The shah was extremely pleased with the invitation. He rode to the ceremony with his attendants and his cannon. A group of Indian army musicians welcomed him with a jolly victory march. Sir John received the shah, took from his inside pocket a piece of chocolate wrapped in gold paper, and gave it to Malijak.

The entrance to the headquarters was decorated with Persian wall tapestries as well as British flags. Beneath the admiring glances of the distinguished guests, Sir John gave a speech in Persian in which he praised the shah for his exceptional cooperation and his friendship with the British royal family. He handed the shah a pair of scissors on a gold tray and invited him to cut the ribbon. This was followed by a tour through the building and past the telegraph equipment.

Over a glass of fresh English tea in the garden of the headquarters, Sir John Malcolm had a surprise in store for the shah.

'On the occasion of this historic event, England would like to offer a present to the children of the shah – especially Malijak, but His Majesty's other children may also make use of it, of course.'

'We are very pleased,' said the shah.

'The present symbolises progress,' continued Malcolm. 'It is an apparatus that has only recently been installed in the parks of London. It's meant for children, but it has been noticed that in London it is being used by both children and their mothers.' With this remark Sir John was suggesting that the present was also meant for the women of the harem.

'I don't know what the Persian word is for this apparatus, but in English we call it a "slide".'

'We shall see,' said the shah, and he looked around to see if the apparatus was in sight.

'The present will be delivered to the palace.'

The next week two large carts carrying elongated objects arrived at the palace. A British engineer and five Indian technicians had made sure the large iron plates were not damaged as they were being transported over the bumpy streets. No one knew what the shining plates were for, and everyone began making wild guesses: 'Maybe they're parts of a telegraph.'

'Looks like the shah is getting a telegraph of his own.'

'This has nothing to do with a telegraph. I think the iron plates are meant to replace the wooden gate of the palace.'

'If they carried these big pieces of iron all the way through the country, it must be something important.'

The shah had decided to have the present placed in the harem, for if the women of London could enjoy it, the women of the harem could entertain themselves with it as well. In the meantime he had come up with a Persian name for the apparatus, an almost literal translation of the English word 'slide': '*sor-soreh*'. A nice discovery, he thought – a word that describes exactly what the apparatus does. 'Sor-soreh: you slide and you keep on sliding.'

All the women of the harem were sent on a pilgrimage to the tomb of the holy Abdoldawood. When they returned late that evening the shah was going to surprise them with his sor-soreh.

The British engineer and his Indian assistants spent a whole day completing their work. They anchored the gigantic slide firmly to the floor and secured it to the walls with iron cables. It was as solid as a house. When all was ready the engineer tested the slide by climbing up the steps and sliding down himself. He was followed by the five giggling Indians.

The present was ready for use and the shah was extremely pleased with this extraordinary piece of British equipment. He gave three gold coins to the British engineer and one apiece to the Indians. Now he was standing all alone beside the massive slide. He had a number of mattresses placed at the lower end. Standing with arms akimbo he cast a glance at his sor-soreh. It was perfect. With great care he climbed to the top, sat down and slid solemnly to the bottom.

'Fantastic!' he said, landing gently on the mattresses.

He waited impatiently for the women to return. The shah received them with a lantern in his hand, and they wondered why all the lights in the harem had been extinguished.

'Ladies,' he shouted proudly, 'the sor-soreh awaits you. Follow me!'

Leading the way he opened the door of the harem. 'After you, ladies!'

The women went inside. By the light of that one lantern, and with the shadows caused by the reflection of the light on the surfaces of the slide, all the women could see was a mysterious monster in the middle of the harem. An extra lantern was brought in. Malijak appeared at the top of the slide, and to everyone's astonishment he slid to the bottom, crowing with pleasure, and flopped onto the mattresses. The shah left the women and went outside.

Behind him he heard his wives screaming and laughing. Two big tears of happiness rolled down his cheeks. 'Maybe it's time we took that trip to England,' he said to Malijak, who was pulled away from the slide with difficulty.

41. Import and Export

The telegraph cables were now running straight through the country on thousands of poles. They were a marvellous addition to the mysterious landscape. The Russians, who had drawn up a treaty with the British during the war in Herat and had left the shah high and dry, had not expected England to be ready with such an elaborate plan for Persia.

The silent power struggle between Russia and England had been won by the British. And once the railway was built from the Persian Gulf to India, the Russians would never be able to catch up. So they did all they could to thwart the construction of the British railway. They hinted to the shah that they, unlike England, were willing to give Persia its own national railway network.

Because of the wars that were constantly being conducted, there was no breeding ground for scientific research or commerce. Little of value had been exported, especially over the past hundred years, and virtually nothing had been imported. But with the great changes that were taking place in the West, ships full of new British products were now stocking the bazaars. The bazaars of the northern cities were still in contact with Russian merchants and sold new products from Moscow and St Petersburg.

Because the British were in charge in the southern port, the Russians focused their energies on the northern and, to some extent, the eastern borders. They came up with a plan to renovate the harbours there in accordance with Russian standards. The Russian ambassador submitted a proposal to the shah for the creation of northern customs stations, which would earn him a great deal of money.

At first the shah wanted nothing to do with the Russians. He was still smarting from the painful experience of the Herat war. But he had no choice – and he couldn't resist the temptation of so much money. His counsellors had advised him to stop ignoring the Russian ambassador in Tehran. They knew that the tsar was under pressure in his own country and that he was prepared to make concessions. The shah invited the Russian ambassador to meet with him.

The story of the slide had reached Moscow, and the Russian ambassador wanted to surprise the shah with his own splendid present. The shah received him with feigned indifference to make sure he understood that the betrayal in Herat had not been forgotten.

Like the British, Russia had sent one of their most experienced diplomats to Tehran to serve as ambassador. His name was Dimitri Chovolovski. He had published a book about the history of Russian–Persian relations.

After the shah and the ambassador had partaken of a cup of tea and exchanged pleasantries, Chovolovski surprised the shah with the question, 'I have brought with me a number of portraits of the tsar's family. Would Your Majesty like to see the photographs?'

The shah was burning with curiosity, but he nodded dismissively. Dimitri Chovolovski took from his leather case a photograph album decorated with gold ornaments, and held up a magnificent portrait of the tsar.

'Handsome,' said the shah. It was the only word that came to mind at that moment. However, the striking likeness of this true-to-life portrait made a deep impression on him. It was totally different from any of the portraits drawn in pencil that he had seen so far. Featured on the next page was a beautiful blonde woman with bare shoulders, undoubtedly the tsar's wife. The shah coughed slightly into his fist and thumbed further through the book with pretended nonchalance.

'If Your Majesty agrees I will commission a Russian photographer to immortalise the shah in his palace, as a gift of the tsar.'

The shah did not respond immediately. He put the photo album away and asked a couple of questions about Russia's plans for the northern harbour. But it was clear from the expression on his face that he had no interest in listening to a detailed explanation from the ambassador.

When Chovolovski took out a roll of paper and began to open it to show him a drawing of the customs building, the shah could take no more. 'Make an appointment with our vizier,' he said.

A few months later a Russian photographer rode into Tehran in a rather unusual coach, getting out at the palace. When the liveryman came up to release his horse, the photographer made it quite clear that his help was not needed. He was an odd character with a bizarre hat, a strikingly trimmed beard and a curled moustache. He gave his horse a bit of water from a bucket he had brought himself. Then he placed a wooden feeding trough on the ground in front of the animal. Finally he walked to the pond with his hands behind his back and strolled through the gardens.

The shah had been watching him from a window. The man acted as if the palace were his own home.

The photographer had enough sense to know that he was not to ask for the shah, but that the shah would come out himself. When the shah eventually did make his appearance the photographer ignored him. The shah walked calmly down the steps. The photographer turned round, tipped his hat, bowed slightly and said, 'Your Majesty!'

For one whole week the shah was photographed in a number of special places in the palace, as were Malijak and the shah's ravishingly beautiful daughter Taj, who was soon to be married. The photographer also immortalised the shah with a chosen group of women, all of them veiled and dressed in burkas.

The Russian realised he was recording a chapter of Persian history, so he patiently looked for unique compositions for his photos. With his considerable powers of persuasion he was easily able to gain access to the harem. This was the first time any stranger had ever entered the building. It was all so spontaneous that even the shah never thought to stop him. Shooting a series of photos of the women, he knew his pictures were unique witnesses to an unknown world. His camera was capturing a moment in time.

There were two scenes in particular that he spent a great deal of time on. One was a group of veiled women sitting in a circle on the floor and smoking hookahs, and the other was a portrait of the shah sitting on the chair on which Cyrus, the king of kings, had once sat.

A long time after the photographer had left, a photo album for the shah was sent from Moscow to the Russian embassy in Tehran. Dimitri Chovolovski took the album, along with the contracts for the Russian–Persian customs stations, and rode to the palace with hope in his heart.

The shah thumbed through the contract, scrutinised a number of sections and asked several questions. He then laid the papers aside and said, 'We have discussed your plans with the relevant persons. Basically we believe it is a solid proposal. Our vizier will contact you shortly. We are very pleased with the new relations between our two countries.'

After these words Dimitri Chovolovski took the photo album out of his case and handed it to the shah, who was overwhelmed by the pictures.

'We are satisfied,' he remarked drily.

He rang his little bell and summoned Malijak to show him his own photo.

'That's you, Malijak,' said the shah.

Dimitri Chovolovski seized the opportunity to give the boy a present. 'I have also brought a little something for your Malijak. If Your Majesty approves.' It was a toy gun.

The shah picked up the gun, inspected it, aimed the barrel at a candle in the chandelier and shot. The gun made a loud pop, and Malijak jumped. The shah laughed.

Dimitri Chovolovski bowed his head.

42. Resistance

After the construction work was completed, the birds recovered from the shock and began perching on the telegraph poles and cables as if they had never done anything else. It was clear from their singing that they were happy. The children were happy too. They pressed their ears against the poles and tapped them with stones to communicate with each other. It was a magical game and they never tired of it.

All the activities that in some way were related to the telegraph system seemed to give everyone renewed strength and hope. Malijak, who detested physical movement, now went everywhere shooting his pop gun at valets, servants, cooks and cats. No one dared stop him. Even Sheikh Aqasi had to watch out for Malijak when he went to see the shah. The fat boy never aimed his gun at Taj Olsultan, however. He sensed it wasn't allowed, and Taj, moreover, had firmly drawn the line.

There was someone else from whom Malijak unquestioningly kept his distance. It was a young officer whom the shah had been summoning with quite some frequency lately. He belonged to the shah's own tribe and bore the same surname. The officer had conducted himself with great courage in the war for Herat, which had not escaped the shah's notice. He had given the brave officer a medal as well as the honorary title 'Eyn ed-Dowleh', which literally meant 'eyes of the state'. This Eyn ed-Dowleh seemed like a most fitting husband for Taj Olsultan.

The shah was far from old, but the wise men of his tribe were pressing him to appoint a successor. Leaving the destiny of the tribe and the country to chance was not a good idea, they thought. The shah was to name his potential replacement, and to do it soon.

Given the relatively peaceful climate in the country he decided to deal with this crucial matter with dispatch. The shah presented his plan to the tribal elders and asked them what they thought of the young officer. They approved him immediately and praised the shah for his judicious choice.

The British engineers had not been standing still either. They were feeling hopeful after studying the soil samples, and they tried to keep the results of their drilling from the outside world. But their presence in the southern provinces, and especially their telegraph cables running straight through and over the tops of mosques, houses, alleys, hamams, rivers and forests, had shaken everyone to their senses.

The shah was concerned about the impact of these external influences on the common people. But behind his back the rich families and important merchants from the bazaars were still sending their sons to Moscow, London, Paris, Bombay and Istanbul. A group of these talented Persian men saw it as their patriotic duty to return and to provide guidance to their fellow countrymen. The most important man among them was Jamal Khan Astarabadi, better known as Jamal Khan. He had been in London when the first trains thundered into the city. He had visited several steel factories in Birmingham, had drunk with the workers in pubs and had attended their meetings.

Jamal Khan had been a friend of the vizier and

corresponded with him when the vizier was still alive. They had met once in St Petersburg and once in Baku. It was this Jamal Khan who had obtained a copy of the French statute book for the vizier.

The death of the vizier had been painful for Jamal Khan, but it did not come as a surprise. Even when they were together in Baku he had warned the vizier that this might be his fate. They both realised that the country needed sacrifices to enable it to move forward. Jamal Khan knew how the vizier had been murdered and where he was buried.

The name of Jamal Khan was not widely known, but intellectuals in the countries of the East respected him as a political thinker. His articles on the awakening of the peoples in the Islamic countries were read abroad with great interest. He had spent several years in Egypt. Then he had moved to Turkey in order to be closer to Persia. Istanbul was a crossroads of new ideas, a place where East met West. Jamal Khan felt at home there, but recent events demanded his return to Persia.

Jamal Khan's father had been a celebrated ayatollah in Tehran, which was why his son had such good contacts in Islamic circles. It wasn't long before he was offered a position as a speaker in the mosque of the bazaar. Every Friday, after the imam of the mosque had finished his prayers, Jamal Khan would give a speech to the mosque attendees, most of whom were bazaar merchants.

He was a gifted speaker, and because the subjects he spoke about were not the standard fare, he was immediately seen as an asset and was received with much enthusiasm. With stories about world trade and about how western merchants earned millions upon millions with the help of the telegraph cables, without having to travel long and tiring distances, he captivated his listeners. He opened people's eyes and became more and more daring, speaking about the corrupt princes and the country's failing power structure. It wasn't long before his name was known throughout Tehran. His words made the rounds, and he was invited to speak in every corner of the country.

One evening he gave a talk after prayers in the Jameh mosque in Tehran in which he attacked England: 'People! We have been humiliated enough. If we cannot have our own national telegraph system, then the British will have to remove the telegraph poles they have put up here.'

It was an unusual message. Up until then people spoke of the telegraph system as something that was none of their business. Jamal Khan was openly expressing his dissatisfaction with having British poles on Persian soil.

'He's right. What good are the poles if they're not for us?' the people said.

'If the cables aren't being used by us, why must they be strung over our houses?'

When Jamal Khan came to a mosque to speak, people fought for a place. After his address long discussions would be held in the mosque courtyard: 'What he says makes sense. There are so many sick people in this country and we have no medicine or doctors.'

'I've never thought about it before, but why are there so many people out of work?'

'If we only had modern industry here everything would be better.'

'He's right. We deserve a better life.'

The people close to the shah were outraged at Jamal Khan, and they issued warnings about his ulterior motives. The shah saw no reason to worry, however – at least not yet. Now that he was enjoying good relations with both England and Russia, his position on the throne was stronger than ever. Of course he made sure he was properly informed about this new speaker, and he asked the chief of the city police force to have him followed. But there was also another matter that required his attention. He had become completely caught up in the preparations for the wedding of his favourite daughter, Taj Olsultan.

It was from her mother, Foruq, that Taj Olsultan heard about the king's choice and the plan for a quick wedding. When the shah called her in to talk about her future husband she threw herself at his feet in tears and said, 'But Father, this man already has many other wives.'

'So do we,' he responded immediately. 'We also have many wives.'

'I know from reliable sources that he is not a good man. He is hot-tempered and he beats his wives.'

'He will not beat you, and if he does I will have him hung.'

'Father, I don't love him,' she pleaded.

'Now you've gone too far,' replied the shah sharply. 'Stop this yammering. Those French books have deluded you with their ideas about marriage. It's not about you. It's about our tribe. You do it for your homeland. Be careful you don't bring down our wrath upon your own head.'

After this reprimand from the shah a group of old, experienced women from the tribe paid a visit to Taj Olsultan to prepare her to fulfil her obligation. They managed to talk her into going to see her father to offer her apologies.

The shah kissed her on the head and said happily, 'Now it's time for a magnificent *ashpazan*.' Ashpazan was a word that the shah himself had thought up. It meant 'the communal preparation of a thick Persian soup'.

The shah loved soup. He always looked for a reason to organise an ashpazan. The women of the harem were happy when the shah announced that an ashpazan was in the making. They saw it as a sign that the shah was in an excellent mood, and because it was a domestic feast it also created a pleasant atmosphere in the harem for a number of weeks. Quarrels and difficulties were set aside in order to satisfy the shah's desires.

Usually they cooked the soup for the shah and their own children, and gave the rest to the palace servants and guards. But this time the shah wanted to pull out all the stops. He wanted to share the soup with the poor of the city as a sacrifice to protect the marriage of his daughter from the Evil One.

On the day of the ashpazan the shah entered the harem early. Just outside the palace a large tent had been set up, and people of the city, all of whom had brought along bowls or pans, fought for a place. In the back garden of the harem twenty large pots had been placed over fires in two rows. The fragrance of the soup filled the air. Everyone was hard at work cleaning vegetables, slicing meat and adding just the right herbs. During the ashpazan the women laughed, danced, sang and joked with each other. The shah's attention added to their pleasure. He complimented his wives on their beautiful jewellery and caressed them.

Taj Olsultan had put on her most festive clothing and spent most of her time with the children. Although all the women were jealous of her they knew she wasn't happy. The shah had invited a group of female musicians to cheer her up. When the musicians entered, playing their instruments as they walked, Taj beamed. Motioning the musicians to stop, the shah turned to the women and said, 'Ladies, soon we're going to celebrate a great feast. Do everything that needs to be done and see that you're beautifully dressed.'

At his sign the musicians raised their instruments once

again. The shah kissed his daughter and walked with her to the pots of soup, blessing each one with a handful of fresh vegetables.

The shah sat down on his couch and was offered a glass of tea and a hookah. He put two sugar cubes in his mouth, took a sip of tea and began to smoke. A bowl of soup was handed to him. He tasted a couple of spoonfuls and let the women see how much he liked it.

In the afterglow of the tea, still a bit dizzy from the hookah and sleepy from the gentle sun, he stretched out his legs and pressed his head into the pillows, preparing to take a nap. But no sooner had he dropped off than he was jolted awake by the bang of a gun. It was Malijak, who couldn't help disturbing the peace.

'Oh, you little rascal!' cried the shah, laughing.

Malijak always tried to get away with more when the shah was around. The sillier his behaviour the happier he made the shah. His main target was the women. They ran away screaming and threw sweets at him to distract him while the king roared with laughter, tears streaming down his face.

At about noon, when the shah, his wives and his children had eaten enough, the women withdrew into the harem. A group of guards brought the remaining soup out to the people. The shah watched from the roof as the crowds jostled their way forward while the guards tried in vain to get them to form a queue. In all the commotion a man in the crowd pushed one of the guards against two other guards who were holding a pot of soup. The guards lost their balance, the pot fell and all the soup spilled out.

Things got out of hand. The guards struck the people with cudgels and the people then turned on the guards, beating them over the head with pans and bowls. The big soup pots fell to the ground and suddenly flames shot up from the back of the tent. In all the chaos the head of the guards began shooting into the air. The people took to their heels and the guards chased them until peace was restored.

The shah looked down impassively at the lucky soup, which was flowing all over the ground.

43. Jamal Khan

The uproar that occurred during the ashpazan worried the shah. There was no question that Jamal Khan and his pals, disguised as beggars, had been part of the crowd the day before. They had caused the unrest and they were the first to come to blows with the guards. One report stated in black and white that Jamal Khan, who was being held responsible for overturning the soup pots, had been staying in Moscow at the time of the popular uprising in Russia. He was also the one who had set the tent on fire. To find out whether such agitators were active in other cities, the shah ordered a full-scale investigation.

There was no organised security service in the country that could monitor the behaviour of suspected opponents. The chiefs of the police forces in the big cities were told to keep an eye on anyone who had been abroad and to report on their activities. That, thought the shah, was where the danger lay.

When the shah received the dossiers two months later he couldn't wait to study them. Every single chief reported on the existence of a group of young men in their respect-ive cities who were meeting on a regular basis to scrutinise the national situation. All the reports noted that at least one or two men in the group had spent some time living abroad.

At first the shah had seen the ashpazan outburst as an isolated incident caused by poor, ignorant people, but as he read the reports he realised that this could be the prelude to a whole storm of protests. He took out his handkerchief and wiped the sweat from his brow, gasping for fresh air. He did not want revolts like those in Russia to happen in his own country. He had always been afraid that the men who had studied abroad would turn against his regime. The incident of the soup pots and the recent reports only confirmed his anxiety.

He pulled out the report on the speeches of Jamal Khan that he had received earlier but had ignored because of the excitement of his daughter's wedding. In one of the dossiers there was a sentence about Jamal Khan that might have served as a warning to him: 'He is a rebel who maintains contact with the leaders of all the Muslim and Indian anti-British insurgent groups from Bombay to Egypt, and he corresponds with them.'

Without further delay he sent for the chief of the Tehran police. The shah could barely control his nerves, but he began by asking the man a couple of general questions about the city. Gradually he brought the conversation round to the soup incident.

'We have read your reports, but please listen carefully now to the questions we are going to ask and give us a straightforward answer. Are you sure that Jamal Khan was there in the crowd on that particular day?'

'Yes, Your Majesty. Actually . . . in the report . . . yes, yes, pretty sure,' stammered the man.

'So what you mean is no,' barked the shah. 'The second question: Are you sure that the man who tipped over the big pot of soup was not a beggar but a man who lived for a short time in Moscow?'

'Actually, our informers . . . I've got it all in the report . . .' said the man with a quavering voice in an attempt to explain.

'So what you mean is no,' repeated the shah.

The man was as white as a sheet. He waited for the next question.

'Get this Jamal Khan!' thundered the shah. 'Bring him here and have him fall on the floor at our feet. Then we'll see if your reports are correct.'

When Jamal Khan came back after spending time abroad he first moved in with his parents in Tehran. He gave speeches in the mosques, which he pretended was his only activity. But secretly he was weaving a network of contacts throughout the country. It was a tedious process because he had to travel back and forth across the country himself. It took more than a year to put the right men in touch with each other. Gradually hubs were created in the big cities where the situation in the country was discussed as well as the political changes taking place in neighbouring India and Russia.

After the order was given to arrest Jamal Khan a group of agents stormed his parents' house in the middle of the night, but they didn't find him there.

The chief of police issued warnings to his men in the big cities and sent them Jamal Khan's particulars, so suspicious characters could be arrested even before they passed through the city gates. But it was difficult to tell from the vague description exactly what the man looked like, nor did they know where they could expect to find him.

Jamal Khan's comrades organised the speeches for him. He would appear at the Jameh mosques unannounced, and as soon as the police showed up he would disappear into the congregation.

At Jamal Khan's first talk he had told the people about developments in other countries and gave examples of present-day life in the West. He underscored how backward their homeland really was.

The people who saw and heard him for the first time were intrigued and didn't know how to respond to his arguments. He reminded them of the prophets of ancient times who stood on hilltops and preached warnings to their people. Oddly enough many people learned fragments of his speeches by heart.

Jamal Khan no longer operated alone. He worked with a core of six loyal men. Fath Ali Akhondzadeh was one of them. He had lived in London and had immersed himself in the English language. He was the first to write a book on the grammar of the Persian language, and in the spirit of the former vizier he preached that all the children of the country should be given the chance to learn to read and write.

Yusef Mostashar Aldoleh had worked for a number of years in the Persian embassy in Paris, but he was dismissed because he had criticised the homeland's ruling system as corrupt. He swapped Paris for Istanbul, where he published a Persian newspaper that he arranged to have smuggled into the homeland.

Zeinolabedin Maraghei was the third man, an artist who had lived in Bombay and then in Rome and had immersed himself in painting. Maraghei spoke Italian and became involved in the polemics contained in the Italian newspapers. He too returned to the homeland to awaken his countrymen.

The fourth was Haj Abdolrahim Talebof, a man from Tabriz who had always lived across the border in Russia and had studied in St Petersburg. Talebof was in close contact with the leaders of the uprisings in Moscow.

The fifth man in the group was Mirza Reza Kermani, a remarkable personality. He was the son of an ayatollah of the city of Kerman, and his father had sent him to Iraq to be trained as an imam. There he came in contact with a group of Egyptians who were struggling against the British colonial power. He travelled to Egypt, where he met Jamal Khan. The two kept in touch and met again in Tehran. Mirza Reza had replaced his turban with a cap, which was being worn at the time by the intellectuals of the Middle East.

The last of the group was Amir Nezam, who years later would become prime minister of the country. Everyone knew him as the young engineer who had served as the vizier's right-hand man. It was Amir who had rescued the vizier's wife and two young daughters after the murder, hiding them in a farm cart and fleeing with them from Tehran. After that he had laid low for a while. His new beard and moustache now rendered him unrecognisable. He returned to Tehran as a repairman, where he met Jamal Khan and began working with him.

The two men always travelled separately, as if they had nothing to do with each other. They came together at various locations and secretly formed a committee that was opposed to the regime.

Six months after the soup incident Jamal Khan gave a speech at the temple of the holy Abdoldawood that was of crucial importance. The speech had been planned for a special place and a special day, when thousands of pilgrims would be coming to the temple to celebrate the birth of the holy messiah Mahdi. Rumours began circulating that Jamal Khan was going to give an important address. This was undoubtedly the best place to stage such an event before a large crowd, since the inner courtyard of the shrine was off-limits to the police. According to tradition everyone within the walls of the shrine was safe – even criminals.

The six confederates had set up a podium for Jamal Khan inside the shrine of Abdoldawood. Those who had heard the rumour tried to stand as close to the podium as they could. The crowd waited impatiently for his arrival. Suddenly there was a flurry of movement. Wearing a green scarf Jamal Khan climbed onto the podium.

A green scarf was only worn by descendants of the Prophet Muhammad. It was the first time Jamal Khan had ever appeared in public wearing it. As soon as the people saw the green scarf they began shouting, '*Salalah ala Muhammad wa ale Muhammad*. Hail Muhammad and his descendants.' The tension mounted. There wasn't a single empty spot in the whole vast courtyard.

'Countrymen!' began Jamal Khan, speaking into a megaphone. 'We have come here today to commemorate the birth of Mahdi the messiah. One day the saviour will come to deliver the world from its misery. But fellow believers, we insult him if we ourselves do nothing, if we just sit back passively and wait for the saviour to come.

'Countrymen! We have rights. Men have rights, women have rights and children have rights.

'People of Persia! It is your children's God-given right to learn to read and write. The rulers of this country have denied us these rights. They treat us all like beasts.

'People of Persia! I am in contact with resistance groups in neighbouring countries. Right now England is in the south of our country, searching for crude oil day and night. There are probably immense oil fields in our southern province, a fact that the British want to keep secret.

'People of Persia, you may not know it, but crude oil is just as valuable as pure gold. It is the fuel that is used to keep the wheels of factory machines in motion. England has bribed the shah and the princes. Those nearest the shah are filling their pockets. They're richer than ever, while thousands upon thousands of parents in this country aren't even able to buy shoes for their children.'

Because he was standing on a raised platform Jamal Khan could see a group of armed men gather just beyond the gates of the shrine. He knew they had come for him and were guarding all the exits to keep him from escaping. But he also knew that they didn't dare come inside.

'People of Persia! You have the right to bathhouses and hospitals. Not everyone can make a living from his land or his animals. You have the right to work. The only problem is that we have no industry in this country. Look around you. Here in this shrine there are hundreds of beggars, blind people, paralysed children and people who are aged and sick. We think it's all a normal part of life, but let me tell you it doesn't have to be this way. They can be healthy. They're supposed to be healthy, just like the princes, just like the rich. People of Persia! The rulers of this land don't think about you. They think only of themselves. Countrymen! Wake up!'

He saw a policeman with a gun in his hand climb up the wall and hide behind the façade of the gate. He brought his speech to a close.

'People of Persia! I must hurry. But there's one more important announcement I want to make. Let me bring your attention to an unmarked grave,' he shouted, pointing to a spot next to the podium. 'That is where the vizier Mirza Kabir lies buried, killed by the shah. We have had a tombstone made, and later we want to—'

He was unable to complete his sentence. Shots were fired, and one bullet struck a pole that was holding up the podium. The police entered the shrine. More shots were fired. People fled. Jamal Khan tried to escape by the back of the podium, but three officers blocked his way. One of them hit him on the shoulder with a truncheon, causing him to stumble and fall. The men bound his hands behind his back, using his green scarf. They pulled him to his feet and pushed him to the gates of the shrine. Then the people turned on the police, refusing to tolerate their presence in the temple. Jamal Khan's five comrades took advantage of the turmoil and began pounding the police with sticks, thereby allowing Jamal Khan to escape and disappear into the crowd.

A group of armed officers forced their way into the shrine and began beating everyone with their rifle butts. Women screamed, children cried and the elderly were trampled underfoot, but the stronger pilgrims took their lives in their hands, grabbed the guns from the hands of the police and kicked them out through the gates of the shrine.

The pilgrims were furious at the officers who had entered the shrine and had even fired shots there. With this misbehaviour they had violated a centuries-old tradition, thereby dishonouring the holy Abdoldawood. The cry 'Allah-o-akbar!' was released from thousands of throats.

After a while peace and quiet returned to the temple. The pilgrims stood in a circle round the grave of the murdered vizier while an undertaker's man recited from the Quran. The comrades of Jamal Khan solemnly placed a tombstone on the grave bearing the vizier's name: 'Here lies buried Mirza Kabir, vizier of great skill.'

44. The Leader

After the episode in the temple all suspicious meetings were closely monitored by special plain-clothes policemen to prevent more unwanted speakers from addressing the public. But since that day it was a long time before any other noteworthy incidents had took place.

The regime's opponents kept their heads down and seemed to have no intention of regrouping, at least not yet. Apparently they had grasped the fact that the shah would be merciless in his response if they were to disturb the peace again.

Jamal Khan and his comrades understood that they could no longer stir up the masses by means of hit-and-run operations. Campaigns that led to violence tended to frighten people, and frightened people lost all interest in the activists' ideas. When Jamal Khan told them their children had the right to a pair of shoes, they didn't understand what that had to do with the shah.

He talked about oil reserves in the nation's soil, but they didn't see what was so important about oil reserves.

He talked about the need for children to have schools, but they were far from convinced that reading and writing were of any use to their offspring.

These were not the kinds of subjects that would win the allegiance of the man in the street. The shah, after all, was regarded as the shadow of God on earth. Jamal Khan and his comrades knew it would be a mistake to borrow and adapt the tactics of the resistance leaders in Moscow or other countries. They would have to develop their own strategy, one that was in line with a recognised Persian tradition. And they would have to end their perilous and exhausting travels and concentrate on Tehran.

During one of their meetings Mirza Reza Kermani came up with a suggestion. Usually he was a man of few words, but whenever he did speak everyone listened.

'I'm not sure, but I think I'm close to a solution.'

'Let's have it,' said Jamal Khan.

'I don't think we're ever going to be in a position to convince the masses. We're not the obvious people to lead them. They don't know us and they don't believe us. What they need is their own leader, someone from their own ranks, a popular leader.'

'But that's just the problem. There is no such person.'

'There are plenty of them,' answered Mirza Reza.

'Who?' asked Talebof.

'The ayatollahs!' cried Mirza Reza. 'Look, in Russia the leaders of the resistance have put all their hope in the power of the industrial workers. But we have no industry, let alone workers. We have the bazaar merchants and the enormous mass of illiterate unemployed. The people obey the ayatollahs. What we need is a powerful ayatollah.'

Everyone was dumbstruck by this insight.

'You forget that the ayatollahs constitute the most conservative force in the country,' said Mostashar Aldoleh. 'The world is totally foreign to them. They have no interest in technology, and the only cities they know anything about are Mecca, where God's house is; Medina, where the Prophet Muhammad is buried; Najaf, where Ali was killed; and Karbala, where the holy Hussein was beheaded. What we need is science, change. We have to be careful that we don't let the country fall into the hands of such conservative forces.'

'That's true,' said Amir Nezam. 'The ayatollahs are insensitive to things like oil and telegraphy. They've got close ties with the royal house, and they really believe that poverty, begging and illness are a normal part of life – that God has so decreed it.'

'We mustn't lump all the ayatollahs together,' said Mirza Reza. 'Surely there are a few powerful clerics who think about the country as we do and are suffering under so much misery.'

'Name one,' said Jamal Khan, sincerely curious.

'I'm thinking of the ayatollah of the city of Shiraz. Haji Sheikh Ali Akbar Mujtahid-e Shirazi, better known as Mirzaye Shirazi. He's never sold his soul to the powers that be.'

'How old is he?'

'Eighty, eighty-five, I believe. Maybe eighty-seven.'

'Eighty-seven!' said Akhondzadeh. 'Then his days are numbered. He probably can't even walk any more. He won't be of any use to us. We need a leader who's strong and young.'

'A spiritual leader doesn't have to be big and tough. He doesn't even have to get out of bed. With just a couple of words he can stir the shah's heart and put the fear of God into him, if he wants. He's got so much power *because* he's old, and I happen to know him personally,' Mirza Reza explained.

'How well do you know him?' asked Talebof.

'He's an old friend of my departed father, and I had him as a teacher for a while in the Jameh mosque in Shiraz. I can put us in touch with him if you all agree.'

'But what are we going to say to him? What can we ask him to do?'

'We've got to have something concrete if we're going to convince a man like that,' said Amir Nezam. 'I've been thinking. We can't talk to him about our country or our people or about telegraphy. But we can talk about religion. We've got to convince him that Islam is in danger.'

Everyone flinched and the room grew silent. Mirza Reza poured tea.

This suggestion was a turning point in their line of reasoning. What could an elderly ayatollah say to turn the people away from the corrupt regime of the shah? How could they convince him that Islam was in danger? Mirza Reza had made an excellent suggestion, but they had to let the idea sink in.

'Let's stop here. We'll continue this discussion next week,' said Jamal Khan.

When they got together a week later no one had come up with a solid plan of action – until one of them said there were rumours of Persian women regularly spending the night with British engineers.

'That may be it,' said Talebof.

'It won't work,' said Akhondzadeh. 'You don't just launch into a conversation about the whores of Tehran.'

'We can talk to the ayatollah about British domination in the Muslim world,' Maraghei suggested.

'It has to be straightforward, otherwise people won't be able to follow it. British domination means nothing to them,' responded Jamal Khan.

That evening the discussion got bogged down once more. But during their next session Amir Nezam and Talebof devised a plan that, if they set about it properly, would cause an earthquake.

Talebof was the first to speak. He was the man who had studied in Moscow and he spoke excellent Russian. He was often called in to act as a mediator between the Persian merchants and the Russian businessmen, and he maintained close contact with the Russian embassy in Tehran.

'Last year the shah sold all the import and export rights for our tobacco production to the British. He receives a small annual percentage of the income, but the British earn a fortune. The man in charge of our tobacco is a Brit.'

'Everybody knows that. What are you trying to say?' said Akhondzadeh.

'Let me explain,' said Amir Nezam. 'This Brit has sacked all the Persian tobacco inspectors and has hired Indian inspectors to take their place. He has lowered the price of tobacco leaves and driven up the price of British tobacco products. The British and Indian employees treat the tobacco farmers very badly and there's friction between the tobacco merchants in the bazaars and the British company.'

Everyone was listening, but no one understood what he was getting at.

'Don't forget that in our country tobacco is as important as bread. Almost all the men carry a pouch or box of tobacco, and all the women smoke hookahs,' said Amir Nezam. His eyes were ablaze.

'Go on,' said Jamal Khan.

'The British boss of the tobacco company is an amusing man. He's fat, a real *bon vivant*,' said Talebof. 'I have met him personally, and he has done something extraordinary, something that will probably be of help to us.'

'Does it have to do with women?' asked Maraghei.

'No, not that. He's not such a ladies' man. He enjoys eating, smoking and drinking and the good times that go with it,' said Amir Nezam.

'Did he drink alcohol in public?'

'No, not that either,' answered Talebof.

'Don't keep us hanging. Tell us!'

Smiling, Talebof took an envelope from his bag and said, 'Finally God has come to our aid. This piece of evidence may be invaluable to us.'

Talebof showed them a black-and-white photograph of a plump imam sitting on a Persian carpet, smoking a hookah and laughingly blowing out the smoke.

'An imam smoking a hookah. What's wrong with that?' asked Mirza Reza.

'That's no imam,' answered Amir Nezam.

'You're joking!'

'It's a Brit dressed as an imam, with a fake beard, a robe and a turban,' Talebof continued. 'I'm serious. This is that British director of the National Tobacco Company. He put on a turban and a fake beard as a joke. And look, he's sitting on a Persian prayer rug with his shoes on. It's conclusive evidence of a religious and national affront.'

'How did you get this photo?'

'I am not at liberty to say,' said Amir Nezam. 'But I'm assuming that Talebof has his contacts.'

Everyone looked at Talebof, but his lips were sealed.

'This photo gives us something to work with,' said Jamal Khan. 'It may determine our entire course of action.'

45. Mirzaye Shirazi

It was early in the evening and still warm outside. Seated in his study on a beautiful carpet at a low table, and in the light of a lantern shaped like a red tulip, the shah was writing in his diary.

To his left, standing at a suitable distance, a servant was waving long peacock feathers to cool his damp brow. Sitting opposite him was a young chronicler who calmly dried the shah's handwriting with an ink blotter, sentence by sentence. Standing to his right another servant with a jug of fresh albaloo juice was patiently waiting for a gesture from the shah to refill his glass.

Sometimes we forget whether we have already described certain events. There's so much going on that we no longer have a mind to call our own. I don't remember what I wrote about Taj's wedding. It already seems like so long ago. But I'll say a few words about it anyway, for besides the wedding there is even more happy news.

Our Taj was married several months ago. We held a feast in a castle outside Tehran. All the wise men of our tribe were there. Taj was distressed – we saw it in her face. But she is still young, and young girls have their own fanciful dreams.

Taj told me again she does not like Eyn ed-Dowleh. But if she has a child by him, that will change. I have discussed this with her many times, but it doesn't do any good. This time I used harsh words. I told her she must stop all this whimpering, that it wasn't about her but about all of us. After that she listened. I told her that we too would prefer not to be shah, but this is the way it is.

Fortunately everything went as planned. The feast was unforgettable. We have also provided her with a lovely home so later she can live a happy life.

He took a sip of juice, thought for a moment, picked up the pen and continued writing.

Now that Taj's wedding is over a great burden has fallen from our shoulders, and we can focus our attention on other important matters.

Sometimes we do not understand what it is we can and cannot do. When we speak to the British, the Russians feel passed over. When we speak to the Russians, the British ignore us.

Yesterday that bearded Russian came to see us – I no longer remember his name. He looks quite amusing. A full beard like that is very becoming on an official. Maybe we ought to ask our public officials to let their beards grow.

The Russians brought proposals for building us a railway. They're acting out of their own interest, of course, for we have no need of a railway. Our horses and coaches are more than adequate. Why should we start riding around on two iron rails? Our vizier, Sheikh Aqasi, agrees with us. Such changes are not in the national interest. But others have warned that we aren't keeping up with the times, that we're going to weaken our position with respect to our neighbouring countries, India and Turkey. We've been taking more walks lately to think things over, and this is why. God will lead us onto the right path: the path of those on whom He pours his mercy, not the path of those He does not favour, nor those who go astray. We are waiting for a sign from God.

In the meantime, albaloo season has arrived. The albaloos are big and red, and they hang from the branches like rubies. Our mouth waters as we write about them. This year is the year of the mouse. A mouse is filthy, untrustworthy and a bringer of calamity, so we must remain vigilant. Praise God and fear Him. Fortunately we have everything under control, and nothing has happened that we have not been able to handle.

There is more important news, but we hesitate to record it here. The glad tidings concern our daughter Taj Olsultan. Her servant has whispered something to us, a royal communication. We are not going to write about it for fear of bringing bad luck. We will wait patiently.

It is warm here. We're going to stop writing and take a nap before the evening meal.

He waved the servants away and went to lie down, after which the chamberlain came in and pulled a thin blanket over his legs.

Soon Malijak came in with his pop gun over his shoulder. He was covered with crumbs. He had just been with the cook and had eaten a whole plateful of butter biscuits with powdered sugar. The cook was afraid of Malijak. Whenever he went into the kitchen and aimed his gun at the poor man, the cook would give him a whole plate of rich, sweet delicacies. It was the only way to keep him quiet.

'Where were you all day?' asked the shah.

Malijak said something unintelligible, put his gun down, crept up to the shah on his hands and knees, lay down beside him and shut his eyes. The shah stroked his head and shoulders and said with a yawn, 'You stink, Malijak. You ought to let them wash you. Don't be so afraid of the water. You're not a child any more. You're almost a man.'

Carelessly he gave Malijak a little nudge, and as he did so he laid his hand on Malijak's jacket. He thought he could feel a piece of paper. He felt again and sure enough it was a little roll of paper.

'What do you have in your pocket?' he asked. He pulled the paper out of Malijak's jacket and said sharply, 'What is this? How did you get it?'

The shah unrolled the paper, glanced at it and shouted angrily, 'Who gave you this? Who put this in your jacket?'

Malijak, who couldn't bear it when anyone raised their voice, looked at the shah with fear in his crossed eyes. The shah pushed Malijak away, at which the boy burst into tears and crept behind the curtain. The shah was trembling with rage. Someone had dared to tuck a pamphlet into Malijak's jacket. The pamphlet called on the people to rise up in revolt against the shah and the British.

He opened the window to call the head of the guards but realised it would be pointless to do so. There were so many people living in the palace, and so many who came to the palace every day, that no one would ever find out who had smuggled the pamphlet in. He would have to control himself and pretend nothing had happened.

It was dark outside and a slight breeze was blowing. He told the chamberlain he would partake of his evening meal out in the courtyard next to the pond. Instinctively he inspected his cannon, which stood in the middle of the courtyard. He strolled to the gate and made sure he was clearly visible to the guards. After that he looked at the horses through the little stable window, walked back to the pond, washed his hands and face, took off his hat and ran his wet fingers through his hair.

The big couch had been made ready for his dinner. But the shah wasn't hungry. He ate a few spoonfuls of each dish and pushed the tray aside. The servants tidied everything up and brought him a hookah along with a tea set and a plate of sweets.

Malijak plucked up his courage and moved cautiously towards the couch. The shah tossed him a sugar cube. With the sugar cube in his mouth he crept up to the shah and laid his head on his lap.

It was a clear night. The moon was shining, the frogs were croaking in the gardens and the bats skimmed over the courtyard.

'A beautiful night,' said the shah, and he took a draw on the hookah. He patted Malijak and blew smoke into the air, which helped calm him down.

The cats began making a racket, and for a moment the shah thought of Sharmin. Raising his eyes he suddenly saw a whole stack of pamphlets flutter down from the roof. The shah pushed Malijak off his lap, turned towards the roof and roared, 'Seize him!'

The head of the guards, who didn't know whom to seize, took a couple of his men and hurried to the roof, but no one was there.

That same evening, and in the same moonlight, Jamal Khan and Mirza Reza rode to the city of Shiraz to meet the aged Ayatollah Shirazi. The British had used money and gifts to purchase the allegiance of the ayatollahs of all the major cities, but Ayatollah Shirazi was too old to be interested in politics any more. So the British had passed him over. Ayatollah Shirazi was seen as an independent spirit, and his authority was acknowledged throughout the country.

Shiraz lay a thousand kilometres south of Tehran. It had once been the nation's capital, and the old Persian kings had built imposing castles and mosques there. The city's bazaar had always played an influential role in the country's various social movements.

Jamal Khan and Mirza Reza, disguised as merchants, entered Shiraz with a caravan and spent the first night in a caravanserai. They awoke well rested the next morning, and as evening approached they went to the city's Jameh mosque, where the aged ayatollah himself led prayers every Tuesday.

Tuesday prayers were less well attended than Friday prayers, and the congregation consisted mostly of elderly people. The old ayatollah took his time and the elderly considered it an honour to be in attendance when he led prayers.

The two men waited for the ayatollah at the door of the mosque. He arrived on an old donkey led by a group of young imams. The small, scrawny cleric with his long grey beard got off his donkey and continued walking with the help of a stick. As soon as he entered the mosque the old men stood up and shouted, '*Salawat*!'

Jamal Khan and Mirza Reza joined them and sat down on the floor.

In the past the ayatollah would climb up to the pulpit to give a talk, but he no longer had the strength for such an exertion. When he was finished he would meet with the representatives of the bazaar or the city officials who had something to discuss with him.

Mirza Reza shot forward, kissed the ayatollah's hand,

and said, 'I am Mirza Reza, your disciple and the son of the late Ayatollah Kermani.'

Shirazi smiled and said, 'God be praised. You look just like your father, like an apple sliced down the middle. Your father was a great cleric.'

'Thank you. I am here with a friend. We have come from Tehran to discuss an important matter with you. The subject is of concern to both the nation and to Islam. We would like to have a private conversation with you, if you will allow it.'

'If it is an important matter come to my home tomorrow afternoon before afternoon prayer,' said the ayatollah.

The next day Jamal Khan and Mirza Reza went to his home, a simple Persian house with a pool in the middle of the courtyard and an old weeping willow that cast a shadow over a nearby bench.

The ayatollah's servant led them to the library, where the ayatollah, seated on a carpet, was waiting for them. They took off their shoes and sat down on the floor beside him. The servant brought each of them a glass of tea and then withdrew.

The delicious fragrance of the tea and the sweet taste of the sugar cubes eased the gravity of the meeting. Shirazi took a sip of tea and glanced at Jamal Khan, who was sitting closest to him.

Mirza Reza was first to speak. He introduced Jamal Khan and gave a brief summary of his travels in many countries and of the fame he enjoyed among the intellectuals of India and the Middle East.

Then Jamal Khan took over. 'Ayatollah,' he said, 'as you are probably aware, the living conditions in other countries are much better than they are here, where almost everyone is weighed down by the cares of a hard life. God will not allow Muslims to live such a merciless existence. We want to speak with you today about Islam and commerce.

'The foreign powers, especially Great Britain, have our country and our religion in a stranglehold. Our simple merchants are going broke, one by one. Even the fabrics our women use for their veils are imported from England.'

The ayatollah listened, but he didn't understand what they were driving at. Jamal Khan was about to enlarge on the oil reserves and the massive presence of the British in the south, but he was afraid the aged cleric would be unable to follow him and would fall asleep. So he started in on the telegraph system, since the cables ran past the ayatollah's own home and continued to the British telegraph office in the centre of the city.

'Ayatollah, you probably know that the British have run some of their cables right through our houses and mosques to make it easier for them to steal from our neighbour India. In India mass demonstrations against the British are being held as we speak.'

The ayatollah straightened his back and looked out the window. A telegraph cable was hanging right over the wall of his home. He put a sugar cube in his mouth and took a sip of tea.

'The British are also hard at work plundering our country. England has already taken the Shiraz bazaar. I don't mean to startle you, but the British have even forced their way into the home of the ayatollah.'

Much alarmed, the ayatollah put down his glass of tea and stared gravely at Jamal Khan.

'These fragrant sugar cubes are not made from our own crops. They come from Sheffield, England. England has enriched no one but the shah, his relatives and a whole lot of politicians. The rest of the population are left in poverty and suffer from diseases that could be prevented.

Who is going to show us the way out of this dreadful situation?'

Ayatollah Shirazi sat staring at them. 'But what can I do for you?'

Jamal Khan nodded to Mirza Reza, who took his turn to speak. 'The people of this land are like a flock of sheep that have lost their way. They need a shepherd with a staff to drive them back together.'

'Exactly,' said Jamal Khan. 'We need a strong leader.'

'We thought of you. We need you, Ayatollah,' said Mirza Reza.

The ayatollah looked at the two men. He was speechless. He had been prepared for anything they might have said, except when they began talking about cables and sugar cubes.

In need of fresh air he picked up his walking stick and left the room. The servant accompanied him. When they reached the pool the ayatollah leaned on the servant's shoulder and dipped his bare right foot into the water. Then he sat down on the wooden bench in the shade of the old weeping willow. After a hookah was brought to him he invited his guests to join him outside. Jamal Khan and Mirza Reza took their places on the bench next to the ayatollah.

'I don't know what you expect from me, but there's nothing I can do about telegraph poles and sugar cubes,' said the ayatollah modestly.

'Let your voice be heard,' said Jamal Khan.

'But I'm an old man with one foot in the grave. I no longer understand the ways of the world.'

'We've brought something with us that you can use as a weapon,' said Mirza Reza.

The ayatollah looked at the faces of the two men as if he were seeing them for the first time.

'The British control the rights of import, export and production of all the major products in the country,' said Jamal Khan. 'Take tobacco. We have no say over the production of our own tobacco, which is used every day by thousands upon thousands of our countrymen. The tobacco dealers and the farmers on the tobacco plantations are having a hard time of it, and many have no money left. The tobacco that the ayatollah has in his hookah right now is a British product. Anyone who buys tobacco in this country is depositing his money directly into the cash box of the British tobacco company. Ayatollah! We need a powerful leader to cry out, "Down with British tobacco!"'

The ayatollah put down his hookah. It was as if he had touched something unclean, and he inadvertently wiped his hands on the carpet. 'These kinds of things are complex,' he said softly. 'We can shout all we want, but it changes nothing. The only thing I can lean on in this world is my walking stick, and I can't do any damage to England with that.'

'Ayatollah, may I show you something?' asked Jamal Khan. The aged ayatollah looked with suspicion at the two persistent men who had shaken his daily rhythm so profoundly.

Jamal Khan took from his bag the photograph of the British director of the National Tobacco Company and handed it to him.

Shirazi held the photo at a distance, but he saw nothing unusual. It was just a photo of a fat imam smoking a hookah in a somewhat comical way.

'Gentlemen, my eyes aren't what they used to be. All I see is an imam, or am I mistaken?'

'You're not mistaken,' said Jamal Khan. 'But the man in the photo is no imam. He's a Brit in a turban who has put on the robes of an imam and pasted a fake beard on his face. This is the British director of the tobacco company.'

The face of the aged ayatollah became instantly ashen. He reached for a sugar cube but pulled back his hand, picked up his glass and took a draught of bitter tea.

46. The Letter

Every Monday afternoon the shah and Sheikh Aqasi sat down to discuss important current affairs. This time, after dealing with dossiers and signing documents, the sheikh pulled a sealed letter from his bag.

'Who is this letter from?' asked the shah.

'From Ayatollah Mirzaye Shirazi.'

'Who is Mirzaye Shirazi?'

'The ayatollah of Shiraz,' answered Sheikh Aqasi.

'What does he want from us?'

'He has also written a letter to me, a letter written in very crude language. I was torn as to whether I should give it to you or not, but I think Your Majesty ought to be kept informed.'

'Read it,' said the shah, and he handed the letter back.

'If it's all the same to Your Majesty I would prefer not to. I suspect the contents are rather uncouth,' said the sheikh cautiously.

'Read it!' repeated the shah, and he leaned back in his chair.

The vizier broke the wax seal.

Besmellah ar-Rahman ar-Rahim,
In the name of Allah the Compassionate and the Merciful.
To the king of the country.
We have already written a long letter to the

vizier dealing with a few matters of national interest, of which this is a summary. The shah has placed the fate of his subjects in the hands of the British.

It is a scandal to Muslims that a foreign power is being permitted to encroach so deeply into their daily lives.

Out of respect for Islam and in the interest of the homeland, we demand that the shah relieve the British of the tobacco trade and return it to his own subjects.

God be with you. Awaiting your reply.

Wassalam

Mirzaye Shirazi

With this brief but severe letter the ayatollah was giving the shah an ultimatum. The shah was furious, but he controlled himself and said, 'This man is old and senile, I presume. There is no reason to respond to his letter in writing. I shall send a messenger to him with a firm answer.'

'I beg Your Majesty to be patient. This cleric is widely respected. First we need to find out why he has suddenly felt the need to take pen in hand. It is a sign that the dissatisfaction among the tobacco merchants of the bazaars is getting out of control. We have to know more before we take action.'

The shah ignored the vizier's advice. 'The tobacco merchants can come and kiss our boots. We have arranged for them to get tobacco that is fully cut and ready for use. What more do they want? We've made it easier for them. The imams don't understand such things. They have to learn that they can't interfere with business. This ayatollah must be put in his place.'

He tore up the letter and added, 'We're going to teach

him a lesson! If we don't, more ayatollahs will start showing up with new demands!'

With the dust of the road still fresh on his face and shoulders, the shah's messenger arrived at the home of the ayatollah a few days later. The servant let him in and offered him tea and something to eat, but the messenger refused and said he wanted to discharge his duty first.

Shirazi was in the library, sitting on the floor at his writing table. The messenger greeted him, bowed his head and took off his shoes.

The appearance of the ayatollah surprised him. He had expected a sturdy, powerfully built man who could stand up to the shah's threats, but when he saw this fragile elder sitting on a threadbare Persian rug, it drained his hard-hitting message of all its strength. He had been on the road for several days and nights, riding straight through the country to put this man in his place.

The ayatollah bade him sit beside him. The messenger knelt at his table and said, 'I have a message for you from the shah.'

'You may give it to me,' said the ayatollah, extending his hand.

Hesitating, the messenger said, 'I'm sorry, but I have no letter for you. I have been told to whisper the message in your ear.'

The ayatollah understood immediately that this was an unusual message. 'You don't need to whisper. Just tell me.'

The messenger glanced towards the door with some uncertainty. He suspected that the servant was standing behind it.

'Don't worry. No one will hear you,' said the ayatollah.

'The shah brings you the following message: "Do not

interfere in royal matters, or I will pay you a visit with a cushion in my hands."'

With bowed head the messenger waited for the ayatollah to respond.

'Was that all?' asked Shirazi calmly.

'Yes, that was all.'

'I thank you for the trouble you have taken. Please have something to eat and drink. Take your time and get some rest.'

Time passed, and the shah was not at all certain what effect his threat had had on the ayatollah. He took it for granted that his message had been clearly understood and that he would hear no more from the cleric.

In the meantime he issued arrest warrants for anyone suspected of having had anything to do with the unrest in Tehran. He slowly began to believe that he had actually torn out the protest by the roots.

Jamal Khan, Mirza Reza Kermani and Amir Nezam remained in Shiraz, using it as the base from which to organise the resistance.

For all the shah knew his hard line had worked, but suddenly he started receiving reports that all the tobacco merchants of Shiraz were refusing to do business with the British tobacco company or to pay their overdue bills. The head of the Shiraz police was given a direct order by the shah to come down hard on the defaulters.

The shah underestimated the merchants' protest. The British, however, took it seriously right from the start. They were afraid the troubles in Shiraz would spread to the bazaars of other cities, and that the merchants would jeopardise the import of British sugar cubes, tea, textiles and other products. Almost immediately the British ambassador came knocking on the door of the palace, advising the shah to come to an agreement with the merchants of Shiraz. The shah asked for time to reflect.

Sheikh Aqasi's religious background made it difficult for him to provide the shah with the right kind of advice. And now that the resistance movement had taken on a religious tone he was becoming even more stricken by doubt. He often simply adopted Mahdolia's opinion.

The shah also regularly conferred with his son-in-law Eyn ed-Dowleh, gradually involving him – as the husband of his daughter Taj – in the governing of the country. But in this situation he needed someone who could untangle thorny problems, someone with experience. He turned to his mother.

Mahdolia was resolute: 'Ignore the advice of the British ambassador and increase the pressure on the merchants.'

Armed guards burst into the bazaar and emptied the tills of the tobacco merchants in order to pay their debts to the British company. One leading merchant, acting on behalf of his fellows, tried to stop the officers, but he was so badly beaten that he fell to the ground and broke his shoulder.

The humiliated merchants turned to the aged ayatollah, who tried to lift up their spirits. Taking up his walking stick, and followed by all the merchants of the bazaar, he went to the home of the wounded man. Upon leaving the house after the visit he urged the nervous merchants to calm down and then announced, 'The bazaar of Shiraz is closing its shops in protest!'

The merchants acted without a moment's hesitation.

In the middle of the night Amir Nezam climbed onto the roof of the bazaar and hung a large banner across the front of the gate. By the next morning a crowd had gathered and were pointing to the text on the banner. Most of these people were illiterate and they asked each other what the banner said. When they finally found out, it sounded like a cryptic message: 'The Shiraz bazaar no longer sells British tobacco. The merchants of Shiraz demand a national telegraph network for the advancement of trade.'

No one knew who had hung the big banner above the gate. It hadn't even occurred to most of the shopkeepers that the bazaar could use the telegraph service for its own purposes. This gave the protest a totally different twist.

The chief of police had the banner pulled down. He also ordered the merchants to open their shops. If they refused, the officers would no longer guarantee the shops' safety. But the order fell on deaf ears. That night the chief of police released dozens of thieves and bandits from prison and sent them to the bazaar to plunder the shops. They forced the doors, took whatever they could carry and threw the rest into the street.

The next day the merchants gathered in front of the ayatollah's home to hear his decision. Shirazi sent a courier to the merchants of the Tehran bazaar, calling on them to shut their shops in solidarity with Shiraz. The merchants of Tehran complied, after which the shah sent in bandits to ransack the Tehran bazaar, just as they had done in Shiraz.

The very thing that England feared was now happening. The protest quickly spread across the entire country. Even ordinary people lent their support. In the meantime the ayatollahs of all the major cities had been sent prints of the photograph of the British director in imam garb. Their verdict was unanimous: Islam was in danger. A collective slogan was chosen: 'England! Hands off our tobacco!'

The shah refused to consent to this demand and, egged on by his mother, he increased the level of violence. But the people only became more resolute. For the first time in history they had the chance to resist the reigning rulers.

The merchants gathered at the ayatollah's house. They could only keep their shops closed for a short time or the public mood would turn against them.

The shah had run out of patience. He ordered that the merchants be driven out of the ayatollah's home and that the aged ayatollah be removed to a secret address.

The police had not counted on the ferocity of the merchants' resistance. Fearing for their own lives the officers opened fire. One person was killed. The people in the courtyard attacked the police, who began shooting at random. The inhabitants in the surrounding streets were awakened and stormed out of their houses, heading for the home of Ayatollah Shirazi. Hundreds of people filled the streets and stood on the roofs, so the police were closed in on all sides.

Shirazi then emerged from the library, accompanied by Jamal Khan and Amir Nezam. Amir Nezam set the ayatollah's reading table in front of him. Leaning on the shoulder of Jamal Khan the ayatollah heaved himself onto the table with difficulty. He raised his walking stick and a deathly silence fell. 'I am issuing a fatwa. From this moment on tobacco is prohibited. No one in the country is to smoke any more tobacco. Anyone here who fails to comply is declaring war on God.'

A fatwa was always used as a form of legal advice. When the Islamic judges were unable to pass judgement on a particular matter they would seek the advice of an ayatollah, who would offer them instructions. These matters always had to do with Muslims and their way of life, involving such questions as eating pork, drinking alcohol and Muslim women associating with non-believers. But this was the first time a fatwa with political overtones had been issued. This fatwa was momentous and sensitive because it was aimed at the shah and the greatest power in the world, England. The old ayatollah had no way of knowing what the consequences of his fatwa would be over the next hundred years, or how his words would alter relations in the Middle East.

Ayatollah Mirzaye Shirazi had spoken, and when he was done he went back to his room. His words would prove more powerful than a thousand cannons. For one long moment it was silent in the courtyard, silent in the alley, silent in the country, silent in the shah's palace and silent in London.

47. The Hookahs

No one could have foreseen the impact of the events in Shiraz. The fact that England was under fire was a godsend for Russia. And because it was becoming obvious that the shah was losing his self-confidence and control, the Russian ambassador in Tehran submitted the definitive contract for the Russian railway to the shah for his signature.

The shah hadn't fully grasped what the fatwa actually meant, let alone that anyone knew how to put it into practice.

Ayatollah Shirazi himself was at a loss. One day, while taking his daily walk, he paused for a rest and looked behind him. There he saw his hookah lying on the bench. Probably the servant had put it there. Shirazi walked back and pushed the hookah over with the point of his walking stick, so it hit the paving stones with a crash and shattered into pieces. The servant witnessed this and took it to be an act of resistance. The report spread like wildfire. Thousands upon thousands of hookahs were thrown into the street and smashed.

In no time at all the country was littered with broken hookahs. Even in front of the British embassy in Tehran there were shards of hookahs lying in protest. To be on the safe side the building caretaker locked the iron gate of the embassy with a heavy chain and the embassy staff withdrew into the residence.

The shah too heard about the hookah actions. At first he thought it was just the work of young mischief-makers, but it appeared that the perpetrators were from all walks of life. What would the ayatollah's next appeal be? Would he dare to set the populace directly against the shah?

At his wits' end, the shah paced through the corridors of the palace. He even went to the second floor, where he seldom ventured. The garments and personal effects of his deceased father and the other kings were kept here. Hanging in this room was a large painting of his father. He knew the painting, which showed his father with his crown and royal robes, gloriously reclining against the throne's gold satin cushions. But only now did he notice that his father was proudly smoking an enormous hookah. It was incomprehensible. Why had he never before seen this remarkable hookah in his father's hand? Only now did he realise that this was not a portrait of the king, but of the hookah.

If the resistance movement's shattering of hookahs were to reach his own palace, there was a chance that even his wives would heed the call of the aged ayatollah. The last thing the shah wanted was unrest among the people closest to him. Every day he sent Malijak into the harem to see whether any hookahs had been destroyed. Malijak always came back with a vague story.

'Did you see the hookahs?' the shah would ask him.

'Yes, the hookahs,' Malijak would say stupidly.

'Were they intact?'

'Intact?' Malijak would ask.

'Were they broken or not?'

'No, not really broken.'

'Are the women smoking their hookahs today?'

'The women? Sure,' Malijak would say.

'Did you see it?'

He would look absently at the shah with his crossed eyes. The shah had the urge to give him a good hiding, but the pathetic spectacle of his little corpulent pet made his anger subside.

The shah could take it no longer. Late in the afternoon, when the women usually got together to smoke their hookahs, he strolled into the harem with Malijak. He greeted the servants in an unusually friendly manner and waited for Khwajeh Bashi, the harem overseer, who was always to be found in his room beside the door. But this time he wasn't there, and his hookah was not where it ought to be, either.

'He's busy. He'll come on his own,' said the shah to Malijak, to reassure himself.

It was oddly quiet. Usually the women chattered with excitement whenever the shah was in the harem, and they fought for his attention. But today there wasn't a woman to be seen. All the hookahs were standing against the wall.

Suddenly one hookah fell from the second floor and shattered nearby in a thousand pieces. Malijak hid behind the shah, who pretended he had seen and heard nothing. If this had happened a month ago the shah would have had the guilty party chopped to bits. But now he knew such a thing was no longer possible. He was sure the women in the harem who hated him were using the fatwa to seek revenge. If he were to punish one of them the rest would complain to the ayatollah and portray the shah as a godless man.

'Khwajeh Bashi!' shouted the shah.

The harem overseer crept out from behind a pile of dirty blankets and bowed awkwardly.

'Call the women! We are going to smoke a hookah,' said the shah.

The servants hastened to prepare the hookahs. Khwajeh

Bashi walked past the women's rooms and called out in an unsteady voice, 'Ladies, the hookahs are ready. His Majesty would like to smoke with you.'

The shah went past the rooms with his hands behind his back. Malijak climbed up the slide, but he didn't slide down. He felt the tension in the air and stayed at the top to keep an eye on his patron.

The women did not appear. The servants who had got the hookahs ready feared for their lives and kept a safe distance from the shah. Khwajeh Bashi went to fetch the shah's chair and set it down next to the fountain. Handing him a hookah, he shouted, 'Ladies, the shah has already started!'

The sound of the bolting of doors was barely audible. The shah inhaled a few times and concentrated on the red and green fish in the fountain. No one was allowed to smoke, according to the fatwa, and whoever did was unclean. The shah had now become unclean, and the women had the right, given to them by God, to ignore him and not to let him touch them.

'Where is everyone?' cried the shah.

The servants shrank into the dark corners. Khwajeh Bashi took cover behind the stack of dirty blankets. Although he was king the shah understood that he was not more powerful than the aged cleric. Even if he were to punish the women more severely than ever, not a single woman would consider touching a hookah or sharing her bed with him.

'I said, where is everyone?' roared the shah.

Malijak climbed down from the slide and approached the shah with hesitation. He took his hand and pulled him towards the door. To everyone's relief the shah let Malijak lead him out.

48. Claiming Sanctuary

The ayatollah's fatwa had brought the country to its senses. You could see hope in everyone's eyes. In Isfahan one of the big tobacco merchants brought his stock to the bazaar square and dramatically set the bales on fire.

The destruction of the hookahs had made everyone conscious of their power. The shah had proved vulnerable, and fear of the country's rulers slowly ebbed away. Merchants in the bazaars of Tehran, Tabriz, Isfahan and Shiraz went en masse to the Jameh mosques in their own cities to 'claim sanctuary'. Claiming sanctuary was a well-known way of going on strike. The demonstrators would take refuge in a place of worship and stay there until their demands were met. As long as they remained in a mosque or shrine they were safe. No one was allowed to trouble them. Even an arrest warrant from the king had no validity. Now large groups of people were entering the various mosques to support the strike.

The people behind the strike kept in contact with Jamal Khan's committee in Tehran. All the supporters made use of the same slogans: 'England! Hands off our tobacco!' and 'Give us a national telegraph network or we pull down the poles and cables!'

Some members of Jamal Khan's group had additional demands. They wanted Persian experts to serve as inspectors at the oil wells. But the others felt it was too early for such a move. Besides, no one had enough expertise to judge the situation properly. For the time being they stuck with attainable demands that people could grasp.

The resistance grew. More and more people came to claim sanctuary with the merchants. The shah pretended to be unimpressed and said that under no circumstances would he cede to the demands of the demonstrators. To do so would jeopardise the deal he had struck with regard to his income. That agreement, and the fixed royal duties being levied on the telegraph and oil-drilling projects, covered the enormous expense of running his palace and his harem and paying for his travels. He didn't want to put his ties with mighty England at risk, especially now that he was feeling threatened at home. In turbulent times like these the British embassy was a more dependable ally than his own ignorant people.

More than ever he was seized by doubt. So he went back to paying regular visits to his old mother, who had helped him before with her powers of discernment. Mahdolia knew her son. She talked to him and roused his flagging spirits: 'These are moments that every king has to endure. Your subjects don't understand what they want from life. It is the shah's job to direct them. Don't forget that Russia is standing right behind you. Your father and I forged a strong bond with them. Don't take a single step backwards, my son, not even when your enemy is closing in on you. The men of our tribe have never feared death.'

His mother never hesitated to remind him of this alliance, but the shah doubted its value. The Russians were not a whit better than the rest. When it came to the crunch they too would think only of themselves. He was determined to endure to the bitter end. He wanted to show England that he was capable of defending their interests. So he gave the heads of all the country's police forces the authority to crush the resistance with violence.

The fatwa issued by the aged ayatollah had not yet had any direct impact on the military. The army had always been unconditionally loyal to the king, and it would take a while for the power of the ayatollah's words to penetrate the thick skin of the armed forces.

In Tehran armed policemen stormed the Jameh mosque and threw the striking merchants out. A few shopkeepers fought back, and one was killed as a result. As the merchants carried the body of their dead colleague to the bazaar mosque on their shoulders, a gang of bandits set fire to the shops. People tried to extinguish the fire with buckets of water to keep the whole bazaar from going up in flames.

News of the arson served as a warning to the other cities. The bazaars were guarded day and night.

In Tehran the head of the police force locked the door of the Jameh mosque and issued an order to arrest anyone found in the vicinity. The merchants continued to claim sanctuary in the small bazaar mosque, however, and countless people gathered on the square of the mosque to protect them.

The police were ruthless. They rode into the crowd, beat them with their long sticks and finally drove them from the square. The merchants were thrown out of their small mosque as well. With such exceptionally harsh measures and violent arrests it became impossible for the merchants to stand firm and united. And although the bazaars were guarded, bandits nevertheless succeeded in sneaking in under cover of night and burning down a shop here, a warehouse or storage area there. The merchants were gripped by fear and doubt. They wondered whether it might not be wiser to open the doors of their shops.

Jamal Khan's committee became aware of their

misgivings and decided to change their tactics. So far now they had followed a policy of passive resistance, but now it was time for a new initiative. It was either that or lose the battle.

After several meetings the decision was made to attack British property all across the country. Tobacco factories and plantations were occupied and the British and Indian employees were sent packing.

England exerted pressure on the shah to provide protection for its people and to safeguard its property and factories. The shah sent in the army to defend the British embassy and to rid the tobacco factories of demonstrators. On the tobacco plantations the farmers showed what they were made of. Armed with nothing but shovels and sticks they attacked the soldiers, and the soldiers opened fire.

The army's brutal response aroused the anger of the populace. Telegraph cables were cut and poles were pulled from the ground and set on fire.

All the Britons in Persia were sent to the southern province, where it was safe. Only the ambassador and his staff remained in the embassy in Tehran in order to be close to the shah and to follow developments as they happened.

In the oil-rich areas several villages sprang up overnight. The British had everything they needed there for the long haul. One look at all the installations, buildings, athletic fields and water facilities made it clear that England was planning on staying in the country for at least a hundred years.

But what the British had feared so long was now about to happen. The shah was incapable of controlling the revolt. At first England had seen his weak power apparatus as an advantage. They were satisfied when the powerful vizier was succeeded by vizier Sheikh Aqasi. But now that their interests were being threatened they began to think differently. In order to secure their position they would have to learn to work together with the country's bazaars. So London instructed its ambassador to speak with both the shah and the leaders of the insurgents. But the shah rejected any form of mediation out of hand.

'We know our subjects better than you do,' he told the British ambassador. 'If we give these ayatollahs free rein, we'll never be rid of them. The businessmen can't keep their shops closed for ever. They'll get tired of striking and start pushing their wares again. Have patience, as we do.'

Jamal Khan and his people reviewed the situation. They saw two possibilities: either increase their attacks on British property in the south or hold a mass march on the palace to put the shah under even more pressure. An attack on the British in the south was not feasible, so the committee decided to turn their attention to two strategic places in Tehran: the British embassy, which they would have to occupy, and the palace of the shah, which they would have to surround.

'The British embassy is out of the question,' said Jamal Khan during their talks. 'They need us and we need them. We have to fight them and at the same time regard them as a partner against the repression of the shah, or we'll lose the battle on both fronts. If we attack the British embassy it will give the shah an excuse to destroy us. I think we have to increase the pressure on the shah and at the same time demand a national telegraph system from the British.'

The plan sounded good, but it was still risky. What if things got out of hand and people began storming the palace? What if they took the shah hostage or, even worse, murdered him? Wouldn't England and Russia take advantage of the chaos and divide the country between themselves? And wouldn't that put an end to the ancient Persian Empire, once and for all? The occupation of the British embassy seemed like the best way forward. It would force both the British and the shah to take further steps.

After a week of interminable discussions Amir Nezam had something surprising to report. 'The British tobacco company is prepared to discuss national tobacco production.'

The embassy had passed on the proposal via a mediator, an old acquaintance of Amir Nezam who met with him regularly in a tea house. As the son of a carpet dealer he had lived in London for a few years. Now he had his own business exporting Persian carpets to England. He was on good terms with the British embassy.

'Friends, we have learned from talks with the mediator that London is not happy with Sheikh Aqasi as vizier. A peaceful, stable Persia would be to their benefit, and they're looking for a way to influence developments. Reading between the lines, I get the feeling that London is prepared to reach a compromise.'

'A compromise about what?' asked Talebof.

'A domestic telegraph network.'

'Were these the mediator's actual words?' asked Jamal Khan with surprise.

'No, not exactly. The ambassador submitted the idea to the shah, but he doesn't want to talk about it just yet. The shah is afraid that if he agrees, he'll lose control of the country.'

Everyone was impressed by this message.

'But what does the mediator want?' asked Mirza Reza.

'Nothing. He just passed it on to me.'

'England seems to be saying they're not happy with the shah and they're looking for a reliable partner,' said Amir.

'England's motives are more complex than we think,'

said Jamal Khan. 'That's why we have to come up with our own strategy and turn the heat up under the shah.'

Amir Nezam wasn't the only one who had picked up these signals. The British were playing a two-handed game. They were afraid that if emergency struck, Russia would support the shah. So they passed a message on to the ayatollah through those who were closest to him: 'England is prepared to give in, but the shah is blocking every option. Your help is needed.'

After Friday prayers the merchants stopped claiming sanctuary and went to the shah's palace, followed by a huge crowd. With one voice they cried, 'Tobacco! Tobacco! Persian tobacco! Telegraph! Telegraph! Telegraph!'

The shah was sitting at his writing desk when a palace guard knocked on the door and said, 'Your Majesty! Your Majesty! Thousands of your subjects are on their way to the palace!'

The shah looked in the mirror and saw himself turn pale.

'What are they shouting?'

'They're shouting anti-British slogans!'

'What kinds of slogans?'

'I don't know, Your Majesty. I just received the report from one of our guards.'

The shah wanted to know whether they were shouting slogans against him as well.

'But what are they shouting?'

'Something about tobacco and telegraphs,' said the man hesitantly.

'Where are they now?'

'They're coming from the bazaar square and they're probably about halfway here.'

'Prepare our cannon,' said the shah. 'Put a row of cannons

on the palace square with the barrels aimed at the demonstrators and warn Eyn ed-Dowleh immediately!'

The shah had appointed Eyn ed-Dowleh military advisor. By giving his son-in-law an important position and responsibility in the army he was securing his allegiance. Eyn ed-Dowleh was brave and trustworthy. The shah hoped that his grandson would inherit those characteristics. Taj Olsultan was almost full term. She was eagerly looking forward to the birth of her baby. As was the shah.

He spoke with Eyn ed-Dowleh in private and ordered him to protect the palace with everything at his disposal.

The crowd had now reached the palace square, but armed guards managed to keep the people at a distance. The head of the guards was waiting impatiently for reinforcements from the army. He had warned the demonstrators that if they took one more step, his men would fire on them with cannons.

When Eyn ed-Dowleh rode onto the palace square with his column of cavalrymen, the head of the guards breathed a sigh of relief. Eyn ed-Dowleh positioned the cavalrymen between the cannons and the crowd. He rode his own great black horse right to the front line. With sword drawn he stood before his troops.

The demonstrators began shouting 'Shah! Shah! Shah!' at the top of their voices. 'Tobacco! Tobacco! Tobacco!'

Eyn ed-Dowleh put his sword away and pulled out his rifle. This awkward threat provoked the masses, who pressed forward.

'Halt or I'll shoot!' shouted Eyn ed-Dowleh menacingly.

No one listened to him.

'Telegraph! Telegraph! Telegraph!' the crowd shouted. 'Shah! Shah! Shah!'

The shah stood on the roof and looked through his

binoculars to see how his son-in-law would deal with this difficult situation.

'Halt!' threatened Eyn ed-Dowleh again.

But no one listened.

'Halt!' he shouted once more, and he shot three times over their heads.

The people were alarmed. They scattered, only to come back together and surround him. Sensing the danger his horse whinnied anxiously and tried to clear a path through the mass of people. The demonstrators blocked his flight and came threateningly close.

'Fire!' shouted Eyn ed-Dowleh, obeying his own command.

The troops behind him opened fire. It was a one-sided battle. The unarmed demonstrators tried to escape down the square's side streets, where new troops flew at them with truncheons. Desperate, the people forced their way into the government buildings on nearby streets and set several departments on fire. No one was in charge. In the chaos everyone did whatever occurred to him. Heavy smoke began to rise, blanketing the palace square in an impenetrable fog. Dead bodies lay everywhere, and the people dragged the wounded to surrounding houses.

This was a development that Jamal Khan and the committee had not counted on. They knew there might be some deaths, but a blind outburst like this had been unexpected. The age-old frustration of an entire people had been expressed in a single day.

The fighting continued all through the evening. Only when it was dark, and the muezzins called the people to evening prayer, did the demonstrators withdraw. The fight had been fought, for now. There was no more shooting or shouting of slogans.

Although it remained relatively calm outside for the

rest of the night, the palace was alive with activity. The shah met with his vizier and advisors, and received repeated visits from the messenger, who was riding back and forth between the palace and his mother.

Another messenger was also riding back and forth in the dark, to and from the British embassy. Behind heavy curtains that kept out even the slightest breeze, the ambassador and his staff were intent on leaving their mark on history. All week long they had been in contact with an ayatollah in Tehran who operated as an envoy for the aged Ayatollah Shirazi.

At the same time the mother of the shah received two visits in her palace from a messenger of the Russian embassy.

The demonstrators had been working deep into the night, barricading the houses and streets around the palace with sandbags. When the sun came up the cavalrymen on the palace square were surprised to find rows of men positioned behind sturdy sandbag bulwarks. They were armed with the rifles they had taken from the soldiers during the previous day's fighting.

The parties stood there, face to face and motionless. They waited until the sun reached its zenith. It was time for afternoon prayers, but the muezzins were silent.

Suddenly there was movement in the crowd. The people were making way for Tabatabai, one of the old ayatollahs of Tehran. It was he who was making decisions on behalf of Shirazi. He had received a special message from the British ambassador the night before and had notified Jamal Khan immediately. Accompanied by seven prominent businessmen from the Tehran bazaar and carrying his walking stick, the ayatollah walked calmly up to the palace, where the shah was waiting for him.

The head of the palace guards received the delegation. The

negotiations continued until late in the afternoon, and all that time everyone patiently waited. When the delegation finally came out the ayatollah waved his walking stick as a sign of victory. A loud cheer rose up from the palace walls. The shah had signed the document spelling out the terms under which the British tobacco company would hand over the tobacco trade to the Persian government.

An agreement had also been reached with the British embassy concerning plans for a domestic telegraph network. British engineers would come to discuss the execution of the plans with the shah. What no one else knew was that the ambassador had also firmly urged the shah to replace Sheikh Aqasi. He was a weak link.

What followed was spectacular. For the first time in Persian history people took to the streets carrying flags, and street musicians could be heard everywhere. The shopkeepers treated everyone to free biscuits and tea, and in all the bazaar squares across the country great pots of food were cooked over fires for the entire population. The festivities lasted a whole week.

49. The Journey

The shah was convinced that Taj would bear him a grandson. He never let on that the thought so preoccupied him, but secretly he had a camel sacrificed at the tomb of the holy Abdoldawood.

Right before Taj was due to give birth the shah dreamed about a young branch growing from an old tree. Suddenly a storm broke and the old tree fell over, but the young branch kept on growing. It grew bigger and bigger. The shah was frightened by the dream. He wanted to ask his dream interpreters about it, but he didn't dare. He kept it to himself and entrusted it to no one but his diary. The birth could happen any minute.

He was standing at the window lost in thought when he saw his son-in-law Eyn ed-Dowleh come riding into the palace grounds. This could mean but one thing: his daughter had given birth to a son. Eyn ed-Dowleh stormed into the hall of mirrors, took the shah's right hand, planted a kiss on it and said, 'God is working for our good.'

It was customary for fathers not to see their daughters until forty days after the birth, but the shah asked for his horse and rode to Taj Olsultan.

According to tradition a wise man of the family was supposed to whisper a short surah from the Quran into the ear of a newborn, but the shah had already forbidden this. He wanted to be the one to whisper the first words into the ear of his grandchild. The shah was received by his daughter's old servant in the residential part of the small castle where Taj had moved after her wedding. It took a while before the midwife finally brought him the child, wrapped in a beautifully worked blanket.

The shah wanted to admire the child, but the baby's face was still covered by a lovely sheer silken cloth, milky white. Before he could see the little boy he had to pay the midwife a *ru-nama*, an admiration present. Smiling, he let a couple of gold coins jingle into her hand. Only now could he pull the little silken cloth away. With a great laugh he gently kissed the tiny hand of the baby, who looked at him with penetrating eyes.

Solemnly the shah took from his coat the collection of poetry written by the medieval poet Hafez. He kissed the cover, closed his eyes, opened the book to a random page, lowered his head to the child's right ear and whispered the melodious poem, which was all about love.

Bolboli barg-e goli dar menqar dasht
Wa andar an barg o nava khush naleh-ha-ye zar dasht.
Goftam-ash, 'dar in wasl in naleh o faryad chist?'
Goft, 'ma-ra jelveh-ye ma'shuq bar in kar dasht.'

After reading the poem he carefully ran his finger over the nose of his grandson and said, 'He looks just like us. He has our nose.' The shah had seen enough.

'Convey our greetings to Taj Olsultan,' he called to the servant when he left. 'Tell her she has made us happy.'

All the way back to the palace he kept seeing the face of his successor.

The shah consulted with people in his inner circle and managed to find a suitable candidate for the position of vizier, someone who was acceptable to both England and to his opponents.

After seeking even more advice and listening to what the wise men of the bazaar had to say, he finally chose Mostovi Almamalek. His mother complained about Sheikh Aqasi having to step aside, but Mostovi Almamalek was from the same tribe as the shah. Mahdolia had no choice but to submit.

At first the shah was going to summon the sheikh and have a long talk with him, but now that he had a grandson he just wanted to get the whole thing over with. During the revolt Sheikh Aqasi had shown that he was incapable of helping the shah in a complex situation. When the demonstrators had surrounded the palace and so many people died, he just sat by and watched, paralysed. The sheikh would have to go.

The shah spoke with the vizier for less than an hour. Then he sent him home and appointed Mostovi Almamalek as the new prime minister, to take effect immediately.

'Whatever the shah decides,' was the response of Sheikh Aqasi, who obeyed the shah without protest. 'I understand Your Majesty completely.'

'But we want you always to be close at hand. Your advice comforts us,' added the shah, so as not to dismiss him too brusquely.

'I served your father, and it will be my honour to continue to serve you as well,' said Sheikh Aqasi, and he bowed.

By letting him go the shah had actually relieved the sheikh of a heavy burden. He had been yearning for the peace and quiet of his prayers, the pleasure of reading old books and meditating in the mountains.

The new vizier was a skilled politician. He had worked as the Minister of Industry and Trade in the cabinet of the murdered Mirza Kabir and had been one of the first young men to be sent to Europe by the old vizier. In Paris he had studied mechanical engineering and obtained his engineering degree.

Mostovi Almamalek picked up where the murdered vizier had left off and continued down the path he had taken. He knew it would be very difficult, since the shah had a hand in everything and would not allow any decision to be made without his approval. The shah's mother and her supporters also tried to influence the new vizier. Mostovi Almamalek was aware of this and thought he had enough experience to resist the shah and his mother. Besides, his family ties with the shah offered him a certain amount of protection.

The shah valued him as a professional politician without a hidden agenda. He felt relaxed listening to Almamalek and gradually granted him more latitude. Deep in his heart the shah actually liked this new vizier because he looked like Mirza Kabir. By working so closely with the old vizier, Almamalek had even adopted some of his gestures and linguistic habits. He wrapped himself in the same long garments and wore the same long beard, but in place of a tall cylindrical hat he copied the headgear of western diplomats.

During one of their discussions Mostovi surprised the shah with a proposal: 'In the interests of the nation it might be wise for His Majesty to travel to Europe, to enable him to see at first hand the far-reaching changes taking place in the West.'

For a moment the shah didn't know how to respond. He rang his little bell and had the chamberlain bring in a tea set and two glasses.

Years before, the former vizier had also broached the subject of a trip across Europe. He had even wanted to take the shah to Russia with him when the shah was still crown prince, but an early and severe frost set in and the journey to Moscow had had to be cancelled. Moreover, the new developments taking place back then were not nearly as visible and impressive as the ones today. With all the recent tension the prospect of such a journey had been set aside for the time being, but now that peace had returned it was a real possibility. This was not just another domestic matter or a personal idea of the vizier and the shah. Europe itself was knocking at the door.

In the past the shah met only with the political representatives of western countries, but now all sorts of foreigners were entering the country, and with greater frequency. These were people who had come in search of threadbare carpets. They went from village to village, showing extraordinary interest in broken bowls and dishes. They packed all this stuff in their trunks and carried it away. Recently a number of them had been found in the mountains, using magnifying glasses to study ancient scenes carved into the rocks.

'What are they looking for?' the shah had asked his son-in-law.

'They're scientists, Your Majesty. They come from Farang [Europe] and they want to record the history of the human race.'

'They can read the history of the human race from our broken bowls?'

'I've spoken to them. They say the great stories of history are hidden away in these small fragments.'

Now the shah understood more than ever why his new vizier would suggest that a trip to Europe was necessary and of great importance. Yet he still hesitated.

'We have given it some thought, but we cannot leave the country unattended,' answered the shah. 'The unrest of the past few years has proven us right.'

'But we really have entered a more peaceful phase.'

'We do not doubt the value of such a journey, but the country has begun charting a new course. We are indispensable. And don't forget that God has given us an heir. We want to see the child grow up and become a man.'

'Preparations for such a journey would take at least a year. That will give the shah plenty of time to enjoy his grandson. The journey itself will last several months at the most. It will be a difficult journey and will be physically demanding. But fortunately the shah is in good health. It would be a mistake for the shah to postpone the journey any longer. On behalf of the nation I beg the shah to reconsider.'

With this serious request the new vizier was letting the shah know that the time was ripe.

'We shall think it over,' answered the shah.

Later, in conversation with his mother, she said, 'I trust Mostovi Almamalek. He is right. But I wonder whether such a journey is wise at the present moment. What does the shah think?'

'We are not opposed to a journey to Europe to visit other kings. Persian kings have always conquered other countries first before taking a deeper interest in them. We would be the first Persian king to break this pattern. Our fear is that as soon as we cross the border, England will put our crown on the head of some insurgent. We would no longer be able to return home and would become a Wandering Jew, a nomad, banished from hearth and home.'

'Now you have an heir. I don't know whether I should encourage you to make this trip or discourage you. We can lay it before the wise men of the tribe. But one thing should be clear to you: if you go travelling, I will guard your throne like an old lioness.'

To whet the shah's appetite Mostovi contacted the Russian, British and French ambassadors and asked them if they had catalogues or photo albums with pictures of their factories and scenes from everyday life.

It wasn't long before three large books compiled especially for this purpose were sent from the embassies. They were impressive albums that were decorated with the colours of the countries' flags and portraits of their heads of state. They were full of images of trains and their passengers, newspapers, lamps, lamp posts, cafés, railways, harbours, squares, fountains, bridges, concert halls, theatre performances and portraits of writers, poets, women, wine and food.

Finally Mostovi got the shah to pen the following words and to seal them with his own ring:

Besmellah.
For us this journey is as inevitable as birth and death. This is something we must experience, which is why we are submitting to it. Our vizier may make the necessary preparations.

Just as the vizier was about to take the letter in his hands, the shah insisted on one condition: 'This is to remain between the two of us. No one is to know that we want to go on such a journey.'

'That will make the preparations difficult. And how are we to explain the shah's long absence?' asked the vizier.

'Once we are gone you can announce that we are going to Karbala to visit the grave of the holy Hussein. If necessary we will reveal where we really were later on. We are doing this for the nation, you understand. Agreed?'

'Agreed!' said Mostovi. The shah did not notice his vizier's slight hesitation.

50. The Light

During the entire length of Ayatollah Shirazi's ban on tobacco the women of the harem gave the shah the cold shoulder because he had smoked despite the fatwa. Now the shah was getting even by refusing to share his bed with them. He decided to hold a *sabuhi*.

Sabuhi was a clever contrivance, a real feast for the Persian kings. They too had been forbidden from drinking alcohol ever since Islam had become the country's official religion. But the kings found it impossible to stay away from wine. They drank nothing but the fruit of the vine produced in the city of Shiraz.

The wine of Shiraz was the wine of paradise, and you had to have read the poetry of the great medieval Persian masters to understand what that meant. As Hafez wrote:

> Make haste, O steward, and gladden my cup with
> wine!
> O minstrel, sing my fate and make it kind.
> My lover's face doth sparkle in my cup.
> The traveller on the road to this café
> Would be a fool to seek another way.

For a king, the shadow of God on earth, drinking wine in public was simply not done. But if the great master had been so warmly inclined towards wine, why should the kings begrudge themselves that pleasure? Life was short and, like the great poet Hafez, they understood that wine and recollections of past lovers were all that remained. So they devised an exception that would allow them to withdraw for a time and to abandon themselves completely to wine and love.

After the ritual they took a bath, asked for God's forgiveness and returned to normal life, where war and treachery prevailed.

The shah had hired an experienced lady for the sabuhi who would provide the women for this occasion. She went to the shah's country house and brought seven women with her. When the shah arrived he sat down among the cushions that had been elegantly arranged for him. Female musicians played their instruments while female dancers moved gracefully to a melancholy song sung by a young female singer who sat behind a transparent green curtain:

Ah, amadi azizam, azizam, azizam
Wa man in-ja montazer azizam, azizam, azizam
You finally came, O my sweetheart, sweetheart,
    sweetheart.
And I waited here so long for you, O my
    sweetheart, sweetheart, sweetheart.
Savage lions stood between us, *azizam, azizam,*
    azizam
And towering mountains, *azizam, azizam, azizam.*

The seven scantily clad women shyly entered carrying wine and glasses. And thus the shah began a week in which he 'celebrated life', as he himself put it. Because he had not slept with his wives for a long time his experience of this sabuhi was very intense.

After returning to the palace the shah received a message from the lady who had brought the women to the sabuhi. She had met an extraordinary young woman. The shah, who was not taken by the thought of returning to his country house, asked her what was so special about this girl.

'She comes from the Russian state of Azerbaijan. She has a Russian mother and an Azari father. The shah can speak either Russian or Azari with her. I have seen many young women in my time, but this girl is unique. I can bring her to the palace.'

The shah was curious, but he didn't want to receive her in the palace. Only when the chamberlain assured him that no one would find out did he finally give in.

'Does the girl know that you are introducing her to the shah?' the chamberlain asked the lady.

'Yes, of course. Otherwise she never would have agreed to come. She is a rare breed, a little jewel. She may look a bit timid, but that is certainly not the case.'

That evening the chamberlain led the girl, disguised as a young man in a hat, up to the door of the hall of mirrors and encouraged her to continue on alone. With some reluctance she went in. She was startled to see the shah standing in the middle of the room in his royal robes. She greeted him softly in Persian: 'Salam!'

The shah studied her appearance, and from his face it was obvious that he had expected something else.

'Take that hat off,' he said with indifference, in Russian.

Timidly the girl took off her hat, letting her long blonde locks tumble over her shoulders.

The shah smiled. 'How beautiful you are. Where did you get that head of golden hair?' he asked enthusiastically.

'From my mother.'

She was younger than the shah had expected, and her very youth made him feel his own age. He turned around and said, 'Please, make yourself at home.'

The girl took off her shoes and walked uncertainly to the mirror, placed her leather satchel on the old royal chair, took off her men's clothing, put on a dress, combed her hair in the mirror, applied some perfume from a small bottle and said softly, 'Now I am myself again.'

The shah turned and stared at her, speechless. There was an air of inexperience and innocence about her that made him feel uncomfortable. She was completely unlike any of the women with whom he occasionally spent time in his country house. She was vulnerable, like a girl from a fairy tale. For a moment he didn't know what to do with her.

'Would we like something to drink, perhaps?' asked the shah awkwardly, pointing to the bottles of juice on the table.

The girl walked to the table, studied the bottles, sniffed the juice and said, 'I like white grape juice. Shall I pour you a glass as well?'

The shah was surprised by this unusual question. Up until now no woman had ever asked him so casually if he would like something to drink.

'No, no. Well, actually, yes. Why not?' he answered.

The girl elegantly poured a small amount of white grape juice into a glass for the shah and handed it to him. Only then did she pour half a glass for herself, drinking it down in a single draught.

'Excuse me. I was thirsty.'

'No, no. No need to apologise,' said the shah.

'It was so exciting coming here to meet you, it made my throat dry,' said the girl.

The shah found her explanation amusing, but it was difficult to carry on a conversation with her. 'There's also food if you're hungry,' he said.

'No, not that. Not now. Maybe later. I've got to catch my breath.'

Now what should he say? He couldn't just take her to

his bedroom. That idea didn't even occur to him. He found her presence delightful, and he simply wanted to enjoy it.

'We were recently given some photo albums as gifts,' the shah remarked, 'but we haven't looked at them yet. If you like we could do that together.'

'What kinds of photographs are they?'

'They aren't photographs but prints. They're about light and other things. We're quite curious ourselves.'

He felt more and more at ease, and the girl saw it as an opportunity to get closer to him. For a moment he wondered whether he should sit on the couch or on the floor, where he smoked his hookah. The girl knelt on a feather cushion and crept up to the shah cautiously like a cat, so he could feel her warm, soft body against his leg.

The shah picked up the Russian album and opened it. The girl bent down to look at the photographs.

'What's your name?' asked the shah, who now felt like a hungry lion beside a young gazelle.

'Anya, Anastasia, Anita, Ani, Antonia, Anisia,' she responded.

'So many names? Even we as king don't have so many titles,' said the shah teasingly.

'I haven't known my name since I was fifteen,' she said. 'The men themselves make up names for me, but I don't mind.' And then she asked him, 'What's your name?'

The shah was caught off guard by this question. No one had ever asked him his name before. He burst out laughing, and with tears in his eyes he said, 'We no longer know our name, either.'

'Really?' said the girl. 'Well, that's all right. You're still a sweet man.' With these innocent little words she touched the shah's heart. No one had ever told him he was sweet before. He took her face in both his hands and planted a kiss on her left cheek.

'Your moustache tickles,' she said.

The shah had to laugh again. 'Who are you, anyway? You're so . . . so . . . How can I put it? There's something familiar about you that makes us feel you're ours.'

The girl wiped the tears from the shah's face with her hand.

'We remember,' said the shah. 'Our name is Naser Muhammad Fatali Mozafar.'

'Are they all titles?' asked the girl.

'They're not titles. They're the first names of my father, my grandfather, my great-grandfather and my great-great-grandfather.'

'Were they all kings like you?'

'Of course. We'll show you. Come here. We can look at the albums later.'

He set the book aside, stood up, took the girl by the hand and led her all the way upstairs, to the big room next to the library where the kings' personal possessions were kept. No one ever came into this mysterious room except the shah's immediate family. The floors were covered with rare carpets, and hanging on the walls were portraits, articles of clothing and jewel-encrusted guns, swords and daggers.

The shah had a little bag of sand from Herat that he kept here in a niche. There were old closets containing the boots and leather slippers of past kings. Woollen socks and handkerchiefs were stored in handmade wooden boxes, and there were special glass caskets containing gold rings and necklaces. Displayed on the great mantelpiece were the kings' writings, quills, scissors and combs. The girl stared in wonder at a series of thin glass tubes in which hairs from the kings' heads and beards were preserved.

The shah pointed at a portrait on the wall and said, 'This is our father. He died of grief.'

'Of grief?'

'The part of Azerbaijan that you come from used to be ours. The Russians took it from us in a war with my father. The grief of that loss was the death of him,' explained the shah sadly.

To show her sympathy she began stroking the shah's arm.

'This is our grandfather, an extraordinary man. He held the country together. He restored our beloved Afghanistan to the homeland and was planning to make India part of Persia as well, but he was killed.'

'Killed?' asked the girl.

'One of his Afghan guards murdered him in his sleep with a dagger. Look, his bloody coat is hanging there on the wall.'

Later that evening they lay together in bed and looked at the catalogues. In the Russian album there were incredible pictures of Russian industries, of impressive tools and of machines with gigantic wheels. How was it possible for men to make such extraordinary devices?

The shah was fascinated by one picture in particular, a photograph of the first train to run from Moscow to St Petersburg. Just before all the uproar in the country he had reached an agreement with the Russians on the building of a railway line from Tabriz to Tehran. But it was only by looking at this photograph that he understood how the combination of a locomotive and two iron rails would actually work. And when he saw a picture of passengers getting out of the carriages he became completely smitten by trains.

'Amazing, don't you think?' he said. 'That people will sit in a monster like this that rides on two iron rails.'

'I've ridden in that train!' said the girl suddenly.

'What? You? In this train?'

'Yes!'

'How? – Or where, we mean?'

'In St Petersburg on the way to Moscow,' she responded.

'You? To Moscow? What were you doing there?'

'I was with those men. I went with them,' said the girl.

Men? What men? the shah wanted to ask, but he didn't. He thought she was lying, fantasising, but nevertheless her story had frightened him a bit. Could she be a Russian spy, someone sent to charm him with her innocence in order to rob him of his royal power?

The girl pushed the Russian album aside and picked up the French catalogue. She thumbed through it and looked at the monumental buildings of Paris, at the Assemblée nationale and at Notre Dame, and the graceful bridges over the River Seine.

'This is something you shouldn't miss,' she said, and pulled the shah towards her. The candle on the bedside table fell onto the bed, and candle wax dripped on her leg.

'Hot!' she cried, and pulled her leg away. The shah picked up the candle, lit it again with another candle and put it back on the bedside table. The girl was disappointed that he paid no attention to her leg, which had reddened.

'You are a king, but you still use candles,' complained the girl. 'Your bedroom stinks. I had expected you to have that new kind of light.'

The shah took the girl's indignation seriously. He ran his hand gently along her bare leg and kissed her hair. He lay down beside her and looked at the picture. It was a photograph of Paris by night. A bridge elegantly connected one bank of the River Seine to the other, and there were two cast-iron telegraph poles standing at either end of the bridge like two works of art. The telegraph cables hung over the bridge like swaying black lines. Part of the photograph was covered by the branch of a tree. In this mysterious environment a young woman in a fashionable black hat was walking across the bridge in the light of an electric lamp.

The girl pointed with her finger and said, 'I've been here and I've walked on this bridge.'

The shah smiled. He didn't want to say it, but he said it anyway: 'You probably went to Paris with those men.'

'No. I was alone, and that night I stood against this pole for a very long time.'

She's not a spy, thought the shah. This girl just has a vivid imagination.

'My girl, you intrigue us. You have so many lovely things in your head.'

'And suddenly,' she continued, 'I heard voices as I stood there with my back against this telegraph pole.'

'What kinds of voices?' asked the shah, amused.

'I pressed my ear against the pole and I could feel movement. Words and phrases being sent from the telegraph office,' said the girl.

The shah ran his hand gently down her back and over her buttocks. The girl turned round quickly, pulled the shah's hand towards her and said, 'Shut your eyes.'

Obediently he closed his eyes. The girl began tapping into the palm of his hand with her finger.

'Can you tell me what I tapped?'

Bewildered, the shah opened his eyes and looked at his palm.

'Shut your eyes and I'll do it again. Then you guess,' said the girl once more.

'We don't know,' said the shah.

'"You are a lovely man" is what I tapped,' said the girl with a smile. 'In Morse code.'

The shah didn't know how to respond. He kissed the girl on the mouth and silently gazed at her.

'Why are you looking at me like that? What are you thinking?' she said. She laid her head on his sturdy chest and began to sob quietly.

'Why are you crying, my girl?'

'You're strong on the outside and soft on the inside. I have never seen such a charming man. When I'm with you I feel like a real princess. I can surrender to you completely, something I've never done with anyone else in my life.'

The shah was silent.

'Say something. Why are you so quiet?'

'We're thinking about tomorrow,' said the shah.

'Me too. Tomorrow you'll send me away.'

'No, we don't think so. Someone who has come so far can never go back.'

'What do you mean by that?'

'Nothing. Forget it,' he said.

The shah put his arm round her and was silent once again.

'You frighten me with your silences.'

'There's something about you that's like trains, like light, like birds that sit high up on the telegraph wires. We like you.'

It was one of the rare times that the shah had told a woman he liked her. His own words moved him. He opened the drawer of his bedside table and took out a pomegranate-coloured velvet pouch. When the girl heard the jingling of the gold coins she sat straight up in bed and said, 'What are you doing?'

The shah opened the pouch and placed the gold coins in the girl's neckline. Taken by surprise she drew her hands up to her breasts and looked at the shah questioningly.

He stroked her breasts, which now made a noise like gold coins.

He got out of bed and said, 'Are you coming?'

'Where?'

'We're sending you away.'

The girl was astonished. 'Why are you sending me away? I thought I was allowed to stay.'

'We've changed our mind.'

'I want to sleep with you tonight.'

The shah hesitated. He looked at her.

'Have I done something wrong?' asked the girl.

While considering her question the shah opened his closet, reached into a small box and took out an old necklace of magnificent green stones from India. He fastened the necklace around the girl's neck and said, 'No, you haven't done anything wrong.'

The shah left the room and rang his little bell.

'Send her home!' he said to the chamberlain, and he walked down the stairs and into the moonlit gardens.

Years later, just before his death, the shah remembered the girl. He heard the golden coins tinkling in her blouse and saw before him the brilliant necklace. These were the last things he remembered before taking leave of this life.

51. The Travelogue

The vizier got in touch with the governmental representatives of Russia, Switzerland, Austria, Germany, Italy, Holland, Belgium, France and England to enable the shah to travel to Europe. To his delight he received highly positive reactions from every country.

The Europeans had all read about the Persians in their history books. They knew the saying 'the law of the Medes and the Persians', and whenever they thought about Persia they thought of gold, flying carpets, mysterious kings, beautiful princesses, the *Thousand and One Nights* and caviar. But no one had ever seen a Persian king in the flesh before.

None of the books made any mention of a visit to a European country by a Persian king. Shah Naser was the first one to make such a journey, which accounted for the great enthusiasm among the European royal houses and presidential palaces. It was so heart-warming that the vizier could no longer keep the good news to himself. He had to tell the shah about the impressive reactions he had received.

'The kings and presidents of the various countries of Europe convey their special greetings to Your Majesty and anxiously await the opportunity to welcome the shah of Persia.'

The shah was surprised, yet he played down the enthusiastic invitations and said with a smile, 'The kings of the

West probably think that the king of kings wants to come and admire their country. What they may not know is that we are merely the king of an endless parade of beggars.'

'What you say is not true, Your Majesty. Your land is one of the most beautiful in the world. We also have affluent people, we have imposing cities, we have Isfahan, which is unique in its beauty. Your Majesty, we have the city of Shiraz, once the capital of the greatest empire on earth, we have mosques that are architectural wonders, we have insightful literature and hundreds of classical works, and our women are the most mysterious anywhere. We have carpets we can fly on. We have saffron, we have the most delicious tea in the world, we have our brilliant tales of the *Thousand and One Nights* and the beautiful royal peacocks. Our fame is legendary. You are the king of the descendants of the Medes and the Persians.'

The encouraging words of the vizier did the shah a great deal of good.

Gradually the journey took shape. First they would travel to Moscow via the Azerbaijan–Russian border, then cut straight across Europe to France, and from there go on by boat to England. After this lengthy state visit they would return home by way of a shorter route.

In an effort to dispel his doubts once and for all the shah consulted the Quran. He closed his eyes and turned to a random page. When he opened his eyes he saw with astonishment that God had given him just the right advice: the title of the surah that he had opened to was 'The Romans'. It was a surah about the Persians who had once conquered the Byzantine Empire: 'Have they not travelled on the earth and seen how the others before them had met their end?' The shah kissed the Quran and joyfully pressed it to his bosom with both arms.

Reassured, the shah began to concentrate on his journey. He invited Pirnia, scion of a prominent business family, to come and talk with him. Pirnia had spent a few years in Vienna, and as a merchant he had travelled back and forth between Austria and Switzerland.

The day was pleasant and warm, and the shah sat on a couch in the shadow of the trees. The servant brought in a tray with a plate of lettuce and a small bowl of syrup on it. The shah loved fresh lettuce. He dipped the leaves in the syrup and stuffed them in his mouth. When he had eaten his lettuce the servant let him know that his guest had arrived.

The young man, who wore a single round eyeglass over his left eye, was fitted out in a most unusual suit. He had put grease in his hair, and his beard was clipped in a remarkable fashion. He bowed his head slightly and greeted the shah. The scent that enveloped him stung the shah's nose, which made him sneeze.

'Please sit down,' said the shah with a gesture.

Pirnia sat down on a cushion, but not on his knees, as was customary. The servant placed a hookah next to the shah, and as he smoked he noticed that the young man was wearing strange shoes that had a black sheen. It looked as if he had rubbed them with the same grease that he had used on his hair.

'We understand you have spent some time in Europe? We know your father. He is a trustworthy businessman. So we have asked you to come here to share your experiences with us. We are listening.'

Without the usual introduction, which was supposed to consist of words of praise for the shah, Pirnia plunged right in with a description of his stay abroad. He gave a brief report of where he had lived and which countries he had visited.

'What exactly did you do there?'

'I traded in rough precious stones, but what really interested me were the local languages and customs! My business gave me the opportunity to travel.'

The man's self-assurance did not go down well with the shah. He found his obtrusive odour particularly unpleasant.

'So you travelled,' said the shah with emphasis. 'Tell us, what did you see?'

'Many impressive things!' responded Pirnia crisply.

'Mention a few!'

'It's difficult to describe a journey in just a couple of sentences. I did keep a travel diary, though. When it's finished I will send Your Majesty a copy.'

'There's no time for that. Just tell me about a few striking things.'

Pirnia, who knew Jamal Khan and had contact with his committee, was aware of the current political situation. He had immediately accepted the shah's invitation and hoped to use the opportunity to discuss the governing of the country with him.

'They had two chambers, for example.'

'Chambers?' asked the shah with surprise.

'Yes, chambers.'

'And what was so special about those chambers?'

'In those chambers they discussed matters that were important to the country and then they made decisions.'

'They? Who are they?'

'The representatives of the people.'

The shah shifted his weight from one knee to the other. He had sensed that the man sitting across from him was an undesirable, and his instincts had not proven him wrong.

'We have already heard about that. Tell us something new,' he answered.

'Another custom that I found strange was the newspaper – or newspapers, rather,' said Pirnia, who noticed the shah was irritated.

'We have them too,' the shah shot back.

'But in those newspapers people write their opinions about all kinds of things and carry on a kind of war of the pens.'

'A war of the pens? What do they fight about?'

'About everything! About politics, about cities, about bridges, about women, about buildings and about art.'

'A war of the pens, fighting about women and bridges. You make us curious, young man.'

'Each of these countries has a book that contains a constitution with all the laws and regulations of the land. All that is allowed and is not allowed is in that book.'

The shah nodded. He remembered the translation of the French constitution that his vizier had made.

'Each country has its own form of government. What one regime does is not universally applicable. On the other hand, a book like that would take a great weight off our shoulders. We'd have our hands free and could spend more time on ourself. Do you have anything else informative to tell us?' He turned to his servant. 'Our hookah is cold!' he snarled.

A fresh hookah was brought in instantly.

Pirnia, who was afraid the shah would send him away if he became annoyed with the conversation, changed the subject.

'Although the East is known for its secrecy and we are the masters of mysterious tales, the West also has something we lack. In the East the secret lies in the past, in books, in our narratives and behind our curtains, but the Europeans have made the hidden things visible. There the secret things can be touched. You can even sit in them. Take the train, for instance.'

'We already know that. In the palace there's a whole stack of catalogues about trains. Tell us, what language or languages did you speak when you were travelling?'

'Although each land has its own language, French is usually spoken within the better circles.'

'*On parle très bien le français*,' said the shah proudly. He smoked his hookah, inhaled a few times and said, 'What do they call the hookah in French?'

'They don't have hookahs.'

'Oh, yes. You're right. How odd!' remarked the shah.

Pirnia had something else he wanted to say, but he saw that the shah's thoughts were elsewhere.

'Bring a glass of tea for our guest,' called the shah unexpectedly. 'You also mentioned the women. Do you have anything special to tell us about them?'

'I don't know how to describe this,' said Pirnia, 'but . . . in the West the women show their faces in public. Everyone is free to show off their eyes, nose, lips, chin and arms. At parties there are even women who leave their necks and part of their breasts uncovered.'

The shah made a gesture of apparent indifference.

'All right, you can go once you've finished your tea.'

Pirnia didn't wait for the tea and left.

'If you have anything else to say that's worth saying, say it now,' the shah called out to him. He had the feeling that Pirnia had not told him everything.

Pirnia paused, and then he said, 'Recently a French engineer has come up with something extraordinary: an incredibly high tower made out of millions of iron beams.'

'How high?'

'Very high. At least as high as that mountain over there!' He pointed to a mountain in the distance.

'Why did they do that?'

'No one knows. It caused quite a sensation. Supporters

and opponents harassed each other in the press. At the same time, hundreds of curious men and women came to climb the tower every day and every night out of curiosity.'

'To climb what?'

'The tower!'

'Stack millions of kilos of iron beams on top of each other and then climb it?' said the shah.

'The engineer who came up with the idea is famous now. He invented a machine, a kind of horseless carriage, big enough for one or two or – I don't know – twenty men. You get in and press a button. Suddenly the carriage starts to move. The amazing thing is that it doesn't go forward or backwards, but up and down. It takes you to the top of the tower in just a few seconds.'

'What do they do when they get up there?' asked the shah curiously.

'Look around. Admire Paris! The view at night is marvellous. You look at the Seine, the river that runs through the city. You see the new street lamps, lights on the banks of the river where the elegant French women go for strolls—'

'All right. Enough,' interrupted the shah. He was watching a peacock who had spread all his feathers for him. 'You can go.' His thoughts wandered off to the girl to whom he had given the necklace. She too had walked along the banks of the Seine.

Preparations for the journey had lasted a year. The day of his departure was coming more quickly than expected. In recent months he had visited his harem more often and spent more nights with his wives than usual. He received them in small groups, arranged them in a circle round him and let himself be indulged. He enjoyed their enticements, kissed them, pinched them, bit them and laughed with them.

He could also be found dining more often with his elderly mother. These were not at all like their normal meetings. They embraced each other longer and exchanged tender endearments.

'My boy, you are my son and my king.' She kissed his hands with tears in her eyes. The shah wiped away her tears and kissed her grey hair.

One day before his departure he went to see his daughter, Taj Olsultan. Since the birth of his grandson he had received his daughter and her child in the palace almost daily, but now he was visiting her.

Taj saw he was sad. She wanted to ask him what was bothering him, but she kept silent. In the past, before she was married, she could speak more easily with the shah and ask him, 'Father, why are you sad?'

But since her marriage the shah had kept his distance, as if she were the girl or wife of another man and no longer belonged to him. It hurt her that their intimate contact was gone and that he no longer wanted to share with her his fatherly secrets. The attention he used to lavish on her now went to her son. Perhaps she was a bit jealous, but she did understand her father. She belonged to another man now. When all was said and done she was glad the shah was so happy with his grandchild that he gave him the love he had once given her.

Taj put her son in the shah's arms and said, 'How lucky I am to have the shah as a babysitter for the prince.'

'My pleasure, I'm sure,' said the shah with a grin. He sat down in a rocking chair with the child on his lap.

The shah always spoke to his grandchild in complete sentences because he believed it was essential for proper brain development. He read short paragraphs from the

Persian classics and enjoyed them himself. This time he told the child a story from a very old Persian book called *Kélilé and Demné*.

'"Once upon a time there was a merchant who lived in Herat. His wife was called Jamis and she was as beautiful as the moon. No one could imagine that such a magnificent woman ever having existed before. Her face shone like the day of victory and her hair was as dark and long as the night you spend waiting in vain for your beloved."'

'"Living in their neighbourhood was a celebrated artist who could work magic with a pencil and brushes. He was having a secret affair with the merchant's wife . . ."'

'Father, why are you telling the child such things? He's only a baby,' protested Taj laughingly.

'He is a child and he is a man. These are things that he must learn early on,' responded the shah, taking great pleasure in Taj.

'Shah-my-Father, there's no need to raise my son with such love stories,' said Taj with a smile.

'He is a man,' said the shah. 'And some day he will be king.'

'And that is why you're drumming the city of Herat into his head, even now,' said Taj.

The shah handed his heir back to her. He knew how important this child was for the future.

Later that afternoon the shah invited Taj Olsultan to go for a walk with him in the garden. As they walked he told her he would be going to Europe on his upcoming journey and not to Karbala.

'Listen, my daughter, only a few people have been told about this trip. Later, during our absence, the nation will be in your hands. Be on your guard, take good care of your child. He already has many enemies. If it were up to me I wouldn't make the journey until he is big and strong. But I cannot put it off. Life has made its decision and I must submit.'

The shah wanted to tell her about the golden treasury in the cellar of his palace. Anything could happen to him during this journey, even death. In the face of such risk it was his duty to share the secret with his heir. The shah took his daughter to the other side of the garden, where no one ever ventured.

'Listen!' he whispered. 'I want to tell you a state secret. It is not meant for you but for your son. If you tell anyone else you will be committing treason. Keep it locked in your heart until your son becomes the nation's king.'

'Father, you're going to live a long life,' said Taj.

'Death can strike us all at any moment. Listen well and remember everything.'

The shah picked up a stick and drew an outline of his room in the dirt. He drew his closet and the hole behind the closet, the narrow tunnel, the stairway, the short tunnel and the next stairway. Then another tunnel, the small door and the treasury. He told her about the jewels from India, and he also told her about the hole and the passage in the treasury through which the king could flee in case of emergency.

Taj Olsultan embraced her father and whispered, 'I thank you, Father, for putting so much trust in me. I will devote my life to the task of passing your message on to your heir.'

The evening before his departure the shah received Eyn ed-Dowleh in his study. Although at first he had decided not to tell him anything about his trip to Europe, he finally realised that as his son-in-law and a soldier of the highest rank, Eyn ed-Dowleh could not be left in the dark. He told him that he was probably going to visit a number of western countries. Then he dictated the following statement: 'We hereby order that all possible dissidents are to be arrested in our absence. When we return, we do not want to hear any more about them. This letter gives you full authorisation to carry out your task.'

The shah slipped the letter into Eyn ed-Dowleh's inside pocket and said, 'Bring Taj Olsultan and her child to the palace regularly. Let them spend their days and occasionally their nights here. It is good for the child to become accustomed to the palace.'

The shah grasped Eyn ed-Dowleh's arm and said softly, 'Protect your wife and your son with your own life. They are the most precious things in the kingdom. In any matter concerning them don't trust anyone.'

The next day the shah began his journey, which would take six months. He brought with him a select group, having warned them beforehand that they were going on a secret mission. The vizier had advised him not to take Malijak, but the shah had rejected his advice: 'That's impossible. If I leave him alone, he'll suffer the same fate as my cat. Besides, we've got to have someone to talk to if we happen to feel out of sorts while travelling abroad.'

The shah had decided to keep a diary during his journey. The book was not meant for people living then but for future generations, when the shah would be long gone. He was aware that he would never be as greatly admired as the ancient Persian kings, that he would not leave his mark on this new age, but he could distinguish himself by writing a travelogue. New machines would be able to print many copies of his book, and one day he would be read by everyone. He wanted to make the journey for people who did not yet exist but undoubtedly would someday.

Late that night he pushed the curtain aside and peered into the dark blue sky and at all the stars. Perhaps this was the last time he would be granted the opportunity to marvel at the Persian night.

Even though he was anxious about the country there was something strangely pleasant about the prospect of travel. He felt as if he were suddenly being relieved of a burden that he had been predestined to carry for the rest of his life. He was a caged bird who was about to be freed, to fly away into that endless blue sky.

Although it had been late when he went to bed he woke up early and took a stroll through the gardens. It was early spring and the trees were putting out enormous blossoms. His patience was gone. In fact he would have happily made an early departure, but he had to wait until his travelling companions were ready.

He wanted to cast one last glance at the harem, but much to his surprise he found his wives standing in the garden dressed in festive attire. They were all holding mirrors in their hands. They wept silently and smiled at the same time. A couple of them stepped forward carrying crystal bowls filled with clear water, and they sprinkled the shah as a good luck token. It moved the shah to tears. The women came closer, touched him and led him to the gate, where his fellow travellers were waiting.

The servants appeared with lit chafing dishes into which they threw fragrant herbs to ward off evil spirits. A group of musicians accompanied a young singer, who sang melancholy songs of farewell. The shah wiped away his tears with his handkerchief and waved to everyone.

Seven royal coaches stood at the ready. The government officials, members of the royal house, a delegation from the bazaar and the British and Russian ambassadors were all lined up at the gate to say goodbye. His mother had already wished him a good journey.

The shah nodded to a few of them, shook hands with others, had a friendly chat with the Russian ambassador and exchanged a few words with his British counterpart. The residents of Tehran also waved him farewell. The chamberlain stood beside the shah with a tray full of new coins, which the shah then tossed to the gathered throng. Never before had he distributed so many coins, but he did it mindful of the fact that these people would never forget him if he failed to return.

Once he had thrown out the last coins he raised his arm in the air and walked to his coach.

52. The Constitution

The shah had been gone for a few months and everyone really did believe he was on a long journey to the holy cities. When his stay lasted longer than anyone expected they speculated that he had gone to Mecca to take part in the annual hajj. As a wealthy believer you had to travel to Mecca at least once and participate in the traditional Sugar Feast.

The shah was now halfway through his travels, and he had sent a few brief letters to Tehran. To his mother he wrote:

> Mother, we were received by our neighbour Russia like a great Persian king. They told us they still have fond memories of your visit to Moscow. They showed us a couple of portraits of you. You never told us that the royal artist had painted your picture. I asked if I could take your portrait with me. Alas, they like you so much that they want to keep the painting in their own collection.

To Taj Olsultan he wrote:

> How I wish I had brought you with us. It is more a journey for you than for us. The women, the cafés, the bridges, the lamps, the churches, the bakeries and the theatres. But it doesn't matter. You are still young, and we will send you to Moscow some day.

We miss our little Ahmad Mozafar, our crown prince. Take good care of him. Feed him with your own milk. Hold him close to your body and talk to him in complete sentences. Don't tell him any foolish stories and don't sing him any common lullabies. Read to him from Hafez. Teach him French songs.

Until we meet again. We are coming soon.

To keep the women of the harem from getting jealous he wrote one letter to all of them:

Wives! The shah misses his harem. We were duty bound to make this journey or we wouldn't have done it at all. The distances are great, the roads are impassable and danger is lurking at every turn. Thank God we didn't bring you with us or it would have been a miserable expedition. We ask you to pray for us. We are coming home soon.

To his vizier he wrote:

The way the people live and work here is completely different from anything we are used to. I keep wondering whether such a life is suitable for our subjects. I am afraid that if we were to adopt all the manners of these people we would end up neglecting our own religion, traditions and customs.

When I come back we will discuss this at length. It has certainly been a useful journey. We have bought cannons and ordered rifles for the country, and we have signed many contracts.

We received a short note from Eyn ed-Dowleh. He writes to us in no uncertain terms that the presence of the shah is essential, which is why we believe it is unwise to stay away any longer. We have decided to cut the trip short. As far as we can judge, we have achieved our goal. The next time we make this journey it will be much longer.

Vizier Mostovi Almamalek suspected he knew what Eyn ed-Dowleh's short note was all about. He had probably told the shah that although everything in the country seemed peaceful, his opponents were busily building up a solid network.

Eyn ed-Dowleh had also warned the vizier: 'You must not think they are gone, or that they have changed their way of thinking. By no means. I have proof that they are preparing to seize power at a suitable moment.'

Mostovi Almamalek had hoped to be able to carry out some of his plans in the shah's absence, but it proved almost impossible to get anything done without royal approval. Eyn ed-Dowleh was a hundred times worse than the shah. He was the ideal watchdog. He had summed up the vizier's position in a single sentence: 'You are not to come up with any new ideas until the shah is back!'

Eyn ed-Dowleh had put together a special military unit to arrest or eliminate opponents in Tehran. He wanted to complete the mission with which he had been charged before the shah returned, but that, as he was gradually learning, would be no easy task. He even believed that Mostovi Almamalek was maintaining contact with the opposition. Almamalek did speak occasionally with Jamal Khan and Amir Nezam, but he was planning nothing against the shah. His purpose in doing so was to win the young intellectuals over to his ideas.

When the vizier had taken office the shah had asked to be shown all legal documents and contracts so he could study them. But because of the sheer volume involved, and because the shah simply didn't want to be bothered most of the time, the papers tended to accumulate on his desk. The vizier had little patience with what he called the shah's lack of responsibility.

Later he would be confronted with the mountain of contracts that the shah had signed unilaterally with European companies and merchants.

The members of the resistance committee had long been convinced that the shah was the biggest obstacle to real change, so they worked steadily on. At the last meeting of the resistance committee in Tehran, the following men were present:

Jamal Khan
Mirza Reza Kermani
Prince Malkum Khan
Abdolrahim Talebof
Haj Zeinolabedin Maraghei
Sheikh Ahmad Ruhi
Mirza Muhammad Hassan Ashtiani
Sheikh Abolhasan
Mirza Soleyman Khan
Mirza Yahya Dolatabadi
Mirza Muhammad Alikhan
Sheikh Ahmad Gherkhani
Mirza Mohsen Sadolama
Mirza Soleyman Khad Dehkade
Mirza Isa Ghaemmagham
Amir Nezam
Abolghasem Lahuti
Mostashar Aldoleh

Most of them were involved in culture, literature, politics or science. Some of them lived in Tehran and the rest came from the other large cities. Their meeting was something like a small national congress at which they attempted to combine their forces.

Jamal Khan opened the meeting.

'Welcome, friends! I consider myself fortunate to see you all here. The fact that we are able to come together this evening is undoubtedly a gift from God. A number of you have travelled a few days to get here, and some of you a week. Once again, welcome.

'Each and every one of you is important for our homeland. Sometimes I worry that our dream will never be fulfilled, that we are doomed to endless misery. But at other moments I feel a glimmer of hope in my heart.

'My friends, I recently went to the south of the country to see what the British are up to. It was not possible to set foot in their territory, but I posed as an interpreter for one of the local officials. What is taking place there is a miracle. The British have erected new installations, machines, engines, appliances and pumps. They have built a long wall and have laid claim to everything, but that wall will not last long. Sooner or later they'll have to work with our graduates and our workers. But right now, we ourselves are the biggest problem. What we need are laws, set down in a statute book. And the power of the shah must be drastically curtailed. We have a long way to go. But when I look at you now, I am looking at the future.

'My friends, when the murdered vizier was still alive he translated the French constitution bit by bit and made a specially adapted version for our own country. I have been able to get hold of the complete text and have had a number of copies printed. It gives me great pleasure to give everyone here a copy as a never-to-be-forgotten gift. Let us study it and make any necessary corrections. This is a dream that will become reality.

'My friends, I thank you for your attendance.'

Mirza Reza left the room and came back carrying a heavy wooden box. He opened the box and handed everyone the first edition of the provisional Persian statute book. Everyone cheered and clapped enthusiastically.

Jamal Khan had set aside one book to take to the house of Ayatollah Tabatabai. He was the cleric who had served as an envoy of the aged Ayatollah Shirazi and had gone with a group of merchants from the bazaar to speak with the shah. After that meeting he had become one of the most important political figures in the land.

The aged ayatollah of Shiraz had retreated completely from public life after the victory of his tobacco fatwa. He wanted to spend his last days in peace and in prayer. All eyes were now on Ayatollah Tabatabai. He had a good relationship with Jamal Khan and had let him know that he could always be counted on. On the evening of the meeting Jamal Khan handed the statute book to Ayatollah Tabatabai.

Someone had also slipped a copy to Eyn ed-Dowleh. Seated among the cushions he thumbed through the book, boiling with rage. The man who had brought him the book had also reported on the meeting of the group. One of its members had probably spilled the beans.

The next day Eyn ed-Dowleh went to the office of the Mostakhberat, the secret service, to discuss recent developments.

'Twenty-five copies of this book have been printed,' said the head of the secret service.

'Where did they have the printing done?' asked Eyn ed-Dowleh.

'They were printed in Bombay and smuggled into the country via Herat.'

Eyn ed-Dowleh had a feeling that this was the work of Jamal Khan. Jamal Khan was often cited as the brains behind all the unrest in the country. But the name of Mirza

Reza, the son of the late Ayatollah Kermani, was also being heard with greater frequency.

There had been nothing personal about Mirza Reza in the report, so Eyn ed-Dowleh was unable to form a clear picture of the man. He had never seen Jamal Khan either, but he had a fairly good idea what he looked like: a man with a drooping moustache who wore a black cap and a black coat.

'A copy of that statute book is lying next to the Quran on the mantelpiece in the living room of Ayatollah Tabatabai,' the head of the Mostakhberat told Eyn ed-Dowleh.

Eyn ed-Dowleh drank his tea in silence.

'The ayatollah has made notes on almost every page,' the man continued. 'This is the latest news, but we also have an unconfirmed report about their statute book. Each one of them was given a copy to take home. They were told to study the text and to come back with the notes they had taken. The ayatollah's copy is proof. We know for sure they're going to meet again, but we don't know exactly when.'

Eyn ed-Dowleh put his tea glass down. This statute book was making the problem more complicated than he and the shah had imagined. That evening he sent a short letter to the shah suggesting that it might be wise for the shah not to extend his journey any longer than was absolutely necessary.

About three months later the members of the committee got together again to talk about the statute book. The head of the Mostakhberat had been informed that the meeting would take place in Tehran, but he was unable to find out the day or the location.

Eyn ed-Dowleh applied pressure. 'These facts are useless. I need concrete information. I want them all behind bars before the shah comes home. I want to show them off to the shah. Think of something. Do something. Give me an address. If we don't arrest them now they'll just grow and grow and we won't be able to stop them. Give me something specific and I'll close all the gates and search all the houses one by one until I get them. I want that Jamal Khan! Pick a day and I'll chain him to the wall with iron shackles round his neck before the shah arrives. I'll smash his face with his own statute book. And the same goes for Mirza Reza.'

The head of the Mostakhberat sent a number of spies to the local inns and stationed his men at the city gates to spot any strangers entering the city and follow them. From all the information they received they concluded that the members of the committee would be gathering within a few days. Eyn ed-Dowleh immediately barred all the gates of Tehran and sent troopers to the inns outside the city. He ordered them to arrest every traveller with a book or even just a piece of paper in his luggage and to put him in chains. The troopers rode as far as the city of Qazvin. They stopped at every caravanserai and arrested anyone who looked suspicious. They found not a single book, but they brought a long row of men into the city in chains. Eyn ed-Dowleh interrogated them one by one and had them locked up.

'If Jamal Khan's men aren't outside the city, they must be inside,' reasoned Eyn ed-Dowleh.

His troopers swept into all the guesthouses un-announced and locked up all the travellers until Eyn ed-Dowleh could question them personally. But they found no suspicious travellers. Everyone had a good reason for staying in Tehran.

On the third day Eyn ed-Dowleh was given a tip concerning the presence of several strangers staying in the imam boarding school behind the Jameh mosque.

Accompanied by his troopers Eyn ed-Dowleh entered the building and forced the doors of all the rooms. In one of the rooms was a man who pushed Eyn ed-Dowleh over and jumped out the window into the garden. It was Jamal Khan. He ran to the gate, but Eyn ed-Dowleh stood up and began shooting at the fleeing man. Jamal Khan stumbled and disappeared into the bushes.

'He's wounded. Get him!' shouted Eyn ed-Dowleh, who still didn't know who the escaped man was.

Three armed officers ran to the place where Jamal Khan had fallen and began shooting blindly in every direction. Just then, from out of the darkness, shots were fired at the officers. They dived to the ground and shot back. Their attacker was Mirza Reza. He was in another room in the building and had opened fire on them, shooting until all the other members of the committee had escaped through the windows and across the roofs.

Eyn ed-Dowleh crept to the room from which he had heard the shots. He kicked the door in and emptied his pistol. Mirza Reza got away just in time. He jumped into the courtyard and hid behind a couple of trees. A few of the officers saw where Mirza Reza had taken cover. Suspecting he had run out of ammunition they ran after him in order to arrest him. One of them struck him hard with his gun and the other two pushed him to the ground.

Jamal Khan managed to escape, but the agents had arrested several members of the group. Eyn ed-Dowleh led Mirza Reza away in chains and had him locked up.

53. The Journey Back

The shah returned after six months away. In answer to Eyn ed-Dowleh's letter he had sent a messenger on ahead with instructions to take occasional evening drives through the city with the royal coach so everyone would think the shah was back home.

The journey had cost the shah more time and money than he had expected. In every country he visited he had bought a great many presents for himself, his wives and his family members. It was a Persian custom to return home with presents for everyone, and the shah observed this tradition. The things he had bought were spectacular: new products, clothing and household items that might never reach the bazaars of Persia. Every time the shah saw something along the way that pleased him he bought it and put it in safekeeping so he could take it back home with him.

By the time he was at his journey's end and had reached the Russian side of the Caspian Sea there were thirteen large, fully-loaded carts being driven behind him. His total luggage amounted to 367 trunks and 32 large boxes containing shoes, hats, coats, books, porcelain, appliances, sweets, toys, pipes, bracelets, photographs of the various heads of state, picture frames, eyeglasses, clocks, magnifying glasses, lamps, walking sticks, fabric, cigars, sugar cubes, gold rings, medals he had been given by the various heads of state, teapots, coffee-making devices, coffee beans, facial creams for the women, mirrors and hundreds of other extraordinary articles.

When his caravan rode past the Russian villages people would run after them and ask for money. To keep his luggage safe the shah would toss out Russian coins. The people had no idea what was being carried in the carts; neither could they have imagined that it was the shah of Persia sitting in the coach or they would never have been content with such a pittance.

The Russian customs office had arranged for the shah to be taken on ahead to his homeland by a Russian naval ship. His luggage would follow later. But the shah, who had seen the greedy people running after his carts, wanted to take his luggage along with him. No one knew why the local customs officials refused to cooperate. They kept coming up with different detailed explanations as to why the luggage could not be placed on the same ship and why the trunks and boxes had to be sent by ferry.

'We don't trust them,' said the shah to his own companions. 'They have wicked intentions – I can see it in their eyes. We cannot leave our luggage here unattended.'

'It isn't unattended. The Russian customs officials will guard our luggage,' said his companions.

'The Russians took more than half of our beloved Azerbaijan from our father and never gave it back. If they find out what is in our trunks, we'll lose it all. We refuse to part with our luggage. We are not going to leave Russia as long as our things do not travel with us.'

The head of the customs office was unrelenting and insisted on first conferring with his supervisor in Baku. Reluctantly the shah agreed to spend the night in an inn that he found far beneath his dignity. That night something happened that, for the shah, was almost worse than the

Russian invasion of Azerbaijan. It never became clear to the shah exactly how, or by whom, but by the next day all his carts had been plundered.

The customs building on the Caspian Sea was located in a harbour used mainly by merchants from the bordering countries. They conveyed their goods to each other's bazaars by means of rickety boats, which is why there was no need to protect the goods separately.

The Russian police had guarded the shah through the Russian leg of his journey, but in all likelihood most of the contents of the trunks had been stolen by local agents, leaving a small amount to the general populace. Shots had been fired that night, but because of the wind and the murmuring of the waves the shah had noticed nothing.

The next day there wasn't a single person in the shah's retinue who dared tell him the disastrous news. When no one appeared to wake him or bring him his breakfast, he sent Malijak to find out why: 'Go and see where everyone is.'

Malijak, who had grown even fatter during the journey, waddled outside with great difficulty and came back short of breath: 'Everyone is gone. The trunks, too.'

At first the shah didn't understand. Then he jumped up from his bed and cried, 'What did you say?'

'Everyone is gone. The trunks too,' repeated Malijak.

There wasn't a soul in the inn, but the harbour was very busy. The carts, which had still been full the night before and stored in the customs building, were all lying empty and in pieces. Bits of broken trunks and fragments of the souvenirs lay scattered all over the beach or floating in the surf.

Utterly distraught the shah called for his advisors, but no one responded. He called for his personal servant

– 'Mashadi! Mashadi!' – but he too failed to appear. Choking, he shouted, 'Malijak!'

Malijak tottered up to the shah and held his hand, crying.

The shah had to spend one more night in the inn in order to speak to the chief of police the following day. The officer arrived early the next morning to pay his respects. He expressed his deepest regret and promised that Russia would pay the necessary compensation. The shah wrote a letter to the tsar and complained about the painful experience he had undergone in his country, ending with the following remark: 'A pack of thieves have managed to cast an ugly shadow on our precious memories of Your Highness the tsar and his beloved family.'

When he left seven cannon shots were fired. A group of officers saluted the shah and accompanied him to the ship. The head of the Russian customs office said, 'We will do everything we can to get to the bottom of this, and we will keep Your Majesty informed. Your trunks will be returned to you.'

Disappointed, distressed and – far worse – empty-handed, the shah and Malijak boarded the Russian ship.

The trip across the Caspian Sea to Tehran was sheer misery for the shah. He spent the greater part of the crossing being sick. Once in Tehran he crawled right into bed. He told the chamberlain that he was to see no one for the next three days. The shah had a fever and his throat was sore. The incident in the Russian harbour had done him no good, but the whole overwhelming journey had also taken its toll.

He had always regarded his palace as a paradise on earth, an idyllic garden that sparked the imagination. Now that he had seen the palaces of the West and knew how the other heads of state lived, his own palace seemed more like a medieval citadel. He couldn't imagine visiting his harem again, having to ring his bell to alert his chamberlain and having to see the same guards, beggars, bazaars and eunuchs.

Everything in his hall of mirrors and in his bedroom struck him as old-fashioned. The closets, the chairs, the tables, the mirrors, the stairways, the shoes and his hats all looked shabby. He pulled the blankets up over his head and wished he could fall asleep and never wake up so he wouldn't have to face another day of this backward life.

On the fourth day Taj Olsultan brought her child to the palace to pay the shah a visit. It was the only way to call him back to reality. Finally the shah agreed to show his face.

'Oh, Father, how thin you've grown!'

The shah kissed his daughter and admired his grandchild, who was sleeping under a sheer, milky white velvet blanket.

'He's grown bigger and he's changed,' he said quietly.

'What do you mean? I can't see it myself.'

The shah pressed a kiss on his grandson's head with his hand.

'Father, what's troubling you?'

The shah immediately started in on the robbery in the Russian harbour. 'We were bringing beautiful clothes for you. We had bought books for you and boxes full of toys for our grandchild. But those Russians have inflicted great pain on us. We had a premonition that they would rob us, which is why we refused to leave our trunks behind. We had bought a gold necklace for you and a locket for the child in Paris. Fortunately we put these two souvenirs in the bag in which we carry our diary. God didn't want me to come back to you and your child empty-handed. Look, here they are.'

The shah picked up a magnificent gold necklace set with little jewels and fastened it round his daughter's neck.

'It's very beautiful, Father, and elegant,' said Taj Olsultan. She held her father's hands and kissed them.

'This locket is for our crown prince. Keep it for him for later, as a memento of our journey.'

The child opened his eyes and stared at the shah. Taj Olsultan picked him up and laid him in her father's arms.

The shah beamed with happiness and said, '*Mashallah, mashallah*, he looks more and more like us.' He kissed the child and held him up high. Then he tossed him up in the air just a bit.

'Don't do that, Father. Be careful,' laughed Taj apprehensively.

'We're careful. Of course we're careful,' said the shah, and he tossed the child so high that he began to cry with fear.

'Father, give him back and tell me: how was your journey?'

'It was an extraordinary experience. We don't know where to begin. Everywhere we went we were received like a true king. The heads of state in the West still think we live in the glorious Persian days of yore. We were surprised to discover that the world knows so much about our past. We kept a travel diary and there are still many details we want to add to it. Later we will give it to you for safekeeping, but do not publish our adventures until after we are dead.

'There are some things, however, that are for your ears alone. Funny experiences. Every time we think of them we have to laugh all over again. In Moscow we were invited to a dinner with the tsar. We climbed the stairs at his side. I was walking upright and was holding onto my sword. Suddenly I felt something slip out of my hand and onto the floor. It was part of my sword, but I couldn't quickly determine which part. Then my eyes fell on a green jewel lying on the carpet. It was the diamond from our sword. What was I to do? We couldn't just let such a precious stone lie there. I bowed down to pick it up. The tsar turned round, but he didn't understand what I was up to.'

The shah took the green jewel out of his jacket pocket, gave it to Taj Olsultan and said with a laugh, 'This is something the Russians weren't able to take from us.'

'Father, you mustn't dwell on that robbery.'

'I know, but they were gifts, for you and for our wives. After all, people expect something from us.'

'Yes, I know. But they'll understand. I'm so curious to hear about what you did on your journey. Tell me everything.'

The shah began to laugh. 'This is something else we can only tell you. Normally our trousers always stayed up round our waist. But while we were in a theatre in Hungary they kept slipping down. We had been invited to attend a concert one evening. When the wife of the Hungarian king took our arm to guide us to the box, our trousers began to fall down. We tried to hold them up with our elbow, but it didn't work. That's when we realised we had lost several kilos along the way.'

Taj Olsultan covered her mouth with her hand to keep from laughing out loud.

'I can just imagine, Father, on such a long journey, without rest and with constant tension. Even so you seem to be bursting with health.'

'In Berlin we visited a zoo. They had lions, tigers, snakes and elephants. We found it very impressive. Malijak enjoyed it so much he didn't want to leave. In the past, when we were young, we ran into lions and tigers in the forests. But these days they're nowhere to be found. We thought it would be a good idea to build such a zoo in Tehran. We'll have one built for your son. It's very good for him to see such creatures up close. Perhaps we can still find lions, snakes and tigers in our own country. We'll have to bring in monkeys and elephants from India.'

'Father, what was it like in Paris? Did you speak French with the people in the street?'

'Of course, but the people in the street speak in a way we're not accustomed to. I believe we speak better French than the Parisians. They speak correctly, but it's a kind of broken French. We've written everything down, since the most interesting things happened in Paris. The Seine winds through the city, and avenues have been built along both banks. One evening we went for a walk there. The river, the avenues and the bridges were illuminated with extraordinary electric street lamps. It was as if we had wandered into a mysterious story. The jewels on our jacket and rings glittered magically and our shadows looked very elegant.'

When Taj Olsultan was gone the shah summoned his vizier, Mostovi Almamalek, who came immediately.

'How was Your Majesty's trip?' he asked enthusiastically.

The shah thanked him for having planned his trip so well.

'All during the journey we noticed over and over again that our vizier had gone to great lengths on our behalf. We had brought back a special memento for you, but unfortunately it was lost in the Russian harbour. The result of this long journey was all in our luggage. But now the luggage is gone, so the journey was made for nothing.'

'I am sorry that the shah has met with this misfortune. But there is more to the journey than presents.'

'Indeed, we did visit a great many factories, building

347

projects, museums and agricultural exhibitions. We still aren't fully recovered, but soon we will talk about all our experiences when the cabinet meets.'

The vizier wanted to know everything about the journey, but the shah limited himself to his visits to factories and the discussions he had conducted with businessmen and important merchants.

'In Germany we visited Krupp, the factory where they make steel and weapons. It was most impressive. The director of the factory let us see their new cannons. We couldn't believe our eyes! I measured the length of one of the cannons with my feet. It was twenty-one steps long. A boy of fourteen could easily crawl into the barrel of that cannon. We ordered a whole series of cannons and a batch of rifles. In Russia, Hungary, Amsterdam, Belgium and France we signed contracts with the owners of shoe factories, porcelain companies, tobacco plantations, clock makers, textile businesses and many others. The contracts stipulate that their representatives will come to Tehran later on to discuss these matters further.'

The vizier realised it made no sense to raise any objections to the contracts now, although he hinted that the shah ought to be careful.

'I am glad the journey was an interesting experience for the shah, but it would be better for the country if the cabinet were to thoroughly examine and discuss the contracts you have signed.'

'That is good. We have new plans ourselves, which we will talk about later on.' The shah stood up. There was one incident that he did not want to withhold from the vizier. The vizier followed him to the door.

'Something happened to us in Berlin that we did not find pleasant. We wanted to pass on a comment to those responsible, but we have not done so.'

'What happened, Your Majesty?'

'In Berlin one floor of a hotel had been reserved for us. It was very good and we were satisfied. Late in the evening, when we had gone to bed after a long day, we heard a group of riotous men. We suspected they knew we were spending the night there. They began to bray like donkeys, low like cows and bark like dogs. We wanted to open the window and urge them to be quiet, but we didn't. We hid our head under the blankets and pillows to block out the noise. The police failed to do anything about it.'

'I fear the men were drunk. People in Berlin drink a great deal. The police in the West have much less power than ours do. Yet Your Majesty acted properly. Every journey has its negative as well as its positive aspects. The most important thing is that the shah is healthy and that we can make use of his royal experience.'

When the vizier was gone the shah went back to his study, locked himself in and focused all his attention on his diary. He sat there until deep into the night and did not touch his evening meal. The shah wrote, leafed through his book, read and re-read what he had written.

Today we wandered around the Kremlin square. It is a large castle with a sturdy gate. There we ate some kind of orange that was red on the inside, which we found quite delicious.

The tsar's wife held us by our arm and the tsar held the arm of a beautiful young woman whose name we have forgotten. We entered a large room. It was a room in which people dance, and occasionally some kind of masked parties are held there. Something like this would also please our wives.

At dinner the tsar's wife sat next to us and the

beautiful woman sat across from us. We very much wanted to speak with her, but the tsar's wife prattled on the whole night and gave us not a moment's peace. Her breath stank. God is punishing us for something.

The shah read this and smiled. He remembered something charming he had witnessed in Paris but had forgotten to write down. Now he added it: 'In Paris we saw a blonde woman reflected in the mirror of our coach, as if her photograph had been framed in the mirror. No woman could ever be as beautiful as she. The coach rode on and the woman disappeared from the mirror. We were prepared to purchase her with gold, but even a king has his limitations.'

It was late at night. Normally he would be in bed by now, reading, but he couldn't stop writing. He leafed back to the chapter he had written about his visit to Holland. His heart almost broke with longing when he read it.

We rode into the Amsterdam train station, and there waiting for us were the mayor, a couple of generals and the city's chief of police. As soon as we emerged from the train, the musicians began playing a deafening piece on their instruments. We immediately felt welcome.

Amsterdam is a beautiful city. The streets are clean and the houses are like biscuit tins stacked on top of each other. You would think the city had been made by children. The king of Holland is ill. He has a young daughter who will succeed him when he dies. If it were up to us, we would have appointed Taj Olsultan as our successor.

We rode through the city by coach, and an enormous throng of people stood along the streets to admire us. We have seen many beautiful women. I believe there are no ugly women in that country.

The people had never seen a Persian before, let alone a Persian king. They waved at us, and some of the women blew us kisses with their hands. This made us feel uneasy, but we enjoyed ourselves.

That night we stayed in an extraordinary hotel on a canal. It was very clean and we slept well. They are refined people, the Dutch. No one brays like a donkey at night. We spent two weeks in that country. We saw a great deal, visited many factories and did business with the merchants. They are well-behaved businessmen, not as insolent as the merchants in our own bazaars.

But in Lahe, The Hague, we looked death in the eyes. We had gone to that city to pay a visit to their parliament and to meet their vizier. Here too the people were extremely happy to see us. The women were visibly delighted. They shouted slogans and welcomed us, clapping their hands. We waved to them and bowed our head slightly in their direction. All those people made the poor horses skittish and nervous. Suddenly they bolted. The coachman was unable to keep them under control. Women and children screamed, and we sat there, powerless, in the coach. The horses raced over the lawns and the doorsteps. The coach bumped against the trees and against the edge of the pavement. I could see the frightened faces. All the screaming drove the horses wild. We thought we were done for. Then the coach ran into a lamp post and got stuck. The guards hastened to assist us and pulled us out. The people looked on in shock, but we straightened our back and waved at them. For a moment there was silence. Then cheering burst forth: 'Long live the shah!'

Our eyes were filled with tears. Lovely people.

The shah closed his diary with a smile.

The next day he lingered in bed, but he knew he had to pick up the thread of his life. This was his life, this was his country and he was the shah, the person who had to provide leadership.

He got up, ate his breakfast and summoned Eyn ed-Dowleh. His son-in-law had heard from Taj that the shah was a bit depressed. His detailed account of the arrest of the resistance group heavyweights would make the shah happy, he thought.

'But you weren't able to catch their leader!'

'According to our information we have apprehended the most dangerous man in the group.'

'Which man is that?'

'Mirza Reza Kermani.'

At the insistence of Eyn ed-Dowleh the shah spent the next day visiting the notorious prison outside the city.

A prisoner in iron chains was pushed outside by three guards. The man put his hands over his eyes to protect them from the sunlight. Eyn ed-Dowleh walked up to him, grabbed the chain and shouted, 'Kneel before the shah.'

The prisoner refused. Eyn ed-Dowleh struck him on the shoulder with his rifle, causing the man to fall down at the shah's feet.

'This is Mirza Reza Kermani!' said Eyn ed-Dowleh.

The shah pressed Mirza Reza to the ground with his polished brown boots and said contemptuously, 'Is this little fellow dangerous?'

Mirza Reza was no little fellow, but the lack of food and sunlight in his damp cell had weakened him considerably.

Eyn ed-Dowleh had expected the shah to say, 'String him up!' But the shah turned round and walked away.

Perhaps it was on account of the journey that he was

no longer able to casually order someone's hanging. Perhaps he wanted to humiliate Eyn ed-Dowleh for failing to arrest Jamal Khan. But it was also possible that fate had something else in mind for Mirza Reza.

54. Cable Complaints

After the fighting in and around the Jameh mosque, Eyn ed-Dowleh had put all the gates of Tehran under surveillance to prevent Jamal Khan from fleeing the city. He had searches conducted in all the houses that he suspected of being places where Jamal Khan might be holed up. The house of Ayatollah Tabatabai was passed over, however – the very place where Jamal Khan had taken shelter.

On the evening that Jamal Khan was shot in the leg, he mustered up every scrap of strength he had and managed to reach the home of Ayatollah Tabatabai. He spent his first months inside the ayatollah's house, waiting for his leg to heal so he could walk again. He let his beard grow and, with the ayatollah's approval, donned clerical robes, put a turban on his head and returned to daily life disguised as an imam.

He tried to convince Tabatabai that the power of the shah would have to be curtailed, and that a *majles* (parliament) and an *edalat-khaneh* (court of justice) were essential for the future of the country.

Jamal Khan then set out to gather his comrades together, but that was no easy task.

The shah had returned with a renewed sense of purpose, and he kept coming up with new ideas. The trip had gone well, he thought, but he was more convinced than ever that the developments taking place in western countries could not be implemented in his own. He stated this clearly at a meeting: 'Adopting their way of life is out of the question, but we can ask them to build bridges for us, or perhaps a hospital. We've seen cannons there that are ten times stronger than what the Russians have. These are the things we need. The Germans have promised us guns. I have spoken with them, and they can make the same kinds of weapons for us that are geared especially for our army. But other changes are not advisable, especially when it comes to their way of life.'

In his own palace, however, there were a number of changes he was eager to introduce. All the western heads of state had their own private telegraph booths, for instance. In England he had discussed the possibility of installing something similar in Tehran, a hope that was realised far sooner than the shah had expected.

Six months after the shah's return Sir James Moore, a young British engineer, appeared at the palace to install a telegraph booth so the shah would be able to receive and send his own telegrams. The engineer gave the shah a letter that said that England was pleased to give him the necessary equipment as a memento. The gift was then brought in encased in a large box. The engineer prised the planks loose with an iron bar and unpacked the contents. The telegraph was a beautifully designed, golden device that glistened in the light.

Two poles, decorated with Persian motifs, were then erected in the palace. Cables ran gracefully from one pole to the other. When everything was ready a booth was built in one of the side rooms off the hall of mirrors.

Assisted by a British telegraph operator the shah sent a test message to the Persian ambassador in London. When the shah was in the English capital he had read a poem in a British newspaper and had thought how extraordinary it was to introduce people to poetry in this way. The shah asked the telegraph operator if he would send one of his poems to the Persian ambassador in London.

> As the moon from the saddened sea doth go,
> My love has left me filled with woe.
> One difference stands: love left no trace,
> While the moon has left us with her face.

The ambassador answered with a telegram: 'It was a masterpiece. If Your Majesty agrees, we will have the poem translated into English for our business relations in London.'

Delighted, the shah responded immediately: 'We give our consent!'

Now that the shah had direct contact with all the big cities he sent daily telegrams to Isfahan, Shiraz, Tabriz, Mashad and Bandar Abbas and asked them for updates. He felt that the country was more firmly under his control. Every day he received reports from local officials, and he read everything with great attention.

He also received more and more reports that he referred to as 'cable complaints'. The merchants sent him endless telegrams expressing their displeasure with local rulers and the bribes they were constantly demanding. They begged the shah to do something about these abuses.

He also received reports from families complaining about police officials, men who had taken their daughters against their will and without the consent of their parents and were holding them captive in their harems.

Cable complaints came in daily by the hundreds, and the shah gave serious attention to them all. It made him feel good to have contact with his subjects. Questions were answered without delay. He sent brief, blunt orders to the officials and helped the families deal with their difficulties: 'Let the girl go or we will come ourselves!'

Every morning he left his bed with fresh resolve and went to the telegraph operator to see if any new reports had come in. He washed and dressed with haste and studied the stacks of requests as he ate his breakfast. Sometimes he would travel to a city unannounced to see whether his orders had actually been carried out. It did him a world of good and he took pleasure in the fairness of his decisions.

Recently he had received a few cable complaints from the Tehran bazaar. A group of shopkeepers had protested to the shah that Malijak was constantly coming to the bazaar to annoy them. It made the shah laugh to see that even Malijak's name was appearing in the reports. He showed it to him and said with a smile, 'Malijak, you've become important, too. Your name has made its way through the cable.'

The rumour that the shah was dealing with the complaints of his subjects by cable spread throughout the country. Villagers travelled long distances by donkey to get to the big cities and jostled their way into the telegraph offices. They sometimes had to wait several days and nights before they could send their complaint or question to the shah. Because the shah's equipment could no longer process the huge number of messages coming in, they were now being sent to the main office in Tehran. The staff at the main office put all the complaints in a sack, which was handed over to the palace guards every morning.

Gradually the shah's unbridled commitment began to waver and turned into a crushing burden. He no longer knew how to deal with all the complaints. People who were oppressed, who were ill, who had seen their harvests wither away, who had been robbed, women whose husbands were sitting out long prison sentences, people who no longer felt safe in their own neighbourhoods, the sick, the blind, the deaf, the lame: all of them kept asking him for help.

The shah became frightened by all the misery in his kingdom. He had done his very best, but he realised he could not help everyone. Slowly his enthusiasm dwindled. He stopped reading the messages, piled the sacks of telegrams in the corner of his study, sent the telegraph operator away and put a lock on the door of the booth.

One afternoon, deeply dejected, he rode to his mother's palace. The late afternoon sun was shining yellow and red against the palace walls when the shah arrived. Mahdolia had been ill for quite some time. Even before dismounting he could see her shuffling along the length of the wall with her walking stick. She still walked with the dignity of a queen, despite her illness. She wore a gold tiara that reflected the light.

The shah had mixed feelings about his mother. Sometimes his love for her was boundless and sometimes he hated her. Now he was fonder of her than ever. He realised he was losing her, that every meeting could be their last. It was his mother, after all, who had made a shah out of him. She was a powerful woman who had hit every possible low point. She was the personification of all Persian women, the embodiment of all the queens before her, a woman who had learned to be as strong as a draught horse, a woman who had been forced to save her own life and that of her son in order to survive in the jungle of corruption.

Her husband had been a weak king, but she had always stood by him. It was she who had forced him to take the necessary decisions. Back when she was a nonentity she would often look in her bedroom mirror and say, 'Someday they'll know who I am. I know all the women of Persia, those who are among the living, who still exist, and those who no longer exist. All the power and all the rights that have been taken from women are now mine.'

She saw in her son both his weak father and his powerful grandfather. Now he was trapped in the cogwheels of change.

'Our greetings to the queen of queens,' the shah called out. The queen mother looked up and smiled.

'The shah has frightened this old woman,' she said.

He got off his horse, walked up to her, kissed her hand, put his arm through hers and guided her along the wall.

'The shah is sad,' she remarked.

He walked beside her in silence.

'Tell me what's wrong.'

'Mother, Mother, I can't go on. People are crying. People are begging. People are dying. People are being robbed. The farmers have been struck by a plague of locusts, the women are being raped, the children are going blind from smallpox, the hair of young boys is falling out. Mother, we feel powerless. Terrible things are happening in the palace. They've made Malijak so fat that the poor boy can no longer walk. I don't know who is doing this to us.'

'Do not distress yourself, my son,' said Mahdolia, and she gripped his arm. 'You are heir to an ancient civilisation. At times we have plunged from the tallest peaks to the deepest valleys. I lived through the reigns of both your father and your grandfather. You rule the land ten times better than your father ever did. It is not your fault, my son. Life is more difficult for you than it was for the other kings. Have patience. I will pray to my God for you. I will go to Him in tears. He will help you.'

'Thank you, Mother. Please don't leave us alone.'

'I am not about to die, my son,' she said. 'I will keep on living until the shah says, Mother, you may go now.'

'You're going to outlive us?' asked the shah with a laugh.

'I'm not going to outlive you. I'm going to stand by you as long as necessary.'

'That's a beautiful promise, Mother,' said the shah.

'Help me, boy. I can no longer climb the stairs by myself.'

He picked her up off the ground and carried her up the stairs in his arms.

'Put me back on the ground,' she laughed, threatening him with her walking stick.

The shah put her down gently and planted a kiss on her crown.

55. In the Bazaar

The years had left their mark on the face of the shah. Whenever he looked in the mirror he no longer dared take off his hat, he had become so grey and bald. Malijak too had visibly changed with the passing of time.

Long ago the shah had talked to his cat to lighten his heart and share his loneliness, but after Sharmin had mysteriously disappeared Malijak took over the cat's job. The shah found him very amusing when he was still small. He never saw the need to teach Malijak to read or write, but he did impart to him the fundamentals of chess. The shah enjoyed Malijak's foolish chessboard moves. As the boy grew older, however, the shah took less pleasure in his company. Malijak still hated to be washed, and he stank. When Malijak was a child the shah himself bathed him, cut his hair and dressed him in clean clothes. But those days were long gone.

The seasons came and went, night followed day, and the shah's travels to Europe now seemed like something that had happened in a dream.

In retrospect he realised that the journey had not brought him happiness but had made him even less happy. His plan to intervene directly and help his subjects with their problems had been more than he could handle, and political unrest was rearing its head once again. As his ambassador in Moscow had written to him in a letter:

What the shah is suffering through in our homeland is actually a variation of the problems that the Russian tsar is struggling with.

There are several groups that want to subvert the power of the tsar. It is their belief that the elite are controlling the state and oppressing the population. These groups are trying to establish a society in which the people govern the state through their elected representatives.

It is a worrying development. They emphasise the rights of the common man, that is, the rights of the man in the street. We believe that the unrest in Russia is going to surface in our country as well, but much more strongly than before. The leaders of the Russian insurgents have spoken with the leaders of the Persian insurgents in Baku. One of them is Aga Jamal.

That evening the shah wrote this in his diary: 'What is happening at the present time is not only our problem. The tsar is having the same difficulties. In Turkey too the sultan realises his power is being compromised. What people in Russia or Turkey do is their business. We will continue to rule in our own way. We are probably destined to go down in history as the last old-fashioned king. If that is the case, we must try to take more pleasure in life.'

Locked up in Tehran's dreadful prison Mirza Reza spent every day applying his mental powers to keep from going mad. He was in with the violent criminals. Most prisoners lost their minds due to lack of light.

The director had been ordered by Eyn ed-Dowleh to subject Mirza Reza to a special punishment. When the guards came to bring him his food they beat him with a copy of his own statute book. At breakfast they beat him once, at around noon they beat him twice, and during dinner they beat him three times.

Mirza Reza knew he must concentrate on his great objective to keep from collapsing in such degrading circumstances. He had a big secret safely tucked away in his heart. It was a secret that burned like an oven, and he turned to it every day to warm himself.

Jamal Khan made several trips to Baku and Istanbul to meet with kindred spirits from Turkey, Iraq, India, Egypt and Russia. He provided his foreign comrades with detailed descriptions of developments in his homeland and exchanged experiences and ideas with them. Slowly he built up a strong network in his own country. Now it was just a matter of waiting for the right opportunity to strike.

Among all the contracts that the shah had signed with commercial firms, businessmen and entrepreneurs during his journey, there was one agreement that proved truly disastrous.

Over a period of twenty years the British had vastly expanded the size of their embassy. They had purchased a large parcel of land behind the embassy building where they constructed a number of houses to accommodate their British guests.

The Russians still lived in their old residence, which dated from the previous century. When the shah was in Moscow this subject came up during a dinner in the Kremlin. The shah, who had already downed two stiff Russian drinks, generously promised a sizeable piece of land to the Russians at no expense whatsoever and sealed the promise with his signet ring.

Nothing else happened. The shah forgot about the contract – until the Russians put up an enormous wooden fence round the promised property. The work was done by a group of local carpenters, and it occurred to no one that the Russians were planning on building a new embassy there. Neither the shah nor the Russians were aware that this was the site of a forgotten burial ground from the previous century.

Jamal Khan was notified of the Russian building plans by his contacts. He went to have a look and was shocked by what he saw. In preparation for the laying of the foundations at the building site all the graves had been desecrated and the bones piled up in a heap. Russian liquor bottles and other rubbish were scattered everywhere.

That evening Jamal Khan took Ayatollah Tabatabai to the cemetery, forced open a length of fence, led the ayatollah inside and cast the light from his lantern over the empty graves, the bones and the thrown-away bottles.

The ayatollah shook with rage as he said, 'Allah, Allah, this is unacceptable. I take refuge in You.'

The shah had made a serious mistake, but what was the ayatollah to do? He had the power to send thousands of people to the Russian embassy to punish both the Russians and the shah. But the ayatollah feared that lives would be lost. So he decided to send a courteous letter to the shah containing the following words: 'We expect the graves to be restored as soon as possible. Allah forgives and Allah punishes without mercy. Wassalam. Tabatabai.'

The shah was livid, but when it came to ayatollahs you couldn't be careful enough. He consulted his vizier. 'It is definitely a serious case,' said Mostovi Almamalek, 'and we must do something about it.'

'It's an old, forgotten burial ground from a hundred years ago.'

'That argument won't hold water. They want the Russians out of there. I'm afraid we'll have to go along with the ayatollah's demand. We have to ask the Russians to abandon their plans for the time being.'

'Out of the question. They'll see us as a weak king. Find another solution.'

'I see no other solution, Your Majesty.'

'Talk to the ayatollah.'

'Talking won't help. There can be no Russian embassy on that site.'

'How do you know that?' answered the shah, who was beginning to wonder whose side his vizier was on.

'Everyone knows that, Your Majesty,' said Mostovi Almamalek. 'And so do you.'

The shah could not put the ayatollah in his place, the vizier knew that a compromise was impossible, and the ayatollah in turn was wrestling with whether he ought to inform the people during a sermon.

Mostovi Almamalek let the Russian embassy know that serious problems had arisen and the new embassy could not be built on that spot. But the Russians, who thought the British were behind all this, ignored the vizier's warning and carried on with their work. Under no circumstances was the Kremlin willing to abandon its building plans.

The vizier paid a personal visit to the ayatollah at his home in order to speak with him: 'I understand your concern, which is why I'm working so hard to find a new site for the Russians. I am asking you to be patient.'

Finally Mostovi Almamalek succeeded in finding another site for the Russian embassy. He sent his messenger to the shah so an agreement on the matter could be reached as soon as possible.

'Not now. Later,' the shah told his vizier. 'We're on our way to Mashad for a working visit. You can come to see us when we return.'

The city of Mashad lay on the Persian–Indian border. The journey alone would take the shah two weeks. It seemed the shah was refusing to acknowledge the sensitivity and gravity of the problem. An outburst could happen at any moment, especially with him away from the capital.

The ayatollah gave the vizier his support and said he was willing to wait until the shah returned from Mashad.

The shah had long ago stopped taking Malijak with him on his travels. It had become difficult for Malijak to put up with the demands of long journeys, so he stayed at home and made life difficult for everyone else. He had a nice collection of pop guns that had been given to him over the years on various occasions. The shah had bought one of the guns for him in Belgium during his European trip. When you shot it at someone the sound it produced was so authentic that the victim would become momentarily confused.

After the shah had left for Mashad Malijak spent every day roaming through the palace with his Belgian gun. His deteriorating eyesight had had no effect on the virulence of the terror he generated. Everyone gave him food and filled his pockets with sweets to stay on good terms with him.

The shah's British doctor, who also treated Malijak, had recently said to the shah, 'He must get more exercise or he'll be dead within a few years.' In order to provide that exercise the shah had arranged for a group of hardy servants to carry Malijak into the hills in a sedan chair every now and then. The servants also had to take a cage full of chickens with them. Once they got into the hills they would release the chickens so Malijak could chase them with his gun. This was supposed to be a playful form of exercise, though it did him very little good.

After such a day in the hills Malijak invariably insisted on being taken to the bazaar. For those seeing him for the first time he struck a remarkable figure: a fat, handicapped prince with strange eyes and a gun in his hand being carried on the shoulders of his servants.

Malijak loved being in the bazaar more than anywhere else because the merchants kept stuffing him with treats. No one there was pleased by these little visits, for Malijak terrorised all and sundry. The merchants had already complained a number of times to the head of the bazaar police that they did not appreciate Malijak's presence and that he constantly harassed them. But the head of the police didn't dare pass the complaints on to the palace. Even sending telegrams directly to the shah hadn't helped.

Now that the shah was gone Malijak ordered the servants to take him to the bazaar even more often. He caused pandemonium day after day – until the shopkeepers decided it was too much. They saw the irritating Malijak as an appendage of the shah. Then the rumour went round that the shah had left Malijak home on purpose just to get under their skin. Their indignation sought an outlet. One afternoon, as if by common agreement, they all began throwing goodies at Malijak. Then the beggars stormed the sedan chair, pushing each other and the servants out of the way in order to get their hands on the sweets.

Malijak was greatly amused by both the hail of confectionery and the fighting beggars. He roared with laughter and shot his pop gun. The bazaar exploded in chaos. The bearers were pushed aside, Malijak's chair toppled over and he fell to the ground with his full weight. The shopkeepers began throwing coins to divert the attention of the beggars, but the mayhem only got worse. In an effort to restore order the police fired a few shots, injuring a number of beggars and shopkeepers.

After the beggars had been chased away the policemen saw Malijak lying wounded on the ground. They put him on a cart and transported him back to the palace. When the shopkeepers saw that Malijak was being treated like a prince while their colleagues were left to fend for themselves, they closed the bazaar in protest and proceeded to the house of Ayatollah Tabatabai, shouting, 'Allah! Allah! Justice!'

Jamal Khan, who had witnessed the unrest and smelled an opportunity, entered the ayatollah's house, knelt down before him and said, 'History is knocking at your door.'

Tabatabai heard the crowds shouting outside: '*Elteja, elteja*, all our hope is in you!' The ayatollah flung open the door of his home, but he had no way of knowing that in doing so he had taken on the responsibility of steering the homeland into a new era. The shopkeepers unrolled carpets and began claiming sanctuary in the ayatollah's house.

Directed by Jamal Khan they fastened a large banner over the door with three short but powerful words written on it: '*Qanun*! *Majles*! *Edalat-khaneh*! Constitution! Parliament! Court of justice!'

56. The Ayatollahs

The first Persian religion was named after the Persian prophet Zoroaster. For the followers of Zoroaster fire was holy. They saw it as the earthly symbol of their god, Ahura Mazda. According to their teaching the very first fire that man ever made was preserved in the Zoroastrians' main temple in the city of Yazd. This temple was therefore given the name '*atashkadeh*', which means 'house for fire'.

The Zoroastrian priests dictated every aspect of human conduct, and the people acted accordingly. When the Arabs invaded Persia under the flag of Islam they banned the religion of Zoroastrianism. They stormed the ancient temple in Yazd to extinguish the fire, but the priests had already taken it away and fled to India, accompanied by vast numbers of followers.

It took a few centuries for the people of Persia to accept Islam, but as an act of resistance they refused to adopt the Islam of the occupiers and instead founded a new Islamic belief. This became the Islam of Persia, now known as Shia Islam. Since then the Persians have had their own clerics, the imams and the ayatollahs, which is the highest religious status an imam can achieve. The ayatollahs introduced new rules and social norms. They led simple lives and did not interfere with the ruling elite.

The aged Ayatollah Shirazi, incited by Jamal Khan and his people, was the first to use his clerical clout to help the destitute tobacco merchants and the farmers on the tobacco plantations by issuing a fatwa. This marked the beginning of the clerics' gradual quest for power. One of these clerics was Tabatabai. After the incident in the bazaar Tabatabai went to the holy city of Qom. He told the clerics there about the violated burial ground, the plans to build the new Russian embassy and the shah's stubborn refusal to take action. Indeed the shah had turned his back on the problem by going to Mashad.

The story of the burial ground had its effect. The Russians' opening of Muslim graves was seen by the ayatollahs as a flagrant insult. They sided with Tabatabai.

The shah returned to Tehran earlier than expected. Assured of Qom's powerful support Ayatollah Tabatabai sent him a sharply worded letter on the question of the burial ground and Malijak's reign of terror. He used these two matters to get to his ultimate demand: 'The people demand qanun, majles, edalat-khaneh.' The ayatollah wanted the letter to be taken to the palace by his messenger, but Jamal Khan advised against it. 'The shah is ignoring you. He'll dismiss the letter as well. I think this calls for a different approach.'

'What do you suggest?' asked the ayatollah.

'Have your letter delivered to the British embassy. With your approval we can ask the British to hand the letter to the shah officially.'

'I don't think that's wise. Why involve England in an internal matter?'

'We have no choice,' answered Jamal Khan. 'And it's irresponsible to wait any longer for an answer from the shah. A constitution is the natural right of any people. England can be our ally in our struggle against the shah.'

A group of seven merchants, representatives of the bazaar, took the ayatollah's message to the British embassy.

None of them spoke a word of English. As luck would have it an important English person happened to be in the embassy that day: Edward Granville Browne. Browne had lost his heart to Persia. He had visited the ruins of all the royal palaces and had made an attempt to decipher the secrets of cuneiform script. At that time it was almost impossible to find anyone as well versed in the Persian past as this Edward Granville Browne. He was a doctor by profession so he was welcome everywhere. He was in his late thirties and had already made three lengthy visits to Persia. He had picked up the Persian language on his own.

The Englishman was still in the southern part of the country when he heard about the unrest in Tehran. He was in Pasargadae investigating the ruins of the ancient palaces that had been set on fire by Alexander the Great. He abandoned his activities and proceeded to Tehran in order to witness the events there first-hand.

Once in Tehran, Browne stayed in the British residence to work on his famous travel book *Two Years Among the Persians*. On that particular day he was standing at the window of a small room on the second floor of the embassy with a view of the bazaar square, waiting for the telegraph operator to send a travel report to a British newspaper. He saw seven men in expensive coats and hats walking solemnly towards the embassy. Because he knew the Persians and their behaviour so well, he understood immediately by their demeanour that something important was about to take place.

The seven merchants had brought along a note written in English that briefly explained why they had come. Browne glanced at the text. He wondered whether he could ask the gentlemen to come in or whether he should warn the ambassador first. He decided on the former. To the amazement of the Persian gentlemen he welcomed them in their own language and invited them in, entirely in accordance with their social conventions: '*Khosh amadid, befarma'id tu'i. Chai tazeh hazer ast.* Welcome, please come in. The fresh tea awaits you.'

The merchants trusted him immediately, and they poured out their hearts to him before they had even left the hallway.

In a state of agitation Browne entered the ambassador's office, closed the door behind him and said quietly, 'There are seven Persian gentlemen downstairs waiting to see you. They're carrying a sealed letter, which they want the British embassy to hand officially to the shah.'

'Why are they asking us to do this?'

'If I understand them correctly, they are being ignored by the shah. Now they want to try going through the embassy to force the shah to respond to their letter.'

'But that's impossible. We are not permitted to get involved in this domestic affair.'

Edward Granville Browne was a free spirit, without political ambition. He had spent almost a third of his life in India and Persia, and he was not pleased with the way the British acted in those countries. Now that the ambassador was saying that he would not receive the letter from the seven merchants, Browne bowed towards him and whispered, 'This is a unique opportunity for the British Empire. Accept their letter.'

The ambassador walked downstairs to where the gentlemen were waiting, all of them standing with great dignity. One of them held the sealed envelope against his chest like a precious gem. They greeted the ambassador, and the man who was holding the letter began to speak in Persian.

The ambassador called Browne to act as interpreter.

The ambassador understood Persian and did not really need Edward Granville Browne, but perhaps he was vain and was thinking about the book Browne was writing. Perhaps he hoped that, with Browne's help, he would go down in Persian and British history.

'The ambassador says it is unusual in the diplomatic world for an ambassador to involve himself in a national conflict taking place in the host nation. But just this once he will take personal responsibility and have your letter officially sent to the shah by messenger. The ambassador stresses that England is not party to this matter and is distancing itself from the contents of your correspondence.'

The man speaking on behalf of the group thanked the ambassador and handed him the letter. The gentlemen bowed their heads and walked to the door.

When the shah received the sealed letter from the merchants, contained in a sealed British envelope, he almost fell off his chair. He summoned his vizier and his son-in-law, Eyn ed-Dowleh. 'The merchants have gone too far. Our last response was too weak, which is why they have had the arrogance to go to the British embassy. We regard it as disloyalty to the throne. England has interfered in our affairs uninvited. We must tackle this evil at the root.'

He asked his vizier to send a letter of protest to the British embassy to show them their place, and ordered Eyn ed-Dowleh to arrest the persons who had sought contact with them. 'Punish them mercilessly, in public!'

'We won't solve the problem this way,' the vizier ventured to remark. 'We're ignoring the contents of their letter. We must look at their demands.'

'What demands? What they are asking is dangerous and illegal. England cannot tell us what to do in our own country.'

'These are not England's demands. They are from the bazaar.'

'And who is the king, we or the bazaar?'

'You are the king, and these are the needs of your subjects – subjects we must listen to.'

'We, the shah of Persia, are not going to sit at the same table with a traitor.'

'That choice will have grave repercussions for the shah.'

'The kings before me have always had to deal with grave repercussions.'

'In your own best interest, I strongly advise you not to use violence in this case,' urged Mostovi Almamalek.

The shah turned to Eyn ed-Dowleh. 'First let us arrest the persons who carried the letter to the embassy. Then we will discuss the letter's contents.' With these words the shah brought to an end any possible discussion.

Eyn ed-Dowleh quickly found out who the merchants were. Accompanied by a group of armed officers he entered the house of the ayatollah where the merchants were claiming sanctuary. Gun in hand he stood in the middle of the courtyard while his officers dragged the seven men outside. The other merchants tried to stop them. '*La ellaha ella allah*,' they cried, attacking the officers.

Ayatollah Tabatabai threw his black turban down at the feet of Eyn ed-Dowleh and shouted, 'I am warning you about your behaviour! God does not allow what you are doing!' and he tried to get to the door to help the merchants. But his path was blocked.

'Allah! Allah!' cried the crowds. 'Anyone who can, come and help!'

People from every nook and cranny came to the house of the ayatollah, where the arrested merchants had been loaded onto a horse cart. Eyn ed-Dowleh and his men were holding the masses back when suddenly Jamal Khan, still dressed as an imam, descended on the horse cart with a group of faithful followers. They freed the detainees, who, along with many others, succeeded in reaching the telegraph office and bolting the iron gate of the building behind them.

In the past people sought sanctuary in the holy places and the homes of the ayatollahs, but this was the first time they had done so in a telegraph building. All Eyn ed-Dowleh could do was have the building surrounded. Then he rode to the palace to inform the shah.

It was already dark, and the officers around the telegraph building had heard nothing from Eyn ed-Dowleh. Apparently the shah had also been overwhelmed by the unexpected twist in the merchants' protest. The atmosphere inside the telegraph building was one of victory. The merchants sent a series of long telegrams to the all bazaars of the country to explain what was going on in Tehran. They signed their telegrams with new slogans.

That same evening the telegraph of the British embassy began to chatter. It was a message to the ambassador. Edward Granville Browne read it aloud to him. 'This is unbelievable. They've made their demands public. They want a parliament, a court of justice and a constitution, and they've asked England to support them in their struggle.'

'I don't know whether this is such a wise move,' said the ambassador. 'I would have preferred to have spoken with them first. I'm afraid it's all going to get out of hand.'

'Maybe, but maybe not. Both the shah and his opponents know how the game is played. The new element is that they're trying to get England involved in their uprising.'

'It's a complicated business. I've explained it to London and we find ourselves in a very difficult situation.'

The shah received the same message by telegram. He

was about to put it on the stack of unread letters when he noticed the names of the merchants. The shock was profound. He gave Eyn ed-Dowleh the following orders: 'Cut the telegraph cables running out of Tehran to end their contact with the outside world. Don't let anyone in. They'll come out begging for water and food.'

News of the occupation of the telegraph building made its way throughout the city. People came by the hundreds to cheer the merchants on. Some tried throwing food over the fences, but whoever did was arrested and beaten by the guards. The merchants in the building cried, 'Majles! Edalat-khaneh! Qanun!'

The crowds cried back, '*Ma hameh ba ham hastim*, we're with you, we're all in this together.' Despite the strict surveillance the merchants did manage to receive provisions. When their superiors weren't looking some of the officers let the people pass jugs of water and food in to the confined occupiers.

Three days passed, but nothing happened.

'*Ya marg, ya qanun*, death or the constitution!' The merchants refused to budge. The crowds responded to this uncompromising rallying cry by taking it over. It resounded in every quarter of the city.

In the evening the shah's wives grabbed their binoculars and climbed up on the roof. They couldn't make out the people very clearly, but they did see their torches and movements and they heard their shouts: 'Qanun! Qanun! Qanun!'

The cries triggered something in the women of the harem. They didn't understand what 'qanun' actually meant or what the advantages of a 'qanun' would be for them, but they hummed 'qanun, qanun, qanun' over and over, and by repeating this strange word they felt a new kind of joy fill their bodies.

The situation seemed hopeless. The shah did not want to use violence and the demonstrators did not want to leave the building. The British ambassador had been advised by London to follow the developments and take no initiative, but to keep all the lines of communication open. London had concluded that the shah could not win this fight, which is why the ambassador had decided that if the worst came to the worst he would give the demonstrators a helping hand.

Jamal Khan and Ayatollah Tabatabai did everything they could to bring the great ayatollahs of Qom to Tehran, hoping that their arrival would signify a breakthrough. When evening came three coaches carrying nine ayatollahs reached the city. People cried, '*Khush amadid, khush amadid. Salalah ala Muhammad salam bar Muhammad.* Welcome, and salam to the descendants of the Prophet Muhammad.'

The officers at Telegraph Square prevented the coaches from going any further. The weary ayatollahs got out and Ayatollah Tabatabai welcomed them. The ayatollahs walked to the telegraph building, but none of the officers even considered stopping them. They knew that if they did anything wrong they would have the crowds to contend with. So they stepped aside and bowed their heads in silence.

When the people in the telegraph building saw the ayatollahs they were deeply moved and cried out, 'Ya marg, ya qanun, death or the constitution!'

The oldest ayatollah, whose name was Behbahani, held his walking stick in the air and moved with the rhythm of the slogan. The other ayatollahs copied his gesture: 'Qanun! Qanun! Qanun! Constitution! Constitution! Constitution!' Then the exhausted ayatollahs went to the house of Ayatollah Tabatabai to claim sanctuary out of protest.

It wasn't long before dozens of other imams began to follow their lead. The British embassy watched everything, wrote it all down and sent daily telegrams to London. They prepared themselves for any eventuality.

When the clerics of Qom came to claim sanctuary it was a shot in the arm for the merchants in the telegraph building, but it did not change the situation. The shah was profoundly unimpressed.

Jamal Khan held a meeting every night to discuss how to help the merchants and the ayatollahs move on to the next phase of their collaboration. A few nights after the arrival of the ayatollahs the committee made an important decision. They would attack the notorious Tehran prison and free their comrades.

The next day hundreds of demonstrators removed the chains from the prisoners being kept in the damp dungeons. Mirza Reza, who was emaciated and weak, rose to his feet like a warrior when he heard the voice of Jamal Khan in the dark corridor leading to his cell. Four prisoners lost their lives in the exchange of gunfire between the guards and the demonstrators. If the guards had wanted to they could have killed dozens more, but it was obvious that some of the guards sympathised with the action.

When news of the storming of the prison reached the telegraph building, the crowd attacked the police. Instead of withdrawing, Eyn ed-Dowleh decided to retaliate. He ordered his officers to smash down the door of the telegraph office using a large, heavy beam. The officers then beat the merchants with their rifle butts. But the merchants put up a good fight, crying, 'Ya marg, ya qanun, death or the constitution!' all the while.

A number of people turned on Eyn ed-Dowleh and completely surrounded him. One young imam leapt forward and grabbed the reins of Eyn ed-Dowleh's horse. The animal reared up and whinnied. Eyn ed-Dowleh aimed his rifle at the imam, but the imam grabbed his left leg and pulled him from his saddle so that he fell flat on the ground with his rifle and sword. The young imam picked up the rifle and was about to shoot Eyn ed-Dowleh but was fired on himself by a nearby sergeant.

Edward Granville Browne was watching it all from the roof of the British residence. In the chaos of trigger-happy soldiers and demonstrators who were fighting for their lives with sticks and stones, Jamal Khan ran through the crowd to the British embassy. He shouted up to the roof: 'Edward Granville Browne, listen to me! Many people are about to be killed. England must assume its responsibility. The demonstrators are being held captive. Open the embassy gate, let everyone in!'

At first Edward Granville Browne did not understand. When he finally grasped the situation he shouted back, 'I shall warn the ambassador!'

London had already given the ambassador the nod to assist the opposition if necessary. Just to be sure, though, he wanted to send one more telegram to London to ask for permission. But Browne appealed to him with great emotion: 'The shah is killing his own subjects before our very eyes. You cannot wait for London. You must decide!' Outside the soldiers were shooting at the defenceless demonstrators.

'Open the gates!' said the ambassador. Browne ran to the gate.

'Everyone flee to the British embassy!' shouted Jamal Khan at the top of his voice.

One after another they all ran into the embassy's huge garden. As the British ambassador dictated a telegram to London he watched the people standing behind the embassy fences, shaking their fists at the soldiers and shouting, 'Ya marg, ya qanun!'

57. The Embassy

The next day almost the entire city had gathered round the embassy. These were ordinary people who, up until now, had only followed the events at a distance. When the gardens of the embassy were full people rolled carpets out over the pavements and onto the square, where new people were constantly coming to sit. The people living nearby opened the doors of their houses so everyone could have access to water.

The shah couldn't believe what Eyn ed-Dowleh was telling him. His lips trembled and his hand reached for his sword. Eyn ed-Dowleh took a step backwards.

'And what did you do?' shouted the shah with rage. 'Stand by and watch? You're nothing but a scarecrow. How else would they have dared to storm the prison? How else would they have dared to enter the British embassy? Don't just stand there in front of me like a puppet in a puppet show. Go and surround the embassy!'

Eyn ed-Dowleh rode to the barracks at once. Then, accompanied by additional troops, he marched to the British embassy. In the meantime the shah had summoned his vizier.

The shah was seething. 'The British are preparing a coup. Either you straighten them out or I'll turn to Russia for help.'

'The shah must think of his health. Anger is harmful to your body,' said Mostovi Almamalek to the shah in calming tones.

'I'd rather die than see the British push us into a corner,' the shah responded. 'Contact the embassy. Order them to send the demonstrators away or I'll regard it as a declaration of war on the part of England.'

'It's not wise to come down so hard on them right away. The problem is not the British embassy.'

'The problem is every bit the British embassy. The British are in league with that so-called Tehran committee.'

'Your Majesty, we cannot keep blaming the British. They have invested a fortune in the southern part of the country. They want a government that will protect their people and their installations.'

'That government already exists,' said the shah.

'What we need for these complex projects are an independent government and a powerful parliament.'

'The vizier is trying to sell us the slogans of our enemies.'

'That's not true. England wants to set up banks in our country. If we have no constitution or court of justice the investors will not materialise. The shah wonders why the British embassy opened its garden to the demonstrators. Your Majesty, England's demands are exactly the same as those of your subjects, that's why.'

'The vizier has expatiated at length, but you've missed one important point in your argument. I have visited a number of European parliaments, but parliaments like that will never work here. Power must be kept secretive and incomprehensible.'

'That will never change. I guarantee it. But I am asking your permission to negotiate officially with the leaders of the demonstrators.'

'As long as they remain at the embassy I will not give you permission. The British embassy is British territory. First they will have to leave the embassy. Then you may begin talks with them.'

'I'll see what I can do,' said the vizier.

'We have patience,' said the shah firmly.

The ayatollahs too were troubled by the new turn of events. If the people were to remain in the garden of the British embassy, it would be difficult for the ayatollahs to provide them with direct support. They would be unable to come to an unequivocal decision. They ended their discussion and went to the courtyard for some fresh air.

Behbahani, the oldest ayatollah, hobbled to the pool, washed his hands and threw some water on his face. He leaned on his walking stick and listened to the bustle in the street with closed eyes. Then he walked up the stairs to the roof. From the edge of the roof he could see the crowds at the embassy, on the pavements and in the square. As soon as the people saw him on the roof they all began to shout: 'Ya marg, ya qanun, ya marg, ya qanun, ya marg, ya qanun!'

The aged ayatollah incited the chanting crowds with his left arm, his right hand on his walking stick. Then he sat down on the edge of the roof. The crowd shouted even louder: 'Qanun! Qanun! Qanun!'

Now the other ayatollahs appeared together on the roof. The people shook their fists and stamped their feet: 'Ya marg, ya qanun!' It made everything at the embassy shake, from the doors and windows to the fences.

A servant rolled out a large carpet on the roof and the ayatollahs sat down on it with their faces towards the embassy. This was how they expressed their solidarity with the people at the embassy without having to go there themselves.

This act of the ayatollahs made things even more complicated for Mostovi Almamalek. First he sent a messenger to the British ambassador and tactfully asked him to force the demonstrators to leave the embassy. The ambassador, who had seen the ayatollahs on the roof, knew that his position was stronger than ever. He in turn sent a messenger to the vizier: 'We have no army to drive the occupiers out of the embassy. Personally, I would be very grateful if you would bring this matter to an end. What England wants is to keep the peace.'

Everyone was expecting that a spirit of gloom would descend on the square, but the atmosphere remained cheerful and lively. Fresh bread began coming in from everywhere as well as vegetables, fruit, sugar cubes and biscuits. The people ate together, slept together, smoked their pipes and discussed things with each other. No one knew how long it would go on.

A great silence hung over the palace. It seemed as if the shah wanted to show that he was still unimpressed by the demonstrations. But he couldn't just stand by idly and watch. The news of people claiming sanctuary in the embassy had spread to other cities, where people had also begun to claim sanctuary in the telegraph offices to support their comrades in Tehran. Prompt action was called for.

The shah, in the person of his vizier, tried to negotiate with the opposition via England. At the same time he spoke with his own advisors and army officers, telling them to prepare for a possible attack on the throne. While all this was going on a Russian messenger was riding back and forth in deepest secrecy between the palace and the Russian embassy.

A week passed. The vizier's negotiations with a delegation from the bazaar, and his discussions with the ayatollahs, had so far proved fruitless. The opposition refused to budge until the shah met their demands.

The shah felt the situation pressing down on his chest,

which sometimes made it difficult to breathe. He had been awakened a few times in the middle of the night by the sound of his own racing blood. He had nightmares. In his sleep he set up his cannon on the embassy square and shot the demonstrators in the embassy garden. No, this could not go on much longer.

'We've got to teach England a lesson,' said the shah to Eyn ed-Dowleh. 'Sweep out the embassy garden. Pull down the fences if necessary and get those traitors out of there.' The shah's order was clear. His son-in-law put a special unit in place – armed horsemen who were skilled with both swords and guns. It was late in the afternoon when he advanced on the embassy. But another development had taken place the evening before. Horse carts full of illegal weapons had been smuggled into the city.

When the special guards appeared on the embassy square the air became electric. Jamal Khan, still in his imam disguise, left the embassy through a back door and entered a house on a side street.

Eyn ed-Dowleh lined up his men and began to speak. 'In the name of the shah I am asking you to leave the embassy.'

'Ya marg, ya qanun, death or the constitution!' cried the crowd in the garden.

'People, listen! I do not want to use violence. I am asking you in a friendly way to leave the embassy.'

'Ya marg, ya qanun!' was the answer.

'People! It is a disgrace to rise up in revolt against your own king under the flag of a foreign power. I am giving you a chance. I am letting you go unharmed.'

'Ya marg, ya qanun!' the crowd shouted at the ayatollahs.

Eyn ed-Dowleh fired a shot into the air and cried, 'Everybody out of here!'

The demonstrators didn't move.

'Sword!' cried Eyn ed-Dowleh. The horsemen drew their swords. 'People! This is my final warning. Leave the embassy!'

'Qanun! Majles! Edalat! Constitution! Parliament! Court of justice!' shouted the crowd.

'Attack!' cried Eyn ed-Dowleh.

Eyn ed-Dowleh rode straight into the mass of demonstrators who were standing on the pavements. When the square in front of the embassy was empty the horsemen blocked all the side streets. Eyn ed-Dowleh turned to the demonstrators in the embassy once again: 'I'm giving you one more chance to leave the embassy without the shedding of blood.'

'Qanun! Qanun! Qanun!' shouted the crowd.

He returned his sword to its sheath, seized his gun and cried, 'In the name of the shah, I am asking you to open the gates or we'll shoot you all down!'

'Majles! Majles! Majles!' shouted the crowd.

'Stand to!' shouted Eyn ed-Dowleh to a row of horsemen directly behind him.

He aimed his gun at the embassy. Not a sound could be heard behind the fences. The ayatollahs stood motionless on the roof and the women fell silent. Edward Granville Browne waited breathlessly at the window on the embassy's upper floor.

'Fire!'

A few people behind the fences fell and suddenly all hell broke loose. The gates swung open and the crowds threw themselves onto Eyn ed-Dowleh and his horsemen. The square became a scene of battle. Jamal Khan, a rifle on his back, had climbed onto the roof of one of the houses on the square. He stretched out on the edge of the roof and took aim at Eyn ed-Dowleh. The bullet hit the man's shoulder so that his gun flew into the air and he fell from his horse. Three soldiers hurried him away.

Suddenly the soldiers found themselves under fire from every corner. They couldn't tell where the bullets were coming from. They let their dead lie where they fell and helped remove the wounded. Now that the people had a whiff of power they moved on to the palace.

Eyn ed-Dowleh was badly wounded, so a senior officer took his place. He rode straight to the palace to make his report. Kneeling before the shah he said, 'Your Majesty! The kingdom is in danger. We have done everything to avoid it, but an armed mob is on its way to the palace.'

'How did they come by these weapons?' asked the shah.

'We haven't any idea. Suddenly our men were being shot at from the rooftops. A couple of soldiers have been killed and dozens have been wounded, including Eyn ed-Dowleh. But many of the army's guns have ended up in the wrong hands. I fear the demonstrators have mounted an attack on our arsenal.'

'We've walked into a trap,' the shah said. 'My father always warned us about England's dirty tricks.' He ordered that a row of cannons be placed in front of the palace gates, and that the entrances to all the streets leading to the palace square be blocked.

When the officer had gone the shah called in the head of the guards. 'Bring out our cannon!' he ordered.

58. An Ultimatum

The shah put on his military uniform, slipped his revolver into his belt and waited for the vizier. He heard a horseman come into the courtyard. It was Mostovi Almamalek. The shah tried to remain impassive. 'I assume you have achieved nothing with your negotiations.'

'Your Majesty is right. Nothing. I come with empty hands!'

'We knew you would. They're traitors.'

'Your conclusion is incorrect, Your Majesty,' responded the vizier. 'The shah sent me without room to negotiate because Your Majesty does not believe in negotiations. The shah wants to solve this complicated matter with violence.'

'It does not become the vizier to speak in this fashion,' the shah remarked.

'Your Majesty, you have jeopardised the safety of the country.'

'It does not become the vizier to speak in this fashion,' said the shah more forcefully.

'The throne is in danger. The ramifications of Eyn ed-Dowleh's intervention are incalculable. The palace is surrounded by armed men. They are no longer ashamed of facing their own king with a gun in their hands.'

It was unusual for the shah to let his vizier speak like this without interrupting him. He poured the vizier a glass of water. 'We understand the vizier's difficult position. What is your advice now?'

'I have a message from them for Your Majesty.'

'From whom?'

'From the leaders of the opposition.'

'Who are they?'

'The shah does not know these people, but they include two ayatollahs, one of whom you met during the tobacco revolt.'

'What is his name?'

'Ayatollah Tabatabai.'

'And the other?'

'Ayatollah Behbahani.'

'Did we meet him before?'

'I don't think so. He is an older cleric who came to Tehran from Qom with a delegation. He is the envoy of the clerics of Qom.'

'What is their message?'

'They are presenting you with an ultimatum.'

'They are too insignificant to present us with an ultimatum!' the shah spat out.

'They are giving you until tomorrow afternoon, until the first afternoon prayer, to agree to their demands.'

'What are their demands?'

'They want a constitution, a court of justice and a parliament.'

'A parliament?' roared the shah. 'What do those mouldy old ayatollahs know about a parliament?'

'Your Majesty, the whole country has risen up in revolt. I'm worried. I'm thinking about you, Your Majesty. As vizier I am convinced that our homeland needs the shah. If the shah were to fall, the unity of the country would collapse.'

'What can we do?' asked the shah.

'I have a feeling that our opponents expect a gesture of reconciliation from the shah. To defuse the unrest, the shah can agree to some of their demands.'

'But which ones?'

'A parliament. It will take at least a year before such a parliament is created. Within that year peace will return to the country and you will have given us some room to think.'

'A parliament? Who will represent this illiterate people in the parliament? The mullahs? What do they know about governing a country?'

'Your Majesty, this is not the time for such a discussion.'

'The ayatollahs are nothing but British puppets!' shouted the shah. 'But we have faced far greater enemies than England. All right, we authorise our vizier to discuss this subject with them.'

The shah went straight to his study, took up his pen and wrote a short note. He folded the paper, put it in an envelope and sealed it with wax. A messenger took the note to the Russian embassy.

Soon the messenger returned, accompanied by another horseman. It was a Russian official with whom the shah had exchanged ideas on many occasions. They strolled together through the garden, and after a brief discussion the shah arranged for the official to be taken back to the Russian embassy.

That night, armed with his binoculars, the shah studied the surrounding area from the watchtower. He couldn't see the demonstrators but he could hear the clamour in the streets. There was a great deal of commotion in the harem as well. The women were standing in two groups, quarrelling and hurling abuse at each other.

'There's never been a time in all of history when women could be trusted,' he said under his breath. 'They're the first ones to leave their bedroom doors ajar for the enemy.'

Then a royal coach rode onto the square, which the shah recognised as his mother's. The coach passed through the gate and stopped at the palace steps. Mahdolia got out, with the head of the guards holding a torch aloft so she could see where she was going.

'Mother, what are you doing here in this madness in the middle of the night?' cried the shah.

'History is repeating itself, my son. This isn't the first time I've rushed to your side to lend you my support.'

'You're right, Mother. History has indeed repeated itself.'

'Except for one thing,' Mahdolia answered. 'The last time I could climb these steps under my own steam.'

'You could have called for me if you had need of me,' said the shah as he helped her into a chair and sat down beside her.

'How could the shah have come to me with all those barricades in front of the palace? Anyway, I wanted to ride past the people to show them we aren't afraid. As soon as they saw me they started shouting, "Qanun, qanun, qanun." But what do these people know about a qanun? They all stink. I had to cover my nose with a handkerchief as I rode past. I still don't understand how they come up with such ideas. Who has put such words in their mouths?'

'We have done it ourselves. We are the cause. The boys who went to Europe to study are now my enemies. We have bred a race of vipers in our own nest.'

'My son, I forbid you to display weakness in the presence of this riffraff.'

'You can see we have not shown any weakness, yet they have presented us with an ultimatum.'

'What kind of ultimatum?'

'They want us to meet their demands tomorrow by the first afternoon prayer.'

'They have gone too far! Clearly they're being given outside help or they never would be hounding us with such demands,' cried Mahdolia, and she produced a document from inside her clothing. She put the document in the shah's hands and said, 'This is the agreement your father and I signed with the Russians. Everything is here in black and white. The Russians are duty bound to help you in time of need. Just ask them for help!'

The shah thumbed through the document, glanced at the various sections and said, 'We are already in contact with the Russians. They know what's going on. But they can't just drop everything and come to our aid.'

'I understand that. We've got to think of something else right now to buy time.'

'Don't worry, Mother, we've taken care of everything,' said the shah.

'Exactly what have you done? What agreements have you made with the Russians?'

Abruptly the shah stood up. He needed the distance in order to speak to her. Mahdolia saw by his bearing that he wanted to say, Mother, I am the king. I make the decisions and I have dealt with the matter. I do not need your opinion.

Yet she repeated her question, 'What have you and the Russians decided?'

'It is taken care of, Mother. We have taken care of it. You don't have to worry about it any more. You need to rest. I will not burden you any further.'

Mahdolia understood that the shah had a secret plan, and that for the first time he did not want to share it with her. What he was saying between the lines was, 'Your time is over.'

Mahdolia was right: the shah did have a plan, and he wanted to keep it to himself. Did he no longer trust his mother and the people around her, or did he want to show her that there were secrets only the shah should know about?

Hurt but proud, Mahdolia stood up, and with tears in her eyes she said, 'The shah is very perceptive: I have grown old and you no longer need me. You are powerful enough to continue on your own. As a mother I am proud of you. I am leaving.'

The shah ate almost nothing the whole day. He was gripped by an insidious fear. He had pushed the old vizier aside with violence, and now, in a more subtle way, he had done the same to his mother. The shah was shouldering all the responsibility – at least that's the way he saw it. But in fact he was now quite alone.

He tried to behave like a real king and not to fear the tremendous events that were taking place in the country. And in this he succeeded. But now that his subjects were armed and standing behind sandbags outside his palace, he did feel afraid. Perhaps the great kings had also been struck by fear in their more solitary moments.

'Taj, my grandson,' he murmured. Why had he not thought of them before? Where was his chamberlain? For the first time in his life he called the man by name: 'Aga Moshir!'

There was no response.

'Aga Moshir!' called the shah again.

The chamberlain was probably not in the building. The shah summoned the head of the guards. The man came running in at once.

'Get your horse! And bring me Sheikh Aqasi.'

The shah went to his study, took a sheet of paper and began to write. He signed the letter and then looked out the window towards the gate to see if Sheikh Aqasi was coming.

Finally the head of the guards appeared with Sheikh

Aqasi. The shah took the sheikh to the small conference room.

'We have neglected something important and it concerns Taj Olsultan and her child, our crown prince. We should have brought them to safety much sooner,' he said.

The shah thrust the letter into the sheikh's hands. 'This is for the Russian embassy. There are two things you must do. First deliver the letter personally to the Russian ambassador. To him and him only. Then tomorrow morning quietly take Taj Olsultan and her child to your country house. Stay with them during this period of unrest. If the situation in Tehran gets out of hand all three of you are to go to Tabriz. If anything should happen to us flee with them to Russia, to Moscow. I have written the rest in the letter to the ambassador.'

Nothing else needed to be said. Sheikh Aqasi kissed the shah's hand in gratitude for his total trust.

Relieved, the shah drank a glass of water. Now he was no longer afraid of the people outside. He was more afraid of betrayal – that people from his own circle would choose this very night to murder him. It was an old fear that he had been carrying with him since childhood.

After having mounted a raid in India his grandfather had been lying asleep in a tent on a hillside in Afghanistan. He was being watched over by his loyal bodyguards. But his most faithful bodyguard stabbed him to death in his sleep with a knife. In the shah's tribe this murder was always spoken of as a lesson. As a child the shah had lived in constant fear that someone would kill him in his sleep.

Tonight the fear was stronger than ever. Perhaps tonight he would be murdered by his obedient chamberlain. Who was this chamberlain, anyway – the man who never spoke? Who did the man have contact with outside the palace?

Who had introduced him in the first place? Indeed, who was this mysterious man who materialised like a ghost every time the shah rang his little bell?

To avoid any unnecessary risks the shah decided to spend the night before the ultimatum in the treasury beneath the palace. Should an emergency arise he could always escape.

59. On the Chessboard

Early the next morning the shah carefully unbolted his bedroom door, put his hand to his ear and listened. It was quiet in the palace. He walked to the hall of mirrors, still wearing his military uniform. The guards marched undisturbed and the soldiers were standing at their post. The chamberlain appeared.

'We're hungry. Call the cook.'

The cook came with a large, round tray. He looked at the shah and waited for him to give his permission to test the food.

'Was there anyone with you in the kitchen this morning?'

'No, Your Majesty,' answered the cook.

'No one?'

'No, Your Majesty. Only the chamberlain.'

'Was anyone in the kitchen last night?'

The cook panicked. 'No, I . . . I don't know, Your Majesty,' he stuttered.

'Then take it all away!'

When the cook was gone the shah walked to the door through which the chamberlain always entered and went into the back room. The chamberlain was sitting at the table having his breakfast. He had not expected to see the shah, and he jumped up with a start.

'You've got the day off today. Go home. We'll let you know when you can come back.'

The chamberlain hesitated a moment.

'Go home,' said the shah firmly.

The chamberlain took his coat off the hook, bowed and left. The shah put the chamberlain's fresh bread, cheese and pot of hot tea on a tray and took it with him to the hall of mirrors.

A little while later the head of the guards came to report that a messenger from the army was waiting at the gates.

'Disarm him and send him in,' said the shah.

The messenger announced that the ayatollahs had called on the soldiers to lay down their arms and defect to the other side. The shah wanted to ask him whether the soldiers had complied with the call, but he held back and said nothing.

'Was that all?' asked the shah.

'Yes, Your Majesty.' The messenger left the room.

The shah went over to the window again. His guards were making their normal rounds and the soldiers were standing on the walls keeping watch. The deadline would be reached in only a few hours. He waited for the vizier, but his patience ran out. He felt the need to pray. He washed his hands and face and turned towards Mecca. When he was finished he picked up the Quran and read the surah called 'The Opening Up', a surah in which God speaks with his Prophet:

> Muhammad!
> Have we not opened up your breast?
> And removed your burden
> Which had left you devoid of hope,
> And exalted your fame?
> Surely with hardship there is ease.
> With hardship indeed there is ease.

The shah could not hold back his tears.

Now the vizier's messenger presented himself. He too had a spoken message. The man whispered, 'I am conferring with the opposition. The negotiations are tedious and they take time. I cannot come.'

Jamal Khan and his comrades held an emergency meeting to discuss the consequences of capturing the palace. If they were to take the shah prisoner and topple him from his throne the reaction of the people and the ayatollahs would be impossible to predict. They all agreed that this would have to be their last resort. They needed the signature and the seal of the shah on their list of demands, but how could they get the shah to agree without bloodshed?

Although they had started by putting enormous pressure on the vizier, now their strategy was to give him more room to manoeuvre so he could actually function as a mediator.

Nor was England eager for chaos. An orderly system of government was to their benefit. They feared that the fall of the shah would give the Russians licence to attack the country from the north. For these reasons the British ambassador supported the strategy of Jamal Khan.

Reading the Quran had calmed the shah's nerves. Now he strolled through the garden, repeating a surah under his breath to stiffen his resolve: '"Muhammad! Have patience! Have patience! Suffer whatever they say to you!"'

The shah sensed that the guards and the soldiers were only there to keep an eye on him, so he deliberately focused all his attention on the plants growing beside the pond. The guards must be made to think that he was completely relaxed. From behind the servant's quarters he went up to the roof without being seen in order to observe the square with his binoculars. The barricades were still there, but to his horror he noticed that they were not all manned. He suspected that some of the soldiers had defected to the side of the ayatollahs. What surprised him was the great silence on the square and in the surrounding streets. You would almost think the demonstrators had given up.

The shah went to the roof of the kitchen. From there he could clearly see that there were people standing behind the sandbags. They seemed to be waiting for an order.

He looked at the harem. It was quiet there too. No one was on the front porch.

The shah felt cornered. He was a good chess player who was better than his opponents at thinking several moves ahead. He had seldom lost to his father. The old vizier was the only one whose superiority he had often been forced to acknowledge. But in real life he was less skilled at overseeing the field. Now the king was in danger of being put into checkmate. He was about to lose the use of his pawns. His horses, his vizier, his elephants and his chariots had all been eliminated. Then his eye fell on his own cannon, which stood idle in the courtyard. He thought of his treasury, of the emergency exit, of the horse that stood ready in the stable.

'When the king is surrounded on the chessboard he has to stall for time,' he said to himself. 'This we have done. Our vizier is talking to the opponents and we have called in the Russians. Now I must act like a true king and have patience.'

Gradually the sun rose in the sky until it stood above the palace. The deadline for the ultimatum had almost passed. Should he wait downstairs and look on as the people stormed the palace, or disappear into the cellar like a faint-hearted lion? He stayed on the roof, which gave him the feeling that he still had some control over events.

His gaze was drawn to the back garden of the palace. He watched as Malijak's sister helped him leave his room and go outside. The incident in the bazaar had left Malijak with a broken left leg and a couple of fractured ribs. Since then he had stayed on his back and had grown even heavier as a result. The shah dropped in every evening to see him. Malijak's sister had placed a chair next to the bed for the shah so he could talk to Malijak if he wanted to. Malijak crept through the doorway on his hands and knees. The shah barely recognised him.

The muezzin of the Jameh mosque called out, '*Allah-o-akbar, hay 'ali as-salat*: hurry to prayer.'

The shah started. The time had come: the deadline had expired. He expected to feel agitation, perhaps even despair, but to his own astonishment the muezzin brought him calm. An end had come to the uncertainty. The thing he had been so afraid of was now going to happen. He had done all he could to prevent it.

'Hay 'ali as-salat,' repeated the muezzin.

Now everyone was expected to lay down their guns and turn to Mecca for prayer. This was the most peaceful of moments. No one would attack him. No one would kill him.

When the muezzin was finished silence fell once again. The shah saw that indeed all the people had turned their backs on the palace and were praying towards Mecca.

A crow flew over the square, and its cry broke the silence. The prayer was over. Agitation spread through the crowd. The shah made sure that nothing escaped his notice. The crowd parted to make room as the vizier, two ayatollahs, seven gentlemen in suits and two foreigners passed through the barricades and walked to the square in front of the palace. There they stopped, talking among themselves.

The shah recognized Ayatollah Tabatabai. The other ayatollah was Behbahani, the old cleric who had been the first to sit on the roof of the house opposite the embassy. The shah also recognised the British ambassador. The second foreigner was Edward Granville Browne, but the shah had never seen him before. He suspected that the other men were the merchants from the bazaar.

He put away his binoculars. As if he himself had summoned the delegation for an audience, the shah went to the hall of mirrors in expectation of the visit. He straightened his tall cylindrical hat in the mirror. Then he went to the window. The vizier was in conversation with the head of the guards, who left to notify the shah.

'Come in!' called the shah calmly in response to the knock on the door.

The man saluted and said, 'The ambassador of the Kingdom of Great Britain, accompanied by a delegation, is waiting at the gate. He asks whether Your Majesty will receive them? The vizier too would like to pay his respects.'

The shah had not yet been put into checkmate. The game was still on.

'Lead them in.'

Vizier Mostovi Almamalek was the first to enter. He took his place behind the shah and whispered something in his ear.

As the guests entered the hall of mirrors the shah positioned himself beside the chair of the great Persian kings.

'Salam, O king!' said Behbahani simply.

'Salam!' responded the shah.

The rest of the delegation greeted the shah as well.

The vizier introduced everyone and returned to his place

behind the shah. The British stood off to the side. The merchants took off their hats. Their place was behind the ayatollahs.

With a royal gesture the shah pointed to a row of chairs that were lined up beneath the great mirror. But because Ayatollah Behbahani remained standing the others did the same.

The British ambassador took the initiative. He took one step forward and said in English, 'Your Majesty, I will spare you my poor Persian. England does not wish to become involved in your domestic affairs. We have been drawn in against our will, but we want you to know that England stands behind the shah. A powerful king is of great importance to us. The role of the British embassy in recent events has probably led to many misunderstandings, but I can assure the shah that England has always taken a passive attitude. Today I speak to you as a mediator. Edward Granville Browne will act as interpreter, to avoid any ambiguities.'

Browne bowed to the shah, and the ambassador continued: 'The attendant delegation has brought with it a document in which Your Majesty is asked to give his blessing to the creation of a parliament. As British ambassador I have been asked to act as witness. This is the extent of England's involvement in the matter.'

After the ambassador had taken a step back old Ayatollah Behbahani pointed at one of the merchants with his walking stick. The merchant stepped forward, bowed his head and handed the shah an envelope. The shah took out a three-page document and looked up. It was impossible to read his thoughts from his face.

Once again he motioned to his guests to sit down. Ayatollah Behbahani walked slowly to a chair, which broke the ice. No sooner had the ayatollah sat down than his walking stick fell from his hand. Ayatollah Tabatabai picked it up, gave it to Behbahani and sat down next to him. The others followed his example. The shah rang his bell and called out, 'Tea for our guests!' But he had forgotten that he had sent the chamberlain home. He said nothing else. Holding the document in his hand he stood there deep in thought.

'Will you permit me to say a few words?' asked Edward Granville Browne.

The shah turned to him, fully attentive: 'You may speak.'

'I am a traveller. I write, and I admire the history of your country. I have lived among the Persians for many years. There is one truth that has stuck with me, and I would like to pass it on to you, if the shah pleases.'

His exceptionally good Persian impressed the shah. He motioned for Browne to continue.

'I have observed that the Persians love their kings. The people who are now standing behind sandbags with guns in their hands – they love you.'

A cautious smile spread across the shah's face. He put his hand in his jacket pocket and was about to toss Browne a couple of gold coins. You could hear the coins jingling. But he kept them to himself. The shah walked to the table, poured himself a glass of water and took a sip. The group followed his every move. The king was buying time in the hope that somehow an opening would occur that would rescue him from this hopeless position. He looked out the window once again, but no, nothing was going to happen. The delegation had given him the document. It was his move.

He walked back to the table, picked up his quill, dipped it in the ink pot, signed the paper and confirmed the contents with his signet ring. The visitors were impressed by the dignity with which the shah bore his fate. The shah rolled the document up and gave it to the vizier. The vizier in turn handed the document to Ayatollah Behbahani. The ayatollah bowed his head, and it looked as if he were about to extend his hand to the shah. The shah ignored him and turned to the vizier: 'If you would lead the gentlemen out.'

'Mr Edward Granville Browne,' the shah called. Browne waited as the others left.

When the delegation had gone the shah said, 'You said you write. What do you write about?'

'I search for traces of history in the ancient ruins, but my real love is for ordinary people. I travel a great deal and I write about my experiences. It goes without saying that this meeting with you has been a fascinating occasion on which I will have to devote quite some attention.'

'You are not interested in politics?'

'No. I write about daily life, culture, customs and practices.'

'When you write about us, write the following: *The shah said, "I decide!"*'

'What do you mean, Your Majesty?'

'You will understand later on,' answered the shah.

As soon as the delegation left the palace the gentlemen of the bazaar held their hats in the air. This was how they let Jamal Khan, Mirza Reza and the other members of the committee know that the shah had signed the document. No one could believe it. No one wanted to cheer before they had seen the impression of the shah's signet ring.

Jamal Khan unrolled the document and shouted, 'Javid Persia! Long live Persia!'

'Javid! Javid!' rose from thousands of throats.

Mirza Reza, weak and marked by his long imprisonment, picked up the tricoloured national flag, climbed onto a platform and cried out, 'The celebration has begun! The shah has agreed to a national parliament!'

'Majles, majles, majles!' cried the gathered throng.

Tehran was overflowing with happiness. Musicians played, singers sang, the people in the street embraced each other and the women on the roofs wept for joy. People danced, lifting the merchants on their shoulders and praising their perseverance.

The two ayatollahs walked along a row of cheering people to the house where the ayatollahs of Qom were still claiming sanctuary. '*Mobarak, mobarak, majles mobarak,*' the people shouted. 'Blessed, blessed, blessed be the parliament.'

Usually the Persians expressed their emotions in words and slogans. It was the first time in history that they had all clapped their hands to show their gratitude. The merchants went to the bazaar to open their shops again after the long strike.

The celebrations continued across the country for a week. 'The air smells of flowers,' people said to each other. And they were right. A kind of spring had burst forth. Everybody felt good. Everybody was happy. Everybody laughed.

60. Majles

In the palace you could hear a pin drop, but the centre of Tehran was bubbling with excitement. The members of the resistance committee, the representatives of the bazaar and the authorised agents of the ayatollahs met every day until deep into the night to pave the way for the first session of parliament.

Calling together the delegates of all the classes and professions in so short a time was simply out of the question, but the committee did want to create a structure for the parliament as quickly as possible now that the time was right. They decided to call to Tehran only the representatives of the major cities so they could create a provisional parliament within a month. That would include the representatives of the six most important classes of society: the royal house, the clergy, the tribes, the bazaars, industry and the men of learning. They also decided that the next session would take place three months later. In this second gathering the shah would sign the acts of the constitution.

They went looking for a prestigious building in which to house the parliament, but every structure they considered belonged to either the shah or the princes, and none of them was prepared to part with their property. It took a great deal of persuading, but finally the shah agreed to release one of the oldest government buildings for use by the parliament. He assumed it would be temporary.

With great reluctance he also ordered the royal print

shop to print 175 copies of the proposed constitution so the representatives would be able to study the text and take it to the second session, complete with annotations. This uncommonly large print run was the first step forced on the shah to accept the views of his subjects.

One month later a great city-wide celebration was held and the delegates walked to the parliament building. The ayatollahs led the way and the princes followed them. Then came the most prominent men of the bazaar followed by the rest of the representatives, all dressed in festive clothing and tall hats. Jamal Khan, his comrade-in-arms Mirza Reza and a few other members of the committee also joined the procession as organisers.

Decorated horses led the way and guards in magnificent uniforms took up the rear. Everyone felt it was a unique procession: the dignified ayatollahs, the princes with their golden canes tucked under their arms, the merchants in their expensive jackets made from English fabrics. But what attracted the attention of the spectators more than anything else were the splendid new black leather shoes all the delegates were wearing. It may have been coincidental that all of them were decked out in such shoes, but they were immediately seized upon as the symbol of a new era.

After the delegates had taken their seats the oldest representative was chosen as parliamentary chairman. Everyone waited anxiously for the shah. They all realised he might not show up at all. A few delegates had already proposed that the parliament be allowed to take decisions if the shah should decide to ignore them. But that was impossible. The presence of the shah was essential in order to make the session legitimate.

The arrival of the king put an end to every discussion. He rode up to the parliament building on a great black horse. There was some confusion as to who would receive him. Jamal Khan appointed Mirza Reza. Mirza Reza, in his brand-new black shoes, walked up to the shah, bowed his head, and said, 'Your Majesty!'

The shah did not look at him, so he had not the least suspicion that this was the same man whom Eyn ed-Dowleh had once thrown at his feet in iron chains. Mirza Reza led him to the platform. The shah cast a glance at the delegates and said, 'We, the king of Persia, have always dreamed of a day like today. We thank God that He has allowed our dream to come true.'

Then he paused for a moment, standing there awkwardly, wondering whether he ought to say something else or take a seat. Nothing more was expected of him. The only purpose of his being there was to legally validate the gathering. Now he could go home. He would have to return to the parliament in a few months to officially ratify the Persian constitution with his signature and signet ring. He stepped off the dais, walked to the door and left the parliament.

Only after he had gone did anyone dare to clap, and everyone followed suit. It was a loud, lengthy round of applause and it did not escape the shah, who was now outside. Standing at the top of the stairs, he paused a moment to listen. Then he calmly descended, passed his cannon, which stood on a cart, and left.

Back in the palace he went to his study and opened his diary. He wrote until his fingers ached.

Before going to bed he took one more stroll across the courtyard. He noticed that the door to Malijak's room was ajar. The candle in his lantern was still burning. The shah went in and sat down on the chair beside the bed. It was hard for the shah to tell whether Malijak was awake or asleep. He began talking to him: 'They've fixed up a parliament for themselves. The mullahs sat there in the first row, beard after beard. Everyone was dressed in fine clothing and leather shoes. They think if they put on expensive clothes it will automatically make them good politicians. They're all puppets, and England is pulling the strings. We gave a little speech. It was a lot of nonsense and it made them very happy, and they all clapped for us. But they don't know what we've got up our sleeve. In the not too distant future they'll get together again. They'll want us to bless their constitution. We'll let them dream, Malijak. You mustn't tell this to anyone. The next time these people meet, death will be there to grab them by the scruff of the neck. Everything is arranged. The Russians are as good as their word.'

The shah heard footsteps. Then he heard the voice of Malijak's sister. He stood up and walked out into the night.

61. Electricity

Russia had gone along with the shah's request because they realised that the English would emerge from the conflict as the big winners once the parliament was officially launched. It was a risky military undertaking, but Moscow saw it as a last chance to gain influence in an area that was gradually being dominated by the British.

In doing so the Russians were honouring an agreement they had made with the shah's father to assist his son in time of need. They let it be known that preparations were proceeding apace. The shah would have to be patient.

To kill time the shah began a study of electricity. After returning from Europe he had introduced a number of changes in his palace. One of them was the installation of the telegraph system, but that had not been a success. For a long time now the machine had been standing idle in its booth next to the hall of mirrors.

Another plan was to furnish the palace with new lamps. In France he had signed a contract with a firm to have the palace wired for electricity. A French engineer had travelled to Tehran before the start of the uprising to discuss the project with the shah. He tried to talk the shah into having electric lights installed in a few government buildings in addition to the palace and to illuminate the centre of Tehran as well, but the shah wanted the electricity all to himself.

The Frenchman had just got started on the project when

Tehran was besieged by strikes. In all the turmoil he was forced to stop work and return to France. Now the shah had asked the French engineer to come back and complete the job.

The man needed one month to build an enclosure in the back garden of the palace, where he would place the turbine generator. Every day the shah would walk with the engineer, chatting with him and thoroughly enjoying the miracle that was taking place. If you hadn't known better you would have thought he was the Frenchman's assistant. The shah would pick up a screwdriver and give the screws a few more turns to make them more secure. He re-measured the cables, studied the copper electrical wires and asked technical questions out of sheer curiosity.

The engineer had brought in hundreds of metres of extra cables and several crates of bulbs. He tried to persuade the shah once again that the generator had enough capacity to provide electricity not only for the entire palace but also for the palace square and the surrounding streets. But the shah was adamant. Only the hall of mirrors, his study, his bedroom and the footpaths in the courtyard were to be illuminated. It was as if his only concern was to get the new lights working as soon as possible.

Everything was ready earlier than planned, and the engineer asked the shah to leave the palace for one day so he could do some trial runs. The shah complied with the request and waited for the evening to arrive with tense anticipation.

In the hall of mirrors the engineer had installed a special gold light switch for the shah on a small table next to the king's chair. When it was more or less dark outside the shah drew the curtains closed and sat down in the chair. With his hand on the light switch he took a deep breath, waited for just a moment and then switched the light on.

A miracle took place. In a flash the darkness disappeared and the room was saturated in a golden light unlike anything he had ever seen before. Completely overwhelmed, the shah remained in his chair and looked around him. The chandelier gleamed, the mirror glittered, the colourful figures in the carpets shone like thousands of tiny jewels on the floor, and the pomegranate-coloured sofas and green curtains took on a lustre of unparalleled enchantment.

He stood up and looked at himself in the mirror. His grey hair was like washed silver under his tall hat. The furrows of his face were accentuated. In this light he looked exactly like his father, and that moved him to tears.

In the days that followed the shah received the women of his harem in the hall of mirrors in small groups. He motioned for them to sit on the floor. As soon as it was completely dark outside he pulled the curtains shut, sat down in his chair and cried out, 'Silence!' He made the women wait for a whole minute, as still as mice. Then he threw the switch and sat back to enjoy their reactions. After the women had recovered from the shock they praised the shah for his lamps and tried to entice him into installing the same artificial light in the harem.

'It will be done,' the shah promised each group. 'But don't tell the other women. I want to surprise them, just as I have surprised you.'

Besides the new inventions he also enjoyed the company of his grandson. Every day after breakfast the little boy was brought to the palace so the shah could spend an hour playing with him. He would get down on all fours and lumber across the carpets with the child on his back. He recited his own poems for him and distorted his voice, which made the child laugh. Hand in hand the shah and his grandson walked together through the courtyard gardens, and he taught him to pay attention to the flowers and the birds.

Akkasbashi, the royal photographer, took dozens of photos of the shah and his grandson: the shah with the boy on his back, on his shoulders, on his desk, on his horse, on his cannon and on his lap, with the shah holding his finger on the electric switch.

Just when the women of the harem had resigned themselves to the idea that the shah was not going to keep his promise, he sent them on a day trip to the mausoleum of the holy saint Abdoldawood. He had a couple of cables laid from the generator to the harem. In half a day he had replaced the harem's old chandeliers with new lamps. The shah asked the engineer whether he had enough cables and bulbs to illuminate the chandelier in the music room.

'*Je peux tout arranger pour le shah*,' said the Frenchman with a smile.

That evening, when the women returned to the palace completely worn out, they couldn't believe their eyes. They screamed with happiness, and when the shah appeared in the doorway of the harem they kissed him and indulged his every whim and treated him to a long night of bliss.

It was still two weeks before the second session of parliament. The Russian troops had entered the country inconspicuously, scattering themselves along the border, and had gathered in the barracks around Tehran. They remained completely unobserved, which the shah saw as a sign that God had taken mercy on the operation.

As the day of reckoning approached, the shah felt burdened by an increasing sense of dread. To take his mind off his worries, and to keep anyone from sensing his agitation, he came up with a pastime that had never been tried before.

In Paris the shah had once attended a *bal masqué*. He decided to organise a Persian version in the music room. One would have thought that the shah had put politics aside for good and had resigned himself to a much lighter interpretation of monarchy.

He selected a group of forty women of all ages, including his oldest and youngest wives. He ordered them to design masks for themselves, to put on elaborate make-up and to dress themselves with great extravagance. He gave them the freedom to do whatever they wanted that evening.

The festivities in the harem were unforgettable. The masked women came out of their rooms one by one. They looked like extraordinary creatures, and among the other women curiosity won out over jealousy. The chosen women walked down a red carpet and into the music room to the sound of loud cheering. It was as if they had come from another planet and had just landed on earth. The shah glowed with pleasure. The masked women did what they normally would never do in the presence of the shah. They moved with elegant grace and made gestures with their hands that the shah found very arousing. A thick cloud of fragrant herbs hung in the room, and three masked female musicians played merry, rhythmic music.

The masked ball went on for one week. The shah kept choosing different women and having them dress up. He enjoyed it – it was truly a feast fit for a king – but it only suppressed his agitation rather than dispel it. The tension had to find a release. He wanted to smash something to pieces, to scream, to weep, to strike out with his fists. Then one evening he came up with a bizarre twist to the festivities.

'Ladies, listen. This evening we're going to play a game

in the dark. Later on, when we switch off the lights, the musicians will begin to play. Then, in the dark, you'll be able to do and say whatever you wish. You are completely free. You can push each other, kick, hit, pinch, bite – whatever you like. Is everyone ready? When the light goes out, you may begin.'

The shah switched off the light. It was pitch dark in the music room and completely silent. The musicians didn't dare play. The women were quite at a loss as to what they were supposed to do. A nervous laugh broke the tension momentarily. Nothing else happened. Then one woman cried out, 'Ouch, don't do that, it hurts.' She had probably been pinched by another woman, so she responded in kind. Silhouettes began to move.

'Get away from me,' they shouted. 'No hitting,' they giggled. 'Don't pinch me. What's got into you?' 'Stop it, I said,' 'Ow, she bit me. I'm going to get you.' They screamed, they laughed. No one knew who was doing the hitting, who was doing the pushing. Years of frustration erupted. The musicians began to play, cautiously at first, then louder and louder. The women tore each other's clothing, pulled each other's hair and shouted, 'Turn the light on, please! Help! They're strangling me, they're beating me to death!' The musicians coaxed hysterical noises from their instruments. The shah laughed and screamed like a madman.

The women pleaded with the shah to put an end to the bedlam until they fell on the floor, tired and spent. The shah waited a moment, then switched on the light. He was shocked by what he saw. All the women were badly beaten. Their clothes were in shreds, their masks in tatters, and black mascara mixed with tears was running down their cheeks. Stupefied they gazed up at the shah. He switched off the light and left the harem.

62. *The Law*

The text of the constitution was ready. The commission had succeeded in including parts of the French constitution as well as regulations from the Quran.

During the second session of parliament the shah – in the presence of all the members – would swear that he would defend the constitution and respect the separation of powers. The shah, who had received all the documents, had thrown everything away unread and let the commission know that he agreed to all the proposed bills.

The committee concluded that the shah understood he could not stop progress. In actual fact the shah was more frenetic than ever. The Russians had not been reporting on their preparations lately so as not to endanger the operation. But the shah felt uncertain, and at the least provocation he would fly into a rage. He sometimes thought the Russians had abandoned him altogether.

Two days before the opening of parliament the shah had almost struck his daughter Taj Olsultan because she had been late in bringing her child to see him for their visit.

'Where were you? Why did you make us wait?' cried the shah angrily.

'I'm sorry, Father. He's been a bit cheeky today,' replied Taj Olsultan.

'No excuses. If you make us wait one more time I will have the child taken from you. You are mistaken if you think you're already queen of the country.'

'I offer my apologies.'

The child, who had climbed onto a chair, fell on the floor and began to cry. The shah had instinctively raised his hand to strike Taj Olsultan but immediately lowered it and left the room in embarrassment.

Late that night a messenger from Mahdolia suddenly appeared at the door. The shah thought it was just another case of pure meddlesomeness on his mother's part and that she was fishing for attention. He received the messenger with indifference. Only when the man pressed a small, sealed leather package into the shah's hand did his eyes light up. It was a secret Russian communication. The shah gave the messenger a coin and withdrew into his study.

The next day when he appeared at the top of the stairs he was wearing his military uniform, and his highly polished dark brown boots were gleaming in the sun.

The night before the meeting of parliament the last troops from the Russian army had been put in a state of readiness. The officer in command was a Cossack, Colonel Liakhov, who had placed camouflaged cannons at strategic locations, in consultation with Eyn ed-Dowleh (now recovered from his bullet wounds).

The sun had not yet risen when Russian soldiers mounted a surprise attack on the city. When the residents of Tehran left their homes they were confronted by an entirely new situation. The roads to the parliament building were closed off, and everyone who lived nearby was told to stay indoors until further notice. Russian soldiers blocked the square of the British embassy. One Russian soldier climbed up the telegraph pole in front of the embassy and cut the cables.

The Russians had kept their word.

Yet the shah's dream would not be fully realised.

Two days earlier Jamal Khan had received a message via the Russian rebels in Baku that an army was headed for Tehran under the leadership of Colonel Liakhov. The only possible explanation was that the shah had enlisted their help to seize parliament.

A group of horsemen kept a lookout on the roads to Tehran. Jamal Khan warned the British embassy. Not long afterwards it was confirmed that a Russian army unit was stationed in barracks outside Tehran.

Time was short and the shah had everyone barking up the wrong tree. The committee had hastily warned the delegates to enter the parliament building at night. While Colonel Liakhov and Eyn ed-Dowleh were directing the Russian troops into Tehran, the delegates furtively slipped into the parliament building. Most of the representatives from Tehran, and those from other cities who were staying in local inns, were on time, but a group of eighteen representatives who had spent the night outside the city walls were too late. The resistance committee did everything it could to get those delegates into the building so a majority would be present.

Also missing was Ayatollah Tabatabai, parliament's most important person. Russian soldiers were posted in front of his home to keep him from going outside. The resourceful Mirza Reza managed to mislead the Russians and steer the ayatollah across the roofs of the mosque and down the surrounding alleys to the garden of a house behind the parliament. But it was no longer possible to get the ayatollah into the parliament building from the roof of that house. Mirza Reza acted with lightning speed. He drummed up three strong men, who used pickaxes to break a hole in the wall, and the scrawny ayatollah crept through the hole and into the building. He straightened his black turban and ran into the assembly room, mud still clinging to his robes.

When the sun was high in the sky Colonel Liakhov reported to the shah. 'The operation is a success,' he said.

The shah raised his eyebrows.

'But some of the delegates were already in the parliament building,' the colonel added.

'We are aware of that,' said the shah coolly. He had already been given the bad news by Eyn ed-Dowleh.

'The parliament is surrounded. No one can leave the building,' said the colonel. 'I do not have the mandate, but if the shah so desires, I can drive them all out.'

'We don't think that will be necessary,' said the shah. 'It's better that the Russian soldiers do not enter the building. I will go with you later on and we will throw them all out single-handedly.' The shah offered him a glass of tea, but the colonel declined.

'When Your Majesty is ready, we can go.'

'We are ready!' answered the shah.

Vizier Mostovi Almamalek had tried to reach the shah a few times, but the shah had told him not to come round until the next day. He ordered him to stay at home.

Surrounded by his guards the shah went out on horseback. Colonel Liakhov rode on his right. To his left, mounted on a cart, was his cannon. They rode to the bazaar square and passed the British embassy in a show of force. All the doors and windows were closed, and there was no sign of anyone in the residence. The shah, who suspected that the British ambassador was spying on him, straightened his back and carried on a conversation with the Russian colonel.

When they came to the parliament building Colonel Liakhov rode up to the officer in charge of the operation, spoke with him briefly and returned to the shah.

'The meeting has begun and the delegates are hard at work.'

'What are they doing?' asked the shah with surprise.

'The officer told me that the rest of the delegates entered the building by way of the walls and the surrounding houses. The hall is quite full.'

'What are they talking about?'

The colonel was unable to answer this question.

The shah gestured to Eyn ed-Dowleh, who was standing beside the cannon.

'You have lost control,' said the shah calmly so the Russian colonel would be unable to detect his rage. 'They have outwitted us.'

Eyn ed-Dowleh tried to say something, but the shah said, 'Shut up. Go inside and order the people to leave the building immediately. Tell them we'll use violence if they don't listen to us.'

Eyn ed-Dowleh did what he was told. Minutes later he rejoined the shah: 'The chairman of the parliament said the following: "We are now in the middle of an intense discussion concerning the constitution. Later we will put the final text to the vote. If the constitution is accepted, we will swear in the supreme court judges. Then a small celebration has been planned to mark this memorable occasion, which will probably go on until the end of the afternoon. At that point, of course, we will come outside. Violence will not be necessary."'

'Go back and say to the chairman: "Get out! Now! Or the shah will come in and drag you out!"'

Eyn ed-Dowleh obeyed and came back almost immediately. 'The chairman says, "The shah's message has been duly received."'

'Was that all?' asked the shah.

'That was all,' confirmed Eyn ed-Dowleh.

The shah gestured to Colonel Liakhov. They rode on a bit to discuss the situation privately. Then the shah turned back to Eyn ed-Dowleh and said, 'Go back into the building and make the following announcement to everyone, loud and clear: "Either you all come out at once or the shah will personally demolish the building with his cannon."'

Eyn ed-Dowleh bowed and carried out the order. Much later than expected he came back out.

'Did you make the announcement?' asked the shah.

'Yes, Your Majesty,' answered Eyn ed-Dowleh.

'Why did it take so long?'

'They were right in the middle of voting.'

'Voting for what?'

'The laws, Your Majesty.'

'I'll teach them a lesson!'

But he stayed where he was and stared straight at the door of the parliament.

Something had to happen. The shah dismounted. With his left hand behind him he walked up to his cannon, placed his hand on the barrel and stood there thinking.

'Aim it at that window,' said the shah to the sergeant, pointing to a stained glass window somewhere in the parliament building.

'Ready!' the sergeant called to his soldiers.

Three soldiers ran up and opened the back of the cart, placed two sturdy planks against it and rolled the cannon down. They moved it to the spot indicated by the sergeant and aimed the barrel at the parliament building.

The shah gave a sign.

The sergeant placed a ball in the cannon.

When everything was ready the shah took his position behind his cannon. Everyone held their breath. The Russian officers did not expect that the shah would actually do the shooting. The sergeant solemnly handed him a linstock. Colonel Liakhov nodded to the shah, who lit the fuse. Fire leapt from the barrel of the cannon with an enormous bang. The ball bored a hole in the side of the building. The ground shook; the horses whinnied and reared.

Suddenly tongues of flame issued from the building and smoke began pouring from the broken stained glass window. The shah waited, the colonel waited, the officers waited, but no one came outside. The shah stood apprehensively beside his cannon until suddenly, out of nowhere, armed men appeared on the roof of the parliament and began shooting.

Colonel Liakhov gave the shah cover and told him to hide behind the cannon cart. The Russian officers, who hadn't counted on this kind of action, withdrew their soldiers immediately to the surrounding alleys, seeking shelter behind the walls.

Fierce fighting erupted all around the building. The armed men on the roof kept up a barrage of fire, thereby enabling the delegates to escape through the back garden.

Colonel Liakhov ordered his troops to enter the building.

Jamal Khan, who had put the approved constitutional articles for the new parliament in a leather briefcase, tried to escape by way of the roof, but he was hit by a Russian officer. Jamal Khan stumbled. The leather briefcase fell from his hand. Mirza Reza fired at the officer, ran to Jamal Khan, picked up the briefcase and escaped. The wounded Jamal Khan crept across the roof and dropped into the garden of a house behind the parliament building.

Fighting in the city continued all afternoon. It wasn't until evening that the Russian soldiers regained control of the city centre.

Late that night Colonel Liakhov appeared before the

shah to make his report: 'The resistance has been wiped out. The parliament building is yours.'

The shah walked over to the mantelpiece, picked up a small box, handed it to Liakhov and said, 'By way of thanks.'

The colonel was astonished by what he saw. It was an old dagger encrusted with glittering jewels.

63. The Shah Has His Picture Taken

The next day the vague sound of demonstrators' slogans permeated the halls of the palace. The shah unconsciously absorbed them, and a few days later he even heard himself humming the same phrases:

> *Az khun-e javanan-e watan, leleh damideh,*
> *Az ma'tam sarv-e qadeshan sarv khamideh.*
> From the blood of our young men that watered
>   the earth
> tulips have burst forth.
> The trees are bowed with sadness.

It took several days before order was completely restored in the city. The Russian soldiers had withdrawn and the Persian soldiers guarded the important places. The shop-keepers minded their own business and the people went back to the bazaar. Seven parliamentarians had been killed, a few were wounded and a considerable number were arrested. How many Russian soldiers had been killed was not known. The ayatollahs and the escaped parliamentarians had all gone into hiding.

When it came to the fate of Jamal Khan no one was really sure. There were rumours that a Russian officer had shot and killed him. But according to reliable sources

Jamal Khan and Mirza Reza had fled to Moscow to stay with their friends.

The shah felt very good indeed. He had received telegrams from all the major cities reporting that the bazaars had reopened and people were going to the mosques for prayer. He had not stood for any nonsense, and everyone had seen what he was made of. The shah's position was strong once again and he wanted to record his victory. He asked his photographer to take a series of photos of himself in the city for posterity.

'Take a picture of us next to that building,' said the shah.

'The parliament building, you mean?' asked the photographer.

The shah emphatically refused to use the word 'parliament'. 'A picture of us next to that hole in the wall along with our cannon, so all three can be seen clearly,' he said. 'Is that possible?'

'That would be difficult. In a photograph the accent can only be placed on one thing. It has to be either the cannon or your head.'

'But we want the hole in the picture too,' said the shah.

'I will do my best, Your Majesty.'

The photographer had the shah's cannon brought to the parliament building, and he moved it around until he found the right composition. When he was ready he alerted the shah. He told him to stand in front of the cannon, with the cannon's barrel pointing at the hole. It was a scene that he had carefully puzzled out with the help of his assistant. The photographer looked through the lens with great concentration. The image was balanced, but the shah's tall cylindrical hat was not completely visible.

'If Your Majesty would tilt your head a little bit backwards. Just a little bit. Stop. That's good,' shouted the photographer from under the black cloth of his camera.

The photographer wanted to take a picture that was reminiscent of the famous painting of Napoleon, a scene in which the wind was blowing, a grey cloud was threatening, a cannon was smoking and Napoleon was looking towards a battlefield in the distance.

'Wait a minute,' shouted the photographer. 'I think the hole would be more prominent if the shah didn't look at the hole at all but in the opposite direction. So look at that tree and raise your chin a little. Place your right hand on the barrel of the cannon, not flat against it, as if you were holding the reins of your horse. Very good, excellent.'

At that moment a man came out from behind a tree. He was wearing a smart suit and a cap. He walked calmly towards the photographer. The shah thought he had seen him somewhere before. Perhaps he was the photographer's assistant, or someone who worked as an interpreter for the Russians. The man came even closer. The shah felt that something wasn't quite right, and he looked to the side. But the photographer, whose head was still under the camera's black cloth, shouted, 'Don't move!'

The shah stood still. 'If the man walks towards us he will have to take off his cap,' he said to himself. The man kept his cap on. He slipped his hand inside his jacket. The shah smelled danger, but the photographer shouted, 'A little more patience! Don't move!' The man pulled out a pistol. The man was Mirza Reza. Before the shah realised what was happening three shots were fired.

The photographer had just taken his picture.

The shah slumped to the ground.

64. Taj Olsultan

The tellers of the old kings' tales tended to take liberties with the narrative of their stories, and when it suited them they always revised the endings in order to close with a flicker of hope. No one knows whether they told the truth or not, but everyone understands that those who related the events of history were granted the freedom to end their stories as they saw fit.

With this old Persian tradition in mind the following just may be true.

Forty days after the death of the shah the delegates of the parliament came together. They appointed Princess Taj Olsultan as regent in place of her little son, who later would ascend the throne.

The beautiful princess arrived at the parliament in her golden coach and entered the building accompanied by a group of guards. All the delegates stood up and clapped for Her Majesty.

Once she was officially sworn in she put her signature on all the parliamentary documents. Taj Olsultan recognised Afghanistan as a sovereign nation and pulled the Persian troops out of Herat. She arranged for housing and allowances for all the women of the harem and sent them back to their families.

During the long life of Taj Olsultan the trains arrived

and all the streets of Tehran were bathed every night in the light of the new electric lamps.

The kings' tales are never really finished, and this is because the storytellers always have to save something for the night that is to come.

Note from the Author

A couple of British characters in this book bear the names of real historical figures. I adopted their names so that their voices could be heard again today. I have always been fond of their books as well as their politics.

Note from the Translator

The storyteller who narrates *The King* has a vast store of classical literature in his head that he recites more or less verbatim, adopting and adapting it as circumstances require. Some of this literature is easily available in existing English translations. The shah's poem in chapter 13 is based on a verse from *The Golestan of Saadi*, translated by Richard Francis Burton. The poem in chapter 24 is from the *Rubaiyat of Omar Khayyam*, translated by Edward FitzGerald. The passages from the Quran are taken from the translation made by Ahmed Ali, *Al-Qur'an*, published by the Princeton University Press in 1984.

I would like to thank R.M. McGlinn for his assistance in transliterating the Farsi texts. Thanks also to Melissa Marshall for her exacting editorial skill. And finally, my gratitude to Susan Massotty for her collegial support and encouragement.